Deviate

THE LIGHT KEY TRILOGY
BOOK TWO

Praise for *Scintillate* by Tracy Clark

"Clark's novel is a powerful, heart-wrenching adventure."
—*Kirkus Reviews*

"Beautifully written. Keep your eye on author Tracy Clark. She's going places!" —Ellen Hopkins, *New York Times* Bestselling Author of the Crank trilogy

"A lush and atmospheric debut with a scorching romance and a metaphysical mystery. It had me hooked from the start."
—Suzanne Young, author of *The Program*

"*Scintillate* is full of unexpected plot twists and turns. A refreshing, magnificent read." —Beth from Tome Tender Book Blog

"If the publishing world is still looking for The Next Big Thing in YA novels, *Scintillate*: The Light Key Trilogy by Tracy Clark hits all the right notes." —The Bookend Family

Entangled Publishing, LLC
2614 South Timberline Road
Suite 109
Fort Collins, CO 80525

Visit our website at www.entangledpublishing.com.

Edited by Karen Grove and Kate Fall
Cover design by Kelley York
Interior design by Jeremy Howland
Cover photograph Ireland (c) Shutterstock/Horia Bogdan
Cover photograph keyhole (c) Shutterstock/Mopic
Cover photograph eyes (c) Shutterstock/antoshkaforever
Cover photograph bokeh background (c) Shutterstock/CHAIWATPHOTOS
Cover photograph gems (c) Shutterstock/Anna Rassadnikova

Paperback ISBN 978-1-62266-523-5
Ebook ISBN 978-1-62266-528-0

Manufactured in the United States of America

First Edition March 2015

10 9 8 7 6 5 4 3 2 1

For Jason

Darkness encroached and you stared it down
I'm humbled and awestruck by the strength of your light

Be near me when my light is low, when the blood creeps,
and the nerves prick and tingle; and the heart is sick, and
all the wheels of Being slow.

—Lord Alfred Tennyson

ONE

Cora

Ireland is a lovely, heartless thief.

Reckless and stubborn, I'd charged into its green and mist and history seeking answers. After a life of being too sheltered, I'd wanted to be brave. My bravery looked like stupidity now. People I loved were stolen from me. Ireland was magical and chillingly mythical, the freaking Bermuda Triangle disguised as heaven.

There, I did discover a piece of me I thought was gone forever. I'd found my mother, saved her from years of torturous captivity, but the unjust trade was my dad, who, because of my rash actions, lay dead on the floor of a dusty tack shed, his body brutally drained of his essence by Clancy Mulcarr. My father's life force, his beautiful pulsing aura, was extinguished forever. I'd lost him.

And I'd lost Finn. My cousin Mari was right when she said love was like lightning. I'd been struck fast and hot. The ruffled edges of my naïveté burned and smoked to cinders.

Ireland robbed me of myself, as well. Everything I had believed to be true about who I was had suddenly been supplanted with one word—*Scintilla.*

The combined force of grief and anger punched a gasp from my chest. I bent forward in the passenger seat of the car and tried to catch my breath. Giovanni clenched the wheel with one hand and squeezed my arm with the other. His gaze passed quickly over me before looking in the rearview mirror. "You okay?" he asked.

I nodded, but doubted that I'd ever breathe normally again. That I'd ever feel safe again. You don't feel safe when you're prey. When you're prey, you duck and swerve, hide and run. You never let your guard down. You fight, even if fighting isn't a normal thing for you. *Thank heavens you're a fighter,* my dad had said to me when I was racked by fever in the hospital.

True or not, if I wanted to live, I'd damn well better fight.

I leaned my head back on the passenger seat but kept my eyes fixed to the landscape outside of the car, wary of being followed. We weren't off Finn's property yet and Clancy could be anywhere. Despite my vigil through the window, images of my father battered me. For so many years, it had just been him and me. Even when our team of two became three after he married Janelle, even when our closeness had been tested by my desire to pull free as I got older, he was always strong and steady. Now he was…gone.

I'd been flung into orbit, spinning and kicking, watching the safety of my ship float farther away, forever out of reach.

Along with Dad, images of Finn intruded on my thoughts. His jaw, shadowed by a shaft of sun filtering through the California redwoods. The angular slope of his shoulders when his hands were stuffed shyly in his pockets. The mischief in his smile. The spice of his kisses. His eyes had their own energy that could laser into me with one look. He'd been my rock-star poet. He'd been my first and only love.

Finn had a way of cracking my shell and exposing the facets of strength and beauty within. And like that moment of wonder and discovery when you break open a geode, for the first time in my life I'd marveled at myself. Now, without my father, and without Finn, I wasn't sure how I would ever scrape the broken pieces together and be whole again.

Was that what life was about? Seeing yourself through the eyes of others until you finally grow up and learn to be your own mirror?

I was sure a mirror would reveal the emptiness I felt. Emptiness wasn't *nothing*. It was a noxious vapor filling the holes they'd left behind.

I opened my eyes and peered through the car window, looking for pursuers. Besides my grandmother in Chile, we were the last three Scintilla I knew of. My mother, Giovanni, and I were running for our lives. The Irish mist we'd waded through when we'd escaped Clancy's underground prison had expanded, rising steadily so that the trees looked as though they sprouted from fragile clouds and we ourselves were floating on a stream of white spray. Giovanni slammed on the brakes as the gate to Finn's family manor materialized too abruptly. It rose high in front of the car, black, imposing, and barred shut.

"It's not automatic?" Giovanni asked, revving the engine. His Italian accent was laced with the panic I felt. We had to get away from this place, this den of Arrazi who lived to kill. Or killed to live.

Semantics.

They were murderers.

I yanked the car door handle and kicked it open. Fog invaded the floorboards like a trespassing ghost intent on grabbing our ankles and pulling us out. Giovanni clutched my hand. "Stay inside. I'll open it."

"No. You stay behind the wheel. We can get away faster if I do it. Be right back." I left the car door open, ran to the enormous iron gate, and pulled on the slick bars. It wouldn't budge. I looked back over my shoulder. The headlights blinded me to Giovanni and my mother, who cowered in the backseat, but I held up one finger to indicate I'd be just another moment. Peering into the mist, I saw an electronic gate box to the side of the gravel drive, right behind the car. I ran to it, bent forward, and with shaking hands, blindly pressed buttons in the darkness. The gate stayed intractably motionless.

"This can't be happening!" I kicked the keypad repeatedly, fear and frustration scraping my skin from the inside. I'd narrowly escaped the Arrazi; no way was this crap piece of technology going to keep me trapped within their reach.

"Cora."

My already aching heart squeezed so hard, I cried out. I didn't have to turn to know it was Finn walking toward me. When he reached my side, he leaned down and entered a code. The chains of the gate growled to life. I sighed with relief but admonished myself for not *feeling* him approach. Terror and grief had numbed my instincts. If I wanted to stay alive, I'd have to be more alert, always.

Looking at Finn broke another piece of me, and I bit down on my quivering lip.

The mist blanketed him, flecking his hair and long lashes with dew that mimicked tears. He was beautiful, but terrifying, too. Because of me, his aura wasn't the sunset of love and desire and strength I'd come to know back in California when our love was a new, sweet flower. All color was gone, and in its place pure white radiated around his body like crystalline snow that was suspended in the air surrounding him and fell upon the curves of his shoulders.

An Arrazi's white aura was deceptively angelic.

"Your *da*?" Finn asked, motioning to the car. I glanced over my shoulder at the outline of two heads in the car. My mother sat slumped in the backseat while Giovanni manned the driver's seat, peering through the rainy windows, trying to see me.

I attempted to answer Finn's question but couldn't say the word that sounded like a slamming door: *dead.*

He understood though. I could tell by the way he held his hands up helplessly and let them drop back to his side and then held them up again. "*Ta sé in ait na fhirinne anois.*"

I didn't know what Finn uttered in his native Irish tongue, but his outstretched hands jolted me, reminding me of his kiss that had almost killed me. He'd held his hands out like that the night he showed himself as an Arrazi. His greedy white aura had expanded from his body and his fingertips, taking up all the space in the room as it had pulled my soul from me.

Instinctively, my feet backed away, toward the car.

"I'll never stop—"

"Don't!" I interrupted, holding up my hand. Finn's beginning hardened me to stone as I grasped the door to the car. I heard only Clancy Mulcarr's deep voice in my head.

I will never stop until I find you. And when I do, you three will die.

My salty tears burned my throat as I choked them off. "That sounds too much like something your uncle Clancy said to me."

Stars, hide your fires; Let not light see my black and deep desires.
—William Shakespeare, *Macbeth*

Two

Finn

Seeing Cora back away from me like that damn near killed me.

I was half dead already.

Not dead enough.

There was a time when those soulful emerald eyes of hers looked at me with trust and curious adoration. All I saw in them now was dark agony and fear. She was right to be afraid of me. I'd nearly killed the girl I loved.

Now she was driving away from me forever. My fists clenched into painful knots as I watched the taillights disappear into the fog. That Italian bastard in the car with her would get to be Cora's knight. I hated Giovanni for what he'd said to her—that what I felt wasn't love. He'd told her not to confuse need with love. That I was only attracted to her because of *what* she was rather than for *whom* she was. How would he know what was in my heart? I'd wanted to be with her from the first moment I met her. She was genuine and beautiful, and the closer I got to her, the more a part of me she became.

Love or need? Christ, it was both.

What knife can flay one feeling of desire from another?

But what if the guy was right? Doubt rode the mist and crept over my shoulders, seeping into my skin. That cloud of doubt was enough to condemn myself with, and while I despised Giovanni Teso for his barbed words, I was glad that Cora wouldn't be alone. He would try to protect her. He would take care of her. He would do what I couldn't.

After the fog swallowed up the car, I turned toward the house. Two glowing yellow lights shone down on me from either side of the front door, watching my lonely trek up the gravel drive. Each step drilled more anger into me, each crunch under my foot ground the loathing deeper into my chest. I was set on one thing. My uncle Clancy was drugged and passed out in our basement. I sure as hell wanted to be there when he woke.

My mother intercepted me at the door, her face drawn with apprehension. She reached her hand out to me as I passed. "Not now," I said through gritted teeth, slipping past her and heading toward the stairs that would take me down to the man who had locked Cora away, intent on feeding off her aura for who knows how long, like he'd done to her poor mother for over a dozen years. What kind of man does that?

An Arrazi man, my mind whipped at me.

Maybe, but not this Arrazi. I'd never do that. I wouldn't be the thing they said I was. And if Clancy's betrayal sliced at my core, my parents' betrayal was worse. To not tell me sooner the full truth about what I was, to let it go so long that I jeopardized the only person I'd ever given my heart to, to let me stroll through my whole life without telling me that I was born just to kill—that was something I'd never forgive.

Halfway down the basement steps, my father spun me around.

"It's no use, Finn. Your uncle's gone."

I sagged against the limestone wall. "Gone? Where?"

His grip on the front of my shirt relaxed and he sighed. The lines on his face drew downward into slack bows around his eyes and mouth. "First, he went to the tack shed where I hid Cora and the others. From there, I've no earthly idea."

"He killed her *da*," I said, putting the pieces together. I could feel the walls of my strength crumbling as I thought of Cora, who must have watched her father die. Damn horrific was what it was. "How'd they manage to escape?" I asked. More to the point, where was Clancy now? Would he catch them again?

"I don't know," my father answered. "There was a fight, though. Clancy's smarmy friend, Griffin, was stabbed to death. Clancy was gone before I returned. The rest of them are lucky to be alive."

"You helped them," I said, churning with mixed-up feelings. "You helped when you could have killed…"

My father's eyes turned soft, sympathetic. "You love her. To kill her would have killed you. I'd not do that to my own son."

"No. You almost let *me* kill her instead!" I shoved my father away from me, causing him to slip awkwardly to the stair below. He braced himself on each side of the stairwell. My mother's shadow stretched down, reaching for us. I shot her a withering glance. "Both of you risked Cora by not telling me what I was capable of. You didn't tell me what *she* was." I didn't realize I was crying until the tears trickled down my neck, meeting the firing pulse at my collarbone.

"We should have told you sooner," my mother said, her tone as cool and impassive as always. Had years of killing made her dead inside?

Nausea stirred my stomach. "Why did you have a child? Why

would you purposely bring another killer into this world? It's unforgivable."

My mother fingered the cross around her neck. "Are we not God's creatures, brought into this world for a reason? We don't kill for sport. We don't kill for lines drawn on maps. We don't kill to support our own brand of righteous dogma. We kill to survive. In this world, we are not alone in that."

I took each step, my eyes never leaving hers, until I stood at her feet. "I know for certain, this world would be a better place without us."

THREE

Cora

"Home," Gráinne moaned again from the backseat, this time more emphatically.

Giovanni and I glanced at each other. My mother had been like this from the minute we escaped the shack, mumbling about home and repeating my father's name over and over again. *Benito. Benito.*

Every utterance of his name drove a spike into my chest.

I had to find a way to stop the Arrazi. I had to find a way to keep us safe.

"Benito…"

Daddy.

"I like to think a part of your father lives on," Giovanni said softly. He didn't look at me when he said it, just stared ahead into the headlights piercing the mist.

"In Clancy?" I spat, sickened by the thought.

"Still."

We were forced to drive frustratingly slow due to the heavy

haze and curved roads. Consumed with the need to go faster, I realized my foot was pressing hard against the floorboard. Clancy could be following us in a car. Using his sortilege of astral projection, he could be hovering in the car with us like a ghost. Where could we possibly hide from his power?

"Go to Trim, Cora," my mother said, sounding surer than I'd ever heard her.

"What's there?" Giovanni asked.

"The house we lived in when I was little." I turned back toward my mother and reached over the seat to touch her leg. "Why? There's nothing for us there. It's not our home anymore."

Gráinne's wild eyes hardened into stubborn glass beads. "It will *always* be our home."

"It can't be safe to stay anywhere they'd associate with her." Giovanni spoke my thoughts exactly.

"I know. I'm trying to find out—"

Suddenly she leaned forward and clasped the antique silver key dangling from my neck. Her fingers spun the red pyramid-shaped crystals, which met at their tips like an hourglass within the top of the key. "This," she said. "You found this. You weren't supposed to. Not you. Everything went wrong after I was given this key. That's when I knew…"

"Knew?"

"Someone out there would do anything to keep the truth buried." She smiled like a madwoman. "Well, I have something of theirs. I can bury truths, too. We have to go home and go digging." Gráinne's words flowed out in a torrent of intense anxiety.

I pulled the key from her grasp and tucked it back inside my shirt. "What does this key open?" I asked. It had obviously meant something to Clancy. It was important enough that my father buried it under the albino redwood tree in Santa Cruz at my mother's request so that no one would ever find it.

But I found it.

Gráinne's flecked green eyes turned skyward and then snapped back to mine. The barest hint of a wry smile curved her thin lips. "Heaven?"

Just when I thought she was thinking more clearly, she lapsed into nonsense. I turned away from her and stared out the window at the lace of fog and fences. My entire body was taut with anxiety.

Giovanni startled me when he reached over and shuffled through the glove compartment. "*Cristo*," he said. "Nobody carries maps anymore. We'll have to stop for one." Soon, he pulled over at a gas station.

"You go in. What if someone recognizes me?" I said, thinking of the airport video of two innocent people falling dead at my feet. My father spoke passionately about the mysterious deaths around the world and his theory about dark energy before he died. I remembered his impassioned words: *The increase in natural disasters is a sign that there is a serious crisis or imbalance in our world…but the more critical sign now is the people who are mysteriously dying.* My father thought the Scintilla were somehow a key to solving the imbalance. But Giovanni and I knew what we saw that day the deaths occurred—the back of an Arrazi, walking away. The Arrazi's aura was white from a fresh kill.

I shielded my face from passersby and practically held my breath until Giovanni returned, map in hand. Danger stalked us from all directions. Hunted by Arrazi, valued more than gold on the black market, and, according to Clancy Mulcarr, we had enemies who wanted us dead more than he wanted to possess us. This mysterious *Society* he was involved with?

I glanced around, watchful. The whole world was full of enemies whose faces we didn't know. We needed to fade into the fog until we could figure out what to do.

Once we were on the right highway to Trim, my mother's whole demeanor shifted from a shaking rabbit cornered by a cat to a child with her nose and hands pressed to the cold window. What must it be like for her after all that time, to be free?

She was a fool if she felt free.

"Turn right," she instructed Giovanni, who had the map spread open on his lap as he drove.

The rain stopped but the roads were still wet and speckled with reflections. Streetlamps cast discs of yellow light on the slick pavement below. I tried to calm my beating heart as we slowed to a stop in front of my childhood home. When Finn had brought me here before, it was sweet and magical. The whole scene was lit in my memory by the light of love and discovery. Returning was like walking from a dreamscape into a nightmare.

Surprisingly, Gráinne didn't jump out when we stopped. She sat, wide-eyed and stunned, as she stared at the cottage—white with ivy curtaining the red trim windows and bright red door as I remembered—the home she and my father and I had shared so many years ago, before she disappeared.

Deep worry lines etched the bridge of her nose. We were all afraid. My stomach settled somewhere near my ankles and Giovanni's eyes darted, both of us looking for someone to dash out and cripple us with their ability to wrench our auras from our bodies. He clutched the black hilt of the knife he'd used against Griffin in the shack.

I couldn't bear to look at that knife. Griffin wasn't the only person who had felt its bite. My neck throbbed where it had sliced into my skin, leaving a line of puckered dried blood. I bit back a sob, thinking of my father on his knees with a scarlet bloom unfurling on his stomach after Griffin stabbed him. His expression had been so disbelieving. I was the last person he had fixed his gaze upon before the life left his eyes.

Was it love I saw in their depths? Or blame?

"What about the people who live here now?" Giovanni whispered as he opened the door for my mother and helped her out.

"No, no," she muttered. "No one should live here. Benito told me he would never let it go." As we walked through the red gate, her slender fingers brushed the metal daisy. "Cora, your *da* gave me that daisy the day you were born."

"Is it strange to call me Cora?" I'd been born Daisy, my name changed when my dad fled with me to the States.

Gráinne's straight black hair hung limp over the hanger of her shoulders. So much about her was lifeless, including her eyes when she looked at me and softly said, "None of us are who we were then."

"I don't feel safe here," Giovanni said, surveying the property.

"I could be in another time zone and not feel safe. Another planet, even," I said.

He nodded his agreement. "Is there a key, Mother?"

"*Mother?*" I mouthed.

He shrugged, a blond curl draping over one stormy blue eye, which was ringed with bruises from the beating he'd gotten when he was captured. "*Somebody* should call her that," he said in his bullish way.

I was about to fire off that he could go get his own mother and quit trying to lay claim to the one I'd just found, but I stopped myself. He couldn't do that. He never could. Though I didn't know the whole story, I knew he'd lost his parents when he was little like my mother had lost hers, and for the first time in his life, he had found two other Scintilla. He was no longer alone. Would it be such a bad thing to let him borrow "mother"?

I thought she'd go to the door, take us inside, and shield us from the enormous sky of stars and the world of shadows. But Gráinne, *Mother*, immediately strode past the house toward the backyard and the wild patch of daisies whose black faces beamed at the moon. I remembered my vision from my first visit here, of her in this yard, planting. But as I watched her drop to her knees now, her long hair curtaining off both sides of her face as she dug with bare hands, it hit me; I hadn't seen her planting in that vision.

I'd seen her burying.

My mother's hands ripped furiously at the stalks of flowers, flinging them aside like a god throwing bolts of lightning. I wondered if I'd looked that possessed the day I unearthed the key from under the albino redwood. It hurt to watch.

"Mom," I said, trying out the foreign word. "Please let one of us dig for a while. We need to hurry and get out of here."

Her arms shook like little stems of wheat trembling in a breeze. Giovanni reached under her arms and lifted her to standing, then dropped to his knees next to me, both of us moving the years of dirt covering my mother's secret.

I flinched when Giovanni used the knife to hack at the dirt, remembering the feel of it nicking my neck and the burn of its mark on my back. I hadn't had time to look at how the knife had marked me, but I knew it had. I had no idea why it sometimes happened when I retrieved memories, but I wore the evidence as a series of tattoos on my skin; strange proof of my power—psychometry—my sortilege as a Scintilla.

That knife held a memory that had gotten us out of the shack when I used the information to bluff Clancy Mulcarr. *Three.*

What was the mystical significance of three Scintilla? Clancy was so triumphant to have captured us. But he was scared, too. He desperately didn't want someone or something known as the Society informed of what he possessed. I needed to find out who or what they were, and I needed to know why Clancy's prize was three.

With both of us digging, we made better progress. The blue-black sky turned milky. A glow of light flared from the horizon. "Your first sunrise out of that place," I said to my mother, thinking of the thousands of moons she'd carved in the wooden floor, one for each day of her captivity. I'd also been branded on the palm of my hand by her moon. The clover ring, the key on my shoulder, the moon on my palm, and whatever was on my back, not to mention the cut across my neck. These were the outward scars of my new life.

I was dizzy with fatigue, struggling to continue digging, to even keep my eyes open, when Giovanni said, "Hey! I think I feel something." We both scraped faster, peering into the dirt. We spotted something like gleaming white stone, then dug faster to uncover it.

I sat back on my heels. "Is that what I think it is?"

My mother, who'd been half dozing against the side of the house as we dug, startled and her eyes flew open. Giovanni flicked the knife underneath the object and used it like a lever to push it up from under the last inch of dirt, then pulled gently.

"What the hell?" he yelled, dropping the thing. We both scuttled back onto the grass.

"Oh my God." I turned to my mother. "You buried a freaking body!"

Four

Cora

"Jesus, Cora. Shut up!" Giovanni hissed, looking around.

"Not a body," my mother singsonged with a smile that froze my blood. "Just a hand."

Giovanni and I shared a look, something like quizzical horror. What on earth had she brought us here for? I could barely control my voice. "*Whose* hand?"

When Gráinne didn't answer, I paced on the grass. My body shook from chill and fatigue, and fear settled on my skin like the fine mist hanging in the air. I was utterly confused and exasperated. Uncontrollable shivers racked me.

"This is ludicrous," Giovanni whispered.

The sky brightened with every passing moment, and the light scared me more than the darkness. In daylight, anyone might see the three of us, industrious and dirty, bloodied and bruised in the backyard, digging up bones with a knife. At least regular people couldn't see the silver light of our auras flickering in the dawn. A light flipped on inside a house next door. The world was waking up around us. "We need to get out of here."

We all peered into the hole at the bones, so slender they were almost elegant, the hand clutching the soil beneath like it was clinging to the dust it would return to. Giovanni reached in to swipe dirt away from the joints of each willowy finger and his movements stirred up a glint of light. From inside the hole, something shimmered and reflected against the rising sun.

"What is that? A ring?" I whispered. It looked like a simple gold band. Every cell in my body quivered with revulsion as I reached in the hole to slide the ring off the end of the finger.

Immediately, I was flung into another time.

A brutal fight.

Savage.

Life or death.

I'd been cast into the violent red energy of a memory held by the ring. I saw my mother as if I, myself, were the wearer of the ring. We fought and rolled and collided against each other. The images hit fast, like blinding strikes of lightning. A confrontation, running and tackling, and one final, terrifying image of my mother swinging an enormous ax, which caught the hand that had risen up to shield against the blade.

The hand fell.

Dropped to the ground with horrific finality.

Fingers splayed open.

The ring was revealed in my memory vision. Recognition punched my breath from me; it was the same ring, with the very same double-triangle insignia, as the ring upon Clancy Mulcarr's hand. And it matched the ruby-red crystalline pyramids that connected at their tips at the top of the key that hung around my neck. What did it mean?

The last image I saw was that of my mother, grabbing the

severed hand and running.

Sister spots of pain burned my forearms. There would be marks from this ring. I could already feel them branding into me. I struggled for breath and swung my gaze to my diminutive mother, her body withered from maltreatment, her mind half baked from trauma and from her aura being drained over and over these many years. God, the things she'd been through. She had such inner strength.

I barely knew her, but life had recently taught me that we can barely know anyone, not even ourselves sometimes.

"You fought for your life," I said, respect welling up.

"I fought for ours," was her answer as she took the ring from my hand and spit unceremoniously on the insignia's flat surface before wiping it off on her skirt. "I buried the hand after I was attacked. The ring meant nothing until I saw it on Clancy's finger tonight. It was a new trinket, one I'd not seen him wear before." With a look of disgust, she handed the ring back to me.

I hugged my mother then, for her ferocity and for her strength. I'd underestimated her. She was ravaged but lucid enough to understand that this ring might mean something. It was important enough to be worn by the Arrazi who'd imprisoned her for almost thirteen years, and had been worn by her attacker. It had to mean *something*.

Too many truths had been buried. She was right to unearth this one.

Giovanni held the skeletal hand from one finger like he was doing some kind of macabre minuet with a dismembered hand, then tossed the bones back in the hole and shoved dirt over them.

"I'll be needing something from inside the house." Without explanation, Gráinne walked toward the back door, carefully slid a rock out from the loose mortar in the house's stone foundation, and scooped a key from the hole behind it. Dogs barked in the distance, birds warmed up their singing voices, the hum of increasing traffic reached my ears. The world continued to awaken.

"Perhaps I should wait outside," Giovanni said. "Keep a look out. Rush her. We've been here too long already."

I nodded and followed Gráinne through the back door. The house smelled like timeworn air and thirteen years of dust. "Hurry," I warned my mother, though in truth, I'd have loved nothing more than to have the leisure to explore the house and trace its memories with my fingers. I'd endure many marks to see my father again.

I lifted my sleeves to confirm the latest brandings from the ring. One black triangle had formed on the soft underside of each of my forearms. I shoved my sleeves back down. It filled me with contempt that I'd forever carry a mark of the Arrazi. Then I thought about the invisible marks my mother carried and tamped down my scorn. My scars were nothing compared to hers.

My mom strode through the kitchen with familiarity and the sureness of purpose. "Does it hurt to be here?" I asked.

"It hurts that my dreams of all three of us returning together are…" She couldn't say the word.

Dreams died with my father.

The kitchen was lifeless—the beating heart of home gone cold. I traced my eyes over its dusty surfaces. An oak table against the wall, crocks that once held flour, sugar, and tea, the square of the root-cellar door cut into the wooden planks on the floor, the farmhouse sink, empty and dry. An embroidered towel still hung from a hook next to it, and I ran my finger over the threads, wondering if my mom embroidered.

A loud thumping jangled the walls and my already taut nerves. I ran out of the kitchen, following the noise, and found my mother kicking her heel at a patch of drywall in an adjacent room. "What are you doing?" I asked, grabbing her by the shoulders.

"Let me be," she said, breathless and still kicking despite my restraining grasp. Small bits of cream-colored drywall crumbled onto the wide plank floor as the wall began to give way. "I have to get something."

"Cora!" Giovanni called to me from the back door. "What in God's holy hell—"

I let go of my mother and ran back through the kitchen to where he poked his head through the doorway. "She's kicking the wall to get something from behind it, I think."

The hint of a smirk played on his lips. "What, like an *entire* body?"

I groaned. "Please, no. I don't think I can handle that right now."

His eyes were sympathetic. "I know. I can't take much more, either. Everything that's happened has rivaled my worst memories. We're lucky to be alive."

"We'll be lucky to stay alive."

We stared at each other for a moment. I was grateful to have found him, another silver Scintilla in a world of color, but I couldn't help but think that we'd made a superhuman promise back in Christ Church that we shouldn't have made—to do everything we could to find the truth and stop all this. How were *we* going to stop all this? Did the lambs *ever* stop the lions?

"Tell her to hurry and that she can't make this much noise. Someone will hear."

"I will," I said, hearing another succession of thumps from the other room. "It must be important. Go to the car. Be ready. I'll get her and meet you out front."

Giovanni exhaled a ragged breath. "You're sure?"

"Yes, totally. We'll be right there."

He retreated down the steps and strode around the corner toward the front of the house. I headed back to retrieve my mother and whatever was important enough to beat down a wall with her feet. I skidded to a stop in the middle of the kitchen.

The cellar door hadn't been open before.

FIVE

Finn

The coarse wooden handle of the shovel chafed my hands as I dug. A heap of soil, blackened by the rain, piled up next to the hole, which was as deep as my waist. I couldn't tell what was mist and what was sweat trickling down my spine. I had to do this. I reckoned that the harder I worked, perhaps the Scintilla energy Cora had transferred into my body against my will would dissipate faster.

The sooner it did, the sooner I could die.

I shivered with the memory of her act as I shoveled, a slowed version of the moment she saved my life replaying in my mind. Cora's dark curls brushing my neck as she'd bent over me, the petals of her lips pressing against mine, the taste of her tears. The essence of her spirit had rolled into me and through me, suffusing every cell in my body with a penetrating spark of light.

Her aura was the sweetest wine.

I'd never felt so alive.

I'd never been so conflicted. My heart and my body were at war.

I hadn't wanted her to save me, but I was too weak to fight

her—too weak in body, too weak of heart. Even as Cora doubted my love, she gave me hers. It was the most beautiful experience I'd ever known…and the most shameful. When I realized what she'd done, as her Scintilla aura infused me with strength, a primal shred of me wanted to grab her by the shoulders and pull every beam of her energy into my body. That survival instinct, that pure ravenous desire, scared the bloody hell out of me.

That's when I knew: in order to prove my love to Cora Sandoval, I had to let her go.

Forever.

It hadn't been the first time I'd had a frightening experience with Cora. I recalled the night her father caught us in her bedroom. That was the moment everything changed. I had this angel of a girl in my arms. Of course I was out of my mind, turned on from rolling together, kissing with abandon in the moonlit bed, but it was more than that. I since realized it had to be the first time I'd unknowingly gotten a direct hit of her Scintilla energy.

I was buzzed with it, reeling, mumbling about how radiant she was. Strange, though… Now that I knew the difference between taking her energy and being given her energy, I saw that night in a new way, and it confused me. In her room, I'd felt like a funnel, her essence pouring into me, like she was actually *giving* to me.

The more heady and befuddled I'd felt, the more compelled I'd been to warn Cora about what my parents had told me I might become. I'd begun to speak, started to tell her the unfathomable truth, when her dad had walked in on us.

I'd run away from Cora because I thought the euphoric state I was in was a signal that I was becoming a monster. I left her house, came to my senses, and ran home to Ireland the next day. Turned out, I couldn't run from fate. To add to my list of self-recriminations, she showed up in Ireland, and I couldn't leave well enough alone.

Damn it—I should have left well enough alone. I'd thought will trumped biology.

For the bleedin' life of me, I'd never understand why we, of all people, couldn't stay the hell away from each other.

I slammed my heel into the blade of the shovel and heaved another load of dirt onto the grass. Cora had once sat in this very spot, reading from her mother's journal, trying to unravel the mystery of herself. We had no idea then how much we had in common. How intertwined were our fates. The worst torture was the feeling that I'd found *the one,* only to be smacked with the cruel reality that it was utterly impossible for someone like her to be with someone like me.

Scoop after scoop, I shoveled until my arms quaked with fatigue, until I caught myself standing in the sunrise, dozing on the crook of my arm over the handle of the shovel.

"Enough of this. Come in now." My mother's stern voice carried down to me, startling me awake. From the hole, I peered up at her outline, black against the approaching day. Holding an umbrella in one hand, she bent and reached down to me with the other. I looked at the grave I'd dug, wishing I could pull the earth around me like a blanket and go to sleep.

"Finn," she urged.

I stabbed the shovel into the dirt and stepped on the blade to raise myself higher. I grabbed her hand and pulled myself from the muddy pit, onto the soaked grass. She waited wordlessly for me to raise myself to my feet. We stood, face to face. I read the look that was in her eyes, the impatient question: *I've come to terms with what I am. Why can't you?*

She took a step closer and peered into my eyes with a searching intensity. "I see," she said with a blink of sad comprehension. It was the first time I could remember my mother's voice cracking. "You have plans to die."

Six

Cora

Had my mother opened the cellar door?

I couldn't recall a moment while I'd been talking to Giovanni when her relentless kicking had stopped. My heartbeat spiked as I sidestepped past the gaping hole in the floor to get to her and get the hell out of there. Bells of alarm chimed in my body, and beneath the ringing sang one persistent note of danger. I felt threat behind me as tactile as a gust of wind and swung around.

His gloved hand was already in motion when I'd turned. Ducking, I narrowly dodged a syringe. Before I could cry out, his other arm sliced through the air in a knife-hand strike to my windpipe, right over the stinging cut. I fell backward and slammed into the refrigerator, clutching my throat, wet with new blood. It felt like my neck had been hammered in half. Stars dotted my vision as I gasped for breath, which was as futile as trying to climb a cloud. Nothing would go in. No sound would come out.

The man lunged at me and I kicked my foot hard, catching him in his right knee and knocking him into the cellar door. That man crashed into another who emerged from below. They both scrambled like black spiders to get to me. I still couldn't scream, could barely breathe. I let go of my neck and pushed myself off the refrigerator, but the man I'd kicked grabbed one of my feet, yanked me down, and pulled me across the floor toward the hole. The gold ring tumbled from my hand and rolled down the cellar stairs.

"Get the other woman!" the man yelled to his comrade.

I kicked at the man's face and pushed my hands against the dusty floor. Sharp splinters of wood pierced my palms. I couldn't let them take her, take us! The man pulled my legs and, with one forceful yank, dragged my body toward him and leaped on top of me, pinning me underneath him. His only distinguishing mark was a harelip scar that pulled his mouth into an uneven sneer. He sat on my torso and once again raised the syringe.

These men weren't Arrazi.

If they were, we'd already be subdued and their auras would flare white in triumph.

Suddenly, the man flew backward off me as though he'd been knocked back by an invisible explosion. He lay in a heap by the sink, unconscious.

Giovanni stood like a warrior in the doorway with one arm extended in the man's direction. I had seen him use his telekinesis on objects before, but never on people. His jaw dropped as if in shock at what he'd done. I scrambled to my feet and ran to Giovanni as the other man appeared from the adjacent room. Giovanni's arm brushed like an elegant tai chi move, causing the man to crash into the wall and slip into oblivion with his companion.

Giovanni immediately caught me in an embrace.

"You did that." My voice came out a hoarse, scraping whisper.

"I had no idea I could," he said, squeezing me tight. His heart thumped against my cheek. "I've never moved anything so big. You okay? I knew I should not have left you."

I coughed my words out. "You couldn't know they'd come up out of the freaking floor."

"Who the hell are these men?"

"Not Arrazi," I said, tearing through the house in search of my mother. "They would have easily just taken from me and my...oh God!"

Crumpled and still on the floor of the living room, next to a small treasure box, lay my mom. I cradled her head in my hands and pressed my face close to her mouth, feeling for breath, holding my own until I felt something.

It was there, a slow heartbeat.

"They had syringes," I said to Giovanni as he scooped her into his arms. I gingerly picked up the spent syringe, put it in the box, and placed the box on her stomach. "It could have been poison, anything." Panic was a rising tide in my blood. Dark shadows already circled her eyes, and she was pale to begin with. How could I know if whatever they'd given her was killing her slowly?

She couldn't die.

Not both of my parents in one day.

The ones who disappear do so forever.

She had written that to my father about her own parents. It was true for Giovanni's parents as well.

The Scintilla—a tribe of orphans.

Both of us ran toward the front door, but I changed course. Giovanni yelled at me as I raced back into the kitchen where the two men still lay, out cold. "One sec!" I had to get the ring from the cellar. It was the only real clue we had as to whom Clancy

Mulcarr was dealing with and probably whom these men were affiliated with.

My heart pumped like it was three sizes larger as I backed down the creaky stairs, my fingers brushing the silky glue of webs on the ladder rungs. A small rectangle of light shone through the cellar window. Luckily the sun had risen higher and I could see enough to scoop up the ring and slip it onto my finger. I curled my fingers around its image.

Another light illuminated the darkness as well. Squinting into the gloom, I focused on a pin of glowing yellow coming from a tunnel dug through the wall of the cellar. A tunnel. Whoever they were, they'd been waiting. And watching. For a very long time.

I climbed back up the ladder and heaved myself onto the kitchen floor. Holding my breath, I lifted the hand of the man who had attacked me.

"Cora!"

Giovanni's cautious warning didn't deter me. There, near the man's head, was his syringe. I grabbed it and ran.

Giovanni cradled my mother like a sleeping baby and sprinted through the door. He poured her into the car's backseat and I climbed in, supporting her head on my lap. She looked so small. "We have to take her to the hospital. Whatever they stuck her with could be lethal. She can't die, G. She can't." Tears streamed down my cheeks. One landed on my mother's forehead like a holy drop of prayer.

"It's like she's sleeping," Giovanni said, directing the car back onto the main road and looking in the rearview mirror constantly. "Maybe they wanted to knock us out, not kill us."

"We can't guess. It could be moving through her bloodstream. It could be killing her while we argue about it. Take us to a hospital. Now."

"If we can get my things from the airport locker, I can call a contact of mine. He's a doctor and might be able to help. Discreetly."

"Might isn't good enough. You take us to the hospital now or get out of this car and I'll take her there myself."

"Damn it, Cora! It's not a question of splitting up. I'm not leaving you. But waltzing into a hospital when—"

I shot him a look that could wither a cactus.

"Hospital it is."

$\mathcal{T}$he waiting room reeked of sick normalcy: crying toddlers, old people slumped over in sleep, an impatient woman with what looked to be a scratch on her arm, acting like it had been cut off.

My mind flashed to the image of my mother hacking off the hand of her attacker. I shuddered and made my way to the desk, squeezing the ring in my palm. When the staff saw Giovanni behind me, carrying an unconscious woman, we were immediately ushered in through the double doors. The woman with the scratch glared.

The nurse barraged us with a flurry of questions. "We were attacked," I stammered. "I have no idea who they were or what they injected her with. We found her unconscious on the floor."

"Injected?"

The nurse flinched and her aura splayed out fearfully when I produced the empty syringe from the box.

"Is your mother a recreational drug user?"

"No!"

"Did you call the police?"

"No."

"I see." She asked me to deposit the syringe in a plastic container and trotted with it down the hallway.

Giovanni and I were asked to wait in an adjacent waiting room despite my protests to stay with my mother. I didn't want her to wake up without me. I prayed she would wake at all. An elderly man walked toward us with his arm draped protectively around a crying woman. They flopped down together in chairs opposite us. Grief was blue-black twilight rippling around their bodies. She dabbed the corners of her red eyes with a cloth handkerchief and inhaled in rapid bursts. A very big cry of very bad news.

Oppressive dread weighted my chest. I'd have to deliver very bad news. Janelle and Mami Tulke had to be told about my father's death. The grieving ache burned with fresh flames. How could I tell his wife and his mother he'd been murdered? Hate also charred me. Hate for Clancy, who'd taken the soul of a man already on his knees, begging for our lives.

My fists clenched so hard they hurt.

Giovanni must have sensed the rage in my aura because he softly laid his hand over mine, giving it a gentle squeeze and an infusion of calming energy. The electric current of our auras merged, making my hand thrum pleasantly. For a brief second, I thought to pull away, but I left my hand under the soothing blanket of his.

The woman sobbed inconsolably, each lurch of her body making me cringe. Giovanni and I glanced at each other and somehow I knew what he would do. He sent his energy, the light of his silver aura, in the couple's direction. They couldn't see what he was doing, of course, but they could surely feel it, as I could, as a warm cloak of comfort.

I tried to do the same, but my aura sputtered pathetically around me. My anguish was a cage, holding back my light.

Thanks to Giovanni, the woman's sobs immediately lessened in frequency, like fading contractions. She curved into her husband's side and closed her swollen eyes, spent. His relief was evident as he rolled his head back against the wall and exhaled.

The waves of my own grief broke less violently. Giovanni's Scintilla energy probably accounted for that. It felt deliriously good to relax and let my body drift into sleep. Exhaustion crumbled me into hard bits. The last time I'd slept was nearly twenty-four hours ago, in captivity, with Giovanni's warm breath on my neck. That was how Finn had found us. It wasn't what he thought when he saw us wrapped around each other in sleep. It was two Scintilla, two caged birds, with our wings over each other for safety.

I woke abruptly, my head jerking forward in panic. Yawning, I noted the clock. We'd been asleep for nearly two hours. The grieving couple was gone, and Giovanni and I were alone in the waiting room with only the flicker of the television mounted from the ceiling. He was sound asleep with his mouth open like a sigh. His hand had slipped from over the top of mine and cupped the inside of my thigh. I lifted it up by his sleeve and set it in his own lap. When I saw what was on the television news, I nudged him awake.

An alarming incident has public health officials baffled. In the heart of New York City, a subway car rolled to a stop at Grand Central Station with three dead passengers. The landmark station was shut down for forty-eight hours afterward for investigation. Other passengers on the train insist they noticed nothing strange and cannot say what might have caused the mysterious deaths. Some passengers are being quarantined by the CDC for medical testing while authorities seek the remaining passengers who had exited the train before the deaths were noticed. "I thought they were sleeping," said one witness. Health officials say they are doing everything they can to determine the cause of the deaths. Similar reports have come out of California and some European countries, causing preliminary concern about an epidemic.

Meanwhile, local authorities are asking for help in finding these two people... They are pleading for the young couple to turn themselves in for questioning.

"They may have seen something that can help us. They could be the key."

The familiar image popped up of me at the Dublin airport, kneeling next to the elderly dead couple. All that could be seen of Giovanni was his arm as he pulled me up and we took off running into the rain. They then showed the blown-up picture of my finger with the ivy marking, the first I'd received when I had the vision of my father talking to Mami Tulke. My stomach plunged as they played the footage from the airport again. I stuck my hand under my leg.

"It's getting worse. What if we turned ourselves in?" I whispered, looking around to make sure no one could hear. "We'd be isolated, safe from the Arrazi. Maybe they would get us out of Ireland."

"You think we'd be safe?" Giovanni asked with a derisive

puff of a laugh. "Ask yourself, why *us*? We're not the only witnesses to the deaths around the world. Why are they so keen to get *us*, specifically, in for questioning?"

"Using the media to get to us?" I asked, my fingers curling into my fists. "If you're right, that's a scary amount of influence."

"Even if I'm not right, if we turned ourselves in, the Arrazi and whoever attacked us today would know exactly where we were. Don't forget, Cora. The Arrazi first found *you* in California. They're everywhere. We've got to find a way to stop them from killing our kind *and* innocent humans. Until the Arrazi are dead, we won't be free."

I crossed my arms. "We're on the run. We're not free now. Maybe another country—"

He smacked his hand on the armrest of the chair. "This is where we need to be! I've been all over the world, searching. Nothing came of it, until I came to Ireland."

"It's amazing how you can go from Sleeping Beauty to Captain Intensity in seconds."

He arched his brows playfully. "You think I'm a beauty when I sleep?"

I ignored that. "What if, through helping to figure out what's going on with the"—I pointed at the television—"*drop-dead people*, we latch onto the way to stop the Arrazi? It could be connected. My father thought it was. I don't know about all that energy stuff, but I think this has something to do with Scintilla and Arrazi. We saw that Arrazi man walking away when those people died at the airport. I bet he killed them. I bet that's what's been happening all over, and the world thinks it's some stupid virus. But if they could see auras like we can, they'd probably see an Arrazi walking away from each scene."

Giovanni looked stone resolute and I didn't understand it.

Both of our auras spiked in pointed jabs at each other. "I don't need your permission to talk to the authorities or leave Ireland," I said, wanting to elude the heft of his domineering ways. Adding *you're not the boss of me* would probably not help. Everyone who says that says it to someone acting like they're in a position of authority, and Giovanni Teso was definitely *not* the boss of me.

Giovanni suddenly grasped the sides of my face with mild firmness; his palms were an electric layer of warmth on my cheeks. He held my gaze and I held his, which, surprisingly, wasn't angry, but intense and afraid. "Stop trying to separate us, would you please? We need each other. I've gone most of my life without knowing another Scintilla, without having someone who understands. Remember how alone you felt when you thought you were the only one?"

I nodded reluctantly.

"How do you feel now?"

Thick emotion welled up in my throat. The improbability of my life now chipped away at my meager bravado. Whose life *was* this? I'd slipped into the current of a bad dream that wouldn't let me go. "I feel lost," I heard myself say, and the tears finally flowed. I sagged into his chest, releasing the pressure of grief and fear I'd held in for weeks, days, hours. I felt helpless and untethered without the rock of my father, without the love of Finn, without any security or safety at all in this bewildering new world.

Giovanni pecked my forehead with a kiss and spoke against my skin there. "Better to be lost together."

"Miss Sandoval?" The doctor approached with a smile and outstretched hand, but I couldn't lift mine to greet her. I was struck dumb by her polished white aura. She was Arrazi, her aura indicating she had killed. Very recently.

Seven

Cora

Next to me, Giovanni sucked in his breath.

I shoved past the doctor and ran the length of the corridor to my mother's room, the tiles of the hospital walls buzzing past. I skidded into her room, banging my hip on the doorframe. Funny how, when you can see life in the pulsing colors around people, you no longer look for other signs. At first, I didn't register the rhythmic beeping of the heart monitor, or the IV dripping consistently into her veins, or the reassuring lift of her chest with each breath. All I saw was her silver—calm as a thick mercury lake—radiating around her body, pulsing in time with her heart.

My mother was alive, beautifully alive. I collapsed over her with relief. Giovanni and the doctor both rushed in. The doctor looked alarmed at Giovanni, whose arm was outstretched as if to ward us from her. She could kill all three of us within minutes. But the doctor couldn't see auras; Arrazi could only sense them, and she didn't know what I knew—that with his sortilege, Giovanni could throw her down with a flick of his wrist.

Unless she chose to take from him first. Didn't people always take down the strongest first? That was what I would do.

"You didn't kill her," I said with disbelief.

Her wary eyes appraised us like we were crazy. "Of course not, miss. Please, be calm," the doctor said. "Your mother is going to be all right. Whoever injected her with the syringe gave her a very heavy sedative—that's all it was. She'll come around very soon." She peered at me and Giovanni, taking in our disheveled appearance, our mud-caked clothes and bloodstains, my sliced neck. "Are the two of you okay? What's going on here?" The doctor took a step closer.

"Don't!" I yelled, holding up my hand. Her shocked response caused me to ease the harshness in my voice. "Please...don't come any closer." Why wasn't she taking from us? Did she not know what we were?

Her head cocked to the side, brows crinkled in a puzzled knot as she studied me. I braced myself for the hit of her hungry energy, like a hook being sunk into the flesh of my chest. But none came. She backed slowly toward the door and shouted something over her shoulder to the nurse sitting at her station. "Code *remedium*."

"Latin," Giovanni said. "In Italian we say *remedio*—remedy. What is that code meant for? Are you calling more like *you*?"

His question stopped her in her tracks. "Like *me*?" she asked in a near whisper. "What can you possibly mean by that?" There was a telling shake in her voice. "If, *like me*, you mean more medical personnel, then yes. I see the tattoo on her finger and it matches the one on the airport security video. I know who you two are."

"Well, we know *what* you are. You will call off your code or we will tell everyone what the Arrazi do to innocent people.

I'll bet you have an unnatural number of deaths on your watch, doctor," I said.

A puff of disbelief came from the woman. She was trying to play it off, but her aura radiated fear. Yellow seeped into the white around her body. "What are *you*?" she asked in a whisper.

Bluffing was the only route I saw to get past her and out of the hospital. "You think you have powers? Your only power is to steal souls, Arrazi. We are," I said, steeling my voice, "your antidote. We *are* the remedy."

"Never mind!" she yelled to the nurses' station behind her. "Call off the code. I was mistaken."

I reveled in the quiver in her voice.

"But, ma'am," the nurse answered from behind her desk, "they're already here."

The IV bag came loose from the pole with a tear. "Carry her," I commanded Giovanni as I pulled the blankets off my mother's thin legs.

"Wait," the doctor said. Her mouth hung open like every thought in her mind vied for priority. Her eyes pleaded with us as we headed for the door, my mother once again cradled in Giovanni's arms. As we passed her, she touched my arm. "You're a different kind," she gasped. "We are not the same. I—I can feel it." She swallowed hard; her hand gripped me tighter. "You're not *normal*. Tell me, what *are* you?"

I shook my arm free. "Your worst enemy, lady."

The nurse gaped at us as we spilled from the room and started toward the elevators at the far end of the corridor. The elevators chimed. Two security guards and a man in scrubs came out and ran directly at us. "I can do nothing without my hands," Giovanni said as he spun around with my unconscious mother and darted in the opposite direction, back toward the doctor, her eyes round with alarm as we ran past her.

"You there, stop!" yelled one of the men from behind us.

I frantically scanned the hall for a stairwell, but all I could see were more hospital rooms with people tipping their heads out to see what the commotion was about.

"This is not necessary," I heard the Arrazi doctor say with a false laugh. "I was mistaken. These are not the people they're looking for." She sounded desperate, fearful, and I was glad for it.

"Then why are they running?"

I looked over my shoulder to see her standing between us and the security personnel, blocking them, but one of the officers shot past her. Suddenly his running stalled and a bewildered look crossed his face. I'd seen that look before. His aura waved behind him like a bride's veil in the wind and flowed into the doctor's body. Our eyes met briefly. Her face was grim, determined. The man clutched his heart and collapsed.

She ran to him, and even as she asked if he was all right, even as she felt for his pulse and seemed to administer medical help to him, she greedily took every last drop of his aura. Her eyes closed. The seed of his humanity bloomed in her own, and her aura exploded in white.

We turned a corner and blasted through the door of an emergency exit stairwell, down the stairs as fast as we could go with Giovanni clasping my mother to him. She moaned, the first sound she'd made since we carried her out of her house. At the first floor, I poked my head through the door. No one was waiting for us. All seemed normal. We walked calmly but quickly out the exit to the car.

My mother was just coming to when we pulled away from the parking lot. She blinked heavily at me as I explained what had happened. My heart beat a mile a minute, but I tried to sound calm for her sake. I turned to Giovanni. "That Arrazi doctor, she didn't seem to know what she had right in front of her."

Giovanni ran his long fingers over his stubble, touched the scab on his lip with a tip of his finger. He looked deep in thought, his brows creased. "No."

"She killed that man. For us—"

He huffed. "For herself."

"Why didn't she take from us?"

He smiled then, the first flash in days lit in his eyes. "I suspect that had something to do with you. You were very convincing."

"I wonder what her sortilege is. She could have attacked us with her power, but she didn't. Clancy told me that the allure of a Scintilla is that our energy gives the Arrazi their powers. He also said it enables them to live longer so they have to kill less frequently."

"That means that many Arrazi have no power at all because they've never tasted a Scintilla's aura. Most probably don't even know such powers exist. If they did—"

"We'd have a swarm of Arrazi on us."

"*Si.*"

Grim thoughts invaded. "We'll have them anyway," I said. "Clancy won't stop hunting us. He wants three Scintilla for some reason, and he'll be hell-bent on capturing us again."

"He'll search. Awake and asleep. Let's hope our trail is lost to him," my mother said groggily through a yawn. She was always so quiet, it was easy to forget her in conversation, and unwise to do so. After thirteen years, she knew more about Clancy Mulcarr than any of us.

I turned to face her in the backseat. "Are you okay?" She nodded but stayed reclined on the seat and pulled the IV from her forearm. I winced. "There's a black market for Scintilla. God, the sickness of it—people paying money for possession of other people." Then I thought about slavery and how people were still bought and sold in this world. The human trade was alive and well. It made my stomach sick. "Not too hard to imagine, I guess. This is the world we live in."

Giovanni's expression turned dark. "We are human diamonds. People do ugly things for precious gems."

"The Arrazi aren't the only ones who are after us," I said. "Clancy Mulcarr said we had enemies in places we couldn't imagine, enemies who'd do anything to keep the truth a secret. He and Griffin called it *the Society*."

"The ring," murmured my mother.

Giovanni nodded. "The problem with trying to find out who or what that symbol stands for is that we might open a box we can't close."

I suddenly thought of Faye and her bookstore, Say Chi's, back home in Santa Cruz. Someone had wanted her to stop looking into silver auras badly enough to vandalize her shop and leave a threatening note. How did they know what she was researching? How would we search for answers without some great eye staring down on us?

Mom bolted upright. "My box!" She looked frantic.

"We have it," I said. "In the trunk with my duffel." She visibly relaxed. "What's in it?" I asked, imagining more keys, or research of hers, or bones. I'd only opened it enough to throw the syringe inside.

"My birth certificate, an old passport," she answered. "And a bit of money. Not much, though. Not enough."

"Enough for what?"

"To survive. To fly away."

"I've got money," Giovanni said. "But we need to go to the airport to get it."

"Are you kidding?" I asked. "The airport, the very place where we were filmed fleeing the scene of two deaths? We can't go there. You saw the news."

He clenched the steering wheel. "I'll go in alone. It's too important. I have money there, a copy of my passport, and a cell phone."

I crossed my arms. "Don't see what you need a passport for if you insist on staying in Ireland," I grumbled.

"Picking fights is your sortilege," he replied, and turned off the highway at a sign marked with an airplane.

A smile bubbled up without my permission.

Giovanni gave me a look then. His blue eyes roved over my hands and the markings there. He reached and opened my palm with his hand. "I'd like to hear more about your true sortilege," he said softly.

"There's not a lot to tell," I said. "When I touch certain things, I see a memory." His eyebrow shot up. "And then it *marks* me."

"Does it upset you?" he asked, still holding my hand. The very palpable singe of electricity was becoming familiar. I felt calmer when he touched me, but invigorated, too. I could see how he'd survived all these years on his own. Scintilla energy *was* a kind of feel-good magic. It had a soft, rolling warmth of happiness.

I didn't know what to make of that. My body burned with the memory of our kiss when he'd regained consciousness after nearly being beaten to death by Griffin. But that had been the response of the pure, primal force of climbing back to life by your fingertips when death was pulling your feet. Giovanni hadn't known what he was doing. I'd been wrong to respond to him the way I had.

"Yes, it upsets me," I finally admitted, trying to focus on the conversation. My jaw clenched. "Very much, and some marks more than others."

We pulled into the airport's parking garage. It took forever to find an empty spot. "I still think this is a bad idea. Leave the keys here. In case." Giovanni got out of the car, then leaned in the window and gave us a meaningful look laced with fear. "Hurry back," I said.

My mother and I quietly watched the tide of people coming and going from the airport. I observed and analyzed their colors, remembering the first confusing days of my ability to see auras. The kids at school were a kaleidoscope of bewildering hues and textures. It felt like too much for someone like me — always flypaper for other people's emotions. I wanted to turn it off, to escape. But there *was* no escape from this, from the evidence of emotion, the joy of people, the illness, sadness, lust, anger — and love.

I saw the color of love all over the place: in the old man helping his wife out of a cab, between the mother and the baby nursing at her breast, between the young couple making out at the bus stop like they were joined at the tongues. People dripped with it.

Love was the most prevalent color in the world.

It was beautiful, the colors between people and the way they vibrated and danced together. There was something else I observed, though. In many people, there was a noticeable drawing in of their aura, a self-imposed barrier, as if the last thing they wanted was for their spirit to rub against anyone else's. The separation was sad to witness, but I could understand it now.

Self-protection.

It was the hoarding of the most beautiful thing about us. I saw proof that the opposite of love wasn't hate but fear. Hate reached out and grabbed, kind of like love did. But fear—it cowered in the corner like a small, terrified animal.

People were afraid of one another.

Now I knew why.

I leaned back in my seat and crossed my arms, thinking that what most people wanted was for their colors to feel the beautiful hues of another, to mix and blend with them and have life be painted better by it.

Connection.

The color of two hearts recognizing each other. I thought I'd felt that with Finn, and I was sure that now my heart beat black with disappointment.

My mom reached forward from the backseat, put her hands on my shoulders, and rubbed them comfortingly.

"Could you see it in my aura?"

"I don't have to be Scintilla to see you're hurting." She smoothed the hair back from my neck. Like—like a mother would. "I can *feel* you, too. Thoughts and emotions have energy of their own. I feel your broken heart."

I turned to face her, dared to let her in. "I've been cracked open. I let myself feel more for someone than I ever have and for what?" Guilt's arrow pierced me. "I shouldn't be talking about this."

She shook her head and a tear flung with it. "What is love but offering pieces of yourself? Falling in love is no tragedy. It simply means you were brave enough to break a piece off and offer it."

"I'm so sorry about Dad," I choked out. How could I moan about losing Finn in the face of that loss?

"I'll never regret the pieces of myself that I gave to your father." My mom stared hard into my eyes for a moment. "He died more whole than he lived the last thirteen years of his life."

"Because he found you…"

"Darlin' Cora," she cooed in her warm Irish accent, "because we were all together once again. Even if for a moment, our broken pieces came back together."

"I'll never be whole again."

She smiled into her eyes. "Aye. You will. Either with yourself, with another, or with God."

"Or all three?"

"Now that's the holy grail, isn't it?"

I liked talking with her this way, when her cobwebs were clear and she had some pieces of her own to offer.

A fresh mass of people washed out from the airport doorways, more than seemed normal. "How long has he been in there?" I asked mostly to myself. It had been too long. Giovanni was supposed to go straight to a locker, get his stuff, and run back out. My heart rocked back and forth in my chest.

I tapped my fingers on my leg and stared at the doors, waiting for a glimpse of his Viking height, his blond hair, his silver aura. A news van pulled up in front of the airport, and a hair-sprayed man and a cameraman got out and ran inside the building.

I squeezed the dashboard. "No…"

What if they recognized him somehow; what if they got him?

My mom shared my worried look as she watched people file out of the airport. She was biting the ends of her hair again. I didn't know what to do. Wait? Go look for him and risk getting caught myself? Drive away?

The engine revved to a growl when I started it. My heart hammered. How could I leave him? How could we stay? How could I manage to drive from the wrong side of the car, on the wrong side of the freaking road, when I barely knew how to drive at all? My hands shook as I placed them on the steering wheel and prepared to put the car in reverse.

Gráinne and I both yelped when my door flew open. With one hand on the roof of the car and one hand on the door, Giovanni radiated alarm. He understood what I was about to do. His jaw set rigid as he motioned for me to move back to the passenger's side. I scooted quickly over but grabbed his arm as he folded his long legs into the car. He wouldn't look at me.

"I'm sorry. I didn't know what to do. There were more people leaving the airport than going in. And then the news van showed up—"

"Volcano," he said, tossing a pair of fingerless gloves into my lap. He looked over his shoulder to back the car up.

"What?"

"Flights were canceled because of ash in the sky from another volcano eruption in Iceland."

"Isn't that totally oxymoronic? Mountains of fire in *Ice*land?"

"It's not the first time. News crews are in there covering the airport closure and talking about the rise in natural disasters."

"Oh, Benito," my mom said to the air. "You were right."

I hoped this wasn't the beginning of her talking out loud to my father. I hadn't even had time to process the reality that he was truly gone. That I had to leave his body. That I'd never see him again. Hearing his name struck my chest with force.

We inched along with the train of other cars departing the airport. People were obviously frustrated as some milled around outside the terminal, hoping the airport would reopen soon. Others bounced their suitcases behind them as they left. The fresh tourists, the last to arrive for the foreseeable future, pointed and looked at maps, confusion evident in the static texture of their auras.

Then I saw something that was so out of context, so incongruous, my mind could barely grasp that it was real. "Stop the car!"

EIGHT

Finn

"What tipped you off, Mother, the grave?" I needn't have asked. Not that I understood all the complexities of being a *different* kind of human, but I knew her sortilege, her specific power, acquired because she'd taken from the rare aura of a Scintilla—Cora's aura. My mother could see my deepest secret the minute she looked in my eyes. Grand. As if mothers didn't already have the inherent superpower to know too much.

"Please, stop this."

"If only I could."

"In time you may come to accept—"

"That's *shite*! When I think of time now, you know what I think of? How it stretches out before me, a road with nothing but loneliness and guilt and more death. I don't want time that includes murdering innocent people. I don't want time without the person I'm in love with. Humans strive to be better than they are, to *ascend*. I don't want a future being a lesser, vile version of who I once was. I'd rather be dead."

Her eyes radiated sadness.

"You should have told me long ago, Mum."

"Why, luv? You have no choice. Wishing you'd known earlier is the illusion of choice. A child can't grapple with this. *You* barely can." The leather of her glove warmed my cheek. "You're exhausted. We all are. What just happened was ghastly. Nothing must be decided tonight. I came out here to tell you…" Her brows narrowed into a consternated line. I wondered how, after the last twenty-four hours, there could be anything else she'd be afraid to tell me.

"What is it?"

"Your uncle Clancy has returned."

The shovel reluctantly released from the mud with a pop of suction as I grabbed it and ran toward the manor and up the rise of stairs to the door, anticipation winding my stomach like a watch, tighter and tighter. I'd unwind on my uncle. I'd thrill to see the shovel sticking out of his wide chest. I'd dig his Arrazi heart out with it.

I shoved the front door open and, with the tool firmly in my hand, strode into the house. "Where are you, you son of a bitch?" I yelled. My voice scraped my raw throat.

"Here," his voice rang out from the library, a low note of fatigue or even…boredom.

Like a shovel being thrust into my own chest, it pained me to walk into the library where I'd attacked Cora. I'd not gone in there since. Pain was soon replaced by aggression when I saw Clancy. The astonishment on his face as I heaved the shovel over my shoulder and swung it at him was brilliant to behold. He jumped backward with not an inch between him and the muddy, sharp metal.

"What did you think?" I yelled, swinging so hard again that

I felt a tear in the muscles in my shoulder. He ducked. As if through a tunnel, I could faintly hear my mother yelling.

The shovel took out a lamp and a glass jar of butter mints. Both shattered on the floor. "Did you think you could just waltz in here for supper? Have a wee chat about how you tortured a woman for a dozen years and then took my Cora?"

I backed him against the bookshelves. With his hands up, an entreating posture, Clancy began to talk, but I punched him full out and he fell to the ground. Books tumbled down around him. My mother was shouting behind us as I stuck the shovel to his fat neck. "You deserve to be killed the way you've killed people, to have your life sucked out of your spirit."

"Like *you* did to *your* Cora?" There was a flicker in his eyes—as quick as the spark from a lighter—as I braced my legs and looked down on him. "Yes. Do it," he choked out.

"You'd kill him?" My mother gasped. For a split second, I wondered if she was horrified or encouraged that perhaps I was embracing my Arrazi nature. "Finn, you *can't* attack him!"

"I won't live life as a killer, but if this is my first and last kill, I'll die a happy man." I threw the shovel aside and focused all my energy, all my hatred for what he'd done, for what we *were*, and began my first attempt at intentionally pulling someone's aura into mine.

My legs swept out from under me. I flew backward through the air as if an invisible bomb had gone off, blowing me into the wall, nearly knocking me unconscious. Stars floated in my vision.

Clancy stood, smoothing his white hair as he did, and picked up the shovel as I lay on the carpet, trying to suck in a breath. He eyed me with derision, then turned his focus to my mother. "See how it plays out, Ina?" he said, using the shovel to point at his sister. "When you teach him nothing? You've left him completely ignorant. He doesn't even know he can't take from another Arrazi. If he were my son, he'd not have been left in the dark."

"If he were your son, he'd be as ruthless as you!"

My uncle Clancy smiled then. Smiled like a secret promise. "He will be."

"He wants to die," she said, dissolving into rare tears. "He's going to let himself wither to nothing."

"Didn't we all say that? Doesn't every Arrazi have their dark night of the soul, questioning their very existence?"

My mother dropped her hands from her face, tears snaking down her thin cheeks. There was a long moment between them, full of memories and unspoken judgments. "You didn't," she finally said. "You never did."

The phone rang somewhere in the house, trilling away the seconds like a shrill bird on the hunt. My head exploded with pain from hitting the wall, but I also felt rattled to my bones. He'd tricked me into attacking him. I wobbled to my feet, dripping defeat.

"I would never want to be a man like you. You sicken me. You tore that woman from her husband and her little child. You stalked Cora until you were sure she was Scintilla."

"Yes."

"You used me," I said.

"Yes. You were bloody brilliant."

"I fell in love!" The words tore from me like an explosion. Didn't he understand the pain he'd inflicted? He gave me the most beautiful thing in the world and then ripped it away.

"You were supposed to, you dense *gowl*!"

I recoiled. My hands found their way to cover my wounded heart. I could barely breathe. I'd been played—my uncle's puppet. Cora had been captured, her father killed. If I'd stayed away from her, none of that would've happened. But I couldn't stay away. From the moment I felt her warmth, she was my sun.

Our housekeeper, Mary, entered the library, her owl eyes taking in the shambles. "You have a phone call," she said to me. "An American girl—"

From the corner of my eye, Clancy edged forward in excited anticipation as Mary handed me the phone.

"Hello?"

"Finn, it's Mari."

Did Mari know how similar her voice was to Cora's? It was wretched, the cold way I had to speak to her, her stunned silence in response to my clipped, one-word answers. They somehow knew about Cora's father's death and were looking for Cora, and when I refused to elaborate, her best friend, Dun, had to get on the phone because Mari began yelling at me. Girl had a gloriously foul mouth on her.

I could say nothing of consequence. Clancy stared at me all the while, his blue eyes boring into the side of my head. They had no clue the danger they put Cora and her mother in by calling the house. For all I knew, Clancy had a way to record our calls, and if he did, he'd know Mari and Dun were on a layover in London, en route to Dublin, due to arrive in the early afternoon. With the quickest expediency, I hung up. Even apart, I was a threat to Cora.

Without another word to my uncle or my mother, I went to my room to gather some things. My mum had indicated that, depending upon my own energy, my need would come fast and strong. I wanted to be as far away from human contact as possible when it came time to kill.

Alone and apart from anyone—that was my goal. And to achieve that, I needed to go to the waterfront. I needed to set sail.

Nine

Cora

The car inched along as I flung the door open and jumped out amid honking horns and yells punctuated by Italian cursing from Giovanni. I ran as fast as I could past the front of the airport terminal, trying to reach the mirage that was olive skin and haughty sunglasses, that was a horse's mane of long, black hair, the sunny yellow aura, and, well…the sequins that could only be Mari and Dun.

They'd come to Ireland, which filled me with shocked elation, followed by confusion, then exasperation.

Dun saw me first. I knew he did because his aura jumped like a bass note when he spotted me. We collided into each other. He lifted me up and swung me in a warm hug. I flung my arms around his neck and melted into him, with his strong arms holding me off my feet. His luminous aura wrapped me in the familiar warmth of brighter days. He set me down, still holding me, and Mari curved around my back as I cried.

I was sandwiched in love.

"How's my girl?" Dun asked.

"I'm not peachy." I sniffed. "I'm not even going to ask how it is you're here."

"Isn't that like asking without asking?" Mari said into my hair. "Are you okay?"

"I'm not okay. I'm never going to be okay. You have no idea what's been happening."

Dun pulled back and looked down into my face. "Is it true about your dad?" he asked.

"How did you—?"

"Mami Tulke told us last night. She just dropped it on us saying, 'My son is dead.' Then she up and walked out the door. Just left. We figured she came here because you and your dad were here. After she left we said 'screw it' and came, too. You shouldn't be alone."

"You have no idea if she actually came?" I asked, tears gathering into a puddle of bitterness in my chest. "I hope not. Ireland is the last place any of you should be." My Scintilla grandmother wouldn't be safe here, of all places. "My dad was murdered," I said, disbelieving the sentence even as it came from me. They stood in wordless shock, the weight of what I said dragging at our ankles. "Guys, there's so much to tell."

"Well," Mari said, pushing her sunglasses on top of her head and fixing me with her dark eyes, glassy with uncharacteristic tears, "we've been traveling all day. You look like you haven't had a meal in a week. Let's get some taters and a pint and you can tell us everything. I'm glad Finn told you we were coming. We were beginning to wonder where we were going to go once we got here. You haven't answered your phone in days."

"Wait." I tried to talk through the rock in my throat. "*Finn* knows you're here?"

"Yeah," Dun said. "Mr. McLoverboy said he couldn't pick us up, though. Rude play if you ask me. He wouldn't say why—"

"He didn't tell me you were coming. He'd have no way to tell me. We only came to get some things from a locker and I saw you walking by. We've gotta get out of here." I frantically pulled their hands, leading them toward the car. Dun was in step with me, but Mari was impossible to pull. She mulishly dug in her steel-toed boots and put her hands on her hips.

"Mari, I will explain in the car, but it is crucial that we leave here, *right now*. Pick up your feet or I'll make Dun carry you."

Mari looked at me with her mouth wide open, then fixed Dun with her *try it buddy, and I'll kill you with my laser vision* look.

"Shall I carry her?" We all turned toward Giovanni. His silver aura pulsed with serrated anxiety. I was sure mine looked as sharp to him. It was bad enough to be at the airport. Way worse if Finn somehow led his uncle to us, even inadvertently. Clancy might figure that we were at the airport right now. Whether physically or astrally, he could follow us. He'd have us. I glanced around.

Mari flipped her glasses over her eyes. "Who's this tall drink of masculinity who *thinks* he's going to be allowed to touch me? Jump back onboard the *SS Plunder and Pillage*, dude."

I gave Dun a pleading look. He was the only one who could get Mari moving. He whispered something in her ear and took her by the crook of the arm. To be honest, I'd never seen him handle her so deftly. A rose color flushed their auras when they touched. They followed me to the car with Giovanni behind us. Dun nodded curiously but politely to Gráinne as they slid into the backseat. Mari's hand flew to her mouth and her eyes flitted back and forth between us when I introduced her as my mother.

"You're alive!"

"Wow," Dun said. "It's nice to meet you Gr— What's your name again?"

"It's an Irish name," my mom said, her eyes and silver aura shifting nervously with the new energy of the strangers in the car. This was more people than she'd dealt with in over a decade. "Gráinne. Pronounce it *grawn-ya*. It means grace." Surprisingly, Mari didn't flinch when my mother softly touched her cheek. "You…you look so much like B…" Her words died on the *B* of my father's name.

"She's my cousin, Mom. Mari is—"

"Eduardo's daughter," my mother finished with an affirming nod. "I held you in my arms once, in Chile."

"Was she wrinkled and screaming like a baby piglet?" Dun asked with his typical good cheer, though the smile didn't reach his eyes.

"Mari was the sweet baby that made me want to have and hold my own," my mother answered. "And I did," she added, looking at me with love, unmasked.

We drove the streets of Dublin in silence, watching carefully in the rearview mirror for anyone who might be following. My stomach grumbled loudly.

"We do need to eat," Giovanni said. It had been at least a day since we had eaten anything.

"And sleep," I said with a yawn. I was so tired that I was queasy and slightly faint.

"Our hotel?" Dun said. "We have a room booked. We can go there."

Giovanni nodded. "Does anyone know where you're staying?"

Mari and Dun both answered in unison, "No."

The hotel that Mari had booked was middle of the road, a block away from the waterfront a few miles south of Dublin. A slice of ocean peeked from in between two hotels across the street. Giovanni handed Mari some cash and asked her to book an adjacent room in her name. She eyed him curiously and gave me a raised eyebrow, but did as he asked. I still didn't understand how he had so much money. He'd made it clear that he'd done whatever he had to do to survive on the streets as a kid. I assumed that was still his life.

We opened up the door between the rooms but dead-bolted the main doors. I left Gráinne staring out the window with her hand pressed to the glass. Her tiny body was in silhouette from the afternoon light. I imagined, for a brief moment, that if my father were alive, he'd stand silently behind her. Be her pillar like he had been mine.

Giovanni showered while Mari ordered enough room service to feed an army.

"Was that everything off the menu?" Dun asked, flopping onto one of the beds.

"Oh, did you want something, too, wiseass?"

God, it was good to see them.

Mari sat cross-legged on the bed near Dun's feet. "There's a long story here, isn't there?" she asked softly.

I nodded.

"And you're going to tell us *everything*."

"Yes," I answered. "But can I eat and shower first?"

Her eyes appraised me. "Been mud wrestling again? You look like you did that day at the redwoods."

I glanced down at my dirt-stained jeans, torn shirt, and dark crescent nails. "Just digging up a severed hand."

They got points for at least *trying* not to look stunned.

"She did say she'd tell us everything," Dun said.

Just then, Giovanni came out of the bathroom wearing nothing but a white towel around his tapered waist.

"Dude!" Mari said, mock-clutching her heart. "Good God, man. Warn a girl." She glanced at the towel tucked into the curved V of his hips.

Giovanni cocked his head to the side. Water dripped from his curls, reminding me of our first meeting in the rain. "My apologies," he said sincerely in his thick Italian accent. "I didn't mean to offend. I have no clean clothes. I was hoping to find a robe," he said, opening the closet doors, finding two robes and hanging the other one in the bathroom. We all tried not to gawk at him. Them, because he was so blatantly...Giovanni. Me, because of the line of bruises arching across the rippled muscles on his back. He'd taken it worse than I thought from Clancy and Griffin.

Mari snorted. "He can offend me any time," she murmured, to which Dun tipped his foot sideways and pegged her in the thigh. *Stop flirting,* he mouthed. His normally effervescent aura fizzled with sage-green jealousy.

"I'm not flirting," she whispered back. "I'm *bonding* with Cora's new friend."

"You two have a story to tell as well," I said, watching their auras interact. "I can see it, you know."

Dun shrugged but Mari wagged her finger at me. "Circumstantial. I told you before, Cora, none of that X-ray vision on me."

"It's not like I can turn it off, Mari."

She started to say something but a knock startled us. Dun jumped up to answer.

"Careful. Make *sure* it's room service," I whispered, Giovanni and I backing into the other room where my mother was resting. Our hands clasped as we stood behind the door and listened. But it was only the food delivery. I sighed and let go.

I went to shower and inhaled the soap-scented damp air of the bathroom. When I swiped the moisture off the mirror, I wished I hadn't. The delicate skin under my eyes was inky dark. My hair hung in dirty clumps of tangled curls. A garish scab ran across my bruised neck. My eyes were swollen and bloodshot. But it was the look in them that shocked me. I didn't recognize the girl staring back. Finn had been right; everyone has ghosts inside them, hidden hurts. My ghosts were a haze that clouded my eyes with sorrow.

I stripped off my filthy clothes. One step out of the puddle of cloth, one pivot, a look over my shoulder; that's all it would take to see how my back had been marked when I'd touched Griffin's knife. I closed my eyes and hung my head back, building my nerve brick by brick into a wall that I could hide behind once I finally dared to look.

I turned.

Opened my eyes.

Down the center of my back was the black mark of a severe, deadly blade.

My fingers dug into the bare skin of my stomach. Wasn't it enough to always have the gruesome memory of my father being stabbed? I had to forever carry the evidence of the knife on my body? I wanted to step out of this hideous shell. I wanted to scratch and claw it off my skin.

The hot shower was a coating of static noise and warm comfort. I sank to the floor of the tub with the water cascading over my back and cried into my knees, letting the torrent wash away my tears. I don't know how long I sat like that, but the water eventually ran cold and chased me out. I pulled back the shower curtain and shrieked. Mari was sitting on the toilet, holding a towel out. I grabbed it and stepped from the shower, feeling sheepish and wondering how long she'd been there. Had she heard me sobbing? Had she heard me cry "Daddy"?

"Sorry I scared you," she said. "You've lost weight."

I knew I had. I didn't feel like myself. I felt weak, brittle. "It's a new weight-loss plan. It's called the fear, suffering, and misery diet." We half smiled at each other.

"Food's here." I couldn't remember Mari's voice ever sounding so gentle. "I'm sorry about your dad. I'm not sure how to take care of you…"

"You don't have to."

"Oh yeah? Why don't I? Because the big Roman Romeo out there is going to? What happened with Finn?"

"It's beyond complicated."

Her foot bounced over her crossed leg. "Waiting."

"The first thing you should know is that you guys can't stay in Ireland. You're in danger as long as you're with the three of us."

"Where do you think we're going to go? We're stuck here anyway until the ash blows over. Besides, I'm *not* leaving your ass. People are worried about you. We need to get a hold of Mami Tulke and tell her where we all are so we can go home."

"We can't tell anyone where we are." I turned to hang the towel and put on the robe that hung from the back of the door. "Not even Mami Tulke."

"Jesus! You have a knife tattoo on your back? What's next? Leather pants and a shag haircut? You don't even wear makeup. I mean, it's moody and rockin', don't get me wrong—"

"I didn't do this." There was a long pause with me trying to decide whether *everything* was too much for Mari to know.

"The knife did," I finally said. I swallowed my embarrassment, dropped the robe, and stood naked before Mari, literally baring all of my new markings.

"Oh my God! Did you join a cult?"

"I—I have an ability to pull memories from objects. But when I touch them, I'm marked by them. Well, not all of them... I don't understand it, really. Seems to have something to do with the intensity of the memory." I turned my back toward the mirror and gaped at the image of a knife, *the* knife, slashing down the middle of my back. How could I touch anything if I was going to wear history like that? I didn't want to think what I'd someday look like, chaotically scarred by random memories, the past written on my skin.

I pulled the robe over my shoulders. "The things I'm about to tell you are going to be so hard for you to believe. Keep an open mind."

Mari held up her hand. "Girl, I spent almost two weeks in a freaking new-agey commune in the hills of Chile with our shaman of a grandmother. You'd be surprised at what I'd believe."

Ten

Cora

My mom had fallen asleep on the couch, curled on her side like a teardrop with her bony knees pulled up to her chest and her head bowed to them. I covered her with a blanket and joined Mari, Dun, and Giovanni to eat and update them on everything that had gone down. To their credit, they listened with rapt attention and without interruption. Neither one questioned the validity of what we were telling them. Neither one made me and Giovanni feel like mutant freaks.

Mostly, they looked properly scared.

After the telling was done, I excused myself to go in the other room. Something impossible needed doing. Something unavoidable. It would gnaw on me until it was done. I had to call my father's wife and tell her he was dead.

A long, cold finger of dread swirled my stomach. I'd never had to deliver news of this magnitude in my life. The reality was so fresh for me that it still didn't seem real. My dad would never be here again. How was that possible? There was an irreparable hole ripped in the fabric of my life. I wanted to reach into the hole and pull him back through.

I sat on the bed with the phone in my hand for a good five minutes before I dialed. Janelle answered immediately. My voice croaked. "Hi, it's Cora."

"Cora! Honey, how are you? What in the world is going on? Your father flew off to find you. You never should have run off like that, you know. I trusted you. I thought we had a deal. And now I haven't heard a word from him. I've been worried sick!"

"I'm—" Shattered. That was the only answer to her question. "I'm not so good. Dad found me…"

"Good." She sighed, relieved.

I forged ahead. "And we found my mother."

Janelle sucked in her breath. Her silence was enormously loud. "He's found Grace? Oh…God. He's not coming back to me, is he?" Her voice fractured. I don't think she meant for me to answer that question. Her fears were bubbling out. She thought he'd stay because he'd recovered his long-lost love, and maybe he would have. We'd never know.

"No, he's not coming back." How could I say it? Her muffled cries filled my ears. Finally I forced myself to utter a harder truth than the one she'd imagined. "Janelle, he's dead."

After telling her through both of our sobs that I couldn't give details just yet but would call again soon to explain, I asked her to try to reach Mami Tulke. I hung up the phone and curled in on myself.

I wanted to dream my dad, to see his face and hear his deep voice. But over and over again all I saw was him on his knees, a scarlet rose of blood blooming on his white shirt, my mother begging Clancy to kill *her* instead. Then, my father's beautiful aura snapping from his body into Clancy's.

Dad falling. Falling.

My consciousness blew like a restless storm from asleep to awake. The next time I opened my eyes, it was in the black of night. I sat upright in a daze, fists clenched in front of my chest, heart pounding. The soft snoring of multiple people reminded me where I was. I wasn't under attack. I squinted into the darkness.

My mother was still asleep on the couch across the small room where she'd collapsed hours before. I could tell from the calm vibration of energy that the body next to me was Giovanni's.

I lay back down, unable to tame my erratic pulse. Images of the deaths I'd witnessed superimposed over my vision, nightmares awake and asleep that tortured me. I vowed these things:

I won't hide the rest of my life. I will find a way to stop the Arrazi.

I will keep my loved ones safe.

I will make Clancy beg me for his life.

I will deny him.

My Scintilla aura flared with pure hate. It radiated above my body, over my heart, the epicenter of my pain. Resentment for what I'd lost and for what my life was now rose up in my body, cresting over any shame I might have felt about wishing someone dead. The girl I was two months ago would never have had thoughts of death and survival and revenge. There was no damage done that I couldn't pin directly on the race known as Arrazi.

Giovanni rolled over with the slackness of sleep. His eyes were still closed but his hand reached out, suspended over me, and rested gently on my stomach, beneath my heart. My breath caught. He still breathed with the heavy timbre of deep sleep. Could he subconsciously feel my deep distress? Did he know that with the press of his hand, my fiery rage would reduce to a simmer?

I had so much to learn about being a Scintilla. I'd have to begin immediately.

It was the only way to become strong enough to keep my vow. There had to be an ability we could use against our enemies. I pressed my hand over the top of Giovanni's and silently thanked him. As maddening as he could be—his boulder of a personality required everyone to be water that moved around him—I was grateful to have found someone I could trust.

He'd already taught me so much about what made us different. I had to believe there was a reason we were created this way, and it couldn't simply be as Clancy had said: that we were lower on the food chain.

Giovanni woke when I gently lifted his hand so I could roll onto my side. A slice of early-morning light shone from between the curtains, brightening his eyes. We faced each other, quietly studying. His brows creased together like he was trying to understand something.

"Why did you save my life?" he whispered.

"Why wouldn't I?"

"In my experience, nobody does something for nothing."

I sighed. Had his hard life made him so jaded, so unable to believe that good people did things because they were the right things to do? "Is everything you do for personal gain?"

Giovanni blinked as if he couldn't believe I had asked such a question, bit his lip, and said a *yes* that I could barely hear. "Mostly."

When I began to turn away from him, he stopped me with his hand on my upper arm, over the mark of the key. Small beats of electricity pulsed from the tips of his fingers into my skin. "Please understand, it's how I survived as an orphaned Scintilla."

The door creaked open. Mari poked her head through. "Breakfast."

The four of us sat in a circle on Dun's bed with a mound of steaming muffins, scones, fruit, and cheeses in the middle, talking softly so as not to wake my mother, who was still sound asleep in the next room. I made a plate for her and set it aside.

"I give you guys the prize for weirdness," Mari said, popping a grape into her mouth. "And you can keep it. These people who are after you, they sound like something out of a nightmare. They're like freaking vampires."

Giovanni uncrossed his legs and leaned forward intensely with his elbows on his knees and fingers clasped. He wore nothing but a pair of jeans that Dun had graciously offered him until we could get some clothes. "Where do you think those stories come from?" he replied to Mari. "Vampires are a fairy tale adapted from an uglier truth."

"Dissing the vampire legend?" Dun said with a smile. "Is nothing sacred?"

Mari's eyes found mine and held. "I can't believe Finn's one of them."

I could only nod. Every thought of Finn was a fresh reminder of what could never be. Another rip in my fabric. You can't be with someone and call it love when every quickening of their pulse around you is only because your aura is nectar to them. I couldn't help but wonder what he'd do when his need for the souls of others became too great. Would he choose to die rather than kill? Or would he reluctantly surrender to what he was? I pressed my palms to my churning stomach. It was impossible imagining the sweet boy I knew murdering again and again for the rest of his life.

Dun rolled on his side, resting his head on a crooked arm, his long black hair spilling over the pillow. "Why are the Arrazi being so stupid as to kill their best source of life force and powers?"

"Clancy could have killed us," I said. "All three of us. But he didn't."

My mom startled me with a touch on my shoulder. I hadn't heard her get up. Her face was pressed with lines from the couch. Her hair reached out like the tangled bare stalks of a winter shrub. She reached past me and grabbed a scone. "Aye, instead of killing, he collected," she said in her soft, lilting brogue.

"Do you know why?" I asked her, hoping to see more of the lucidity that leaked out from her once in a while now that she was away from her prison.

She shook her head, her eyes going to a faraway place before she said, "He nearly did kill me, many times. But he always stopped short."

I reached to touch her arm. I knew the pain of my aura being ripped from my body against my will. I couldn't imagine how many times she'd felt that pain over thirteen years.

"He shared me with people," she said, voice small. "I presume so that they could get their sortilege. They'd take from me while I was blindfolded."

Sickening. It had been even worse than I'd imagined.

"You don't know who they were?" Giovanni asked. "Men? Women?"

"Both," she answered. "One young woman used me repeatedly. She was especially cruel about it. There's a legend about killing Scintilla," my mother said, and my mind skimmed back to when she yelled for Clancy to kill *her* instead of my father.

Take me to the death. You know what could happen…

Rumors, he'd responded.

"He told me once that when an Arrazi takes a Scintilla to the death, they never have to kill again. Our death is their cure."

"I hate to ask this, but why wouldn't he want a cure if he could have it?" Dun asked.

Giovanni stood and paced the floor. "There are very few Scintilla left, so it's likely that he doesn't want to kill something so valuable when the legend might not be true. And possibly, Clancy wants something more than to be cured."

"He wants something he believes having three of us will give him." I reached for my mom's hand. "Do you know what that is?"

She slipped from my grasp and walked to the window. "Three…" she repeated. We hung on what she might say next, but the silence stretched out. Finally she turned toward me with a bit of sparkle in her eyes. "Three is a magic number in this world, did you know that?"

Giovanni exhaled in frustration. His pacing was beginning to agitate me. We were all caged, and his restless prowling reminded me of that fact. My mother crossed the room, stopping in front of him. He rested his hands on his hips and looked down into her childlike face.

"*Three is the mystery come from the great one. Hear, and light on thee will dawn,*" she said to him.

"That's written in your journal," I said.

"Bible quote?" Mari asked.

"No." My mom's head turned to me. "Do you still have my journal?"

"Clancy has it now," I said, a barb of regret piercing me. "I'm sorry. What does that quote mean?"

"It's from an ancient text called the Emerald Tablets. I found it while trying to find information about the triple spiral at New-grange. I was grasping for anything back then. My whole world was a search for answers, and I'd focused for a time on threes—triunes." She had said all this as she came to kneel on the floor in front of me, eyes wet with tears. "I was so obsessed. It caused them to find me. I hurt everyone so much. That's not what I wanted."

She was beseeching me to understand her long-ago choices. I did understand. I'd had the same obsessive drive when I sneaked off to Ireland to find out what had happened to her. We both had regrets. Neither of us would ever recover what was lost in our searching.

"Newgrange seemed very important to you. You wrote 'origin story' on one of the pages. Why? Did you think that's where our"—I searched for the right word—"*species* originated?"

My mother's eyes were so penetrating; she was looking at me as if I had the answer to my own questions. "Yes, I believed strongly that our kind had once populated that place. Then we disappeared without a trace."

"Yes, the tour guides told us that the inhabitants vanished."

"We always disappear," Mom said.

"Did you find proof that it was an important place in the history of Scintilla? Evidence of *any* kind?"

"No," she answered sadly. "But that's where I was abandoned as a baby. It had to mean something, I reckon."

"Maybe it just means that your parents wanted to leave you someplace with lots of tourists, someplace you'd easily be found," Mari suggested. "So that you'd be okay."

Gráinne gave one nod, considering. "Indeed not. It wasn't yet the attraction it is now. I was found on an early morning by workers excavating the site. A note left with me said only that I was home."

Eleven

Cora

Mami Tulke was still not answering her phone, but a young woman finally did and told me in her broken English that she thought Mami Tulke might have hiked to the temple in the mountains to grieve her son. So, she hadn't come to Ireland? How my grandmother knew of Dad's death was beyond me. We'd speak eventually. Maybe that was better, anyway. She couldn't help me from Chile.

There were a few shops along the waterfront, so Mari had accepted more money from Giovanni and left with Dun to go buy clothes for him, my mother, and me. They'd been gone for a few hours already. I'd maintain a state of mild anxiety until their safe return. God only knew what Mari would choose for me clothes-wise, but I had one edict: no sequins. The more drab and inconspicuous, the better. I was sparkly enough even if she couldn't see it.

"I hate to be nosy," I said to Giovanni, "but since we're running for our lives together, do you mind telling me how it is you have so much cash to throw around?"

Giovanni didn't look away from the television news to answer me. "Odd jobs. I save most everything when I do make money. I can live cheaply."

"Yeah, but you don't."

That earned me an annoyed look. "A simple *thank you* would do."

The key swipe on the door beeped and Mari and Dun rushed in, breathless, tossing bags on the bed. "Get dressed," Mari ordered. "We need to get out of here."

"Why?" Giovanni asked. His hand rested protectively on my shoulder. My mother dug through the shopping bags with the same childlike excitement I'd seen when Clancy brought her new things. She scurried off to put something new on.

"Because," Dun said, his normally kind, almond eyes widening with agitation, "we just saw Finn."

I was already in motion, dumping clothes out of bags and gathering up what was most obviously mine: jeans, a sea-green T-shirt, and basic athletic shoes. My heart was on fast-forward. I tossed a black T-shirt to Giovanni. "Did Finn see you?"

"I was waiting for Mari outside an—an underwear store— and he spotted me. We had, like, a full-on conversation," Dun said, throwing up his hands. "It was kind of unavoidable."

"Oh my God, I should have never let you go out there, Dun," I said, motioning to him. "Look at you with your long black hair and brown skin. You look like some kind of six-foot Native American God plopped in the middle of Ireland."

"Well, I wasn't going to let Mari go alone," he said defensively. "All this talk of aura-sucking killers. That would have been completely unchivalrous of me."

Giovanni was pulling the T-shirt down over his chest. I

glanced away. "Does he know you're with Cora?" he asked. "Does he know where we're staying?"

Mari threw up her hands. "Yes, indeed. I invited him for tea and scones, you—"

"Actually," Dun jumped in, "Mari threatened him."

This stopped all of us in our tracks.

Mari beamed.

"Yeah," Dun said. "Told him that while she was aware he could suck the life out of us, if he ever came near you again, she would kick his ass before he got the chance."

I closed the bathroom door but yelled out to her. "Mari! He could've killed you!"

"It was kind of sad, actually," Dun said. "I always liked Sir Shamrock. He looked like crap, too."

Giovanni huffed.

"Don't feel bad for him," my mother said with unusual ferocity. "They killed my husband."

I opened the bathroom door and tossed the robe on the bed. "Finn didn't."

Why I'd defended him, I didn't know. It was too quiet then and everyone's eyes were averted but Giovanni's. "No," he said, his blue eyes tearing into me. "He nearly killed *you*, instead."

"He walked away," Mari said. "Tail between his legs, dejected, like a sad little aura-stealing puppy. But before he did, he said to please tell you something…"

Biting my lip, I waited to hear his message.

"He said he was wrong. He said, 'This tale *does* have an end.'"

All the breath left my body. *Feels like a tale with no beginning and no end.*

Only pure strength of will stopped me from sinking to my knees. Finn hadn't changed his mind. He was going to let himself die. As an act of love, I'd done what I could to save him once. I was powerless now. Why'd this have to be the tale of my first love? He'd always be another of my ghosts. I'd have to find a way to let Finn go, to release him from my heart, or be haunted by him forever.

"Dun and I ran around for a while to make sure he wasn't following us," Mari said, snapping me back to the present danger. "We returned when we thought it was safe."

"They have freaking superpowers, Mari! And Finn showed zero ability to control it. It's never safe. Don't forget that."

"You have powers, too."

"Yes. My ability to pull memories from objects is *really* going to help us." Sarcasm wasn't the best tactic with Mari, but she and Dun didn't seem to get how dire our situation was.

"*That's* your sortilege, child?" my mother asked, astonishment clear on her face. "Uncanny."

"Why?"

"Mine is to transfer memories *into* objects."

Our sortileges were opposites on a pole. A warm feeling of connection wound through me. My silver aura emulated that, reaching across the room for my mother.

Mari zipped closed her backpack and carried it to the door. "My power is to be awesome. But you already know that."

"I knew that," Dun muttered, a crushed-berry hue creeping into his cheeks and his aura.

Within minutes, everyone had a backpack with meager supplies and a few personal items. We piled into the elevator and watched the floors tick slowly down to the lobby. Dun broke the uncomfortable silence. "I once heard that they put mirrors in elevators so people would be less impatient."

"I see the mirrors and I'm still impatient," Mari said. "How are the mirrors supposed to help?"

"Because people are entertained by looking at themselves."

"We're all entertained by looking at you," Mari told him.

All I saw in the four-sided, mirrored box was what looked like an army of us, multiplied into infinity, and shimmering with colors: silver sparks and too much yellow. Too much fear. I wished we *were* an army. We needed to get to the car and get as far away from Dublin as possible, which, in a country the size of Indiana, was no easy feat. And an island to boot. Clancy was as slippery as smoke, and if he knew where Finn was, he could find us too easily.

"The two of you can't stay with us," I said again. "I won't let you."

"You can't stop us," Mari said over her shoulder. "We're in this together until we can get you away from all this nonsense."

"Where do you suggest we go? My dad is dead. I can't go back to California. They've probably got someone watching to see if I do. I tried to tell you that nowhere is safe until—"

"Until they're all dead," Giovanni said, grimly.

"We'll get you all to Chile. Mami Tulke will know what to do. We're family, and family's got your back. Besides, I have an Aztec god as my bodyguard," she said, smiling up at Dun. I wanted to flick the back of her hard head.

The elevator chimed and the doors slid open.

White light filled my vision.

Twelve

Finn

There was fear in their eyes. Fear of me. A skinny Irish git who'd never hurt anyone on purpose. Cora had obviously told them what I was. It twisted my gut into a pathetic sack of coiled dread. Well, Mari may have attempted to conceal her fright, but I could hear the staccato of fear in her voice when she boldly threatened me. I had to respect her for that. Seeing her and Dun only confirmed my resolve; I'd never want to watch a person's eyes pool with fear before me, then empty, as I drained the life from them.

I carried my supplies: two small cans of paint, two brushes, some favorite foods and…whiskey. The lack of human energy would kill me eventually, but I wasn't going to die without food and whiskey and the guitar on my back. I was doing a service to the world. Why should I suffer any more than I would? Call me a coward, but I had no idea how painful it might be to die from needing the life force of others. Hunger, dehydration, fire—those forms of death had to suck. Drowning never scared me. Sailing, like music, was my passion. I could die doing that and die happy.

However, dying because I had no spark in me, no inner flame to keep me alive—well, that I didn't fully know. I had a taste of it, to be sure, after I took from Cora and refused to take from another. It felt like my every cell was frostbitten. Every bone was hollowed of its marrow. The need choked off all good feelings. It felt like the icy breath of death was blowing on my embers. I'd go cold from need. At least the whiskey would warm me some before I died, and the food would be a reminder of the pleasures of life.

I'd starve to death on my boat, just a different kind of starving.

And what did it mean? That I had no light of my own? Why would there be a need for a breed of humans who could only plug in to others' wattage and take? I was pointless.

I walked through the coastal town of Dún Laoghaire, where my boat was stored at the yacht club. I'd left a note for my parents, telling them that I'd gone west, to the Cliffs of Moher. Perhaps they'd figure I'd jump from the knuckles of the craggy cliffs. Maybe I'd fooled them and could sail away to die in my own way. Though fooling my mother was not a task easily accomplished. I kept a watchful eye out for my parents as I approached the marina.

Hopefully, they wouldn't give Mary a hard time. Poor woman was obviously charged with the onus of watching my bedroom door. When I'd crept out in the early hours, I'd discovered her leaning against the wall in the hall, sound asleep on her duty. I'd blown her a kiss and hurried past.

People walked along the harbor and I mixed in, taking in my last sight of the ocean from the vantage of dry land. The breeze kissed my skin and I inhaled a ragged, salt-filled breath. Loading my provisions on board took all of five minutes, then I got to work removing every item in the boat with its previous name on it. If my parents suspected where I'd gone, I didn't want it to be so easy to find.

The white paint easily covered over the letters I'd stenciled on the hull when I first got her. *Amber*. People assumed it was named for some girl, but the truth was, I got the idea after a crusty Polish fisherman told me a Lithuanian legend about the goddess Jurata, and how she fell in love with a fisherman. This angered her father so that he changed her into sea foam and destroyed her underwater palace made of amber. Baltic amber that washes in from the sea is said to be the ruins from her palace. I figured I'd name the boat in homage to what the goddess lost for love and because she is ever-present in the foam of the sea.

For the new name, I'd chosen a green paint that was the closest approximation to the eyes that haunted me. Free-handing the script helped to tick the time away. The meticulous work gave my restlessness a hub to spin around, each brushstroke a meditation. I lost myself in the curve of Cora's name until a chill passed over me, raising my hairs and making my hands shake. I wasn't certain whether the ghostly shiver came from within or from the brackish wind whispering that the sun was sinking.

I asked myself, for the hundredth time, *do I really want to die?*

No matter how many times I asked, it came down to choice. I wanted to be normal, but I had no choice in that matter. I was a killer. If the choice was between my death and the senseless deaths of innocent people, then it was no choice.

I slipped my arms into the supple sleeves of my leather jacket and stood on the undulant dock, admiring my paint job. At sunset, I'd be carried away by *Cora*. I sipped Jameson from the bottle, the vaporous tawny liquid doing its best to warm me from the inside. Intense shivering rattled me again. It was definitely not the ocean breeze. I recognized *this* chill.

Because the customs of a sailor should always be observed, I christened the *Cora* with a liberal pour of whiskey and tipped some more into the gray sea—a gift to Manannán mac Lir. He once gave the gift of a golden cup that broke if three lies were told over it and was repaired by three truths. I always loved that idea, being put back together by truth.

The buildings and hotels of the waterfront I kept to my back as I sailed out of the harbor. My eyes were fixed on the eternal sea. As I stood and stared, a line from an E.E. Cummings poem came to mind:

> *For whatever we lose (like a you or a me), It's always our self we find in the sea.*

My epitaph.

The craft took to the waves like she was eager, bobbing easily on the water as I sailed northeast. Howth dipped ahead on my left, its lighthouse winking at me, and beyond that, the Irish Sea. I lost myself in the motions of sailing, of handling my rig, of the elements and movement. My last dance with the sea.

It's not every day that you get to attend your own death like a guest. Rolling out the good memories of school chums and mischief, the sweet taste of strawberries and kisses, how laughter was a wild eruption, how falling in love felt like dropping and flying all at the same time. I held a smooth green apple and smelled it. I played my guitar, the notes louder in the cupped hands of the boat, the ocean calming as if it were listening intently to my song. I supposed it was.

Hours drifted with me. A countdown.

I played until my hands shook so violently that I couldn't

keep a chord. That was one of the sadder moments; letting the last note—a fitting D minor—rise up and carry away behind me with the wake of the boat.

Every life leaves a wake.

Numbness spread slowly through my arms and legs, creeping like a sluggish, cold wind up my extremities and into my torso. It started as a vague longing that blossomed into intense need. The way a man in the desert aches for water, or the drowning lung clutches for air, that was my desire for the presence of an actual person.

The sun set on my trembling body and I lay there, humming a new, unfamiliar tune, and staring at the vast sea of stars. One of the things sailors know that those whose feet are firmly fixed on soil do not is that there are times in the still of night out on the ocean, when the stars and water reflect so brilliantly, you find yourself floating in the vast expanse of limitless distance and limitless time. It's not small you feel, but enormous. You are the center of the universe for one infinite moment.

It's possible that feeling like death made me morbidly poetic.

A powerful wave of nausea and trembling hit. I imagined that, to the wind, I must look like another pitiful, quaking leaf barely clinging by a thin, dry vein.

I wrapped myself in a plaid blanket, the tartan of the Doyle family, and pressed my shaking fear and ravenous hunger against the solid curve of the boat. Hot tears slid from my eyes and I swiped angrily at my face. I wanted to be valiant. I wanted to be a man about this business of dying. But how do you fall into the stars when no one will be there to catch you?

As I fixed my eyes on the constellation Boötes, I set my thoughts on Cora.

Around her, I'd felt warm and comfortable, like I could drop every preening, false affect and just be me. Our time together was a contradiction. Everlasting and short. When I first saw her, it felt like the universe had been holding its breath, waiting. And when we met face-to-face, it sighed a breath of eternity. I loved her like I loved my music, because it was a part of me. Was she a part of me because I had sipped her aura like syrup? That conflicting thought made me lie there and question if I understood love at all.

I didn't know how long I'd been lying on the seat of the boat, staring up into the night sky. I'd drift off, weakness so heavy that it was the arms of giant gods, grasping me, pulling me down. Each time I came to for a brief moment, my first thought was of Cora. Each time I slipped under, her name was on my lips. I wanted the memories of her light and sweet love to carry me from this place.

THIRTEEN

Cora

I gasped, instinct pressing me against the back of the elevator, away from the brilliant white light.

"Hello, pet," Clancy Mulcarr said to my mother with a slimy smile. Flanking him were two men I'd never seen. Their bulk filled the doorway, trapping us inside. "We were just coming to collect you."

"Finn," I said, more an accusation. How else could they know where to find us?

"You need not be worryin' your pretty curls about Finnegan," Clancy said, bitterness spiking his words so they stung. "He's got a date with death, he has."

All breath left me. *Death.*

Before I could react or act, Giovanni's left hand swiped the air and my mother skidded sideways like a chess piece, right into me, knocking my chin with her head. He stood defensively in front of both of us, ready to protect.

But before he could, Giovanni clutched his chest and bowed

forward toward Clancy like a servant. His beautiful silver aura raged and swirled—a whirlpool of sparks in front of him, as he fought the pull. I felt the yank of Clancy's aura stab into my own chest. Surely my mother was being attacked as well. She whimpered with her arms crossed over her heart and tried to turn away from Clancy, toward the corner of the elevator.

I'd never conceived an Arrazi would have the power to take from three of us at once.

Without word or warning, Dun's body sprang forward, black hair spreading like a skirt, and he slammed a punch into Clancy's face. Clancy stumbled backward onto the floor, grasping his nose.

Mari thrust something at me behind her back. I grabbed the small black cylinder with one hand and my mother's hand with the other. I knew exactly what it was and how to use it. My father had made sure I knew. I never told him I'd stopped carrying one long ago.

Mari shoved through the elevator doors, with me and my mom behind her. As we passed, I sprayed the closer of the two men in the face with pepper spray. I tried to hit Clancy with a shot. He lurched to grab me, and I slipped forward into the stinging mist. We rushed toward the doors at the front of the hotel. My eyes and face burned from the pepper spray. My mom's hand remained clasped in mine as I pulled her like a child. Clancy cursed in Irish as we bolted away, past shouts and scuffling sounds, causing everyone in the lobby to gasp and point. I dared a look behind me.

Through watery eyes, I could see the other man had snagged Mari by the arm, pulling her roughly toward the elevator. "Not her! I don't care about her!" screamed Clancy, coughing and pointing at us with blood dripping from his nose into his white mustache. "Them!"

Dun crashed into the man holding Mari, knocking them

into the mirrored doors of the elevator. Shards of glass cascaded around them, raining onto the polished floor. The man lost his grip on Mari and she darted in our direction with Dun following.

My eyes weren't on them running toward us but beyond them. I watched, helpless, as Clancy used his power to weaken Giovanni to his knees. His mouth hung open like he was fighting for air. I screamed.

Dun whirled around to see what I was screaming at as Mari crashed into my mother and me and pushed us out through the glass doors into the fading sunlight. As good as it felt, as unbelievable as it was that we might escape, I fought to get back inside. I had to help Giovanni and Dun. Mari held tightly to my wrist. "Mari, let go! Clancy will kill them!"

I wrenched free from her grasp and reached the door to go back inside. I couldn't imagine them taking Giovanni—or what they'd do to him if they let him live. His first impulse had been to protect my mother, to protect me. Now he needed protecting. But before I could open the door, Dun and Giovanni spilled out of it, breathless and frantic. Giovanni limped with one arm draped over Dun's shoulder as we ran aimlessly through the streets of Dublin.

"Are they behind us?" I asked after enough time and distance had passed and when it became clear that Giovanni needed a rest, if only for a few moments. He'd have to keep running though, as Finn's father's car was back at the hotel and out of our reach. We were officially on foot, with only the possessions we'd concealed on our bodies or shoved into the backpacks. I looked around, recognizing nothing. I'd never felt more like a stranger.

"I don't see anyone," Dun panted, looking behind us. "I slowed that man down with a good kick to his shillelagh. He shouldn't be able to walk normally for a while, let alone run."

Giovanni bent forward, catching his breath, then eyed me. "I don't think they expected five of us. Where'd you get pepper spray? It's illegal in the UK and Ireland."

My eyes darted to Mari, who shrugged nonchalantly and said, "You can obtain anything if you know where to shop."

We turned another corner and walked into a crowded boulevard with no cars, only shoppers and tourists everywhere. I recognized this place. I'd seen it before while walking with Finn from the park to the pub the night we were reunited.

Stupid, meddling fate.

"The church," Giovanni and I both said at the same time. Christ Church was nearby and would be teeming with tourists. We'd be anonymously concealed in a crowd. "Maybe we could wait there until it closes," I said. "We have to get off the streets and out of sight."

We shuffle-walked a bit more, surely looking like a band of paranoid tweakers. The peaks of the medieval cathedral rose in front of us like a granite mountain, grayish-brown and imposing. Together, we stepped forward, but I faltered. "Maybe we shouldn't go in there," I said, feeling a flurry of trepidation in my stomach. "There are a lot of people—and—we could be seen. Maybe we should find another place to hide."

Every choice I'd made since deciding to go to Ireland had led to disaster. I looked at the four other people surrounding me, each of whom I was bonded to. What if coming to the church led to one of them getting hurt, or worse, like my dad?

"Don't do that," Giovanni whispered, pulling me aside. "I can see it. You're wrestling with your demons right now. The *real* demons were back at that hotel. Don't doubt yourself. Doubt is the enemy of action, and we have to act."

I looked up into the steady blue of Giovanni's eyes. He

always seemed so sure. I envied that about him. "I don't want anyone else to die because of me."

Giovanni placed his palm on my cheek, his face softening. "What happened to your father was not your fault. No choice has a guaranteed outcome. Your father died because they are devils."

I wanted to believe him, but loss hammered at my confidence. First my father, and now—grief pressed me—Finn. Did he really go off to die? It hurt to breathe. "When I saw Clancy taking from you, I thought I might lose you, too," I admitted, and realized as I said it that it would shatter me to see Giovanni's light go out. How many more people would die before this was over?

His fingertips traced under my chin as he stared intently into my eyes. His look sobered as he curled his fingers into his palm and dropped his hand to his side. "You're the first person in my life, since my parents, who has cared if I lived or if I died."

What a sad thing to say.

I reached for his hand and squeezed my fingers around his, wanting him to know he wasn't alone anymore, and in doing that, I realized that I wasn't, either. We were lost together.

We nodded a silent, resolute agreement and led the group past the ruins of the chapter house and through the wooden doors of the oldest church in Dublin. Cool air hit my skin and goose bumps flared on my arms. Missing nothing, Giovanni ran his hand down them, the warmth caressing my skin.

Everyone walked calmly and as inconspicuously as possible across the shiny tiles into the large cathedral. Dun and Mari verged away from us toward something that had caught their eye. Neither of my best friends had admitted to crushing on the other, but it was obvious. Perhaps stronger in Dun. The yellow fear that had been so prominent in their auras moments ago faded to a mix of honeyed emotions connecting across the few feet between them. They were never apart, even when they thought they were.

I wondered: if everyone did that, let their auras blend with others, would there be any separation between us at all? How far could people expand their energy? How close did an Arrazi have to be to kill? Seemed that we had run about four car lengths from Clancy to be out of his reach.

"We need to get to a new age bookstore or something," I said to Giovanni. "I'm not going to spend my whole life running. I'm going to spend it looking for answers about energy until we end this."

He nodded, a beam of admiration shining from his eyes.

Triangular panels in the arched ceiling stretched overhead like the billowing sails of a massive Viking ship. The more I looked at the pattern, the more it reminded me of the design on the key and on the ring underneath my gray fingerless gloves. I held the underside of my arms out to see the triangle markings again. There was one on each forearm, but facing different directions. Triangles everywhere.

Trailing my gaze past the ceiling and down to the Gothic stained-glass windows, my pulse quickened when I noticed a white stained-glass window inlaid with red glass, forming a banner. In the middle of the banner were two intersecting gold keys. The keys so closely resembled mine, both the real one and the marking on my shoulder, that I gasped. I lifted my sleeve, peered again at the marking of the key, then back up to the window.

My body was becoming a map, but to where? "This has to mean something…"

My mother brushed my arm. "I reckon it might."

"Your journal said something about the 'Scintilla holding the keys to heaven.' That's what the key is about, right? You think this key will open something that will tell us about ourselves?"

"A key is but half a puzzle. We could search our whole lives for what it opens and never find it." My mother's eyes turned sad.

"And for how many lifetimes has that key remained hidden?" Giovanni murmured. "It could mean nothing now. It could open nothing."

"The images it holds mean something, though," I said to both of them. "I saw the memories in this key. If there was one predominant message," I said, tracing its shape through my T-shirt, "it's a vague message about threes. And it's a warning to anyone who tries to decipher it."

Giovanni listened with his hands on his hips. "That number again."

"Yes."

My mother tapped me on the arm and motioned for us to sit on a couple of the many chairs filling the cathedral. Giovanni and I had done that very thing once, when we talked in urgent whispers, knee-to-knee, one Scintilla to another. That was the day I vowed to continue my mother's search for answers despite my growing fears.

It seemed a true decision doesn't happen in one flagrant moment of daring. If you're tested, you have to choose, over and over again.

My mom patted my leg as I sat down and blew my worries out in a big exhale.

"I married your father here," she said, her eyes glistening with new tears, her aura glistening, too, as if her whole being was crying.

I squeezed her hand. "I know you did. I found the invitation. I bet it was beautiful." A frond of longing uncurled in my chest. It would have been achingly sweet to see them sit here now, quietly, hand in hand, reliving that memory together.

My mother's eyes traveled to the front of the church, watching her own memories from long ago. Quickly, she snapped her gaze back to me with a rare, delighted grin. She clasped my hand and closed her eyes.

My mind twisted into a memory.

The church filled with beams of color from bright sun striking through the stained-glass windows. The church also filled with the colors from the auras of the guests who had congregated to watch the special event. I looked down at bare feet poking out from a ruffled hem of ivory lace. When I looked up, I saw my father standing before me. He beamed at me, or rather, at my mother, with such an expression of pure love that it could be called *holy*.

Marrying her was his most sacred act, a sacrament of the heart.

My own heart fluttered with the delicate grace of a small bird. Tears filled my eyes as the scene played in my mind. This wasn't psychometry or object-memory that I was picking up. This was my mother using her sortilege to infuse *me* with the memory of their wedding.

They clasped hands in front of a metal cage affixed to the wall, which held an old wooden heart behind its bars. They spoke about true love never being bound like that. No bars separated their hearts from each other. They then walked together down the aisle. My father escorted her because she had no father to do so. He was her family now. A tiny woman bound their hands together with a satin green ribbon in a ceremony known as handfasting. I knew her as my father's mother, Mami Tulke. Hanging from the shimmering ribbon was the key I wore around my neck. It had been a gift from my grandmother to her son's bride, a rare woman who shone silver—like her.

The vision faded. Tears streamed down my face and dropped onto a lion tile at my feet. She reached up and wiped my cheek. "Thank you." My words came out through a dam of emotion. "It was like I was there with you and Dad. I'd love to see the wooden heart."

"It's no longer here. Someone stole the heart from its cage. I read about the theft a few years ago, in a paper Clancy brought to me."

Weird. Why would someone steal an old wooden heart from Christ Church? "This key came from Mami Tulke? Did she tell you what it's for?"

"She didn't know."

"Where did she get it?"

"She wouldn't say. She only said that some people bury with shovels and others bury with keys. She told me to guard it, always, because she took it from someone who'd guarded it for centuries."

"We've got to get a hold of her and ask," I said. "I saw so many memories in that key. Did you put them there?"

"No. I had it with me when I hid my journal at Trinity Library, and I knew only that that moment was being recorded in the key."

"When I found your journal, I expected a memory to spring from it. But there was nothing."

"I had to write the words so that *anyone* could see the truths I was uncovering. Words are humans' most powerful sorcery." Her head dipped. "The woman who wrote in that journal is gone now."

"No," I said, ducking to look in her face. "Only if you decide she is. If that woman is gone, then what are we doing? Why not run from Ireland and run the rest of our lives?" I was grasping at the tangled edges of obsession, wanting desperately to have freedom, but also to have answers, an end to all of this. But I couldn't truly have one without the other. Freedom is a land of answers, not unanswered questions.

Giovanni came to our sides, concern in his eyes. I wondered if he was alerted by the craze in my aura.

"You are doing what I was," Gráinne said, "fighting for more than yourself. For the lives you might save. For the children you will have." Her eyes flickered from me to Giovanni. She had the wrong idea about us. "So no more Scintilla will disappear." My mother had stood again but now slipped to sitting, more like her legs giving out than a purposeful act. "I feel useless. I'm a bird with broken wings."

Dun wandered back to us and sat down quietly next to my mother as she spoke. He wrapped his arm around her and pulled her close. I envied the ease with which Dun reached for her, his ease of giving to others. He was practically a stranger to her, but she didn't seem to mind. Their long black hair mingled. It made me think of auras and how people didn't realize the ways they touch.

"You were caged too long. Some birds grow to like the safety of their cages," Dun said to the little bird under his wing. "But not you. Not your daughter, either. My grandmother used to say, 'A bird has two mothers: the mighty wind, and the one who teaches, by example, to ride it.'"

I smiled at them and scanned the room again, paranoia making it a habitual need. I tracked the clipped walk of a very polished woman carrying a clipboard in front of her silk blouse. She stopped to speak to a church employee near us and leaned in with a practiced smile to whisper, "The cavern looks very well appointed for the party. The Society will be pleased that the church has taken such care to arrange things."

Every sense amplified. My heart pounded the familiar beat of alarm. My eyes took in the tourists nearest me, assessed their auras. The candles crackled in their votives. The first time I'd heard those two words, a knife had been at my throat. I glanced from the woman to the ring on the underside of my finger. *The Society…*

FOURTEEN

Cora

The man's face showed no emotion as he replied to the woman, "All due to your superb event planning, I'm sure."

She inclined her head.

"C'mon," I said, pulling Giovanni up from the bench and across the aisle of chairs toward the pair.

As we approached them, she said, "I will, of course, be back in the hours before the event to check on things and see to it that all runs smoothly."

"Of course," the man replied.

"Excuse me," I said in a squeaky voice while tapping lightly on her shoulder.

The woman turned with a question in her eyes.

"I'm sorry to interrupt, but it sounds like you are just what we need," I blurted. My hand pulsed in Giovanni's. I could feel his eyes on me, but was afraid to look at him. I hoped he was savvy enough to play along. If anyone was, it was him. "I—we— are getting married and will be needing an event planner of the highest, um, quality." *Deep breath.* I needed to calm down. "Do you do weddings?" I asked. In the history of voices, none was higher.

The woman's eyes raked over our disheveled appearances with a quick flick of her eyes before she tipped the clipboard forward to get her business card. She pressed the clipboard against her chest too quickly and held the crisp ivory card out to me. Damn! I needed to see that piece of paper.

Giovanni squeezed my hand, pressing the ring against my skin. A whip of energy lashed past me and the woman's board suddenly dropped to the ground.

"Oh!" Both of us bent to the floor, her fingers hurriedly scraping papers into a pile. She was quick, but not quick enough that I didn't get the most pertinent details. *Bal Masqué.* Friday night at 8:00 p.m.

I handed the invitation back to her. The woman stood, obviously annoyed, which she tried to mask with a hasty smile. "I'd be happy to discuss your wedding with you. Give me a call. Best wishes." She gave a quick nod to the church employee before walking out.

"I don't know who this *Society* is, but they have a connection to the Arrazi somehow and I'm going to find out what it is."

"How?"

I looked up at him and grinned. "Looks like I've got a party to crash."

"You can't do that."

"Watch me."

"If this is the same Society, it's too dangerous, Cora."

I slipped my hand from his. "We're in danger just getting out of an elevator! We're in danger walking down the street. We are in danger no matter where we go because they are looking for us, *everywhere,* all over the damn world. Clancy will not stop. Do you understand that? We have to find a way to stop *him*."

"But—"

Holding up my hand, I said, "No. Clancy is a part of this Society. Why else would he have a ring with their symbol on it? But by keeping the three of us, he was doing something secretive. He was nervous for them to know what he was up to. If I can find out why, then we'll have some kind of leverage on him."

Mari and Dun had come up next to us. Giovanni sighed in surrender. "Then we'll go together."

"Bad idea," I said. "It'll be hard enough for me to crash the party. And it would be stupid to simply hand them two of us if we're caught."

"Party crashing? I like the sound of this," Mari said.

I turned away from Giovanni's furrowed brows. "You should," I said to her. "You finally get to put some sequins on me."

We got more than a few suspicious glances throughout the early evening from the workers in the church. As darkness fell, we were politely swept out like leaves into a cold wind that smelled of salt and dust, reminding me of the Santa Cruz boardwalk on a rainy day.

"Now what?" Mari asked.

We were all thinking it.

"I say we pool together some cash and find a room off the beaten track, but close enough to town that we can get a party outfit for me and have access to an internet café or a library. We've got research to do, and we need a place we can hole up until the party."

"I'm urging you, Cora." Giovanni stood behind me, whispering into my ear. "The scientist I've told you about, he will help us, and with any luck, find a way to stop all this."

"I'm not ready to put my trust in someone I don't know," I said, turning my face a little too quickly, causing my lips to brush the scruff on his jaw. The familiar sensation set off pangs of hurt. I raised my hand to his cheek. Lips have keen memories, and the sensation reminded me too much of Finn. "You should really shave," I said.

Giovanni's brows bent in an amused smile, but he didn't move. I dropped my hand and tried to look away, but he adjusted his body and tilted his face into my line of sight, forcing me to look into his eyes. Those eyes were a relief because they were nothing like Finn's. Giovanni's were the wild ocean glinting in the sun, versus Finn's honey-dipped earth.

My heart shuddered. *He's surely dead by now.* Somehow, I felt it. Like the golden thread between us had slackened. I knew better than to believe anything Clancy Mulcarr said, but hadn't Finn promised me himself that he preferred death? Even if we were forever apart, I couldn't imagine a world without Finn in it.

The night breeze blew my hair against my neck. I shivered. Mari cleared her throat and snipped the hold of my tormented thoughts. "Dun's stopped a cab." She gestured over by the street where Dun bent to speak with the driver, then motioned for us all to climb in.

"Jolly" would have been a good word to describe the cab driver, though I'd be the last person to trust how people physically appeared. Auras were harder to see in the dimming light, but it was his rippling aura that set me at ease. A cool green, almost minty color, rolled off the man, who introduced himself as Patrick. He clasped the wheel with sturdy-looking hands, the kind that could plow a field all day, then just as easily pat the head of his dog at the end of it. He spoke in an Irish accent that was different from the people in Dublin. It took a bit of concentration to understand what basically sounded like a series of run-on sentences with his words skipping happily across the surface of his deep voice.

"We need a place with a bit of privacy," I said. "A hotel isn't exactly our first choice."

"You're local," Dun said. "If you had family coming into town who wanted to be near the action but far enough away from it to have some privacy, too, where would you take them?"

"Home," Patrick said with a laugh. "Though I'm not sure what me wife would say to showing up with five strangers right at suppertime. Skin me like a rabbit, I reckon. Come to think of it now, I have a neighbor with a cottage that he sometime lets out. I can give him a call, see if it's vacant."

Dun patted him on the shoulder jovially. "That'd be awesome, dude. Thanks."

"You're not dodgy types, are ya?" Patrick asked, eyeing the rest of us in the backseat through his rearview mirror. "We don't want any sort of trouble in our neck of the woods."

"Trouble is the very thing we're trying to avoid," Mari said. I nudged her.

My mother said something to him in Irish as we flashed him our sweetest smiles. He told her with regret that he didn't speak Irish, but he seemed placated by the fact that she did and got on the phone to arrange for us to stay in a private cottage on the outskirts of Dublin.

No one spoke much as we stumbled by the light of a flashlight up an uneven path to the cottage behind the owner's house. I kept my mom close to me, afraid the big world was making her nervous. She'd begun biting her nails in the cab. As everyone filed into the house ahead of me, I stared up into the dark sky dotted with stars. For some reason, they made me think of Finn, and they made me incredibly sad.

FIFTEEN

Finn

Flying from darkness into a swirling vortex of light.

I felt like a comet racing from the blackness of space toward the only target that mattered—Life.

Life was warm. Life was light. Life was shafts of sun in a redwood forest. Life was the glint of green eyes, love-infused kisses. Everything in me hurtled toward the beauty of *being*.

I snapped violently back into my body, gasping.

Hot, fast breaths hit my face from above. Someone was leaning over top of me; their weight was heavy as a steel block on my chest. I tried to see, but everything around me was a smudged charcoal shadow of movement and confusion. My hands reached and clasped hairy wrists. Fingers gripped the front of my leather jacket as I clung to them like a life preserver. Was I drowning? I scraped for breath, or what felt like breath. Drawing life into my body was like sucking a tornado through a straw.

I didn't realize until my blood pumped hot with life and adrenaline that I was subconsciously fighting for my own survival. My body had taken over where my will left off, coming alive without consent. The steel block abruptly lifted from my chest. I rolled to my feet, balancing like a surfer in the rocking boat, the ocean slapping a rhythm, like slow applause, on the hull.

I looked down. A man lay at my feet, his arms crossed protectively over his chest. I bent to feel for a pulse, but something in my body knew his life was mine now. Inside of me, the flicker of his gentle soul burned like a star. His boat floated next to my own. He must have seen mine and stopped to check on me. He'd only wanted to help. My heart broke with realization; my life came at the cost of someone else's death. Cora's face flew to the front of my mind.

I dropped to my knees next to him.

God, forgive me.

Sixteen

Cora

"Amighty flame follows a tiny spark."

"*Excusi*?" Giovanni whispered into the dark night. Nearby, the quiet purr of breathing rose from the others, who were already sleeping. I envied them. My mind cranked out questions one after the other so that I couldn't sleep through the noise.

"They're the first words Griffin ever said to me."

"The Arrazi I killed? I know those words. It's a line from the greatest poet in Italian history." Pride filled his voice. I could tell by how his Italian accent became more pronounced. "The line is Dante's, from *The Divine Comedy*. It's from the third *cantica, Paradiso*."

I sat up in bed. "*Paradiso*? Finn had a painting from *Paradiso* in his house."

"That's quite a coincidence."

"Two Arrazi that I know of have a connection to the work. We don't have a whole lot to go on, so it's worth looking into. Tomorrow, in addition to investigating the symbol from these

Society people, I need to get my hands on a copy of *Paradiso*."

I was the last to sleep and the first to wake. Though I think I might have slept more if it weren't for my mother's restlessness. After one tormented whimper of my father's name, I was up for good.

Mari woke up and saw me looking in the empty cupboards. "Gives us an excuse to go get us some real breakfast. We need fortification for the shopping," she said through a yawn.

"I'm going to have to trust you to get something for me to wear. Size ten-ish, or whatever the euro equivalent is here," I told her. "I've got some research to do. If you and Dun can take care of the party, the rest of us can start looking into this symbol." I flashed the ring at her. "And we have to find out why Clancy wants three Scintilla."

"If this is the same Society, it's totally oddball that a bunch of killers would have a swanky party at a church, don't you think?" Mari asked.

"You'll need a mask for the party," grumbled Giovanni, appearing suddenly in nothing but boxer shorts.

"A mask?" Mari and I both said in unison.

"On the paper, it said *Bal Masqué*. Did you not see it?"

"I was kinda focused on the day and time," I said defensively.

"I'm kinda focused on the fact that he's pantsless," Mari said.

"I didn't know what it meant." Nor did I understand why the party was being held in the most famous church in Ireland.

Giovanni interrupted my thoughts. "It means masked ball."

"Savage," Mari said with a grin.

"Dante," Giovanni said to me. "Don't forget we must look into that, also."

Mari tilted her head. "Dante? As in books-my-teachers-want-to-torture-me-with Dante?"

"That's the one."

"Why?"

"Just something I'm wondering about. Could be a long shot. But when all you've got are long shots, you take them all."

Finally Dun and Gráinne were up, everyone was showered, and we headed into the quaint little town for a huge breakfast.

"I think Gráinne here ate us all under the table," Dun joked. She sat back against the booth with her hands on her belly, a look of pure satisfaction across her dainty features.

"Mari, in the name of all that's holy, please don't get me something skanky, freaky, slutty, tight, or too noticeable. I need to blend in. Think *boring*. Think head-to-toe camo so they won't recognize me."

She gave me an offended look. "This is a masked ball, not a freaking hunter's convention. Camo has its own rugged beauty, yes, but this calls for something more festive."

I groaned. "Ugh. There's gonna be sequins involved, I know it."

"I still don't understand how I got nominated to go dress shopping," Dun said. "I'd rather be on the investigative side of this operation."

Mari rolled her eyes. "I'll model all the slinky dresses for you."

He jumped up. "Let's do this."

"No slink!" I yelled as they exited the restaurant, a hint of bubbly happiness rising up in me. It was good to have them around, even if being around me was the last place they should be. I sighed. "I have to get them away from all of this," I said, watching their retreating colors head down the street. "I can't have anyone else's death on my hands."

My mother's hand landed lightly over my own. I knew what the touch meant. *Don't blame yourself for your father's death.* The very thought of his death filled me with such sorrow that I could hardly breathe.

"Cora?" Giovanni asked.

"I'm okay," I said, waving them off. "I need a bit of air, that's all."

"I could perhaps make the pain better."

"Not this pain," I snapped. Hurt flashed in his eyes, and it softened my anger. "I know you want to make me feel better. But some pain is meant to be felt. That which doesn't kill you, right?" But inside, I didn't feel stronger. I felt like grief was a ravenous monster eating away at me.

Giovanni insisted on paying the breakfast tab, even though my mother had a bit of money of her own. "We can't keep spending like this," I warned.

"Let me worry about that," Giovanni answered in a clipped tone. Back was the high-handedness that had shown itself when we first met. Fine. If he had secret reservoirs of cash, that was his business. We asked for directions to the only internet café in town and walked there in silence. My mother's head swiveled, taking in the countryside, the window displays, the smiling faces of passersby. She smiled at me, but her hand grasping the hem of my hoodie betrayed her anxiety.

The internet café also doubled as a Turkish market, with the savory smell of roasting lamb and various spices like oregano, allspice, cumin, and mint mixing with coffee. I settled my mom into a seat with a screen in front of her, a pen, and some paper we'd brought from the cottage. I figured that the best way to reach her was to engage the researcher within, that part of her that quested for answers so many years ago. If I could bring that woman to the surface, maybe the damaged woman would retreat behind the curtain. I logged her on to the computer. She gazed up at me with questions in her green eyes.

"I may have lost your journal," I said to her, "but I found *you*. You can help now. Can you start looking into this symbol? I drew the triangles on the paper. We need to know more about who is allied with the Arrazi. Are you up for it?" She nodded shyly. A good start.

To Giovanni, I said, "Who better to tackle the great poet of Italy than our resident Italian?"

"You wish for me to read *Paradiso*?" He shrugged. "Not such a bad assignment."

"You might detect nuances that I wouldn't. It could be a dead end. Who knows?"

"What will you research?" he asked.

"Why does Clancy want three of us? We know there's a rumor that taking one Scintilla to the death means they'll never have to kill again. So, what does he think three will do? The number three keeps popping up over and over, especially in the images I saw from my key. What is the significance of three?"

We worked quietly for a while, sipping Turkish coffee and tapping away on the keyboards. It took discipline on my part not to be distracted by the auras of the people coming and going. I still found it fascinating to observe and assess the colors I was seeing. I caught Giovanni watching me with a bemused expression. He wasn't one to quickly avert his eyes when caught staring. I had to do the looking away. It was like playing chicken—with eyes.

"*Interessante*," he said in Italian. He often spoke Italian when he was absently thinking to himself. "Listen," he said a moment later, pointing to some lines on the screen, which, unhelpfully, were in Italian. "This is from canto twenty-seven in *Paradiso*. Dante has just witnessed Saint Peter change color." Giovanni gave me a pointed look. "Saint Peter has something to say about changing color and it basically translates as, *If I now change my color, do not be surprised, for as I speak, you shall see all these souls change color, too.* After that, Saint Peter goes on a rant about the church. He's angry that the keys entrusted to his keeping should be put upon a banner used to wage war against the baptized. He calls some popes out for being 'rapacious wolves disguised in shepherds' clothing'. He later urges Dante to tell *the truth* in his writing."

"The truth?"

"It doesn't clearly specify, but doesn't it sound like he was writing about auras?"

"I suppose, yes," I admitted. "If Dante sees souls' colors change, it seems to mean that he can see auras like we can."

"What have you found?" he asked.

I sat back down and rubbed my eyes. "My mom wasn't kidding when she said that three was a magic number in the world. It's everywhere. In nature, in science, in nearly every religion or creation story in the history of man—"

"Examples?"

"Okay, so, three is the first prime number. There are three parts to the atom: proton, neutron, electron. Birth, life, death. Unconscious, conscious, superconscious. Beginning, middle, and end. Id, ego, superego."

"Triangles," my mom said, like it was a game.

I nodded. "The Christian trinity is one example, but almost every major religion seems to have a prominent triune concept." My brain hurt. "The oldest recorded creation stories came from a civilization called Sumer, and guess the significant number," I said. "There are the triple deities in nearly every civilization throughout history—Greek, Egyptian, Roman, Middle Eastern, Norse, and even here, in Celtic mythology. In the Torah, three is the number of 'truth.' Triple gods and goddesses are everywhere. Like the vision from the key," I said. "When I touched it, many of the images had to do with this number."

"So, the key and three are connected?" Giovanni asked.

My mom rolled her chair closer to us. "Don't forget the triple spiral," she added.

"Yes. An important three to us, I'm guessing."

We lapsed into silence, lost in our own research, when Giovanni called out. "Dante actually uses the words 'scintillation' and 'scintillating' in *Paradiso*!" He swung toward us with a pen tucked into the curls behind his ear and a look of amazed disbelief on his face.

"That's incredible. Coincidence?"

"If it is, I think it's an uncanny one in light of writing about the colors of souls."

"I found nothing on the ring's symbol, Cora," Gráinne said.

Giovanni waved his pen at her. "Why would you? Secret societies aren't secret for nothing."

"Ever notice how everyone seems to *think* they know about them, though? There was an episode on Edmund Nustber's show once, about these famous secret societies, and how people believe they're in control of all the governments all over the world. I remember asking my dad about it. I said, 'If they control the governments, then who is the *one* person at the very peak of it all? Wouldn't that person control the world?'"

My mom's forehead creased into little lines. "I'm going to follow the spirals like a labyrinth. See where they lead. Years ago, they led me to your *da*."

I patted her arm. "Okay. Good idea," I said, trying to ignore the feeling that we were just throwing darts into a tornado, hoping to hit something.

"Good God!" Giovanni said moments later, leaning forward

with both hands on the sides of the computer monitor. "In canto thirty-three, Dante writes of empyrean...*heaven*." He began to read aloud. "*Of the deep Light appeared to me three circles, of one dimension and three different colors. One seemed to be reflected by the other, rainbow by rainbow, while the third seemed fire breathed equally from one and from the other.*"

Giovanni looked intensely thrilled, both physically and in his aura, which flared and buzzed with excitement. "Dante's version of heaven is three circles. All I can think of is the triple spiral. I don't want to read more into this than, perhaps, Dante meant. But there are surely verses in *Paradiso* that could be interpreted in a way as to suggest that Dante knew about us, or at least very much believed in auras and the power of three."

In keeping with "the power of three" I suddenly wondered if there was a third breed of human besides regular humans with traces of Arrazi or Scintilla blood. Incredulity pressed to shut the door of my mind. I fought to keep the door open. The Arrazi and Scintilla were breeds of humans that had been around for who knew how long...maybe as long as humanity. Certainly, people knew of us. I'd never considered that famous people might have.

What a colossal secret to keep hidden.

Who had power enough to hide something so huge?

"This is older and bigger than the three of us," I said, to my mother's emphatic nods. I was impressed that Giovanni picked out these nuggets when my eyes were glazing over from all the online searching. Considering that he raised himself and schooled himself from an early age, his intelligence was impressive. I liked the way his brain worked. "The way Dante writes about 'seeing colors' makes me wonder..." I bit my thumbnail, and then pressed on. "I feel like a colossal wack job for suggesting this but...do you think Dante could have *been* one of us?"

SEVENTEEN

Finn

First, his legs. Then, his upper body. Dead weight. He was a big man, this stranger I'd killed. I reckoned it wouldn't matter to him or his family that I cried over him as I hefted his body back onto his own boat, which he'd tied to mine when he, presumably, had stopped to check on me. I could have offered up his body to the sea, but then I imagined his loved ones forever wondering in anguish what had happened to him.

Not knowing had to be worse. In matters of death, answers trumped questions.

The gentleman had a robust spirit. I felt it in me, swirling smoothly through my body, like stirring sweet milk into black coffee. Shudders of revulsion passed over my skin. Not because of his energy. But because it felt so good. It felt good to be alive.

Before I'd decided to put him back on his boat, I'd pondered whether to tie something to his leg and drop him into the depths. I'd also pondered doing that to myself. That would be a death I surely could not recover from. But just as Cora had been my last thought as I slipped from life, she was my first thought when I rose up again. Shame was a million demon voices hissing at me about my first kill. Since I'd become an Arrazi during my time with Cora, all I seemed to feel was utter, black shame.

I realized I also felt shame for another reason. Had I abandoned Cora when I might have helped her? If I'd died, she'd have one less ally in the world. Could I possibly be of help? To keep her safe from me, though, I'd have to stay far away from her. Banish all thoughts of someday.

You've been a bloody, self-indulgent git, Finn Doyle.

The sun had long risen over the city. The question of whether I'd live or die seemed to have been answered, through no conscious accord of my own. To assuage my good ol' Catholic guilt, I'd figured that if I'd let myself die of *natural* causes—through lack of other people's energy—then I might not be condemned to hell. Seemed I wasn't meant to die. Not yet, anyway.

So, as I sailed away from the gentleman's floating casket, my new question became, *why?* Why was I made this way? If I feared a god that would condemn me for murdering, why would he have created me to do so?

Suddenly, I needed the answers with a fervor that rivaled my need for that poor man's energy. And if I could find answers, then perhaps I could help Cora, help all of us.

Sometimes, a git needs a purpose greater than the one he'd envisioned for himself.

Driving up to the manor was paradoxical. I approached my family home, altered. I'd walked through some kind of fire on that boat, and it burned in my belly. Every question I wanted answered was a puff of breath, stoking the flames. Paradoxically, coming home was also like nothing had ever happened. The same massive stone steps that I'd raced up, fallen down, and sat on for countless photos welcomed me as I walked toward the manor.

No doubt my parents would be overjoyed to see me alive. They knew me well enough to know that I hadn't been making an idle threat when I'd said good-bye. It had hurt like hell to see my father cry. I think it made me love my mother more, not less, to see *her* console *him* and stoically accept that I had the right to live—or die—on my own terms. It was probably the greatest act of love she'd ever shown me.

As soon as I entered the house, I heard yelling.

And my uncle Clancy's voice.

I'd not thought out how I would react to seeing him again so soon.

"Jesus, Ina, you idealistic twit! Do you not grasp the danger this family is in?"

"I don't care. I've lived this long without being under anyone's thumb. I've lost my only son. Your pursuits and ruthless ambitions are nothing to me!"

Clancy growled in frustration, his footsteps ticking off a worn path back and forth as they argued. "I know, for a fact, that when Arrazi do not cooperate with the Society, they suffer from a sudden attack of *dying!* Jesus, Mary, and Joseph, we're all in jeopardy if we don't at least *appear* to cooperate with them. Finnegan's cowardice has only made it worse."

My nostrils flared in bullish anger.

"Do not speak of him!" my mother roared. "You've given me no facts about this group you call the Society. Only threats. You're afraid and you don't truly know of what or of whom."

"I know they are powerful. I know there's no place too high

for their reach, and no place too low they won't go to get what they want."

"And what *is* that, exactly?" I asked, pushing the library doors open and striding in.

"Finn!" My mother gasped. She was dressed all in black and was on her feet, already gathering me in her arms, making me feel like a little boy when I most needed to man up. "Oh, my son," she whispered. "Know only that I love you." She tilted my chin up and looked into my eyes. Her elation was smothered by a quick, passing cloud of understanding. She saw my blackest hole.

I was now a murderer.

I tore my gaze away and stared past her, at my uncle.

His simpering smile iced my blood. "How robust you look, my lad," he said, rocking back on his heels with his arms crossed over his drum of a chest. "I'm proud of you, boy."

My jaw clenched. "Don't be."

"Can I dare to hope you've come to your senses?"

We stared at each other. This was a critical moment. I couldn't bow down and swear to be a good little Arrazi killer. But I had to make him believe I could be an ally—of sorts. It was a balancing act. Too contrite and allegiant, and he'd be suspicious. Too angry, and he might dismiss me altogether. I wished I'd had more time to prepare.

In order to help Cora, I had to be *in* with Clancy, close enough to keep tabs on him. "If my family is in jeopardy, I want to do what I can to protect them," I said, hoping I didn't sound as monotone out loud as I did in my head. "But," I said, as Clancy opened his mouth to speak, "I will not help you find Cora and her mother, and…her friend." I became aware of the rise in my blood pressure at the thought of Giovanni Teso.

"I don't need your help. I found them yesterday."

An anvil of terror and dread swung hard into my chest. "Where are — ?"

"Unbunch your knickers, boy. They escaped." He ran his hand over his mustache and I noticed the fresh cut on the side of his head. "For now. Either we find them, or someone much more dangerous will."

I shrugged, trying to keep my composure despite my racing heart. "Their blood will not be on my hands, then."

Clancy stepped close. "Aw now, nice sentiment but," he said with a menacing smirk, "the passive often have more blood on their hands than those who wield the sword."

"You and I both know it would be a lie for me to walk in here and tell you that I'm suddenly motivated to help you capture the girl I love and hold her prisoner for the rest of her life. I won't do it."

"This isn't about prisoners, boy. The Society wants all the Scintilla *dead*. All of them. Every. Last. One."

Knots of fear and apprehension twisted in my gut. He was suggesting genocide. "And what? You're working for them? Killing a race of humans that are more beautiful and special than we could ever be?"

"I don't want to kill the Scintilla."

"What *do* you want them for?" It was a direct question. He should *have* to answer it. Clancy couldn't resist my power before. My sortilege to get the truth had helped me save her once. Perhaps… I held my breath.

My uncle threw up his hands in frustration. "I sympathize with your anger at me, at your parents. It's why I never had children of my own — foiled many a romantic prospect, I can tell you. I am just like you, we're the same."

When he saw the disgust that must have been evident on my

face, he softened his tone.

"You have been like a son to me. I know you can drag the truth out of me against my will, so let me be honest with you so we can start over. I don't want any more deception between us. The Society has asked me, and all Arrazi allied with them, to seek out and kill any Scintilla they find. I want the three, yes. I always did. But not to kill them. That is the truth. If I wanted to kill Scintilla, I'd have killed Gráinne years ago. She was always more valuable to me alive. They would have been better off with me, even in captivity, than dead, which is exactly what they'll be if the Society gets a hold of them first. I'm forced to play two games here. Mine *and* the Society's. Three is this family's insurance against Ultana Lennon, the most powerful Arrazi in the world. I want three because *she* wants three."

"I see," I said.

"Finn, you don't have to entertain your uncle's notions for another minute. Nor do you have to join with him," my mother said.

I ignored her and locked eyes with him. "I understand."

"Do you, boy?" he asked, grasping my jacket. "I hope you do. Because it's not just their lives that depend on how we play this."

EIGHTEEN

Finn

Clancy left us in the sunlit library, where the fire sputtered like an old man.

"I want to know everything about our kind. And what you know of the Scintilla, as well."

My mother smoothed her hand over her forehead. "Your life depends upon using the life source of others to sustain you," she began, sounding very antiseptic. I wondered if this was how she sounded when she delivered bad news to her patients. "At first, your needs will be urgent and come quite frequently. The space between kills," she said, ignoring my grimace, "will lengthen as you mature. You require more energy when you're young."

"Why do the Scintilla affect us differently than regular humans?"

"Scintilla energy is especially potent. Their energy is such a perfect match for ours that it lengthens the time between our necessity to kill. It also gives us our sortilege."

"But we still have to kill, even if we're regularly taking energy from a Scintilla, as Clancy was doing?"

She sighed. "Yes. But *much* less frequently."

"And if we take a Scintilla's life? What happens then?"

"If you kill a silver one, you will gain *their* sortilege as your own, and never have to kill again. That is the rumor, anyway."

"Clancy knew this, and he didn't kill them? Why?"

"I don't know why my brother didn't kill Cora's mother. As he said, he hoped to find three of them. I've never met an Arrazi who's killed a Scintilla. We thought they were extinct, remember? We'll talk more later. You'd better go see your father. He's upstairs. He's been disconsolate since you left."

"I'm sorry."

My mother sighed heavily. "Nearly every Arrazi has been there. Not all of us return."

I turned to go but stopped with my hand on the door. "I'll go let Da know I'm okay."

Her smile was tight-lipped and grim. "We'll have visitors tonight," she said. "That's how the fight started with your uncle. The Arrazi woman, Ultana Lennon, from one of the *old* families, who is evidently quite enmeshed with this Society." Her hand waved on the word like it was a triviality. "She is coming to speak with your father and me. I can't imagine what she wants. We've kept to our own all these years. I'd like that to continue."

"Kept to your own? What do you mean?"

"You are from one of the oldest Arrazi families known. There's no hiding what we are from other Arrazi. Families talk. But now, they wish to drag us into their politics. I don't want any part of it. I've sheltered us from that because I don't want *you* to have any part of it. You can't be serious about cooperating with him?"

Hence, her overprotectiveness all my life. I'd not answer aloud. Who could know the ways my uncle had of spying? But the look I gave my mother was pure seriousness. I went upstairs to find my father.

His door was shut so I gave two light taps before entering. He slumped at his desk by the window overlooking the sea, chin resting in one hand, face drawn. The other hand played idly with a gray stone. Shock rounded his eyes when he saw me walk in. Wordlessly, I crouched in front of him. He simply took my face in his hands and pressed his forehead to mine. It was startlingly intimate. I ached. My father had always been the softer of my parents.

"Forgive me, Da. I didn't know what else to do."

One lone tear raced down his cheek and suspended like an icicle from his stubbled jaw before dropping down. "I questioned everything, too, when I was your age, but came to one conclusion—it's not as though the Arrazi created ourselves, son."

"Maybe not," I admitted, begrudgingly. "But *you* created *me*."

He simply nodded. So many words filled the room that silence was the only communication that made any sense.

"You have to be careful, Finn, about taking what you must. How you do it. Where you do it. Now you understand why your mother and I became doctors—to work around sick people. It seems more…humane. But sometimes we are forced to take wherever we can. It can be done quickly, more expediently." He thrust his hands out in front of his chest, holding the stone out to me.

"What're you on about with this?" I asked, turning the smooth rock over in my palm. It was engraved and painted with a strange marking: a green lotus flower with a hexagram in the middle of it. "Go on, Da. What's this about?"

"It is called *anahata*. It is the Hindu symbol for the fourth chakra, the heart chakra."

"What's the meaning of the hexagram?" I asked, fingering the triangles within the symbol. "Is it the Jewish Star of David?"

"It looks like it, but no. The two triangles make up the *shatkona,* the Hindu symbol for the union of the opposites of the masculine and feminine forms."

"I'm sorry," I said, placing the stone on his desk. "What's this got to do with anything?"

"It has to do with how you can be less severe when taking what you need. Imagine a funnel of energy from their heart chakra, right where the heart — "

I wanted to cover my ears like a child. "Don't bloody tell me how to kill!" I was already heading for the door. "There is nothing more *severe* than killing someone."

"You can make it easier on them."

I looked over my shoulder at him. His eyes were imploring.

"Tell that to them, Father. I don't want to know how to efficiently kill someone. I want to know how to stop it."

My mother wasn't waiting for me in the library as I'd hoped. What did I expect? In my mind, I returned to this house something other than their boy and they'd treat me differently. I'd killed a man. You're never a boy again, after that.

Being alone afforded me the opportunity to peruse her books. I'd always ignored these new age books, thinking they were the silly hobby of a woman in need of diversion from her hectic professional life. As I scanned some of the titles, I caught myself thinking, *Do people really take this stuff seriously?* But those thoughts belonged to another time — a time when I thought I was normal and that magic and mysticism were only make-believe.

Most of the books were about the energy around people—the science of it, the seeing of auras, how to "cleanse" your aura. There were books about chakras with colorful illustrations for each chakra. I stared at the page for the heart chakra, *anahata*, the one with the triangular *shatkona* my dad said to focus on when killing. I blew out a ragged breath as I looked at the beautiful symbol.

"His books are some of the best I've found," Mum's velvety voice said from behind me.

I looked at the author's name on the spine. "Edmund Nustber? Hm. Why do you have so many books about auras if Arrazi can't see them?"

Mum sat in her wingback chair and crossed her legs. My mother was the most deliberate and composed person on the planet. "I wished to train myself to see them, especially when I was younger. I foolishly thought that if I could see auras, I'd be able to pick and choose who I killed."

"Why is that foolish?"

"It's like picking fruit, only I wanted the spoiled ones. The ones who were already sick, or…rotten."

"I don't think that's foolish."

She took a sip of tea and set the cup down on its saucer. "It's foolish to want what you can't have."

"So, we can't see auras?"

"I know of no Arrazi who can."

I gathered a few of the books under my arm. "Can we talk more later?"

She inclined her head. "Of course."

"I'm going to my room." I needed peace, rest, and some privacy to do a little digging on my own.

I flopped onto my bed, sinking into the white pillows. I scanned the familiar room with new eyes: a variety of guitars, clothes slung over a wide chair, framed album covers of B.B. King and Stevie Ray Vaughan. I berated myself for the comfort it gave me to be here. The man I'd killed would never again feel the simple comfort of slipping into his bed at the end of a long day. If I had to carry his gentle soul within me, I vowed never to take it for granted.

For quick information that might have been more current, I did a computer search before diving into my mother's books. The internet was a rabbit hole of speculation masquerading as knowledge. As I suspected, there was nothing about "Arrazi." I typed in "Taking energy from people" which immediately rendered results about "energy vampires" and how to protect yourself from the "energy parasites, energy vampires, psychic vampires" of the world.

My stomach sank.

So, this was a phenomenon that people had surely felt, though it seemed clear they didn't know the *whole* truth. Neither did I, for that matter. For instance, our origins... Were there always Scintilla and Arrazi? And if so, how was it possible that others didn't know about us?

My mother was right about the author, Edmund Nustber. He was everywhere. On the surface, especially in videos, he came off a bit of a mentaller. Right-wing conservatives constantly attacked him for claiming to be an expert on scripture and for his claims that there were loads of secret messages in the Bible and in the gospels that were left out of the official canon. He loved conspiracies and even believed the Sistine Chapel was full of surreptitious messages encoded in the paintings. But if you ignored all that and concentrated on the energetic stuff, he seemed to know more about the phenomenon of giving and taking energy or auras than anyone else.

Nustber wrote about how psychic vampirism was actually

the forerunner to the folktales about bloodsuckers. Soul eater, energy predator, pranic vampire, psychic vampire, and parasitic vampire were some of the ugly names they had in place for what we were *really* called. I couldn't blame them. Damn accurate, they were.

I read about Hindu vetalas, spirits who fed on the *prana* of others, exhausting humans' brilliant light to fuel their own abnormal embers. Hours were spent combing through books and sites. Enough of the truth was out there that there was no denying; the belief in those who took energy from people had been around for thousands of years.

What I couldn't find at all was a cure.

On the nightstand, my phone buzzed with a text. Mother, informing me I should clean up and ready myself for dinner. Our Arrazi guests would be arriving soon. As much as I rebelled at the thought of raising a glass with a bunch of other *energy vampires*, my mother's comment that they were sticky with the Society was enough to get me moving. If I was to help Cora at all, I needed to find out everything I could about the mysterious club and why they wanted the Scintilla stamped out.

Nineteen

Cora

"It's *silver*."

"Right!"

"Are you trying to be funny?"

"It's rad, you know it is."

"My aura is pure silver. It's a freaking neon sign, pointing right at me!"

Mari pursed her lips. "Not to the ninety-nine point nine nine nine percent of people who can't see auras, stupid."

"This doesn't look so bad, though," I said, holding up the very *sparkly* dress. It shimmered with infinitesimally tiny silver beads. She couldn't help herself. I sighed in relief at the cut of the dress. It was short, yes, but not too short. Long sleeves. A neckline that actually lived up to its name. I was surprised at the modesty of Mari's choice. I spun the dress around on the hanger that was looped over my finger to see the back. "Um, Mari, where's the back? This dress completely lacks a *back*." As in swoosh and swoop, bare skin—right down to my ass.

"That's the best part, aye? I'm taking to saying 'aye' now. Totally sexy. The dress, I mean. Nothing is hotter than a modest front and then BAM! The rear view, baby!"

"I can't wear this. You realize my entire back is going to show. The knife…just…no."

"Has anyone seen that marking?"

"No. No one but you."

"So you can't be identified by the knife tattoo. And I don't know about you, but I'd seriously think twice about messing with some masked chick with a freaking knife on her back, even if she was hot."

"I'm not going there to be hot. I'm going there to find out more about who in the hell these people are. I have to blend in."

"Well, I'm guessing that in a swanky masked ball, *hot* will blend in. Want to see the mask? I've got to make a few alterations to it." Her dynamic orange aura pulsed as she rambled on, pulling out feathers, little crystals, and a bottle of glue.

I headed for the door. "I'm walking away before you start gluing sparkles on me."

Whether the cottage owner liked it or not, my mother was outside pulling weeds from the little patch of scrawny flowers by the front door. The door was open, letting in a warm breeze and the sound of my mother's humming. Dun crashed on a couch that was half the length of him. His legs hung off the end, one shoelace untied.

Giovanni read in a chair positioned in front of the window. His head bent forward, curls springing more wildly on top of his head than at the nape of his neck. I tiptoed toward the chair, intent on surprising him, but the closer I neared, the more erratic his silver aura became until he said, "Hello, Miss Cora."

Damn. "I'm never going to be able to sneak up on you, am

I?" I said, leaning over the back of the chair to see the book on his lap. A used bookstore had a worn red hard copy of *The Divine Comedy*. He'd been intently reading ever since we returned.

"Never. You still have no idea how potent your aura is. It's going to make that party very dangerous for you if any Arrazi are there."

I chewed my lip. "I know."

He reached for my hand, which had been resting on his shoulder as I stood behind him. "Please let me go with you, or maybe Dun?"

"We've already talked about this. No." I slipped my hand from his — the zinging energy of his agitation was like tiny needles. "You're out of the question, and Dun is way too conspicuous to blend in. My goal is to stay as far away from everyone as possible. I'll watch and listen. Fade into the shadows."

"Do you think Finn's uncle will be there?"

Finn's name was a hammer, splintering me like a block of ice. It took me a moment to trust myself to speak without crying. "I hope not." I gestured to the book on his lap. "Anything interesting?"

"You believe three to be a significant number. I find it fascinating," he said, his accent tipping and swaying with the words, "that the last line of *Paradiso* is the thirty-third." His blue eyes flashed up to see my reaction. "It was written in what's called in Italian *tiri gondi,* or third rhyme. There are nine circles of hell. Three times three equals nine. And the whole damn thing, *The Divine Comedy*, he wrote in *three* books! And, I see that each section, in each book, is thirty-three stanzas. *Three* was very important to this work."

My breaths came faster. It was uncanny. "Obviously that's all intentional. But why?"

Giovanni flashed a brilliant smile. "There's always a why, isn't there?" He dipped his head back down to continue reading.

I used Mari's phone to call Mami Tulke again. I'd have little peace in my heart until I spoke to her about my dad. Also, I wanted to ask her about the key.

She still wasn't home, but to my utter surprise, they had heard from her. She had called to let everyone know she was in mourning and would be out of reach. The same girl I spoke with before said Mami Tulke had sounded dismayed that Mari and Dun had left for Ireland. She wanted to know if they had heard from me, where I was, and if I was okay. She said that if we should call to tell us...*be safe.*

I hung up, unsatisfied and slightly irritated. I knew my grandmother was eccentric, and of course she was in mourning. My mom, Janelle, and I were, too. But to be so out of touch when we needed her was frustrating.

I went outside and sat on the bottom step where there was thick green grass edging the path up to the door. It was lush and cool on the pads of my feet and pushed up through the cracks between my toes. A tingling surge of energy seemed to rise up through the earth into my soles. I wiggled my toes, wondering if I was imagining it. I always loved walking barefoot. It settled me. That got me to thinking; I still had so much to learn, and I had two Scintilla who might be able to teach me how best use my abilities. The party was coming very fast. I needed to know more.

"If there's nothing we can do to protect ourselves," I said, stabbing my toe into the ground, "are we helpless?"

My mother yanked hard on a thick weed and flung it aside, wiping her brow with her forearm. The weed lay on the grass with its roots curled like a claw. She kept digging. It was like she could think better with her hands in the dirt. "Helpless..." The

word drifted past us like a cloud. "We were made for one thing."
I waited for more and it seemed more might not come. But then
she started talking again, her brow furrowed like it took extreme
concentration to think straight. "Keep yourself strong, so that
when they *do* take from you, you can survive it."

"How?"

"Keep your thoughts on positive things. Don't think thoughts
that weaken you or make you sick. You must raise the vibration
of your entire being and keep it high. It'll make you stronger
because, darlin', you're never safe. Unless an Arrazi has just
killed, their auras will look normal. You won't know who is the
enemy and who is not until you learn to *feel* the difference. Be
ready to be taken from again."

I recoiled. That was something I never intended to let
happen. And if it did, it might be the last time. I'd die fighting
them. "That's not exactly a positive thought."

"I said to try to be positive to strengthen your energy, not be
unrealistic. He'll find us. He will. Be ready."

I shivered, disbelieving that she could say that to me. Way
to *raise my vibration*, I thought bitterly. With Gráinne, though, it
was senseless to condemn her for the things she said. I was still
finding it hard to negotiate her mental swings. She seemed more
consistent since we had escaped. Though sifting through her
mind was like panning for gold. Every once in a while a nugget
of truth would filter out. "So how do I raise my vibration?"

She gave a chin-lift to indicate my feet. "You're grounding
yourself, there. You might not know it, but that's what you're
doing, instinctively tapping into the energy of the earth and
drawing it up into yourself. Do it every day."

"That's what you're doing, too."

Her eyes crinkled into a smile as she dug. "Aye."

"And you're saying I can make myself stronger with my thoughts? Really? Thoughts are just…thoughts."

"We are energetic beings and everything about us is energy. Thoughts have energy. They are the wands we wave to create our reality. Your body aligns with your thoughts. The world would certainly be different if people knew how much power their thoughts have."

"There's a famous essay," Giovanni called out to us from his chair inside. "'As a Man Thinketh.'"

I smiled. Giovanni had a breadth to him, like he'd skimmed so many surfaces in his life as a wandering orphan, he couldn't help but pick up on a wide array of interesting information. It was a worldliness I didn't possess. My father had seen to that.

Dun had awoken sometime during the conversation and stood in the doorway, listening and stretching his long arms over his head. His aura was a bit more extended than it had been, like the nap had rejuvenated him. "My grandmother," Dun said after a roar of a yawn, "said people walk over to a wall and flick a switch with the intention of turning on the light. Not even thinking about it. Autopilot. We take for granted that we'll get the result we intend. She said we don't give half as much thought to what switches we're flicking in ourselves."

"Okay, back up," I said. "Positive thinking? This is our grand plan for protecting ourselves?"

My mom sat back on her heels and sighed. "It's not as simple as thinking positively. It's about your thoughts and your vibration being in harmony so your spirit will be stronger."

"So, after everything that's happened, I'm supposed to waltz around feeling happy and it will make me strong enough to fight an army of Arrazi who want to *kill* me? You wanna know how I'm vibrating? I'm *vibrating* with pure terror! I'm supposed to rein in my negative emotions after Finn's uncle killed my father? After he said that Finn is likely dead by now?" Though I didn't quite feel the noose of sadness I'd felt the previous night when I'd thought of Finn. I wondered why. "How am I supposed to raise my vibration when all I feel is sadness and hate and grief?" I took a shallow breath, trying to calm myself. It didn't work. "If our safety depends on me being happy, we're freakin' screwed."

Giovanni mirrored my thoughts. "We can't fight this darkness with wishful thinking. The darkness will disappear when we eliminate it. The tables must be turned on them."

"All I could do to make myself stronger when I was taken underground was to center my thoughts on love," my mother said. "Otherwise, I'd not have been strong enough to withstand the repeated attacks. When I failed to do this for myself, it was much worse. Those times, I rode death like a black horse into the darkness."

My blood ran hot with anger, then cold with fear at the thought of how she'd been hurt for so many years. Fear was my magnetic north right now. How could she center herself around love while going through that torture?

"Love is the strongest binding in this world. Love is the key." Her simple statement seemed to answer my question, even if it was impossible for me to believe.

Love didn't save my father. Love wouldn't save Finn.

TWENTY

Finn

Mother always liked formal occasions, but I could see her disdain as she inspected the table Mary had laid out so carefully with the china and crystal normally reserved for holidays. Mother also inspected me, but I raised my eyebrows, daring her to mention my casual dress. Dark jeans and a clean shirt would do. She was lucky the shirt had buttons.

I acted aloof about dining with this Arrazi woman who Clancy had indicated was his connection to the Society, but I wanted nothing more than to nick information from her. Now that I'd decided my path, I wouldn't be satisfied unless my feet were moving in that direction.

I'd pursued Cora that way. I was completely besotted. She was all I'd wanted.

I wished it had been that pure. I envied those for whom love was.

The Society wanted something else entirely—*all* Scintilla dead. If Ultana wanted three, as Clancy had said, why would she insist the Arrazi kill any Scintilla they find? Clancy wanted them alive. I assumed it was to use them, live off them, as he'd done with Cora's mother. Christ. The hunt was on and Cora was in their crosshairs.

Jittery anxiety surged up in me at the thought of how close Clancy came to getting his hands on Cora again. If he'd found them once already, Cora and the others wouldn't have much time.

I wondered how he'd found them and if it had anything to do with me. Likely, Cora would have thought the same thing. Her cousin runs into me on the street and then Clancy almost gets them? I sighed. Let her think that. Maybe then she'd never get near enough for me to be a danger to her.

"Finn, would you get that?" my mother asked in a weary voice after the doorbell chimed. "They've come to gawk at you, in actual fact. Might as well get it over with."

"Why me?"

"The newest Arrazi, of course. That, and she sees you as a perfect prospect for her daughter. It's an antiquated thing among the old families."

"I'll be goddamned," I said, barging out of the dining room.

"Finn, please."

I entered the foyer and took a deep breath—this was bloody critical. I swung open the door. Three people waited expectantly, though I could only barely see the two young people behind the imposing woman who greeted me. Blimey, I thought my mother was commanding. This woman had *presence*. Not in a beautiful way, though she may have been beautiful once upon a time, long ago, in a land far, far away. She was round with age and excess, but there was something strange about her, too, something off about her clothes, her manner; it was like she couldn't settle on a decade or had stepped into this time from another.

"Hello. I'm Ultana Lennon." She shook my hand, holding both it and eye contact unnaturally long. It was everything I could do not to snatch my hand away from her hungry reach. Sensing energy was an ability I'd supposedly refine over time. Even through her red leather glove, I knew I'd just *felt* what it was to be fully and completely Arrazi. I inwardly recoiled. Would I become *this*?

She gave me the creeps.

"You must be Finnegan Doyle," she said, scanning me with satisfaction evident on her face.

"I am," I said, straightening taller. "Pleased to meet you, Mrs. Lennon."

Ultana nodded perfunctorily and stepped aside. Her full-length, gothic-looking black coat swished about her ankles. "These are my children."

How different from each other these two looked! "How'ya," I greeted them more casually, burying my surprise beneath a blank mask. The young man I instantly recognized. Lorcan was his name. He frequented Mulcarr's Pub. He didn't sit right with me—an aggressive drinker with an aggressive temper. We had a rousing tussle some months back when I was managing my uncle's pub one night and had to throw him out. He was a great deal bigger than me, both in height and weight, and had a mouth that grew exponentially depending upon how many pints and how many friends he had. I never understood why Clancy tolerated him in the pub. Until now.

His sister, in contrast to her brother's towering bulk and dark coloring, was a pixie of a girl. Everything about her was wispy. Her tiny face peered at me shyly from beneath a hood, her ginger hair glowing like a light against the black fabric. Pulling the hood back, she introduced herself. "Saoirse," she said with a nervous smile. The "sare-shuh" pronunciation was a breathy, feminine whisper of a word. Even her voice was wispy. She had startlingly light eyes, blue...or...green? They flickered up to her mother as if seeking approval.

The ladies stepped past me, through the door.

"You're not as big as I remember," Lorcan mumbled. The faint smell of whiskey wafted from him.

"Big enough to toss your rowdy arse out if I need to. Like before."

He chuckled and knocked my shoulder as he passed. My parents greeted everyone in the foyer, and we stood for an awkward beat until Clancy appeared, booming a hearty greeting, though I could swear there was a hint of an uneasy shake in his deep voice. I listened to voices the way I listened to my guitar. They could reveal a great deal.

"May I take your coats?" my father asked. He slung them over his arm and waited for Ultana to remove her gloves, which she slapped into his hand. It was then I realized there was only one glove. Only one hand.

"Thank you, Fergus," she said to my father in an accent I couldn't quite place. Irish, certainly. But something else. "It's been a long time. You don't look quite well."

"It's been a trying few days, Ultana."

Her gaze landed on me. "Yes. But this one came to his senses, obviously. We need more strong, young Arrazi men among us."

I bristled. Both at being talked about like I wasn't there and at the accusation of being weak. "I'd rather die with morality than live with depravity."

Ultana's eyes glinted. "You'll get over it, boy."

My mother led the group into the dining room. The chandelier cast shimmering light upon us, and I saw something I hadn't seen in the dim light of the foyer. It looked as though Ultana had a remarkable letter-shaped scar on the left side of her face. I tried to get a better look without staring, but each time I caught a glimpse, she'd turn to say something to Clancy or my parents.

"It's a birthmark," whispered Saoirse.

Heat rushed up my neck. "Sorry. I shouldn't have been staring. It looked like—"

"The letter *V*?" She smiled. "It does. Your markings are a bit more deliberate," she commented, her eyes—startling seafoam green, I realized—darting to my neck where the arches of my tattoo curved up like a wave before diving back down beneath my shirt. "Do you mind if I ask what it is?"

"Sure. The triple spiral."

A flash of something like understanding lit up her eyes. "How apropos."

"What do you mean?"

Before Saoirse could answer, our attention was drawn to the other side of the table where the conversation had already taken a heated turn. Ultana leaned forward on the table, spine erect, head cocked like a warning, one finger punctuating her words. "Ina, I've often regarded your reluctance to associate with your own kind as a futile wish to deny what you are."

My mother, never one to shy away from engagement, or from her own truth, smiled with composure, but her voice had an unmistakable frost. "On the contrary. Only a wish to not associate with you in particular, Ultana." Her lashes fluttered once, and I nearly laughed.

"Ina Doyle," Clancy hissed, but tried to hide it with laughter. "Now play nice, sister." His expression was reproving. He'd warned us about this woman and her connection to the Society. It seemed to me she was on a fact-finding mission of sorts, to see where the Doyle family stood.

My mother continued, despite her brother's warning look. "You come around with the singular aim of securing a place within our family…"

Saoirse shifted next to me.

"Is it not our responsibility to ensure the survival of our great race?" Ultana asked.

My father, who'd been quiet up until then, said, "While you endeavor to make extinct another?"

"You have aligned yourself with a group we know nothing about, which has an agenda that makes no sense to us," my mother said.

Ultana's eyes shot to Clancy with a look of anger and then back to my mother. Clearly she wasn't pleased with Clancy for telling us what the Society's aims were.

"Their presence causes discord among Arrazi who compete to find and possess the ones who remain. The Scintilla are nothing. Beneath us."

"The Scintilla are the most beautiful and extraordinary beings on this planet!" I was pinned to my seat with the threatening look that Clancy shot me.

"And how would *you* know this, young man?" Ultana asked, scrutinizing me with her penetrating stare. "Clancy informed me that your parents have told you next to nothing. Not about the Arrazi *or* the Scintilla. You speak of the legendary Scintilla as if you'd actually met one," she said with a condescending laugh, as if that was the most preposterous thing she'd ever heard.

My mother interrupted, likely to save me from exposing what I now realized was Clancy's secret. He didn't want Ultana to know about Cora and the others. "For as long as I can remember, the Scintilla have been rumored to be no more. *If* there are any left, their numbers must be so small as to guarantee their own demise. They can't possibly be a concern. You are hunting an already endangered race. Explain the threat. Make me understand."

Ultana was slow to respond, guarded. "The Scintilla are no threat to the Arrazi."

"If that's the case, then they're a threat to someone else," I said. "Or else someone wouldn't want them dead. Why does the Society want them dead?"

It was then that my mother played her hand. "If you'd like us to be allies," she said, her voice dangling the promise that Ultana needed to hear, "please, act as an ally and tell us why doing so is in our best interest."

Everyone in the room seemed to hold their breath, waiting for Ultana Lennon to answer.

TWENTY-ONE

Finn

"There's a great deal of money and power at stake," Ultana said. "That is all I can tell you."

"We don't *kill* for money or power," my mother replied.

"Would you kill for survival?"

My mother smirked. "We already do."

"That's kill or die. This," Ultana said, taking a slow sip of red wine before setting down the glass, "is kill or *be killed*."

No one spoke as the threat hung heavy in the air.

My fork clanked to my plate. "Be killed by the Scintilla?" It was preposterous. How were they a threat to us?

"Of course not," Ultana snapped. "The Society has made it very clear that the Arrazi are to cooperate or join the Scintilla's fate. We can be killed just as methodically or we can join with them and serve at their right hand."

My father tipped his head back as if to throw a silent laugh to the ceiling. "Serve as supernatural henchmen, you mean," he said. "Of course this is merely a tactical question—I am in the

Defense Force, after all—why are we bowing to anyone when we have the ability to silently and invisibly kill? The Society does not fear the Arrazi will turn on them?"

Ultana smirked. "You do not know who you're up against," she said. "Are you not tired of slinking in the shadows of humanity? We are promised exaltation. Baser humans will be kept in line where they belong, and the Arrazi will no longer have to kill in secret like criminals. It's time we took our seat at the head of the table."

"I don't see the big deal. The Scintilla are our enemy. Always have been," Lorcan said, stuffing a wad of beef into his mouth. "And we've obviously annihilated the enemy or there'd be more of 'em, wouldn't there? We get rid of the rest of 'em. Done."

The handle of the knife I held dug into my palm. I wanted to hurl it at him.

Clancy pulled at the bottom of his vest. "Since they're thought to be nearly nonexistent, we don't have much to be concerned about, do we now?" One white eyebrow shot up at my mother. "It's high time our families were on speaking terms again and that has been done. Let fate deal its hand."

"Fate will have nothing to do with it," Ultana said with a lift of her glass. "I control my own fate."

As do I, I thought, turning to Saoirse. "Would you and your mother like to have coffee with me tomorrow? I need to go into the city, and would like to hear of the many things my parents neglected to tell me."

Throat clearing from my father. Stony silence from my mother.

"They've told you nothing? Denial or duplicity, Ina?" Ultana's eyes sparkled with victory. "Ah. The boy can play nice. Smart lad. I can't possibly, however. Business."

Damn. I thought she'd jump on my invitation.

"I'm sure Saoirse would be happy to fill in the gaps," she said. "I didn't keep my children in the dark about who they are. We have a rich legacy, Finn Doyle. In my opinion, it's high time you knew about it."

"**W**hat did you think you were doing?" my mother fumed. "Ultana Lennon is a viper. Her son is a dodgy brute, and her poor daughter is a pawn in her mother's scheming. She wants *you*, Finn. And you've played right into her hands."

"Or she into mine."

"Ah," she said, after a moment. "Make her think you're at odds with me and your father. Ingratiate yourself." She stepped close, her voice low. "Don't get cocky, young man. It's a dangerous game, and you're playing *way* out of your league." She crossed her arms and paced in front of the fire. "There isn't an ugly story I've heard that didn't have Ultana connected with it. I don't know what her history is, but I can tell you this, she knows more about the Scintilla than any of us."

"How do you know? Did you see her secret?" I asked excitedly. I'd honestly forgotten that my mother would have been trying to use her new sortilege to see what Ultana didn't want her to.

"She has so many. I fell into a pit of them when I looked into her eyes, but it was like writhing snakes in a well, impossible to read just one. How can a person have that many secrets in one lifetime?" Her pacing stopped and she uncrossed her arms to touch my cheek. "Sleep, son. You'll need to be sharp for your lunch tomorrow. In Saoirse's case, I pray the apple *does* fall far from the tree."

"Night, then." I was happy to leave the library and go to bed.

Every time I went in that room, the weight of memory crushed me. I'd had the most beautiful moment of my life in there with Cora. Right before I tried to kill her.

"I'm glad my mother isn't with us," Saoirse confessed, her hushed voice shy. She curled her lips around the straw in her iced coffee, took a sip, and said, "Because I find myself wanting to say something that I could never say in front of her."

This was the most she'd spoken since I'd picked her up at home. Suddenly, she pierced me with a stare. She'd been doing everything but looking right at me the whole time. She couldn't be called pretty, exactly. Saoirse was *fascinating*. Her eyes were a little too close together, her nose pointed like a dart above bowed lips. She was a breathing caricature of a fairy. In the daylight, her sea foam-colored eyes were even more startling, especially against her flaming hair.

But this was not my Cora. Would never be.

The look Saoirse gave me was intense, searching. She had something big to say. My nerves fired with anticipation.

"My mother has been pushing the idea of you on me like you're the second coming of Christ. I know your parents told you this, and it was *painfully* obvious last night. So I'm putting it out there in the open so it doesn't have to be awkward, or forced. I have zero interest in her matchmaking schemes. I just wanted you to know, um, God…I'm not *after* you, Finn."

I feigned a dagger in the heart, which got a chuckle out of her. All of that came out in a hurried tumble, but I was impressed. Took balls. I didn't think Saoirse had it in her. Then again, maybe my sortilege had compelled her to be so honest. I exhaled, relieved. I didn't want to have to pretend to be interested in her romantically. It didn't seem right. Though it'd be a lot easier to be a two-faced git if she was anything like her mother. I rather liked Saoirse so far—in a friendly way. Liking anyone for real would be impossible. My heart was forever taken.

"Okay. You're not after me. I can live with that." I smiled to set her at ease.

"But my mother is, and she's formidable when she wants something."

"Why are you telling me this?"

"I figured if I aired it out," she said, "then maybe we could be friends. *Real* friends. It's hard to be friends with *regular* people when you know you could kill them. Our secret is too huge. Besides my brother, I don't have anyone I can talk to about all of this."

"Of course we can be friends," I said. "I'm getting over something serious with someone anyway, if you want to know the truth. I'm damaged goods, I'm afraid." My heart ached just admitting to it.

"Aren't we all?" she said, and we both smiled sadly. It made me wonder what her damage was. "I'm happy to tell you everything I can. I don't want you to pretend to like me just to get information."

Wow. This girl was shrewder than I gave her credit for. A dainty, delicate appearance did not equal a mousy spirit. Lesson learned. "You're right. I want information. I have respect for your honesty. I'd like to be friends," I told her and was surprised to feel a splinter of truth in the words.

"Grand." Her voice became stronger, like a barometer of her comfort level. "No fakey romance. That's the *last* thing I want."

"Wow. The mere thought of romance with me is repugnant,

huh?" I teased. "Friends aren't supposed to make friends feel like shite about themselves."

"Sorry to disappoint you, but it *is* repugnant," Saoirse said, a deep blush flaming her pale skin. "I don't want to be forced into something that should be natural. And I'm—I'm not ready. My mother will be a problem, though. She's quite intent on us being together."

"Why?"

"Two reasons, I reckon. One, she's impatient for me to change. To"—she made quote fingers—"*blossom* fully into what I was born to be." She rolled her doe eyes. "And often, it's powerful feelings for another at this age that bring it on."

Cora... I bit my lip.

Saoirse noticed, her eyes flickering to my mouth and then away, but continued on. "If I understand the theory, we have the connection to our parents as children, but it's our first love that causes us to want to forge a connection with another. It's the first time that we *choose* for our energy to reach out for another's. Our intense longing to connect with that person is a trigger."

When she said that, I immediately understood her rebellion. "You're reluctant to get involved with anyone because you don't want to turn."

She looked away, her gaze wandering and then settling on a young couple a few tables over who'd left their pastries uneaten because they were too busy chatting with each other as if the world didn't exist outside of them. "I know I'm *supposed* to want it to happen..."

I couldn't be sure if she was talking about romance or becoming a mature Arrazi.

"Anyway, I've heard that intense hatred for another can also bring it on."

"I'll be careful not to piss you off, then. And the second reason your mother is pushing me on you?"

"It's your family, your mother's side to be specific. She makes it sound like the Mulcarrs have been around since the beginning."

"The beginning?"

She cocked her head, a shock of red covering one eye. "Yes. Brú na Bóinne…Newgrange."

TWENTY-TWO

Cora

"Those blithe souls flashed out like comets streaming from the sky, Whirling in circles round determined poles. And even as wheels in clock escapement ply, In such fashion geared that motionless, Appears the first one, and the last to fly."

We sat around the table, having lunch as Giovanni read aloud from *Paradiso*. He slapped the book shut and stared at us with this amazed kind of expression that, frankly, perplexed us all. Dante wasn't exactly easy reading.

Dun slurped from his bowl of soup and set it down. "Dude. Ancient, old Italian fella said what?"

"Yeah, it's like a secret that you're the only one in on even though you just told it to us. I think you have to read that, like, twelve more times for me to even understand what the hell he was talking about," Mari said. "Whirling circles and flying?"

"Who is Beatrice?" I asked him. She was a key figure in *Paradiso*.

"Dante's heart and soul. His love. In this canto, they are

watching this celestial event together."

"What is it, child?" my mother asked. She'd apparently been watching me mull it over. Her eyes crackled with curiosity as she waited for me to answer. I think our quests were bringing her back to herself.

"It reminds me of that painting in the Doyles' manor. A man and a woman, standing together under this spiraling mass of angels. I wish I could see it again, because that's what this quote makes me think of."

I wish I could ask Finn about it. I wish...

I wished too many things, like that I could see Finn once again and talk about our bizarre lives, ask him what his family knew about Scintilla, ask him about the Dante painting, the Dante quote about flames and sparks, and why Griffin had said it to me in the hospital. I wished to look into Finn's warm brown eyes, feel his lips on my cheek as he whispered to me. I wished to feel the way I felt when we were innocently falling in love. Well, it was love for me, anyway. I wished for his life to be different so he wouldn't have preferred to die.

I wished for the thousandth time to save my thoughts of Finn for *someday* when I could process everything without it feeling like a kick in the heart.

I pushed my soup away, too troubled to eat. Morbid, negative feelings soaked through me. Although I'd been told to keep my thoughts grounded and positive, I'd been feeling worse. I tried working on making myself stronger in preparation for the party, in preparation for the unknown, for the attacks that Gráinne said were sure to come, but my body or mind or freaking *vibration* wouldn't cooperate. My heart sagged with sadness. My limbs were heavy with anger. I buzzed with fear. None of that was going to make me stronger. It was like pulling myself out of quicksand with one hand.

Giovanni's silver aura grew and swirled around his body, flowing from him toward me as he neared. "Stop that," I snapped, feeling the hit as an appealing mist rolled over my skin. "You won't always be there to give me strength or make me feel better. There will be times when you can't give me what I don't possess for myself. I *have* to learn this."

"Cora, you had to have massive strength to save my life. I know those men almost killed me. I felt myself floating out of my body. I was dying." Giovanni touched my shoulder, sending warmth and waves of crackling energy down my arm. His voice softened. "You're stronger than you know."

"You saved his life?" Dun said, mid-bite.

"Don't sound so astonished."

"*How?*"

"With a kiss," Giovanni answered, a smile in his voice. I think he was trying to lighten the mood, but it felt like taunting. And I didn't want Mari and Dun to get the wrong idea.

"What?" Mari practically yelled. "How very Sleeping Beauty mash-up of you!"

"I didn't save him with a kiss. I saved him with thoughts of you guys, of the people I loved." I pushed out of my chair and left the room.

Mari and Dun followed a few minutes later. I was glad they did. They—they were normal. They were pre-bizarre. They were home. And the only way I could go back to that home now was through them. They climbed on the bed, one on each side of me, and we all lay there like sardines, silent, staring up at the cracks in the ceiling. Hot tears flowed onto my temples.

"I know you're scared," Mari said, the hush of her voice taking me back years to our "whisper time" in a darkened room when we were supposed to be sleeping but would lie awake and share our dreams and secrets. Whisper time was a sacred bubble.

"I'm kinda scared," Dun whispered. "I keep doing that thing I do when I leave the movies, you know…where I feel like what happened in the make-believe world of the movie is happening outside of the theater?"

"You're dumb," Mari whispered.

"Am not. You are."

I could have lain there all night and listened to their stupid-awesome chatter, but I found myself mystified by the zings of pinkish-gold radiance flying over top of me from one to the other. I felt like I was in a love cross fire. When were they going to admit to me that they had the hots for each other? I could deal. Maybe, it occurred to me, they hadn't admitted it to themselves.

"How are we going to get you out of here?" Mari asked, bringing us all back to harsh reality.

"First, we need to get you and Dun out of here and back home."

"I'm not leaving this island without your fully realized butt."

"If you don't, Mari, you might never leave at all. This isn't a movie. This is real life and people are trying to kill us."

Dun gently nudged my side. "Is that more of the positivity you're supposed to be working on?"

"What do you suppose Dante meant by 'a mighty flame follows a tiny spark'?" Giovanni busted our little dome of quiet. He stood in the doorway, book in hand.

I sat up. "Clancy called me 'little silver spark' once. If we were the tiny spark, then I suppose Dante could have been talking about the Scintilla being pursued my something much bigger and mightier, if he was talking about us at all."

"I believe he was. And in the canto with that quote, he speaks of lifting up a prayer 'that Cyrrha may reply.' Cyrrha is widely thought to be code for Apollo, god of light and truth. I want to go back to the internet café and do some looking into Dante's life."

I scooted off the end of the bed. "Let's go. I want to see if I can find that painting online." I gave Mari's leg a squeeze. "You guys wanna come?"

"Nah," Mari said, rolling her head to peek at Dun. "Are you taking your mom?"

"I don't know. It's not smart for the three of us to be together all the time. We're a beacon to the Arrazi, especially together."

"Do you think it's like that?" Dun asked. "That you put off some kind of mojo like one of those silent dog whistles and all nearby Arrazi come sniffing?"

Giovanni answered. "They can sense us, yes. We're in danger because we don't know they're Arrazi unless their aura is white or we are close enough to feel their peculiar energy—"

"Energy that I haven't yet learned how to detect," I interrupted.

"You might be surprised," Giovanni said, looking down at me. "You've been attacked by two and have known one other, quite intimately." He looked away from me, pursing his lips together.

Intimately. An assumption on his part, but one that still made my stomach cave. I'd never feel Finn's unique energy again. My father's and my first love's distinctive and gentle energies were lost to me forever.

My mother wouldn't be put off from going with us to the café. "Don't make me useless, I don't want to be separated from you, Cora," she said, softening my resolve with sadness.

Truthfully, I didn't want her out of my sight, either. I'd worry about her constantly.

The three of us walked down a patchy grass path from the cottage to the main road that led to the small town. The crumbled ruin of an old home rose up from the knee-high field grass behind a stone wall. Mari had previously taken to exclaiming, "Beautiful random old shit!" every time we passed a decaying remnant of the past.

I wondered what she and Dun were up to back at the cottage, all alone.

Giovanni hooked my mother's arm in his after she slipped on a patch of uneven ground. She smiled gratefully. Content to be alone with my thoughts, I strolled a few steps behind them until we reached the Turkish coffee shop. Orhan, the owner, greeted us warmly when we walked in. Giovanni bought coffee in little demitasse cups and baklava to eat while we worked. There were many more people occupying the row of computers than before. We settled into a booth, waiting for one to free up. When it did, my mother elected to stay in the booth until a computer freed while Giovanni scooted a chair next to mine so we could share the single terminal.

"Look up Dante's life," he said. "What? Why do you purse your lips together?"

"You're bossy."

"I prefer decisive."

"I prefer you to get your own terminal."

He laughed. "I prefer your lips when you're sleeping. Full and parted slightly when you are relaxed. Better than pinched together and telling me I'm bossy."

He's studying my lips when I sleep? "You shouldn't watch people when they sleep. It's creepy."

His head tilted sideways, as it did when he found something I said perplexing. I typed Dante's name. Giovanni leaned in. "You call for them in your sleep."

My fingers paused above the keyboard. I didn't need to ask for whom. My shoulders curled forward as Dante Alighieri's history popped up on the screen. Nothing in the poet's life in the Middle Ages suggested that he'd had special knowledge of other breeds of human. No, it wouldn't, right? Someone wanted us to be a secret. It wouldn't be *that* easy. Banished from Florence for his politics, many believed *The Divine Comedy* to be a thinly veiled arrow of resentment that Dante launched at the Florentine government while in exile. I pulled up *Paradiso* on the computer while Giovanni thumbed through his book. As I read, I couldn't help thinking it was so much more than a poem.

It seemed a disguised message.

"Interpretation is always filtered through the perception of the individual," Giovanni said after I told him my thoughts. "I agree that his writing seems to speak of us, but I want to be sure I'm not grasping for what I *want* to see."

"I don't think both of us are seeing things in *Paradiso* just because we want to. It's not every day you talk about people's colors changing."

"I told you, talk of auras was once very common. Look at the religious art throughout history. Auras galore. But it fell out of fashion. A belief in auras, he very well may have had. But can we truly say he knew of Scintilla or Arrazi?"

I chewed the pad of my thumb while, with the other hand, I scrolled through artwork inspired by Dante. "No, it's not proof," I conceded. "And we might be wasting our time. Though, the connection to threes…" I threw up my hands. "Maybe we're better off sticking to what *heaven* this key opens, why Clancy wants three of us, or how the Arrazi are connected to a secret society that wants us dead."

He didn't look up from the book. "*Si.*"

An image rolled past on the screen and I stopped, my heart flaring and thundering in my chest like it gave off an audible hammering to everyone within earshot. "G," I said, barely containing the shock in my voice. "Look at this." The black-and-white painting that hung in Finn's house filled the screen. The same two people, gazing up into the sky where the same spiral of whirling angels circled in the clouds. "The painting is by an artist named Gustave Doré."

"Mmmm," he said, glancing up.

"Look! The name of the painting. It's called *Scintillating Host of Heaven.*"

TWENTY-THREE

Cora

Buzzing. All three of us were buzzing. Yes, we were three Scintilla looking for clues or meaning. Vague perceptions of truth or evidence were bound to happen. They were flimsy strings of ideas we tried to clutch in the wind. But these were more than co-incidences. Even my mother, whose sanity had been stripped and sanded with the years of energy-battering, covered her mouth in wonder when we showed her the painting.

Our silver auras erupted and glowed around our bodies, melding together in a symphony of excitement. We were so potent that I couldn't calm my racing heart. Thank God the effect of us together couldn't be seen by regular people. We were walking silver fireworks! I became paranoid when I noticed a woman repeatedly walking past and slowing near us for no reason. We had to get out of public and to the privacy of the cottage. Again, I was glad the airport video showed only my profile with a hoodie over my head.

On the stroll back, someone abruptly opened a car door in

front of us and my mother gasped, jumping vertical like a startled kitten.

"What is it?" Giovanni asked, looking around with panic in his eyes.

"I was taken right off the street," she answered, breathless. "When I disappeared."

Giovanni's face suddenly became an impassive mask, but his aura churned and spit like a silver fire. I put my arm around her shoulder. "What happened?"

"One moment, I was walking down a sunny street. I remember hearing a car door open right behind me. I started to feel faint and was having trouble walking. I remember thinking I might be getting sick. I became so weak, like my skin was thin. Then I passed out. I came to and I was Clancy's prisoner. In one moment, I lost my family. I lost everything."

Giovanni remained quiet after that. We walked in silence until we came upon a little grocery store. He slipped inside for a few minutes and returned carrying a grocery sack. When we arrived at the cottage, he set the bag on the counter and pulled out a bottle of red wine. "I need to relax," he announced while rummaging through the cabinet drawers for a corkscrew. His aura and body language broadcast high excitement of our discoveries, but also agitation.

"Research went that well, huh?" Dun asked.

Giovanni uncorked the wine like a pro. "Mmm-hmm. All my years of searching for clues to our history never turned up something so exciting. Always hints, but nothing that felt so concrete and real."

"Auntie," Mari said to my mother, "when you were researching years ago, did you ever find something that made you feel this excited?"

Mom pulled a loose string on her sweater and began tying little knots in it like a rope. "Nothing was more exciting than meeting others like me in Chile. I found out I wasn't alone," she said, a trace of wonder still evident in her voice all these years later. "I never knew my parents. Until then, I had no idea if I was the only one. It felt so good not to be alone."

Giovanni stopped mid-pour. He nodded slowly, but his aura retracted as she spoke. Even if I couldn't see auras, I could see the hurt that warped his features. He raised his glass to an invisible guest and downed it.

Hours later, after the simple cans of chili we heated and the bread we used to stretch the meal were eaten, the house quieted enough for me to fall asleep. It wasn't long before I woke though. I was sure someone had said my name in the darkness.

"Yes?" I said, but no one answered. The soft fall of footsteps outside made every nerve tingle with alertness. I listened harder. Someone was definitely outside. Careful to stay away from the window, I tiptoed in a half crouch to the kitchen and felt around for the knife we'd used to cut the bread. Holding it at my side with shaking hands, I walked slowly toward the wide-open front door.

Moonlight cast a disc of white at the front door and to the steps beyond it, illuminating Giovanni's dirty-blond curls against the darkness. He sat on the step, back hunched, head bowed. My brain thought for a moment that maybe he was reading *Paradiso* by the light of the moon. But I was wrong. As I stepped closer, I realized his wide shoulders shook with quiet tears.

I set the knife down and stepped through the door, past him, my feet hitting the night grass, cool air playing on my skin as I stood in front of him. He didn't look up at me when I bent to place my moonlit hand on his shoulder. *Should I go?* I started to back up, but his hands circled my waist. He pulled me forward and buried his cheek against my stomach, clutching me to him like a little boy clutches his blankie. My breath hitched. The gesture was so intimate, but so innocent, too.

The dampness of his tears pressed through my T-shirt to my skin. Suspending my hands above his head, I clenched my fingers, unsure. Finally, I wound my fingers into Giovanni's curls and cradled his head against me as he cried softly. I imagined he hadn't been held or comforted much in his lonely life. How sad that was. Everyone needed a trusted friend they could cry with.

His hands curled into the ridge at the small of my back as he fought to regain his composure. He finally looked up at me, and when I felt the beat of his aura change from small and wounded to something stronger, I stepped back, brushing his wet cheeks with my thumbs as I did. "What's wrong, G?"

His hands slid from my back, past my hips, and grazed my outer thighs before he dropped them into his lap and looked away. I shivered from the track of heat his fingers left on my skin. "I was with them when they disappeared," he said, voice ragged.

"That must have been awful." I wanted to hear the story but was afraid at the same time. Too awful, and I'd add it to my rotating mental list of the horrors that might await me. I knelt down in front of him and waited to see if he wanted to talk more.

"I wasn't young, like you were when you lost your mom. I was old enough to remember them, to have pictures." He tapped his temple. "Clear pictures of love and family, of what it was like to *belong*. I see them every day in my mind."

"It's wonderful that you have those memories with them. My mom was a stranger to me when I found her. We're just getting to know each other now." In fact, I felt the first surges of real love for her and it scared me. Would I be strong enough to handle it if anything happened to her?

"Yes. But no matter how beautiful my memories are, the one that haunts me, the one I can't forget, is the day they were taken from me."

I sucked in my breath. "What happened?"

"We lived in Cortona at the time. In a hillside villa, a golden dream of a life all together. Olive trees and lemons grew outside the kitchen door." Giovanni's eyes turned wistful. "My mother was washing dishes at the sink while I sneaked pine nuts from a jar. Her belly was round with a baby. I remember hearing a car drive up, and her humming stopped abruptly when she looked out the window. A black van had parked close to the door. Three men jumped out. I hid in an electronics cabinet like my father told me to. He said if the Arrazi ever came, to hide there so the frequencies might mask my Scintilla energy. She told me to not come out no matter what. 'They'll keep looking for you,' she said. 'Never let anyone find you. Never. Don't trust anyone.' Her voice was so shaky, Cora. So scared."

Like his, now.

"My father heard them kick in the front door and he came running down the stairs. I was so glad he was coming to save us, but afraid for him, too. I wanted to yell out to warn him, but covered my mouth to stop myself. I watched through the crack between the cabinet doors, but didn't know what was happening to my mother. Her back was to me, but as she fell to her knees and curled herself around her big belly, I saw the man's aura pulling her silver from her like a long thread. I hadn't known such a thing was possible.

"Their thieving energy hit my father as soon as he skidded into the room. He knew one of the men, said his name as he fell to his knees. I watched his spirit being yanked from his body, too, until soon he was on the floor next to my mother. She lay a few inches from where I hid. She rolled her head toward me. Her eyes were open, but she wasn't seeing me." Another tear rose in Giovanni's eye and fell as his voice cracked. "Her eyes were open.

"I've hated myself every day of my life since then. I did nothing to stop them. I hid like a coward and watched as my parents were carried out of the house. The men, they looked for me and then they left. I knew they would come back again. I don't know how long I stayed in that cabinet. But after dark, I got my backpack, put as much as I could carry inside, and ran away."

"You were *not* a coward. You were brave, and just a little boy. What she told you saved your life. There was nothing you could have done differently except share their fate. God, Giovanni," I said, reaching for his forearms, which were hugging his knees. "You're alive because you listened to her."

My own throat was thick with tears. I knew the pain of watching an Arrazi pull my father's spirit from his body. But I wasn't a little kid. I wasn't all alone.

"Yes, I listened to her. I never trusted anybody, and I was never found."

I leaned forward on my knees and hugged him. With a gentle lift, he pulled me closer, settling me in the space between his thighs. His hug was so hungry, I wondered how many times since that day he'd hugged another person. I said, "I'm glad to have your trust—"

"I *don't* trust you." Equal parts offended and hurt, I tried to pull away, but his arms held me to him. His mouth was against my neck when he murmured, "You terrify me."

"I don't understand."

Giovanni let me go then, almost a gentle push away from me. He stood, ran his fingers through his wild hair, and began pacing the grass. "I've always had to rely only on myself. I had no reason to ever trust someone else. Then, I meet *you*. You, who are like me, who understands without me having to explain. You, whose mere physical presence lights up my energy in a way I haven't felt since being with my parents.

"But I can't control you," he continued, his arms waving. "You are your own person—an incredibly willful one at that. You're taking a risk with that party that I don't want you to take. And yet, I respect you more because you won't let me stop you. You never let things stop you. I want to do anything I can to save you from ever being locked up again. And I want to lock you up myself, to keep you safe."

"Don't even joke—"

He stepped forward. "No, no. I'd never do to you what *he* did."

That pushed an aching sigh from me.

Giovanni gestured toward the cottage. "I never again thought I'd feel like I have a family. I'm—I'm terrified to lose it again. It's why I want to fight back against the Arrazi. If I could, I'd kill them all." His jaw set in a rigid line and his fingers coiled into fists. "You've no idea how badly I want to kill them all."

"It would be a lie to promise you won't lose someone again, but I don't think that waging all-out war on the Arrazi when we're outnumbered and defenseless is a smart option. And Clancy said they aren't our only enemy. We don't even know what we're up against with the Society."

His head bowed, nodded. "I should perhaps trust you for your cruel honesty," he said, looking up at me with a wry smile.

"I promise to always be honest with you, G. You do the same and we're good. Deal?"

"Deal." A flicker of something passed over him, so quickly I might have mistaken it for a secret.

Twenty-Four

Finn

"You said that my triple spiral tattoo was *apropos*. Now you're saying that Brú na Bóinne is pertinent to our history? My mother took me there constantly as a lad. I loved the spirals, loved the zigzags and art all over the rocks. She used to tell me that she felt like there was a message in the spirals for our family, but that's all she would say. Maybe it was all that she knew."

Saoirse lifted an auburn eyebrow. "I'd venture she knows more than that."

"Aye. Perhaps. She hasn't exactly been forthcoming with information. I got the tattoo because I loved the mystery of the triple spiral and thought it was cool. Even as a child, I knew that ancient site was magic. Please tell me what you know."

Talking about the spiral brought Cora to mind. We'd spoken of it. Bumps flared on my skin with the thought of how she yanked open my shirt and ran her tongue over my tattoo. I clenched my jaw. My last message to Cora was my good-bye. That there was an end to the tale of the triple spiral. If she understood, then she'd believe I was dead now. It was probably for the best.

My chest and stomach curled in with the ache of heartsickness, so much so that I bent forward with pain. I took a breath, straightened, and focused back on Saoirse.

"You all right there?"

"I am, thanks. Go on."

"My mother told Lorcan and me that it was the origin, the birthplace for our kind. Well, not *just* our kind. But also those others they were talking about last night."

"Scintilla."

She nodded emphatically. "Mmm-hmm. Mother says we conquered the Scintilla as we were meant to, claiming their powers and Newgrange as our own, ruling there for centuries after." Her eyes took on a faraway glaze. "I like the sound of that, ruling, as if the Arrazi descend from nobility."

"I don't call conquering noble," I said, thinking hard about what she was telling me and feeling both irritation at the arrogance of some Arrazi families and excitement in my chest. "If we came from the same place, that means we somehow coexisted at one point. Or," I said, my excitement deflating, "do you think the Arrazi came from someplace else?"

"Originally? I don't know. But there are a lot of us around here. If you placed a bull's-eye map over top of Brú na Bóinne, you'd see that the closer in you get to it, the more concentrated are the Arrazi families."

It was information, but not information that was going to tell me how to cure us of our need to kill, or how to save the remaining Scintilla. I rubbed my forehead. "Your mother's work—with the Society—what is that about? Why are they out to eradicate the Scintilla?"

She shrugged. "I'd always thought her work with them was

for the advancement of our kind. She's always talking about research the Society is paying for. Honestly, last night was the first I'd heard of trying to find any remaining Scintilla and killing them. Listening to it was appalling if you didn't know what we were, or that they'd always been our natural enemy."

"They're defenseless. How can they be *our* enemy?" I scoffed.

"My mum was right. You haven't been told a thing about your Arrazi heritage, yet you seem to know an awful lot about the most mysterious part of that heritage. It *is* as if you've known one personally or something." Astutely, she stopped talking and let me sit in the pause uncomfortably long.

"They are more of the magic my mother told me about as a kid. I thought she was making up stories…" Beads of sweat rose on my upper lip. I hoped she wouldn't notice.

"Do you think there are any left?" Saoirse asked. "My mother says that one drop of their energy will give us extrasensory powers."

A nervous laugh. "Did she? Superpowers, eh? Now who's making up stories?"

"You don't wonder what your sortilege would be?"

"I only wonder how to stop us from having to take energy from others at all."

Brows pinched together, she looked at me. "That's like saying you're going to find a cure for breathing. There *is* no cure."

We finished our drinks and walked around aimlessly until I had to get going. I planned on reinserting myself into my job at the pub so I could keep an eye on Clancy. I suspected he'd not refuse me. We were watching each other, no doubt.

The ride back was not unlike any other "first date," with Saoirse telling me about her school, and cello lessons, and dreams of travel. She surprised me by talking of learning to navigate by the stars and wanting to charter a boat someday to take herself around the Caribbean.

I pulled up to the Lennons' home. Ultana Lennon did very well for herself. My mother said she'd never been married, that she knew of. I wondered what she did to earn the spectacle of a mansion.

A chill fingered up my back as I opened the door for Saoirse. Her mother approached from inside the house and called out to us. "Back so soon?"

I stuffed my hands in my pockets and tried not to tip back and forth on my feet. The woman made me bloody edgy. "Aye, work, ma'am."

"And where are you employed, Finn?"

"My uncle employs me at his pub."

She tsked and narrowed her eyes while stepping closer. "Your family is intent to keep you small. Have you ambitions?"

We held eye contact. I couldn't help but feel that something depended upon my answer. "I have ambitions, Mrs. Lennon."

"Good."

I cocked my head. That was it?

"I have a marvelous idea!" Ultana exclaimed. "There's a party coming up. My family and I will be there along with many other *distinguished* families in the area. Why don't you attend with us? You can chaperone Saoirse, and I'll introduce you to people who might help you up a rung or twelve from that haybarn of a pub you're working at."

"Mother. I'd planned on going alone to the—"

Ultana's head whipped back to her daughter. The look she gave was venomous. "Nonsense. What could you be thinking?" She didn't wait for an answer but returned her gaze to me. "Join us. It's an annual fund-raising bash. The best, most exclusive party in the city, I guarantee."

"Thank you," I said. "I'd love to come."

"Of course you would." Ultana breezed past Saoirse as if she weren't there and entered the house.

Saoirse crossed her arms and glared at her mother's back. "I'll get you a mask." When she saw my confused look, she said, "Anonymity is preferable to many of the guests, so it's a masquerade party. All of the Society's parties are."

TWENTY-FIVE

Finn

The night of the party, I was told a car would be sent to pick me up.

The driver, gruff and looking more like a bodyguard than a chauffeur, came to the door. "I take it this isn't your average party?" I joked, looking past him to the limousine parked in front of my house, though I had known it wasn't an average party when I'd been instructed to wear a tuxedo. The driver gave a small smile, tight and a bit lopsided from a scar that hooked his lip up below his nose.

The car door was opened for me and I slid in next to Saoirse, who looked very pretty in a green satin dress. Except, all I could think was that the emerald of her dress was so like Cora's eyes. Lorcan strained the seams of his tuxedo. Ultana had on an odd black dress that reminded me of Victorian England with its poufy shoulders and lace and ruffles. "My favorite era," she remarked, when she saw me looking her over. I was sure I couldn't care less, but I smiled anyway.

Everyone had elaborate masks over their faces. Saoirse handed me a simple black one to put on. Her own was made of teal and green peacock feathers. Her eyes blended eerily into the circles within the green feathers so that it nearly looked like multiple pairs of eyes staring at me.

I wasted no time on my mission. "Ultana, you said this party is a fund-raiser for the Society. What does the Society use the funds for?"

"You're a stickybeak," Lorcan snapped. "Mind your own business."

"Now Lorcan," Ultana admonished him, "Finn is smart to ask questions. It's only natural to be curious when one has been kept ignorant for so many years." I fought to keep myself from reacting. "The Society has many investments and interests. It takes a great deal of money to fund some of their more philan-thropic work."

"Philanthropic? Like killing the Scintilla?"

"Enough," she said, throwing the word down like a gavel. I could see she was used to being able to wield her words that way. She turned toward the window. "Excellent turnout," she said of the long queue of people waiting to get inside Christ Church. I expected the limo to pull into the string of cars dropping masked partygoers at the entrance, but it continued west, past the church, and turned onto a narrow side street off Saint Michael's Hill.

"Where are we?" I asked when the limo pulled over.

Ultana smirked. "Hell."

"Don't let her vex you," Saoirse whispered after her mom climbed from the car. "She's only referring to this place's his-tory. Used to be a seedy place known as *Hell*. This is where the gate was," she said, pointing. "At the entrance, there used to be a wooden statue of the devil."

"Brilliant. The gates of Hell overlooked the church?" I asked, surprised I'd never heard this lore about my city before.

Saoirse patted my cheek, mockingly. "Aye, dear Finn. Maybe the devil and God like to keep an eye on each other."

I followed the Lennon family up the sidewalk, under an arch, to a plain, unmarked door. Ultana pulled a key from her pocket and unlocked it, ushering us into a small entryway with a flickering square light in the ceiling. The sounds of Dublin traffic abruptly ceased when she slammed the door shut, and we began walking in single file through the narrow passageway.

The floor descended sharply like a ramp, which led down under the streets of Dublin. The sound of rushing water ran nearby. We kept close together as we walked downward until the ramp leveled out and we arrived at another door. Ultana pushed a small button, like a doorbell, and within moments, a robed church official opened the door, ushering us into a private room within Christ Church. With a meaningful look, the man handed Ultana a folded piece of paper, which she read, saying only, "A gracious invitation, indeed. Please convey my acceptance," before stuffing it into her skirt pocket. We were then shown to a private door leading to the party in the crypt under the church.

I couldn't help but wonder how she garnered such privilege.

Twenty-Six

Cora

"How you gonna get in?"

Mari's question poured more anxiety into me, making my nervous level rise to where I thought I couldn't hold any more. "This ring is the only key I have for getting into that party."

"I feel sick to my stomach," Dun said, with a groan. "How do spies even handle this kind of stress? I think I should go in with you for protection."

"Dun, you'd stick out like a sore thumb, even with a mask. I keep telling you, the remarkable way you look…not a good idea, even if Clancy *hadn't* already seen you and fought you in that hotel lobby."

Everyone stuffed belongings into our backpacks. After Clancy's attack, we agreed that we should never be without the essentials, especially on a day like today. The plan was for them to drop me near the church and then wait for me at a nearby pub.

When Giovanni slouched on the end of the bed next to where I was packing, I smiled to try to ease his worry, and maybe my own. It was useless. I could only think of one thing. "If anything happens to me tonight—"

"Cora," Giovanni said, imploring me not to finish.

It had to be said. My tongue felt coated with ash and I swallowed past the lump in my throat. "If it does, I'm counting on you. I need you to take my mother and my family—our family—and get out of Ireland."

"**B**limey," Patrick said as we neared Christ Church in his cab. "There's a long chain of swanky cars up ahead."

"Drop me here," I said. "I'll walk up to the door." My knees felt weak after I paid him and slid out. Like Mari had practiced with me, I lifted my chin and did my best confident strut down the sidewalk, or, as confident as I could in those heels. I knew I looked like a giraffe on roller skates. Honestly, death by stilettos might be preferable to what I feared could happen if Clancy was inside that church. My plan was to stay out of sight and if Clancy somehow spotted me, to make him believe I'd been invited by the Society. My bluff had worked the night of our escape from the shack when I'd told him that people from the Society were on their way. He'd been shocked that I knew about them. Maybe it'd work again.

I shivered and cursed Mari when the breeze hit my bare back. An Irish breeze is always cold as midnight sea spray.

People lined the walkway to enter. I eyed the crowd, then slipped behind an elderly couple. Maybe it would be assumed I was their granddaughter. Every cell in my body flared with apprehension when people flashed their invitations to the serious-looking man at the door. He didn't just inspect the invitations;

he used a scanner and held the paper up to it. When he ran the scanner over the paper, triangles came into view. I was right! The symbol on Clancy's ring and on the ring I unburied was the symbol for this secret society. One that Clancy had warned was an even greater enemy than he was.

How crazy was I, to march straight into the enemy's camp? I saw no alternative. In order to disarm one's enemy, sometimes it was necessary to head to the front lines.

My chest rose and fell unnaturally fast as the guard nodded his approval and the couple passed him and went inside. I had no invitation. This wasn't going to work. My palms and pits were soaked. His eyes roamed from my studded silver heels, past my wobbling ankles, and settled on my eyes. "Miss, I cannot possibly—"

Desperate, I flipped my palm over in a dramatic gesture of fake confidence and showed him the gold ring with the symbol. He paused, pulled my hand toward him, and scrutinized it.

I sighed impatiently, trying to affect the bored, entitled stance that spoiled celebrities give. Finally, he gave me a reverential bow and ushered me through the door.

I thought I was going to faint before I even got through it.

A series of turning stairs led me down into the primeval crypt of the church. People going up the stairs passed me and nodded in greeting. Thank God for the mask to hide behind. Too bad that anonymity went both ways. I wouldn't clearly see the faces of my enemies.

Color surrounded me and I turned awkwardly on my heels, scrutinizing the crowd. The partygoers couldn't hide their spirits behind a mask. Auras wafted around people's bodies as they mingled, drank, and danced. I had to be careful not to get caught up in the kaleidoscopic beauty of it. The air above the party was like the aurora borealis. I scanned the room for pure white auras. No one glowed with the conspicuous all-white of an Arrazi, but that could be misleading as they only glowed white when they had recently killed or taken from a Scintilla.

When I asked my mother why they turned all white when they killed, she said she didn't know for sure, but she always believed that it was the absorption of *all* wavelengths of color from another's aura that temporarily illuminated them to white. It seemed a cruel joke that the color most often associated with innocence and purity was actually the consuming black hole of a human killer.

I did as my mom instructed and took deep, calming breaths. As I blew out, I imagined a pole from the crown of my head, down the middle of my body, and out my feet. This was supposed to *root* me. The more grounded I was within myself, the more I'd be able to feel the energy of others. If I couldn't see the danger of an Arrazi, perhaps I'd feel it, *sense* it.

Arches of stone blocks curved around the twelfth-century crypt. I hid behind one. It was cold to the touch, and I whipped my hand away when a wisp of indiscriminate history bubbled from the surface toward my hand. It was the first time I felt it coming. The last thing I needed was to get hit with a memory, become a woozy spectacle with spontaneously erupting tattoos, and draw everyone's attention. Apparently, this place had once been everything from a city market to a tavern. There was history here so palpable, I felt it within a foot of the walls, strong enough to raise goose bumps. I slunk around the arches for cover but stayed wary of them as well.

Conversations I overheard were mundane for the most part, limited to surface party chatter and pretentious egotisms. An influx of guests arrived. My toes tapped to a Nat King Cole tune as I hid and watched, then I froze completely as an aura of white came into view. A throng of people blocked the Arrazi so that I couldn't get a good look. They pressed in like adoring fans, auras blending into one collective mound of insistence for the Arrazi's attention.

I moved away from the wall to the other side of a vaulted archway. From the center of the colorful group, like she was the wick and her white aura the burning flame of a candle, stood an older woman. I studied her from behind the stones and from behind my mask.

Most of the women, I'd noticed, had elaborate, feathered masks like a flock of birds. Her mask was fashioned out of something that looked like black chain mail that curved down her cheekbones. She wasn't young, but her presence was demanding. Everyone seemed to treat her like royalty. I studied her odd Victorian dress and her necklace made of dozens of tiny locks. It had to be heavy. It made my hand instinctively fly up to the key beneath my sheath dress. How strange; an Arrazi with locks—a Scintilla with a key.

This woman looked like she'd stepped out of another time. Her blinding white aura was alarmingly strong, as if she lived off a steady diet of murder. The only weakness in her aura appeared near her left hand, where it was more of a chalky smudge. I realized there was a phantom aura of a hand—like the spirit knew only her wholeness—but her arm hung limply at her side, stationary and unanimated.

The vision of my mother struggling against an attacker flew forward in my mind. She'd violently hacked off the person's hand. I'd *assumed* it was a man. I never saw the face. This Arrazi was at a party for the Society, which used the very symbol on the ring that pressed so hard into my palm it was starting to hurt. I closed my eyes and sifted through the ring's memories and got a flash of the rustle of someone's cardinal-red skirt, slipping the ring onto a waiting finger. I opened my eyes and fixed them on the Arrazi woman.

My heart beat a steady rhythm, as if to keep me aware of the flimsiness of life. *Boom, boom. Alive. Alive.* My heart knew what it felt like to experience the draining, the agonizing slowing, as an Arrazi sucked the life from it. Like a tribal drum of alarm, it beat out a warning in my ears that I was too close to my enemy.

The woman stopped mid-sentence and looked around the room as if she'd heard her name being called. Or heard my drum. Like a second hand ticking off digits, her gaze flickered methodically from spot to spot in an almost mechanical scan of the people in the crypt.

I stepped slowly into a curtain of shadow to my left. My heart stopped hammering and froze as her relentless, searching eyes landed on the spot where I was hidden.

Twenty-Seven

Finn

Once we were inside the party, Saoirse pointed discreetly around the room. "He's an Arrazi. And that older couple over there. And that woman there…"

Blimey. I was one of them and they scared me. Did the innocent people in this room know what surrounded them? *Were* there any innocent people in this room?

As far as parties went, this one was brilliant, held in a medieval crypt of all places. Funerary monuments sat in recessed alcoves beneath the arched walls and ceilings that looked one substantial breath away from crumbling. World War II–era music would have normally lifted my spirits, if I weren't so on edge. My muscles coiled, ready. I reminded myself that if there was any way to find out why the Society wanted all Scintilla dead, then being here among these treacherous people would be worth it. *You are one of the dangerous people,* my head scolded. I constantly had to remind myself who I was, *and* who I wasn't anymore.

My aim was to talk to as many guests as possible. Ask as

many questions as I could. Get more information on these phil-anthropic ventures and ingratiate myself to whoever was in charge of this group. Ultana seemed fixed on helping me get an *in* with the Society. I didn't care much about her motives.

I had my own.

Lorcan, Saoirse, and I followed Ultana through the crowd. Saoirse dutifully affected a merry and attentive expression when introduced by her mother, but would turn to me privately and cross her eyes or stick out her tongue. I poked her in the ribs when a man with a bit too much ale in him practically drooled on her feathers. Lorcan noticed, too, and stared at him with a malicious glint. The man stumbled. Was Lorcan taking from him? Confusion passed over the old codger's face. He swayed and hastily excused himself. Though her back was to us, Ultana immediately turned and scowled at Lorcan. I was right! And she could feel it! Her sensitivity was fascinating. And disturbing.

"Why didn't you bring a date, brother? Everyone turn you down?" Saoirse teased.

Lorcan scowled. "Why bring a sandwich to a banquet?" he answered, downing a glass of champagne. "For example, that hot piece over there." He pointed toward a flicker of silver. "She's alone, see? Pretty little wallflower needs plucking."

I squinted toward the alcove cloaked in shadow. If she was a wallflower, she'd found the perfect spot. But if she wanted to hide, she was woefully underestimating her allure. Her beaded silver dress draped over her hourglass shape in just the right way. Scooting around the shadows, she shimmered like a star in the black sky.

A flash of her profile stuttered my heart, but she turned away before I could get a better look. "Excuse me a moment," I said to Saoirse, who nodded curiously before another acquaintance of her mother's pulled her away. The trio disappeared into the crowd.

This girl seemed intent on watching Ultana. I barely got a glance at her back—completely, tantalizingly bare, but for the most interesting, wicked tattoo—before she disappeared around the side of the arch like a fugitive. What kind of girl has a bold black knife etched right down the middle of her back yet hides in the shadows of a party?

I was intrigued. Guilt etched the outline of my heart like it was being burned out. There was no other person on this planet I wanted more than Cora. Why was I approaching this dark-haired stranger with such interest? I stopped in my tracks. What was I doing? I shook my head, sadly. It was energy. Curiosity and the pull of a captivating energy. I *had* to learn to control my impulses in this new body. I was only being a slave to my Arrazi nature.

As I was about to override my inquisitiveness and attraction to her and walk away, she backed toward me from around the pillar again, peering to the other side.

I smiled, despite myself. It was comical, and sort of adorable, the way she was playing peek-a-boo with an unknown partner. Unbidden by me, my heart raced as I watched her. Once upon a time I'd felt magnetism like this… The closer I got, the stronger the sensation was. It was like a perfume I'd inhaled before. A whiff of energy intoxicated me, rattled my composure, made me feel more alive than I'd felt in days. This surge of spirit, melding with mine, was so familiar, I was heady with it. This didn't feel the same as dying from lack of taking someone's aura. The need, however, was just as strong.

I was compelled to be close to her.

I reached my hand out, to touch the gleaming skin with the deadly tattoo, when she spun around.

TWENTY-EIGHT

Cora

The Arrazi woman had such an inscrutable gaze, I felt like she could see through four feet of thick stone to where I hid. My body blared with warning signals. She could kill me so easily. She could reach in and snap my soul in half, probably from where she stood. And there was nothing I'd be able to do about it.

This paranoia draped over me, sagged my body with a heavy surety that her Arrazi energy was reaching out for me, even as I watched her chat and sip wine with her one good hand. Chills crept over the skin on my back. I forced myself to stay calm and breathe deeply. Only one scrap of conversation was thrown at my feet: that the Society was fund-raising to continue supporting vital research. Into what, I had no idea.

I felt the creeping shiver of attention that raised the hair on the back of my neck. It wasn't from her. Someone loomed behind me, I could feel it. It was the menacing energy of an Arrazi. I spun around, ready to punch, kick, and scream my way out if I had to.

Molten amber eyes met mine. Even through the black mask,

I recognized him. I could have been blind and I'd recognize my first love.

Every drop of strength I had dissipated out through my legs. I gaped at Finn in a black mask and a well-fitting tuxedo. "Well, don't you look as ripe as a peach." My words were clipped and choked from the shock. I'd been grieving the boy I loved. Now, the Arrazi Finn stood before me.

He recoiled like I'd hit him. "You'd rather I be dead?"

"I—I thought you were."

His eyes turned sad. "Why'd you come here? You've entered a den of snakes. If you had any sense of self-preservation at all, you'd never have come."

His words made me sick with remembrance. "Funny. Your uncle said something like that to me once…about you."

If you had any sense of self-preservation at all, you'd have never let Finn near you.

"Why are *you* here?" I asked. I didn't want him to be here. I didn't know what I wanted.

His tone was steely. "I was invited."

"I bet you were," I said, stepping close, the fire of adrenaline and anger coursing through my veins. "What, is your dear uncle grooming the next heartless killer in the family?"

Finn glanced around and pierced me with a warning gaze. His voice was deep and low. "Arrazi can *feel* you. You're not safe here."

"I'm not safe anywhere. Your uncle could be following you with his sortilege. He *did* attack me, right after Mari and Dun ran into you. Maybe he's watching us right now, listening. Maybe he—"

"No." The pupils of his brown eyes expanded in alarm.

"No? What do you mean *no*?"

Finn looked over my shoulder. "I mean that he's not using astral projection, because he just walked in. You need to get the hell out of here."

I didn't dare turn around. My knees began to shake. Even my chin quivered. Being this close to Clancy Mulcarr fired off every distress signal in my body.

Finn's brows pinched together. We both knew how scared I was. "Cora, I—"

"There you are!" Dancing up to us was a girl, all whipping flame and ragged wind. The teal of her feathered mask drew out her startling aquamarine eyes. This tiny exotic thing hooked her arm through Finn's, that one move stabbing my heart all the way through. She pecked a kiss on his cheek.

My energy bled through my chest; I could feel it leave me. I had no control. No access to the positive vibes that my mother urged me to work on. No grounding in earth. I was a puddle at Finn's feet. It was all I could do to stand upright. I swayed, staring hard into his eyes, hoping my epic eye-speak would tell him that my heart couldn't stand any more breaking. I wasn't sure I could talk.

"Saoirse," he purred, saying her name in his exquisite voice. "I'd like you to meet…" His voice faltered. "I'm sorry…what was your name again?"

Oh my God.

I thought I might be sick.

Saoirse smiled warmly, though her eyes probed Finn's face, looking for something in that way that girls do when they are measuring their possessive prowess. "I'm glad my brother hasn't found you yet," Saoirse said, holding her petite hand out to me. I somehow accepted her handshake. "He's had eyes for you already. I hate to malign my own brother, but you look like a nice girl, and he's not the sort of fella you want—"

Her words clipped off as we clasped hands. Her tiny head cocked to the side, red brows furrowed, like I was a puzzle she held in her hands. Her little rose of a mouth hung open, like a question was poised on her tongue. I tried to politely pull away but her grasp, like her dominating vibration, was firm and much stronger than I'd have supposed. She *felt* like a frenzied young dog fighting against its leash.

"Thanks for the warning," I choked out in a voice as thin and diluted as my spirit. "There are a few guys in here I know enough to be wary of."

Saoirse didn't seem to want to let go of my hand. In fact, she stepped closer, peering at me. Closer still, uncomfortably close so that I could feel her puffs of breath on my collarbone and the cloying smell of her expensive perfume. Her other hand grasped mine so that she seized it between them like one would catch a lightning bug.

Finn's long fingers reached up and affectionately skimmed the back of her neck before reaching under her chin and turning her face to him. I knew the feel of those fingertips. He bent and inched his face toward hers. I slipped my hand from her grip and backed away. Was he seriously going to kiss her? Was he going to make me stand there and watch? I stumbled, but caught myself, realizing too late that I was shaking my head no.

It was whispered words rather than a kiss. His hand pressed against green satin on the small of her back as he led her away. She looked back at me.

Finn did not.

No part of me functioned properly. I couldn't walk. I couldn't breathe. He appeared, snuffed out all the light in the room, and walked away, leaving me in the dark. He was alive and I couldn't even rejoice in that fact. He had been so cold. So unmoved by my appearance. He had plainly and effortlessly moved on.

A hand I hadn't felt coming ran the length of my bare back. Shivers skittered down my spine. "You look lost, doll," a guy whispered in my ear. Relief hit me; it wasn't Clancy's voice. But ice flowed through me when my energy registered his.

I knew the impression of an Arrazi.

Twenty-Nine

Finn

Cora's pain was the weapon I wielded upon myself. I was stabbed by the agony I saw in her emerald eyes peeking through the delicate silver mask that looked as though it was a web spun by magical spiders. I was tortured with the hurt that made her head knock sideways as if she'd been slapped. The anguish in her voice, in her spirit. Did she think I couldn't see it, *feel* it? The agony rolled off her in sorrowful waves, and that was the needle I used to carve a new groove into my soul. My God…she didn't deserve to hurt like that. Not after what she'd been through.

I wanted so badly to tell her what I was up to, that I wasn't here because I *embraced* my damned nature. I was trying to help keep her safe, for Christ's sake! And she waltzes in here, a flash of silver and shimmer. A beautiful light in the darkness.

No wonder I was drawn to her. My heart *knew* it was her. My body knew it was her.

A soul knows its home.

"I feel strange, Finn," Saoirse said, her nose crinkling between her eyes. Her voice had gone soft, dreamy. "Blurry, like I've been drinking, but I haven't touched a drop."

Saoirse was reacting to Cora in a primal way. She may not have changed yet, but she obviously had the ability to sense the pulsating energy of Scintilla. She'd latched onto Cora immediately, seizing upon her unique vibe. The girl didn't want to turn, and she had a Scintilla, literally, in the palm of her hands.

Problem was, Cora had no idea how she affected *regular* people when she walked into a room, let alone the Arrazi.

I'd done what I had to do to scratch Saoirse's record. I had to break the connection. It was awful—brutal and cold.

To save Cora's life, I had to break her heart.

Thirty

Cora

"I'm not lost," I said, already extricating myself from the reach and energy of the Arrazi who swaggered like he owned the place. Maybe he was just hitting on me and would give up when convincingly rejected. I didn't want to draw attention. Clancy could *not* see me. That would be disastrous. Deadly. It was already deadly.

"Don't be like that," the guy said, and grabbed my wrist.

I turned around to face the blocky guy, older, maybe early twenties, with the sour odor of too much alcohol on his breath. I straightened my back, trying to feel less small, less vulnerable before him, but it didn't work. He was a stone wall.

"What's your name?" he said, moving closer, his hands getting way too familiar with my hips. I squirmed from his grasp and prayed to stay out of the clutch of his Arrazi power. Hopefully, he was too stupid or too drunk to know what I was. Again, he put his hands on my hips, his fingers grazing the bare skin of my back.

"Okay, here's what you need to know," I said, shoving him

away, my fear replaced by hot anger. Arrazi or not, this guy was an ass. "I'm not lost, I'm *leaving*. My name is none of your business, but it's definitely not *doll*. And if you put your hands on my body again, I'll make you wish you were wearing a suit of armor." I stomped away from him and ran up the stairs and out of the building.

I walked briskly, wrapping my arms around myself, and looked behind me to make sure he wasn't following. I had to make it back to the pub where everyone waited anxiously for me to arrive. This night was a fiasco. The only other knowledge I'd gained was information I didn't want to know about Finn. My heart had leaped to see him. He was alive! My soul sprang up inside me, a flame of love I forgot I was supposed to squelch. His soulful eyes, his mouth, his sweet face. Then it all came crashing down. For a brief moment, I wondered if I *did* prefer the idea of him being dead.

What did I think? That he'd suffer as much as me? That he'd at least wither away some first before jumping into the world of killing innocent people? That he'd see me and his love would show so undeniably that I'd never be able to question it? Now I *did* question it. I questioned everything. Being an Arrazi was bad enough, but he couldn't help that. Being a jerk was totally optional.

Looking up to make sure I had my bearings, I turned the corner heading toward the pub where the others were eating and waiting for me. I hated the thought of telling them I'd accomplished so little. The only thing I'd confirmed was that it was indeed the same Society Clancy had spoken of, that they were raising money for research of some kind, and that the Arrazi were in thick with them.

As smooth as fog, a dark figure slipped out of the shadows

right in front of me. I gasped in surprise. That same grabby Arrazi seized my arms. "I don't know your name and I don't need to," he slurred. "But I'm going to have a taste of you."

I struggled to wrench free from his tight grip, ripping off his black mask as I did so. He pulled me to his chest, nuzzling his face in the crook of my neck. I started to scream, but as the sound reached my mouth, my chest heaved forward toward him, and the knife of his slashing Arrazi energy drilled my upper body and pulled at my aura as if I bled from my chest directly into his.

I tried to knee him in the crotch, but my foot felt leaden, and my kick landed more on his shin. He didn't seem to notice. His strength expanded as mine dissipated.

"You have the most delicious energy," he panted with his toxic cloud of breath. "Like nothing I've ever felt."

Cold whipped through my body, numbing my arms and legs. My legs wobbled and I started to slip down, but he held me up and close to him as he continued to take from me. I wished the taking would quiet my mind as it quieted my body. It was like a slow icing over. Instead, my body was becoming paralyzed with the lack of energy, while my mind was on overdrive. Would he be able to stop? Did he have any intention of stopping at all? I'd never make it back to the others. My poor mother... They'd always have questions...

Even with my face pressed up sideways against him, I saw that his aura glowed stark white and projected really far from his body. I turned my head toward his face, and in a last moment of desperation, I bit his cheek. He howled and stumbled back, his chest heaving with exhilaration. He had that same dazed look Finn had when he first took from me. Nausea built as I fought to stay standing.

He was on me before I knew it, pushing me backward. I

fell hard onto the grass where he pounced on me, pinning me underneath him. With every bit of strength I had, I pushed my hands up toward him, trying to get him off me. I didn't think I touched him before he scrambled off me and gaped, alarmed.

"A Xepa ring?" he asked with surprise and fear in his voice. "Why didn't you say anything? Jaysus, I'm so *fooking* screwed! Just—just who—who in the hell *are* you?" He sat back on his heels and laughed. "I don't know whether to run, or whether to finish you off so they never find out what I've done."

Thirty-One

Finn

My uncle sidled up next to Saoirse and me with an amiable smile, which she returned in too easy a way. But I knew him. He had something urgent to say to me alone. His pull on my forearm confirmed it. I hoped to God he hadn't seen Cora, and I tried to back myself against the wall so he couldn't face the crowd.

"Ultana just gave me an urgent message from the head of the Society," he said in a whispered rush, his tone insistent. "An Arrazi in Kilsallaghan thinks they've run across a group of people who might be the ones we're looking for. She asked around and traced them to a rental cottage." His eyes darted as he spoke. "Let's be goin' now."

I'd backed against the wall to divert him from Cora, but now I wanted to walk away and my uncle had me cornered. I had no idea where Cora and the others were at that moment, but I sure as hell didn't want to sniff them out for the Society to pick them off. I started to protest, but Clancy's fingers dug into my arm.

"It's dicey enough that we're going on orders from the Society.

If we *do* find them, it'll take both of us to apprehend them and make sure the Society is none the wiser. If you care about the safety of your family, you'd at least *pretend* to be looking hard and fast for the Scintilla." Clancy's head tilted as he assessed me and blew out a breath. "If you care at all about that girl, you'd know she's safer in our hands than roaming free for anyone to get at her. How will you help her then? Want her to be sold and bartered on the black market like a brasser, to be used by whoever has enough money? Or she could be killed right on the street, giving yet another Arrazi their sortilege and taking hers as well. If you love her, find her, because if anyone else finds her first, she's as good as dead."

Was there a chance I could warn Cora? I scanned the crowd. If she was still at the party I couldn't see her. Clancy looked over his shoulder to see what I was searching for. "Fine. Let's go," I said.

Kilsallaghan was on the outer edge of west Dublin, not an area I'd ever been to. I wondered why the Scintilla didn't try to get farther away. But then, she knew about the party and that meant she was searching for answers as hard as I was. "Does the Society have a network of Arrazi looking for the Scintilla?"

Clancy crooked his jaw from side to side like he was cracking his neck, but I knew it was him struggling not to tell me the truth. The fact that people could feel when I used my sortilege meant I had to be careful whom I used it on. Ultana, in particular. My sortilege would confirm for her that I'd encountered a Scintilla before because I'd not have my sortilege otherwise. "Aye," he said. "The Society has a mass of Arrazi whose singular focus right now is finding them. It's not easy, though. They'll be needin' to feel for energy most of them have never experienced."

"Won't there be a risk that someone will take them for themselves?"

That earned me an appreciative glance. "Glad to see you finally using your head. Now you see why we had to run right out here and take a look." He glanced at the road, then back at me. "Your hands are shaking. You scared? Or is it hunger?"

I grit my teeth. I'd been increasingly shaky and cold over the last twenty-four hours. I thought it was too soon to be my need, but the signs were there. "I'm nervous," I lied. "To see Cora again."

"I've no doubt you'll see her again."

"You'd love that, wouldn't you? To use me to get to her again?"

My uncle clucked his tongue. "Now, now. I deserved that, but you misunderstand. Not everything I say is meant to be malevolent, lad. I only meant that you two seem to have a particular talent for colliding, like it's fated."

If he only knew.

"And yes." He sighed loudly. "To a certain degree, I'm counting on that." Truth.

He checked the address and made a turn onto the main street of the town, pointing at a Turkish coffeehouse as we passed. "That is where the Arrazi woman thought she felt peculiar energy from three people. The descriptions were spot-on. We're lucky Ultana passed this on to me rather than to someone else."

"Feels the furthest thing from lucky."

We drove up a grassy drive where two houses perched on a hill, one in front of the other. The house in back was dark, but the main house glowed against the black sky.

"You believe the Society will kill Arrazis who don't march in line?"

Clancy parked in front of the house. "The Bogue family—"

"They moved to London."

He smirked. "They sure did, in caskets. Come," he said. "I keep telling you that the safety of our family depends on how we handle this. Come with me to talk to the owner of the cottage. This might be a good opportunity to feed. It's deserted as can be, and you'll be needing your strength in case we find them. Wouldn't it be a twist if I had to stop *you* from attacking the Scintilla?"

"I'm not going to the door with you."

"Suit yourself, you stubborn *gowl*." He patted his stomach like he'd had a holiday meal. "My needs are well taken care of. You'll be facing the truth again soon enough by the look in your eyes. Aye, then you'll beg me to take you for killin.'"

"Don't count on it."

He slammed the car door and walked to the front door. Moments later, a middle-aged man wearing overalls and a woolen cap greeted my uncle. Warm yellow light from the house slanted out from behind him. I rolled the window down to hear. Clancy asked about rental of the cottage in back. The kindly man confirmed that he did indeed let out the place. He said that the group that had been staying there had checked out this evening, but that it hadn't yet been cleaned. My uncle feigned disappointment and stepped back a couple of paces with his hands in his pockets. I expected him to turn around and come back to the car. What I didn't expect was for the kindly man to bend at the waist and topple forward.

Clancy was attacking him!

Every human instinct to help, to save someone in distress, had to be quashed as I watched my uncle silently kill while the man reached for him and whimpered, "Help me, sir." As Clancy spun on his heel, the man jerked forward and crashed to the ground in a heap. Clancy looked up at the starry sky and whistled as he walked to the car.

"What the bloody hell was that?" I yelled as he started the car. "You said your needs were taken care of. You didn't need him." I slammed my hand on the dash. "You didn't *have* to kill that man."

"I didn't kill him for his energy, *eejit*. I killed him for his silence."

"Jaysus!" I kicked the floorboard. "I don't want any part of this! That was the most cold-blooded thing I've ever witnessed." When Clancy didn't respond except for his hands grasping the wheel a bit tighter, I said, "You make me sick. Let me out of the *fookin'* car."

"What, in the middle of bloody nowhere?"

"I don't care. I want out. Now."

He screeched over on the highway. A truck screamed past and shook the car as I got out. "You'll be singing a different tune when you have to kill."

"Sure," I said, leaning in the passenger door. "When I *have* to. No matter how much you want me to be like you, I never will be. And you know," I said, my throat closing around the words, "I used to admire you."

A quick flash of hurt betrayed him as he said, "Turnin' Arrazi is just one of the changes you'll go through. The other change is to accept the power you were born to wield." His bushy white brows lowered above his eyes as he leveled his gaze at me. "The Arrazi are not villains. We are simply doing what we were born to do. What other creature is expected to do as it was created, yet do it in secret, as if it should be ashamed for how it was born?"

He sped away. I wrapped my arms around my shaking body. The night wasn't cold, but I was, and that wasn't a good sign. My teeth chattered as I walked and thumbed for a ride back to Dublin. Before long, a hardened-looking gentleman pulled his car over and offered me a ride. He eyed me and my tuxedo with scrutiny as I opened the door, as if how I looked mattered. I realized for the first time that I no longer feared any stranger.

I feared myself.

THIRTY-TWO

Cora

The Arrazi got to his feet and stood over me.

"Don't kill me," I said, and looked down at the ring that had somehow spared me, at least for the moment. He thought I was part of the Society and was obviously anxious he'd attacked me. "You didn't know." I mustered up the strength to climb to a wobbly stand. Affecting a superior tone, I said, "I should have said who I was. Ignorance can be forgiven. Blatant disregard for—for how things are, that won't be pardoned so easily."

My bluff had better work. He was still eyeing me with a questioning yet predatory stare. He wanted more. "Take your mask off," he demanded.

"No." He was either going to kill me or he wasn't, but I was not going to give him a full look at my face if I didn't have to.

His hardened expression folded to a scowl. He nodded some kind of acceptance. "Fair play to ya. We'll meet again. I'm sure of it. Being as how we travel in the same circles."

"Don't worry," I said, trying to sound patronizing. "When

we do, I'll happily pretend I don't know you." Then I did what
I thought I would never do—I turned my back on an Arrazi. I
walked away.

As soon as I could no longer see him, I slipped the damned high
heels off and ran on rubbery legs all the way to the restaurant.
Everyone looked up as I blew in through the door. Giovanni was
on his feet as soon as he saw me. He slipped his arm around my
waist. I was grateful for the solidity of him. It was hard enough to
hold myself together.

"*Merda!* Damn it! What happened to you?"

Mari reached up and plucked a piece of grass from the side
of my mask, her dark brows furrowed under rage-filled eyes.
Shivering and clattering teeth made it difficult to talk. My diluted
energy weakened me so that raising my shaking hand took effort.

My mother calmly lifted the mask from my face and peered at
me. "She was attacked. Look at her aura, Giovanni." They walked
me over to the booth where my mother ordered tea. I recalled her
first words to me in Clancy's underground prison: *drink the tea.*

"What happened?" Dun asked, slipping his jacket over my
shoulders. His sweet face was concerned. However, his jagged
mustard aura had a bit more fear than his face and calm tone
revealed.

Words stuttered out of me like a skipping stone. "I had the
misfortune—of running into an Arrazi. A couple of them. Finn—
he was there as well."

Mari gasped. "Finn is alive? He did this to you?"

I shook my head. "No. Finn didn't attack me. But he's alive,
yes, and doing *juuuust* fine." I bit back tears. "I don't know the

guy who attacked me. He was big and maybe a few years older than us. He only stopped when he saw this ring."

"Ah," Giovanni said. "So we were right—it *was* a party for the very same Society. Because you had the ring, he thought you were someone important."

I nodded. "He also said a name—sounded like *zeh-puh*. Once he backed off, I had to put on a show to prove I wasn't afraid of him so he'd think I really was part of the Society."

"Do you think he followed you?" Mari asked, looking worriedly toward the door.

"I didn't see him following," I said. "But then again, I didn't see him before he stepped out of the shadows and attacked me, either. I have no idea how he even got there ahead of me."

"He'll have his own sortilege now, if he didn't already," my mother said. We were all quiet for a moment, probably wondering what kind of freaky superpower this already deadly Arrazi was going to be capable of because he'd stolen from my Scintilla energy. If he had killed me, he'd have my sortilege, too.

Giovanni rested his forehead in his hands. "The Arrazi get more dangerous every day." He leaned back and crossed his arms. His aura flared with so much protective intensity, I could feel it pressing on my own. "It's why we have to kill them. I've had enough of this."

"Yeah," Mari said. "Why don't we run on over to Grenades and Uzis R Us and pick us up some supplies? We'll kill all those bastards!"

"Shhh!" Dun hissed, earning a scowl.

"Why can't we do that?" she asked, dripping sarcasm. "Oh, because we can't seem to get our hands on any guns in Ireland." My head shot up. That meant she'd been looking. I shouldn't have been surprised. "Oh, and the fact that our trusty aura-seers here can't always detect who is an Arrazi and who isn't unless they've recently *killed* someone. Or, if Cora or Giovanni happen to be close enough to feel their special sauce, in which case they're probably going to die anyway."

I slammed my tea down. "Mari, shut up. You're not helping."

"Hey, I'm not the one talking about trying to kill the supernatural killers."

"You don't have an edit button, do you?" Giovanni said to her.

Dun smirked. "You're just now noticing?"

Everyone looked surprised when I scooted out of the bench. "Let's go. Being this close is making me very uncomfortable. I don't want to be anywhere around here when that party ends."

"Okay, I'll call Patrick to see if he's free to take us back to the cottage, if they'll let us rent it again tonight." Giovanni pulled out his phone. He'd barely gotten the question out when he was cut off. I couldn't hear what Patrick was saying, but Giovanni's face was a pane of alarm. "I'm so sorry," he said. "No, don't worry about us. We'll figure something out."

After he hung up, he explained. "Patrick says that the owner of the cottage was found dead right outside his front door. His wife said only that he'd answered the door, had a brief exchange with someone about the rental, and then she heard the sound of a car driving away. She found him only after he hadn't come back inside."

My hand flew to my mouth. "They knew we were staying there? But how?"

"Hey," Dun said, "maybe it wasn't the Arrazi. Maybe he had a heart attack. It could be a coincidence." But even as he said it, his eyes and his aura belied his opinion. He was petrified. We all were.

Gráinne dropped her head forward into her hands. "We have nowhere to go…"

THIRTY-THREE

Finn

The driver refused my money when he dropped me off. I wanted to warn him about being more careful of people like… like me. But we were the worst kind of predator. Normal people had no way of recognizing an Arrazi or of knowing how deadly we were. I suddenly saw how easily an Arrazi could keep this secret. Our lives depended on the ignorance of regular humans.

I'd asked to be dropped at a bookstore in town. My mother's books were a good source, but I wanted to check for myself if there was anything she didn't have. Something new, perhaps, that might help me find a cure for this…*affliction*. Watching my uncle ruthlessly kill that man was prime motivation. I couldn't get away from him fast enough.

Bookstores would be closing soon, if they were open at all. I didn't have much time.

Murphy's Books was a wicked odd place and lucky for me, open until midnight. Every disdainful comment I'd ever made about my mother's taste in books came rushing back at me.

Embarrassment was my penalty for being so arrogant. Now I needed these books to save Cora's life, to save countless people's lives. Redemption for killing would never come, but that didn't stop me from turning over every stone looking for it.

I bought two books, one of which was a new release from the prolific Edmund Nustber, which I didn't think my mother had. I slumped down on a bench to read.

There was a wealth of information on how to protect yourself from someone like me—an *energy vampire*. The books talked about "shielding" your aura, creating a loving bubble of light like some kind of force field. I didn't mean to scoff, but it sounded bloody dippy. No amount of shielding was going to stop an Arrazi from taking an aura.

Finally, I found references to people who know they are *takers* of energy and wish to stop it. My heart pumped a bit harder. Maybe I'd found something useful? The book said that some of these people would frequent malls and shopping areas and take from groups of people at once. It galled me to admit it to myself, but reading about it made me painfully aware of my own swelling craving. The idea was worth a try, though, as my need was growing and would only do so until I was out of control, like the last time.

Immediately, I went to the busiest nightspot in Dublin, Temple Bar. It was constantly loaded with hammered tourists. There, I could slip within the crowd, attempt to take from groups without them knowing, and see how it would tide me over. Everything in me resisted this idea, but I had to try. My other option was murder.

The first group I came upon was already plastered: three blokes, four girls, all of 'em swerving and teetering through the busy street. They laughed with careless, oblivious ease, never suspecting that a breed of human followed close behind, intent on sipping from their spirits. They wouldn't believe it even if I told them.

I stuffed my hands in the worn pockets of my leather jacket to quell their shaking and followed close enough to feel the unique blends of energy that trailed behind them like the wake of a boat. It was this picking through their auras—like one might with flowers—when I realized that there might be levels to people's energy, wavelengths that varied with each person. I sensed that some were more potent than others, more...*vibrant.*

As my attention to their vibes focused, my need increased. Too soon, an experiment in how to extract what I needed without killing turned into abysmal hunger.

I was new at this and alone. I'd have to somehow control myself.

My stomach felt hollowed out. Nerves frayed so that I became edgy and irritable, wanting to clout everyone who bumped me or looked at me sideways. My limbs grew cold and no amount of walking or rubbing my arms would warm them. Shame forced my head down so I'd not look anyone in the eye.

I hated this new hunt.

When the group turned into a crowded pub, I followed behind, close enough to hear which drink each preferred. Close enough to listen to the harmony of their jokes and laughter. Close enough to gently pull the strands of their auras braiding toward me.

I couldn't say for certain from whom the spike of sweet energy came. It was like smelling a familiar intoxicating perfume on the wrong person. There was something vaguely *Cora* about it, effervescent and light. Pain constricted my heart. I shut out the din of the pub, closed my eyes, and took the energy in, inhaling with my whole body.

Shattering glass nipped me from my reverie.

The laughter stopped as friends gasped and congregated around the young man who'd dropped his drink. Onlookers would simply think he'd had too much in him. I knew differently. His was the sweet energy I took too much of. He was still alive, I saw with relief. I slipped from the pub. Once I was out of close range, I ran.

$\mathcal{T}$he energy was short-lived—a snack when I needed the meal. I rolled in my bed, punched the pillow over and over. I had to take to the death or it'd be like never having enough to eat.

I needed to kill again, and soon.

THIRTY-FOUR

Cora

Giovanni bent to me. "Cora, it's time to call my contact. I've been telling you—"

"Yes, I guess it is," I said, more resigned than decided. I'd said no enough times. I didn't know what to do, but we needed somewhere we could stay undetected. I hated to see the fear in my mother's eyes. "We'd be risking your contact's life," I warned.

"He wants to help us," he said. "It's his life's work."

"Really? Okay, call him." Maybe the Scintilla did have friends in the world.

After a long, antsy hour spent fidgeting and stirring coffees that had grown cold, a gray van pulled up in front of the pub. Giovanni spoke briefly with the driver through the passenger window. To my surprise, a young woman stepped out and slid the van door open for us. She wore a black fedora and introduced herself as Teruko Yamagata. Sweetly pretty, with expressive eyes and full lips pursed as if there were a surge of words she'd trained to hold back.

I felt a subtle spike of energy when I passed Dun and Mari. It was like walking through a light spray of perfume. Were they nervous about this newcomer? The feeling didn't feel like fear, though. More magnetic. This feeling had pull, like…attraction.

Teruko dipped her head in a courteous nod as we climbed in the van and slid the door shut with a clang. I instantly felt co-cooned behind the tinted windows. It was exactly what I needed to feel: unseen, concealed. Perhaps going to Giovanni's friend was a good idea.

"They are preparing for your arrival at the institute," Teruko said. "You'll be quite comfortable."

"There are rooms?" Mari asked. "'Cause I need a bed like bacon needs eggs."

"There are rooms, yes. Most of the staff is from Japan and lives at the institute full-time so it is fully equipped for guests. Including eggs," Teruko added with a smile.

"Do you have many guests?" I asked.

Teruko's eyes briefly met mine in the mirror before she returned her gaze to the road. "They come and go."

Soon, too soon, we pulled up to an office building in what looked to be a hardly used, old industrial section of Dublin. A dilapidated storefront with awnings like droopy eyes stood watch across the street. More of the streetlights were dark than were lit, and the ones that were lit flickered irregularly. There was no name on the outside of the building. It was as nondescript as a smudge of gray lead on paper. A black security gate yawned open, and as we drove into an underground parking lot I glanced out the back window and the gate shut behind us. I noticed my mother staring at the gate, as I was.

We didn't like anything resembling a cage.

Once inside, we were asked to sign in on an electronic visitors sheet, which also took our fingerprints. Then we were shown into a large, opulent waiting room—a gorgeous mix of sapphire blue, black, and white. Four curved white love seats formed a broken circle around an illuminated blue floor. Teruko asked us to sit and make ourselves comfortable. We all gaped when we realized the sofas circled a saltwater aquarium built right into the floor.

Dun knelt down, pressing his hand against the glass as tiny purple fish darted up to greet him.

"Honey, I'm home," Mari sang as she flopped into the white cushions and leaned her head back. "Look at this place! More swanky than any hotel I've ever stayed in. Do you think we'll be safe here? By the way, how do you suppose that squat Irish elf found us at the hotel anyway?"

"Finn." The metallic taste of ire coated my tongue. We'd managed to go some time without pointing the finger, but it had to be said. It had to be said by *me* because I was the reason nobody else had said it already. "It's too much of a coincidence. You and Dun run into him on the street and later his uncle shows up."

"I'd kill him if he wasn't going to do it himself," Mari blurted, but her eyes quickly turned apologetic and she looked away from me.

"I think his plans have changed," I said.

Soft Japanese music floated on the air, recounting centuries of drops from soft rains. Giovanni yawned and slid down in his chair, fatigue etching his watchful eyes. The more relaxed this place tried to make me, the more on edge I felt. Our eyes caught.

"You've been here before?" I asked him.

Giovanni nodded. "It's had some noticeable improvements since," he said.

Teruko returned. "The doctor is ready for you now." She spun with crisp precision and, with the push of a button, opened a wall panel I hadn't even noticed was there. Polished. That was the best word to describe not only Teruko Yamagata, but the entire atmosphere of this facility.

I whispered into Giovanni's shoulder. "Someone invested big money into the place. Which means—"

A disheveled man appeared through the open wall panel. He was everything his facility wasn't: rumpled lab coat and stained tie, smudged glasses, and nose hairs in serious need of trimming. Or…braiding. The only thing polished about *him* was his bald head.

I scanned his aura for the darkness of bad intentions, the cloudiness of covering up, the mud of confused feelings. I'd watch this stranger for the black smoke of lies. Instead, he radiated the blue of high intelligence and inquisitiveness, reminding me of my father. There was one thing I'd never encountered—patchiness in his aura around his head.

He greeted Giovanni first with a two-handed shake. "I'm glad you're all right, I certainly am. When I hadn't heard from you, I feared the worst."

"I know," Giovanni said with a nod. "It's been some time. We've run into trouble."

"'Course you did. 'Course you did. Your kind always does. You'll have to tell me all about it, later. Would it be too optimistic to assume you're all Scintilla?" he asked, beholding us with his brows raised in hopeful anticipation. Mari and Dun shook their heads. He greeted each one of us in turn, expressing gladness that we'd come to him. But when he came to my mother, they looked at each other with wary recognition. "We've met before?" he asked her. "You look *very* familiar."

"Yes. I—interviewed you once a—a long time ago."

Realization struck. "Dr. M?" I asked. "*The* Dr. M? From

your journals?" I'd wanted to find him.

The doctor put his hands on her shoulders and spoke in a low, concerned tone. "I'd always wondered why you never came back. You were supposed to—"

"I was attacked." My mother wrung her shirt in her hands, but she didn't look away.

Dr. M threw his hands up, startling us. "Awful. God-awful business what's happened to your kind. I fear if we don't find a way to stop the slaughter, there will be none of you left. This dark world is no home for the givers of light."

"Light is exactly what's needed when things are most dark."

Everyone stared.

I said it with less conviction in my heart than my voice portrayed. It was a highly idealistic thing and sounded like something my father would say, something he tried to impart before he died. It felt true, though. I just never thought *I'd* be a torch in the world's darkness. Being a light was for other people, like Gandhi and Mother Teresa, and…Bono.

I stepped forward and extended my hand. "I'm Cora Sandoval, Gráinne's daughter."

He looked back at her with his hand still holding mine. "I don't recall you saying you'd had a child. No, you wouldn't, would you? To protect her. And the father?"

"Dead."

"Was he—?"

"No," my mom said with a shaky voice. "He was not—like me."

The doctor nodded sympathetically and swept his arm toward the elevators. "I'm sure you're all in need of rest. Teruko will show you to your rooms. Please, feel at home. This is a sanctuary, your refuge. No one will come after you here."

I hadn't taken a deep breath since I'd arrived so I tried to force myself to relax. As I blew out my fear in one long exhale, a question came to me. "But we can *leave* if we want?"

Dr. M stopped and turned. His aura flared with a bit of muddy seaweed color, which curved toward me. "Why would you want to? It's not safe out there, don't you agree? You'd be foolish to leave, and we mustn't bring them back here, to us." He leaned in, his aura reaching in the hooklike way of someone who wants attention. "The Arrazi won't stop, you know?"

"How do you know about all of this?" Mari asked.

"Because I'm—"

Each of us flinched.

"No, no! Oh, dear. I mean to say, I believe I am of that bloodline, like so many regular humans who have traces of either Arrazi or Scintilla. But, no. I cannot suck your life's energy from you." Then, he smiled wryly to himself. "Though my ex-wife might argue that point."

"Isn't it rare for someone who is just a regular guy to know about all this?" Dun asked.

"There was a time when my research on the energy field of the human body led to some very suspicious things happening to me, or to my facilities, my computers, and even people I had met." He gestured to my mother. "You, for instance. You were the first self-professed *giver* I had ever encountered, and until you brought your daughter in today, I'd despaired that I'd never encounter another pure female giver again. If you recall, I wanted to conduct further tests. But then you disappeared and I feared the worst."

"And yet you kept at it," Giovanni said, sounding impressed.

"Few people can resist the allure of a locked box. Don't you agree?" Dr. M continued on without waiting for agreement. He seemed to do that a lot. "The more trouble I encountered, the more determined I was to know what was being hidden. It wasn't until I obtained the support of investors that the funds were there and security was truly tightened so that I was safe to do my important research, chiefly, how to generate a synthetic form of your unique energy. Now then," he said with a clap, "I should like to meet with you tomorrow. You have no idea how glad I am that you've come to me." He looked at Giovanni and they shook hands before we filed into the elevator.

We rode in silence to the top floor. "Penthouse?" Mari whistled.

Teruko spoke without turning around, but the amusement in her voice was evident. "I think you'll like it very much up there."

Once the doors opened, the first thing I saw were five people, two men and three women, dressed in black pants and white shirts lined against the wall. Teruko said something in Japanese. They gave her a bow and, in turn, peeled from the wall and introduced themselves to each of us.

"This way, please," said one of the women to me, her arm gesturing to the hallway on our right while the guys were already being led to the left by the men and soon turned a corner, out of sight. Gráinne and Mari were obediently following their attendants. My mother looked nervously over her shoulder at me so I quickly followed.

Giovanni hadn't looked back. I couldn't help but wonder, if he had found such a refuge, why had he ever left this place at all?

Thirty-Five

Cora

My mother and her attendant stopped in front of a door just as Mari and the lady leading her stopped in front of another. "It looks like you're right next door to Mari," I said reassuringly, despite my own misgivings about being separated. I kissed my mom on the cheek. "I'll see you in the morning." She nodded and the door closed between us.

I was led around another corner and mentally mapped that we had gone two right angles turning left both times, like a square. My heart fluttered with every step away from the others. Being alone felt strange now. Trust in Giovanni's judgment was the only thing that kept me from resisting the arrangement.

Serenity was a concept I thought I knew until I walked into that room. Candles glowed in wall sconces, casting yellow circles onto the walls. A delicate pink bonsai tree stood on a pedestal that looked to be part of a tree trunk. I traced a finger over the spirals of age lines in the wood. Low to the ground and covered in downy white blankets was a platform bed. The woman slid a rice-paper door aside. "Your toilet," she announced, but it was more than that. It was heaven. A circular soaking tub sat in the corner, surrounded by small lanterns. Someone had already filled it with water. Jasmine steam rose lazily into the air.

The woman bowed at the doorway. When closed, the door beeped and a red light flashed on the pad. I heard a metallic click of the lock. I instantly reached for the handle and yanked the door open. I exhaled.

The woman turned to see why I'd emerged. "Need something, miss?"

"I—I wanted to say thank you," I said and shut the door again.

A white silk robe hung on a wooden peg next to the soaking tub. My beaded dress fell to the floor. I stepped up the teak steps and stared into the still water, round like a pupil, reflecting my face back at me. Sliding slowly into the soothing water, I let it ease the tension from my legs, my shoulders, neck, and jaw—which I hadn't even realized had been clenched.

Relaxation was a gift, and I silently thanked Dr. M for it. His intensity and passion for his work reminded me of my father. Longing fisted my insides. I had to add Dad to the list of people I was doing this for. One of the last things he said to me before he was killed was that he believed I was the key to the energetic imbalance in the world. Crazy. But if he believed it, and his idea showed promise with blood tests, then maybe I should try to believe it, too.

What a responsibility belief was.

Reluctantly, I got out of the tub when the water had grown too cool and wrapped myself in the robe. I padded with wet feet on the smooth wooden floor toward the bed. Blackberries filled a white bowl on the side table. I ate the entire bowlful and fell onto the bed with the memory of a warm summer day on my tongue.

Water ran somewhere outside. The last thought I had before I drifted to sleep was whether it was rain. I thought of Finn, standing in the rain with pained eyes the night we escaped. I had a heart hangover from seeing him at the party and finally, alone, I could let myself cry. And I could finally allow myself to decide that our love story was over.

I woke with a start. The shadowed figure of a man showed through the rice paper on the wall. Sunlight streamed in behind him, pushing his shadow across my legs. There was a *tap tap* and then Giovanni's rich Italian voice said, "Cora, I've got something to show you." It was an uncharacteristically singsong manner for Giovanni to speak in. I swung my legs onto the floor and slid open the door.

The sound of water was louder with the door open, but Giovanni's broad chest and shoulders blocked my view around him. He had on some kind of white pajama bottoms but was shirtless. He cocked his head sideways. "You missed breakfast," he said. "I've been relaxing in a chair up here with Dante's book, but I began to worry."

My stomach growled loudly in response. We both laughed.

Giovanni's face turned serious for a moment, and he reached out and touched my hair. "Wild tangle of curls," he murmured, "like vines around a flower."

"A flower?"

He released the black coil of my hair and closed his fingers. "Your face."

Warmth rose up my neck and onto my cheeks. "Shut up."

His brows furrowed. "Compliment one-oh-one, in which you learn how to gracefully accept kind words about yourself." He shrugged. "I speak the truth. You are the most wildly, naturally pretty girl," he said. "It's rare to be so comfortable in your skin."

The way his voice softened and his eyes swept my face, my lips, then found a resting spot on my collarbone, kicked up a nervous feeling in me. My skin felt decidedly *un*comfortable all of a sudden, like soft fingers brushed across it.

"I also wanted to ask what you were going to say last night about what it means that Dr. M has investors."

"Oh, um, I think it shows that someone *else* knows the truth. Someone else knows there are different kinds of humans, and they have their own reasons for wanting to pay for his research and security. That makes him an employee. Don't you want to know *who* he works for?"

"Smart girl. I *would* like to know, yes."

"We'll have to find out, then, because the only talk I could pick up at the party last night was of money and research and it's making me nervous. What if they're connected? We already know from Clancy that the Society knows about us. Who else does? What if the Society is behind Dr. M's research?"

"That's a worst-case scenario."

"Those are the only kinds of scenarios I think about."

"In the five years I've known him he's only ever been good to me. I've come here twice before and nothing bad has ever happened. I learned never to simply trust just anybody."

"So have I." The hard way. I pushed past him into the sunlight. "So, what did you want to show—" I stopped and gasped.

Our rooms were in a square, as I'd guessed. But I never anticipated what was in the middle on the top floor of this warehouse building. Bright sun shone in through glass panels above us, reminding me of my school's greenhouse back home. Below the panels, a rooftop courtyard stretched out before me into a spectacular Japanese garden.

Giovanni's arm brushed mine. "It's like someone transported a slice of Japan onto a rooftop in Ireland, no?"

"Yes," I said, breathless. "It's gorgeous." A tiny arched bridge led from my patio onto a path, which wound through Japanese maple trees ablaze in gold and red. Small waterfalls cascaded into miniature koi ponds. Rock statues were placed upon the path with water dripping from bamboo reeds onto the stones below. Birds flew in and out of the roof through small holes in the glass. Across a red bridge, a pagoda stood regally in the middle.

I walked barefoot through the garden, stopping to notice a spiral design someone had made on the ground from river rocks. I bent to peer at it, and when I stood, Giovanni's hand was pressed to my back over the knife marking. My silk robe had slid down, exposing my marking. His voice burned with soft intensity. "So, you got this from the knife that night?"

I didn't turn around. "Yes."

His hand radiated a sweeping current over the spot where I'd been marked.

"I hate that the memory is written on my body."

He leaned in. "I'm sorry this happens to you. *Il tuo dolore è il mio dolore...*" he whispered in Italian. "Your pain is my pain."

Suddenly, I felt the soft brush of his curls on the nape of my neck. My breath caught and bumps flared on my arms as he bent and tenderly kissed the marking of the gruesome knife in the middle of my back. Unbidden fissures of pleasure spread from my back and radiated out, but still I didn't turn around. I couldn't. Doing so would have been a betrayal to my still-grieving heart, because it wanted nothing more than to turn and see Finn standing there.

That could never be. That could *never* be.

My body remembered what it was like to kiss Giovanni, to feel the weight of him on top of me and the electric pulse of our energy together. I pushed that memory away. My head needed to have supreme rule over the rest of me.

The pressure of Giovanni's lips on my skin lightened and I felt his energy recede. When I looked over my shoulder, I knew he'd be walking away from me. Sure enough, a trail of silver wound through the trees behind him. Surprising though, was the dark, tarnished-silver color of pain in the middle of his aura at his back.

He'd been sincere. My pain *was* his pain.

THIRTY-SIX

Finn

hunger. I loathed thinking of it like that, but the sensation was truly—hunger. An empty belly, the need for sleep, the craving for a kiss, a thirst so desperate, you'd suck on bitter green stems of grass to quench it—that's how I woke. I was *need* with two arms and two legs. I was a walking, talking appetite.

I bolted upright in bed. *Green stems of grass…* Nature! Both my mother's books and the books I read from the store last night had mentioned rejuvenating energy by spending time in nature. There had to be a reason for that, and the only reason I could think of was that nature was a source of energy.

Slipping my legs over the side of the bed, I tried not to curl in on myself. Even though I'd just slept, the fatigue of needing to feed had hit me hard. My body was shaky, off-balance. I put on a clean shirt and shoes and went outside.

It was an unusually cheery morning. Bright sun glinted off every rock, penetrated through every green leaf, warmed my skin as I walked toward the woods on our property. Returning there snapped me back to that night, to the horror of realizing what my uncle had done to Cora and, worse, to her poor mother.

It might be a good idea, I thought with some trepidation, to investigate Clancy's hidden den. If he'd ever tried to keep someone captive there again, I'd want to know about it. I'd want to stop him. He couldn't enslave another like that.

My inner voice mocked me. *No, but he can just kill them? That's more humane, right?* Being an Arrazi was a lose-lose situation. What was the damn point of us?

After walking for what seemed like forever, I came upon the granite wall that had caught my mother and I so unaware the night we found Cora. We'd followed a path worn down over time by the trod of Clancy's horse and buggy, and by the wear of feet. In the darkness, amidst the thick trees, I had smacked right into the wall. Now, in the daylight, I could see how impressively tall it was. Smooth as glass and impossible to climb. Even if you figured out how to scale it, barbed wire looped around the top. None of us ever came to this part of our property, and Clancy had his own entrance at the opposite side. Still, it must have been quite a production to build his secret fortress. A fortress right in the middle of our very large plot of land. We were lucky to have found it at all the night we helped Cora and the others escape.

The skylight in the ground was hard to find because it was obscured by foliage. But it was the fact that there was a bare rectangle in the greenery that drew my eye. I brushed a few fallen leaves from the glass and knelt to peer inside. Cupping my hands around my eyes, I tried to focus on the dark room below me. Nothing but shadows. For a brief moment, I thought I saw a flutter of movement. I stayed very still and watched, but saw nothing else.

When the sound of cracking twigs startled me, I jumped to

my feet and ran as quietly as I could to hide. I listened longer but heard nothing more. Likely, it had been some creature dashing through the brush. Clancy would be an utter fool to use the underground prison again. He had to know I'd be checking to make sure he didn't. If it were up to me, he'd have been cut from our lives altogether.

I wandered through the knee-deep ferns and tall trees, deciding which form of plant life to experiment on first. I chose a young fern, small in comparison to the others around it. I sat cross-legged on the forest floor, in front of that wee plant like it was an altar, and focused on the spot in my chest where I felt the energy of others enter me. It was a mind game of sorts, imagining a tendril of my energy reaching from my body out toward the variegated fronds. I stared at the curled fiddleheads, marveling at their spirals, noting how many items of nature were spiraled: seashells, snail shells, ferns, succulents, hurricanes, our solar system…

It was like meditating, not that I'd ever been into that sort of thing, but I realized I'd lost my focus and directed my attention back to the plant. A tickle of energy threaded onto my own as I pulled from it. I watched in fascinated horror as the once-emerald fiddlehead curled tighter in on itself and began to turn brown. A light burst of vitality bubbled in my chest, then dissolved. I sighed. It would take the whole damn forest to quench the craving building inside of me.

Trees might be a better alternative. What's bigger in nature than a tree? The biggest trees I'd ever seen were in the California redwood forest with Cora. I'd love to take a hit off one of those beauties right about now. The albino redwood she showed me was extraordinary. A sour pit of sadness lodged in my chest. I remembered looking at her as she stood on the forest path with giant shafts of sunlight trained on her like a spotlight, and wondering what it was that made her so irresistible. At the time I'd thought to myself, *she glows from within.* Now, I wondered if I'd been sensing her Scintilla spark. I threw a rock at a nearby tree. I'd rather believe in the love story.

Seeing her last night had been cruel torture. Everything in me yearned for her. My love—the beautiful, shimmering half of my soul—was right in front of me. But she was no longer mine; could never be. I never thought I'd see her again. Hurting this way, I wasn't sure I could take it if I did.

Focus. The tree I finally chose to experiment with was a foot or so taller than myself, its branches more sparse the lower they went. The sun shone from above. Naturally, that was where the healthier, thicker leaf growth was. All living things reach for their source.

Why did *my* source have to be people?

I placed my hands on the cool trunk. My fingers ran over a patch of mossy growth on the shadier north side of the tree. Almost immediately, I felt the energy of the tree rising up through the trunk like a hose, funneling it from the ground. This could work! What if I could siphon enough energy to keep me from needing to kill? I closed my eyes and focused all of my thoughts on the energy running through that tree, imagining it pouring through my hands and into my body. My cells sang!

How long I stood there, clutching the tree like a stiff dance partner, I don't know. I opened my eyes when my ears registered a sound like the patter of rain, but I was dry. The sun was still out. The sound was leaves, hundreds of leaves, hitting the ground, landing on my head and shoulders. I fingered one. In the dawn of summer, it was brittle and brown. The canopy above me was completely bare.

"**W**hat on earth have you been doing?" my mother asked. Keys dangled from her hand, and her purse was looped over her arm.

"Killing trees."

"Oh, Finn." She sighed. "Don't you think that's been tried before? You're not the first to try to find an alternative source of energy. There isn't one. A human soul is our only true sustenance."

"I'm going to my room."

She stepped in front of me. "You don't look well. I'll have your father take you out later. How bad is it?"

I didn't respond. My choices were die or take. My stomach turned.

"What happened at the party?"

"Nothing," I said, avoiding her eyes. She stepped in front of me and turned my cheek toward her. I pushed her hand away. "You don't have a right to use your sortilege on me just because you can." The last thing I wanted her to know was that I had seen Cora at Christ Church. The less anyone knew of Cora's whereabouts, the better.

"Something happened…"

"I met some people. I don't know what may come of it, but Ultana seems very keen to have me become one of her minions. She introduced me to quite a few of the guests."

"Arrazi?"

"Many. Saoirse had to point them out to me."

"Be careful. I can't say I buy Ultana's reasoning for being involved with the Society. When she speaks of money and power, it would have to be a great deal more than what she has already.

Ultana Lennon is one of the wealthiest women in the UK."

That surprised me. I wondered how she'd amassed that kind of wealth. "I'm being as careful as I can, but don't forget," I said, turning my back on her to stare out the window toward the ocean, "I'm willing to die. Dangerous liaisons don't seem so perilous by comparison."

"But we're past that now, aren't we?" she asked, hope lifting her words. "Throwing away your life is a waste. There's so much you can do. Your father and I, we kill because we have to. But we've each saved many more lives through our profession. Think about that."

"After everything, you're still on about me becoming a doctor? Enough. I know my job, and that's to help Cora and find a way to end this *fooking* madness for all of us."

"If you tell me what's going on —"

"No, Mum. The less you know, the better. Your brother could inadvertently use you to get to Cora."

She dropped her purse and keys on the hardwood floor. "Finn Doyle, you are still my child and I won't be put in the dark." The toe of her shoe hit an insistent note on the wood.

I would still not look directly at her. "You don't like being in the dark?" I asked, hoping she caught my sarcasm. "Turnabout's fair play."

THIRTY-SEVEN

Cora

The Japanese garden on the rooftop of Dr. M's was a peaceful refuge from the fresh hell of my life. Because of us, the owner of the cottage was dead. Another life snuffed out by people who believed the souls of their fellow humans were theirs to take. I wish I knew how they'd found us. Ina Doyle's words from the night Finn nearly killed me were an insistent shout in my head—*that girl's not safe anywhere.*

Massive security measures were in place at Dr. M's. Hopefully, we wouldn't be so easily found. Hopefully, we could trust this doctor who claimed with a little too much pride to be of Arrazi descent. Some people get off on the idea of being anything but normal. I wanted nothing but. He did seem very earnest about helping, though. Passion for his work was obvious. He and my father would have been thick as thieves.

I wanted to look into my father's theory about dark energy and the people dropping dead. More accounts were in the newspapers that were left under my door. Worldwide, the incidents were increasing. I still believed it was Arrazi being more brutal and blatant about their killing, especially in light of the fact that their best source of energy was nearly extinct.

I found an attendant who led me to a common area one floor below the garden and our bedrooms. I spotted Mari deep in conversation with Teruko. Their auras interacted in friendly and animated hues. My mother was on the other side of the room, happily rearranging the cut stems of a lovely flower arrangement on a buffet table. Her soft humming grew louder as I neared. She turned before I reached her, a smile already crinkling the edges of her eyes. "I like it here," she said.

"I'm so glad. I'm going to go find Dr. M. Have you seen him?"

She nodded. "I had an appointment this morning."

"Appointment?"

"Yes. He had many questions about my time with the Arrazi. He wanted to have a physician examine me. They took blood and—"

"They did what? Be right back." I hadn't even had the chance to decide whether to trust this doctor and he was already drawing blood from my mother? I strode to the elevators, seething. Someone from the institute, wearing black and white, stood by the elevator door. "Take me to Dr. M."

A sterile pause blanketed the eyes of the worker before he nodded curtly, punching in a code in the elevator keypad. I gritted my teeth. After a short ride down, the elevator doors opened to a long corridor with a series of lab and exam rooms along each side. Dr. M strode out from one room, startling us and nearly knocking me over. "Oh! Ms. Sandoval. I'm glad to see you," he said with a darting look at my escort. "I very much want to conduct an interview with you, run some baseline tests, and—"

"That's why I came to find you," I said. "Don't run tests on my mother without my approval."

"Pardon? That would be up to her, would it not? She's an adult. She consented." He said this with a smile, but the kind that an irritated grandfather gives to his least favorite grandchild.

"She has been through so much and she's not well enough —"

"Precisely why I wanted to have her looked at. I'm concerned for her well-being."

"Don't interrupt me again."

Taken aback, Dr. M stared, then nodded diffidently the way his workers did. He hugged some files to his chest and waited for me to speak. His aura did not flare with fear or smoke. He was calm, yet highly alert. Curious, even. But I again noticed the holes in his aura. I had no idea what that meant.

"My mom's body is fragile, and I'm sure she needs care in order to be stronger. I want that. But her mind is fragile, too. And in her case, I think it's best if you come to me first before you examine her and run tests. I want to be with her when you do."

"Yes, yes. I see. This is quite a role reversal, isn't it? The daughter managing her mother's care?"

"It doesn't matter how we started. It's where we are now. I'm doing what I have to do to protect my mother."

"Very admirable. I am sorry to have upset you. I sincerely do wish to help."

"I know." I didn't want to start off on the wrong foot. "I appreciate your understanding, Doctor."

He motioned for me to follow him down the hall and I did, shooting glances at each room we passed along the way. "Is it possible," Dr. M asked, "that your mother is stronger than you think?"

"What I think," I said, following him into an exam room, "is that my mother is the strongest woman I know. You try having your energy drained near to death, month after month, for twelve years."

He shook his head. "I can't imagine it." Then his face brightened considerably. "*Your* strength is apparent. Working with you and Giovanni is going to be very exciting. Two young, perfectly pure specimens to study..." He gazed, daydreamy, at nothing, then snapped his attention back to me. "We are going to find answers together. Trust me."

"To be perfectly honest, Dr. M, I don't want to offend you. But trust is becoming a really big hill to climb."

He led me into a lab room and began with a penetrating list of questions. I would answer only those that I determined couldn't be used against me. If this were my father, I know he'd want absolute clarity about my history and my abilities, but... this wasn't my father. I gave the date of my last period, my recollections of the illness that preceded my ability to see auras, and blood samples. I refused to give information on my sortilege and markings. He could start with the human side of me. The supernatural side was mine.

I did feel that Dr. M should know about my father's theory about the drop-dead people and how he believed the Scintilla were somehow the cure, the answer to the world's ills. Dr. M sat in a chair next to me and scribbled furiously as I spoke, even though I was pretty certain I was being recorded. A small camera in the upper corner of the ceiling of the exam room was trained on me.

"Is there any way we can gain access to your father's work?" he asked. I honestly had no idea if or how we could, certain that the company he worked for would keep its data private.

"Do you believe it's possible?" I asked. "That dark energy is causing disasters all over the world and causing people to drop dead? I don't even understand what it is."

"Your father is not the first to suggest that dark energy is a malevolent force in our system. There have been increases in natural disasters on Earth. Blame global warming, dark energy, or any other fault of the month. I'm more fascinated by the people who are dying and his tests showing that *your* blood looked to be a remedy, bringing balance back into the cells of the affected. That's an astonishing premise. That indicates there's a direct relation to your energy and the mysterious sickness that's overtaking people. If we run on the assumption that your father was right, then your diminishing breed would be saviors to the whole planet. Good Lord, if the world knew of his research, your kind would be even more sought out."

"We already are," I said, thinking of the airport footage. I wouldn't elaborate.

He dropped his pen and whipped off his glasses, rubbing his eyes wearily. "I strongly urge you," he said, putting his thick glasses back on, "to stay within the safe confines of this facility."

"I won't be a prisoner again," I said through tight lips.

"There is a distinct difference between being a prisoner and seeking asylum." When I didn't answer, he added, "Ultimate safety lies in finding a way to stop them from hunting and killing the givers of light. Our work together might be the best chance we have to do that." He reached for my hand. "Are you in, Cora?"

He looked so sincere, so eager, so...*fatherly*. I nodded. "I'm in."

Setting his clipboard down, he slapped his hands on his knees and rose to his feet. "Let's get started then."

"I thought we had."

He chuckled. "That's just the beginning. I will summon Giovanni and, with your permission, your mother as well. I want to familiarize you with my biometrics facility."

Giovanni, my mom, and I were escorted into the biofeedback lab. We ate a private lunch together while Dr. M explained his latest research to us. He had recently acquired sensitive instruments to detect our biomagnetic fields, and I volunteered to be the first to be hooked up to a magnetometer he called SQUID.

"Like an antenna, you project biomagnetic pulses that we can measure and record on our computers. For instance," he said, pulling Giovanni to stand behind me, "watch the screen. Giovanni, I want you to run your hands over her, but do not touch her physical body. Use energy to manipulate her astral body."

I couldn't see Giovanni's face, but I felt him as sure as if a storm blew against my back. Flickers of increased energy developed around my body on the screen as his hands hovered over my shoulders and slowly ran down my arms. A cascade of bumps flared on my skin. My aura spiked. I felt the tickle of his energy as one hand brushed over the nape of my neck and up over my head. In my periphery, his fingers caressed the air near my cheeks and jaw. I tried to ignore the stroke of his energy as it skittered across my lips. On the screen, my own aura surged with stimulation and blended with his.

Thankfully—as I wasn't ready to meet his eyes yet—Dr. M moved Giovanni into a small, enclosed room behind a partition for our next experiment. I was told to close my eyes and maintain a receptive attitude and to report whatever I felt, if anything. "My toes tingle," I reported. "My right knee is throbbing. My— ouch!" My thumb felt like someone had jabbed a needle into it. I opened my eyes and saw that my pain was reflected on the computer—the area around my hand fizzled and spit. I stood. "I want to speak to Giovanni, immediately."

I'd asked to speak with him privately in an adjacent lab room.

"Dr. M wanted to test how astrally connected you and I were and whether the connection penetrated walls."

"Did you let him hurt you? On purpose?"

Giovanni smirked and crossed his arms. "Only a little. But I'm appreciating your evident concern."

"Why would you do that?" I understood the need to run tests and experiments, but I wasn't willing to let Dr. M get all Dr. Frankenstein on me. It was worse that I was in the dark about the experiment.

"Because when he posed the question, I wanted the answer as well. Dr. M and I had a fascinating debate earlier about 'unity consciousness.' Cora, we can see with our own eyes that there is less separation between humans than normal people realize. But I feel an even closer connection with *you*. I wanted to know if it was measurable."

"Okay." What Giovanni did with his own body was his business. The fact that my energy responded from another room *was* interesting. "But do you truly believe this New Age *we are one* stuff? Why does it matter?"

"Because we are energy, and our entire situation is about energy. Information is power. If it's true, then our idea of separation is false. If it's true, then what I do to you, I do to myself."

Your pain is my pain.

"Are you being all sciencey on me?" I asked, noting the way

his aura expanded with light-tipped silver as he spoke about it. I liked his curiosity to learn. *My* mind was stretching to accommodate the new ideas I'd had thrust upon me the last few weeks. But I needed a more tangible grasp of this slippery idea of *oneness*. "I believe in connection. As in 'I feel ya.' But if I'm holding on to one end of a long rope and you're holding the other end and you shake it, I'm only feeling your movement on my end. It doesn't make us *one*, the rope just connects us."

"Perhaps it's more like we are in this limitless pond of energy. Like water, it surrounds us, moves with us, adapts to our shape, and what ripples outward cannot help but ripple to another in the pond."

"Or," I said, my hands on my hips, "maybe we are like fish in the pond, inescapable from the energy surrounding us, but we are not *one* fish. We are many, in the same pond. If this is part of the riddle, I want to solve it, to help us."

He threw me a smile that doubled as a challenge of some sort. Maybe he didn't think I could grasp what he was trying to explain. "I shall try a new way to describe," he said, rubbing the blond stubble on his chin. "Consider me now, the *subject*, looking at an *object* of beauty." I felt heat rise up my neck as he held hard with his eyes. "That's the first level of experience, that we are physical beings, experiencing each other as separate. Subject, object. See?"

"Go on. This had better matter."

Giovanni stepped closer, his silver aura reaching beyond his sculpted edges, expanding and contracting with each breath. My pulse skipped, my aura beating in unison with his. "You and I, Cora, we see another level of reality. We see the spiritual essence of people, their feelings rippling through their energy field like watercolors, staining their auras with emotion."

True. Beautiful. He took another sure step toward me. The look in his eyes made me breathe faster. I wanted to kick my aura's ass for being so in sync with his.

"I can see your emotion right now. I'm causing you to feel nervous and"—his aura flared and his voice coaxed—"a bit excited?"

I blushed and looked away. "You are not."

"Science already has proved that there are other levels of reality that people cannot see with the naked eye, not even you and me. With the help of microscopes, we can look closer and see that we are billions of cells vibrating at extreme speeds. Molecules, atoms. Beneath what appears to be two separate beings are really clusters of energy dancing together in this space."

He stepped even closer now, and I tried to account for my rapid heart rate and dropping stomach. "And the truth is," he said softly, standing so close I could feel the caress of his aura brush my skin, "molecularly, there is no separation at all between us. My energy field is experiencing and appreciating your energy field, and since our energy comes from the same infinite source, we *must* be one."

We stood a breath apart, auras and cells and molecules, or whatever, dancing and swirling. My heart hammered with the energy of it, with the fascinating and bewildering truth of what I could see and feel.

Giovanni's nostrils flared as his gaze met mine for a few beats, roamed over my face, then fell to my lips, lingering too long there. My body was a storm of confusion. Feelings rose up in me that felt forbidden. My arms tingled. My stomach fluttered. My lips pulsed with want, and I became acutely aware of the tickle of each breath that passed over them.

I had to remind myself that this was our Scintilla energy together. This was no different from what I'd done to Finn. Giovanni and I had no choice but to feel *charged* around each other, right?

I'd never trust what normal people took for granted. Attraction meant nothing when you were a walking magnet.

I put my hand on his chest to stop the forward tilt of his body, but I wasn't fighting only him. I had to fight myself. Things didn't need to get more complicated. "If what you're saying is true," I said, "then, biologically, on a cellular level, *we* wouldn't just be one." I cleared my throat and tried to shove a deep breath down my chest to calm myself. "*Everyone* would be connected."

Giovanni eyed me suspiciously, like a chess player already assessing my moves.

"We'd be one with our enemies as well," I concluded.

His silver recoiled a bit and he stepped back, blue eyes flashing with annoyance.

"What, you hadn't thought of that? That it's not just 'Kumbaya' and oneness with those we—we care about. It's oneness with our enemies, too. It's being one with the people you most want to kill."

Giovanni gave a little half shake of his head and his eyes opened wider. I could tell he hadn't quite thought of that. "I was looking for a way to protect ourselves, for information that might help us. You're looking for a way to intellectually one-up me," he said.

"I'm not, I'm just—"

"What then?" His voice lowered as he gazed into my eyes. "Looking to think your way out of what I make you feel?"

He walked out and left me there.

Alone.

THIRTY-EIGHT

Finn

"I didn't know who to call." Saoirse's voice was thin, weary. She'd woken me in the middle of the night from a troubled sleep. My whole being burned with need. "I feel so strange," she whispered into the phone. "Like I'm hollowed out. A shell."

I rolled over, tucking my knees up against my stomach. Even if she wasn't sure what was happening to her, I was. She was turning. I didn't know what, if any, intense emotion had brought it on or if it was just her time. But she sounded very scared. Becoming an Arrazi was like being told you were a cancer, the ravenous parasite of humanity.

"Please come over, Finn. I'm scared. I don't want to call my mother on her business trip in Rome, and I can't confide in Lorcan. He'll run to her with his big gob. I don't want to be alone. Christ," she cried. "I can't do this."

What could I say? To tell her to hide away, to do nothing, would be to condemn her to death. She already knew that. I didn't want to encourage her to kill, either. It was still a reality so abhorrent to me that I'd been wasting away trying to suck the life from groups of innocent pub crawlers and *fookin'* trees. Now, to save my new friend's life, I'd have to help her become a murderer. I'd also have to help myself get through my first murder when I wouldn't be half dead, semiconscious, and crazed with need. I'd be cognizant and aware.

That was worse.

I also needed Saoirse alive to keep close to Ultana. Guilt swirled in my gut like brackish silt. My head pounded as I sat up and swung my feet over the side of the bed. "Aye, I'll come. But I don't know how helpful I'll be. I'm likely in a worse state than you."

The Lennon family lived about forty minutes away, and the drive afforded me the time to listen to music and think, and avoid the intrusion of my mom's questions and seeking eyes. So, Ultana was out of town on business. Perhaps this was the perfect time to pay a call to her house, though snooping with Saoirse and her lout of a brother around might prove difficult.

There was but one light on at the house when I arrived. Following Saoirse's instructions, I walked quietly to the front door and let myself in.

"I'm in here," Saoirse called to me from a nearby room. I found her huddled on a large chaise, clinging to a blanket like a child. Her fearful aquamarine eyes followed me as I approached and sat down in front of her.

"I'm not well at all," she said, though that I could see for myself. Dark circles rimmed her eyes, and her small hands trembled as she curled them into the downy fabric.

"I know. There's no way around it. It's ghastly."

"You really think that's what's wrong with me?"

"From what you describe, yes. It's how I felt. It's how I feel right now."

"I don't understand why this has happened," she said with desperation. "I've done everything right."

I laughed. Couldn't help myself. "I don't think there *is* a right or wrong. You can't stave off the inevitable."

"Ever since the masked ball…" she said, her words twisting my gut into a tight wad. It was meeting Cora that caused this. It had to be. "I felt something stir in me, a restlessness I couldn't quite put my finger on. My body wouldn't calm, even in bed. My legs were so damn twitchy, I thought I could run to Galway and back and they would still crave exertion. I'm exhausted, too. I feel like I've been leached of all motivation…except one."

"I understand," I said, feeling that same agitated ache in my own limbs as we talked. I tried to keep my eyes on Saoirse's, which was difficult because I wanted so badly to look around. Saoirse had said Lorcan was out getting knackered, so it'd be a good time to try. *Patience,* I reminded myself. "There's only one answer for both of us."

The look she gave me was utterly tortured. Huge tears rose in her eyes before spilling over. She closed her eyes, but that didn't stop more tears from coming. "I *can't.*"

Forcing more steel into my voice than I felt, I said, "You will."

We stared hard at each other, silent, yet I wanted to rail about the unfairness of it all, the unjust position we were born into, the dreadfulness of what we had to do. She leaned her head back and closed her eyes.

After some time, Saoirse seemed to fall asleep. The blanket drooped around her waist and her mouth parted slightly. She mumbled something unintelligible and rolled her head to the side. I covered her and stood to go see what I could of Ultana Lennon's home. I didn't know what to look for. Something. Anything.

I left the sitting room where Saoirse slept and ventured down the hall, my feet creaking on the ancient wooden floorboards as I crept in the dark. I pulled my phone out and held it up as a light. Most doors were wide open to cold, spacious rooms, opulent in the way that only loads of money can buy. Some of the artifacts could compete with the National Gallery.

There were paintings, of course. More interesting were the daggers and swords from multiple cultures and many eons. A locked glass cabinet housed clusters of very old coins that were nonchalantly strewn into a varied assortment of church collection plates. Ultana Lennon was ironic; I'd give her that.

Farther down the hall, an old wooden door bore a full-scale replica of the triple spiral carved into the grain. Obviously, other Arrazi saw the symbol as important to their family history. Unlike the other doors, it was closed. I wiggled the handle. Locked. Fishing through my pockets, I produced a silver guitar pick, but only the tip would fit into the lock and did nothing to work it open. I wanted to kick in the door. How many bloody chances would I have to rifle through Ultana's private rooms?

Feverish desperation made me trip twice as I went out to my car. There'd once been a multi-tool in there somewhere. If so, perhaps I could get the lock open with that. My exertions were making me dizzy and out of breath. The tool was there. I grabbed it and ran back inside.

There were a couple of apparatuses that fit into the keyhole, but neither would unlock the damn thing. My hands weren't steady at all. I was increasingly nervous I'd be caught by Saoirse or Lorcan, if he arrived home any time soon. My concerns for myself paled when I thought about Cora somewhere out there, being hunted like game.

I thumped my forehead on the door in defeat, the useless tool dangling from my hand. Then I thought of something; it was a risk but I had to take it. I used the tip of the screwdriver to push up the hinge pins on the door, first the lower, and then the upper. With a hefty pull, using more strength than I thought I had in me, the door came free. I'd made a fair bit of a racket, though, and stilled to listen for anyone coming.

Behind the door was an opulent office with a two-story coffered ceiling of wood so saturated in color, it looked coffee-soaked. Within each square was a relief of the three hares. I've looked at that image countless times, as my uncle had a boss in the ceiling of the pub with the same design. He used to tease me with a riddle: *three hares sharing three ears, yet every one of them has two.* Later, I'd learned that it was an ancient symbol but with inconsistent meanings; some called it a hieroglyph of "to be" and yet others believed it represented the holy trinity, as it was often used on church buildings.

The room had the musty smell of old, forgotten things. I was damn shocked to see a large wooden carving of the horned head of the devil staring down at me from the wall behind the desk. Could she *really* own the devil statue from "Hell" that Saoirse had told me of? It was a rare piece of Dublin history and had to be worth a fortune.

The large mahogany desk lorded over the room and was as imposing and scratched as the woman who used it and the devil who watched her back. I still wondered if the V on her face was truly a birthmark. Why or how would anyone get branded like that?

I stopped on the thick rug and listened again for sounds, but it was still quiet. The lamp I clicked on cast a glow in the otherwise dark house. A few notes and papers scattered across the desk, some as mundane as bills and as vague as two-word reminders on ripped scraps of paper. I jiggled the desk drawers, but each one was locked. To add to my dismay, her computer had a fingerprint detector attached. Ultana was serious about maintaining privacy. Only someone with big secrets would keep them so severely guarded in their own home.

The fire to know her secrets burned hotter than my need for energy, and kept me moving even though I was exhausted. I inspected bookshelves, marveling at the antique collection she had. One volume was situated sideways in the middle of a high shelf, and I reached to pull it down. It was Dante's *The Divine Comedy*. Some pages near the back were dog-eared with underlined passages. Peculiar. My mother also had a keen interest in Dante. I remembered gazing up with Cora at the painting in our hall, and the eerie feeling it gave me, like we were staring up at a mirror image of ourselves.

Dust flew out of the book when I opened it, as well as an irregular triangle-shaped piece of paper that had been tucked inside between the front flap and first page. I picked up the paper. Something was inscribed in Italian and signed with three interconnected circles drawn with the flourish of a quill. It said: *Abbiamo tutti le nostre illusioni ei nostri misteri.*

I didn't speak Italian, but I could puzzle out two words— something about illusion and mystery. On another wall was a reproduction of a drawing—a profile of an oddly masculine yet not unattractive woman, with an odd fish-scaled cap of some sort, and braids protruding from the sides of the cap. I stepped up to it, studying the woman with the overtly masculine profile, very strong nose, and slightly disappointed set of her mouth. The printed caption titled the drawing *Ideal Head of a Woman* by Michelangelo.

Strange thing was, she looked uncannily like a younger version of Ultana Lennon. Perhaps that's why she fancied it. I stared at the drawing, marveling at the resemblance. There was an odd triangular shadow on the print as if the corner of the original drawing had been ripped off and so the image on the reproduction was incomplete. A piece missing in the shape of... I held the scrap of old paper with the Italian words written on it. Even more incredible, the triangle fit exactly.

Was it even possible I was holding a note written by *the* Michelangelo? If so, why didn't he sign his name? And what was the meaning of the three connected rings? That was boggling enough without trying to understand how a drawing that old could look so much like Ultana Lennon. My hairs stood on end. I took a picture of the note with my phone and put it back in the book before replacing it on the shelf.

I scanned the room one last time. I needed to put the door back on and get out of there before I was caught. As I walked toward the door, something above it caught my eye, if only for the oddity of it. It was a crude wooden heart-shaped box, about the size of a baby's head, dangling from a chain on a nail above her doorway.

Scooting a chair under the heart, I plucked it off the nail and pried it open. Two identical yellowed envelopes were tucked inside alongside two purple velvet pouches. The gold thread of one pouch crackled with age when I pulled the top apart. I feared the delicate thread might disintegrate in my hands as I peered inside. It held a strange, grimy powder. I pocketed one envelope and one pouch, figuring that if Ultana looked inside the heart, she'd not realize that both weren't still there. Then I replaced the wooden heart on the nail.

I quickly returned the chair and moved into the hall to put the door back on its rusty hinges. As the bottom hinge slid into place and I shut the door, a piercing scream rocketed down the hall toward me, shattering the silence of the night. Over and over, screams of terror and the word *no*. As fast as I could, I ran into the sitting room where I'd left Saoirse and found her scrambling in her half-awake state, terrorized by whatever ghastly dream had awoken her.

"God, it was awful," she cried. "There was a line of faceless people for me to kill. They stood frozen, waiting for me to suck the life from their bodies, and when I did, they fell at my feet into piles of dust. There were so many." She recounted the dream in sobs. "My one lifetime will ruin so many lives. So much dust."

While Saoirse trembled and cried, I settled myself next to her on the large chaise, tucking her against me and covering us both with the blanket. I pulled her into a hug and tried to quiet her. It was strangely soothing to know that I wasn't the only Arrazi who found their gruesome reality too hard to bear. It felt like the most unnatural thing in the world to do, and yet we were *naturally* created to do it.

The only things that ever felt right and natural were my music and my love for Cora. Thinking of her was another reminder that part of me would always be missing. I was sure that if she looked at my aura once again, she'd see the gaping hole in front of my chest. She'd see where she used to live. She'd see the part of me that died with our good-bye.

I'd feel that void every damned day for the rest of my life.

As Saoirse's cries and ragged breathing quieted, the door slammed. Lorcan strode in, swaying on his feet. The minute his eyes clamped on us, he smirked. "Aww, would you look at that. Mum'll be so pleased," he said, tipping his head back in silent, mocking laughter. "Though I don't think she envisioned your romance would, er, blossom so quickly. Snogging on the couch together already?"

"Shut up, Lorcan." Saoirse sniffed. "I asked Finn to come talk to me about something."

"Uh-huh."

"You'll not tell Mother anything, hear?"

Lorcan shuffled closer, peering down at us with slightly out-of-focus eyes. "What the hell is wrong with you both?" he slurred and leaned forward, placing his hands on the foot of the chaise for stability. "You look like you got a bad dose. Baby sister, are you in need of some soul blood?" He laughed.

"I'm not talking to you about this!"

"Back off, man," I said, laying a calming hand on Saoirse. "You'll keep your trap shut or I'll shut it for you."

"Say that again and you'll not be able to walk for a day."

I jumped to my feet and stuck my nose in his piss-drunk face. "I'll speak slowly, so you understand. She's trying to deal with what's happening, right? Give her time. Back off, and keep your *fooking* gob shut, or I swear, I will shut it for you."

No sooner had the words left my mouth than my legs gave way beneath me. I buckled and fell forward to the carpet, knocking my head against Lorcan's knees.

What the bloody hell?

THIRTY-NINE

Cora

The damn attendants wouldn't leave me alone. After Giovanni stalked off from our we-are-one conversation, I wanted to find my way back to the common area with a side order of snooping around. No luck. As soon as I left the biofeedback lab, an attendant materialized to escort me to dinner.

Dinner was served in a sleek rectangular dining room on what seemed to be the world's longest black lacquered table. Rectangular vases displayed clusters of chartreuse flowers down the middle. I stopped short when I entered the room. I hadn't expected to see new faces, but I was excited. Finally, I'd get to meet some of the other guests. Two groups bookended the table. My peeps sat in a cluster at one end, auras wafting upward like the steam from the dishes in front of them.

The other group intrigued me. It included a wizened-looking old man, Japanese, I guessed. He was Scintilla. His silver was calm and steady, flowing around him in a beautiful current. Next to him sat a little girl. This girl, younger than the age of the kids at the Boys & Girls Club where I used to volunteer, watched me as I watched her.

Her aura was colorful and bold. She wasn't uneasy about the new additions to the clinic. Not a bit. Instead of her aura retreating with hesitancy, it reached out farther than any I'd seen before. It swirled around her, a corona of energy and pure life. What shocked me more than the almost aggressive reach of her aura, though, was that every so often I detected a flick of silver, like someone striking a lighter, before it melded into her unique blend of astonishing *strength*.

The little girl actually made me nervous. I tried to disarm her with a smile as I entered the room and sat down next to Mari, but she only stared, poker-faced, flinty. Okay, a tough nut to crack. Reminded me of little Max from the Boys & Girls Club, except when I started seeing auras, his was so smudgy and gray, sad. Not this kid. Hers was the eye of a silent storm.

"Look at how she's staring at you," Mari mumbled. "I never thought I'd say this, but *creepy child is creepy*."

Dun grinned and whispered, "You? Scared?"

"I was plenty scared when those guys attacked us at the elevator. Good thing I didn't show it." Mari shrugged. "I'm calm under pressure like that."

"Depends on whose pressure you're under," he teased, for which Mari kicked him under the table.

"This is the strangest room," Giovanni remarked, looking around at the smooth, glassy black walls. There were no sconces on the mirrorlike surfaces, no artwork, nothing but four sleek walls surrounding us and square recessed lights in a line above us. "I don't recall it from my previous visit."

The doctor entered behind me and sat down near the middle of the table. As soon as he did, the little girl hopped up and ran to him, bouncing onto his lap and tucking her blond curls under his chin. He patted her back and smiled. "Claire, how are you today, my little bundle of kindling?"

Claire shot a glance toward us, a coil of blond winding over one eye. "Who are these people?"

"These nice people have come to visit us. They are helping me with my work. Go on now, say hello."

We all smiled and waved like a bunch of parade princesses. Claire scooted off Dr. M's lap and walked over, examining each of us like a lawyer might approach a juror's box. She reached up and pinched a strand of Dun's long hair between her fingers, sliding them down the length of it as if it were a silky ribbon for a dress. Mari was trying not to look at her, but when Claire stepped into her peripheral, Mari gave her a sideways chin-lift. "'Sup, kid?"

After greeting my mother by placing both hands on top of hers, Claire approached Giovanni and me. Staring into her oceanic blue eyes, it looked as though she had three tiny dots in each eye—three pupils!

Looking past her uncanny eyes, I noticed Dr. M observing us with his finger tapping his mouth and an analyzing stare. Claire shook both of our hands and lifted her chin proudly, regally, and skipped back to her end of the table, whispering into the ear of the older gentleman who was introduced as Abraham, Teruko's grandfather.

"No whispering. We have no secrets here, Claire," Dr. M admonished. Claire jerked back from Abraham and sat down. The doctor turned to me and he said, "On that note, I'd like for you to tell me more about your special *gifts*."

My gaze flickered from Giovanni to my mother. One of them had said too much.

"I understand Giovanni is capable of telekinesis," Dr. M said, with a nod to Giovanni. "Was this something you could always do? Even as a child?"

"I found out I could move things, draw them to me, by accident. I was young and hadn't eaten in a couple of days. I found myself staring longingly at a half-eaten baguette on a plate at a café table in Paris. The baguette flew to me. Landed at my feet. It wasn't until very recently that I realized I could move large things, such as people. It was during a threatening situation," he added, looking at me.

"You move things? With your melon?" Dun gasped. "Do something."

Immediately the napkin in front of Dun spun and skipped across the table where G put his hand over it, tapping his fingers casually. Claire clapped her hands and heels together gleefully.

"My ability didn't come on until recently," I said through clenched teeth. My sortilege was *my* business.

"Interesting," Dr. M said, moving his food around but not eating it. "That you can pick up strong memories from objects, vibrational imprints, as your mother told me she can place memories *into* objects. Extraordinary. Tell me, Gráinne, how did you *know* you could do that? If you can't retrieve as your daughter can, how did you realize it?"

"I—I didn't know for certain that I could until I was older," my mother said. "When I went to Chile, I met a clairvoyant who confirmed it. And…" She studied her fingers on her lap. "A person knows when a piece of them has been left behind."

"Extraordinary," he said again. "Dun and Mari, I assume, can do nothing special?"

Mari raised an eyebrow at him. "How would you like a special kick in the—"

"Tssst," I warned. "Stop it. He's trying to help us."

Just then, a man rushed in and told Dr. M of a news report of a devastating typhoon in Japan that had killed more than two thousand people, and the death toll was rising. The doctor reacted with grave somberness, shaking his head and pursing his lips together.

"My father warned about an increase in natural disasters," I said.

"This hits very close to home," Dr. M said. "Most of my staff has family there."

"I'm sorry. I hope they're okay. Dr. M, may I ask what's your biggest goal here? You have money behind you." I glanced around. "Obviously. So what do you hope to discover with your research?"

"It has certainly become a new goal to find a way to prove your father's theory. Since our conversation, I've thought of little else but what might happen to this world and the people in it, if the only beings that can save us are exterminated forever. Don't you see? If you father was right, our entire existence is threatened and might be dependent upon the survival of your kind.

"Up to now, I've been trying to learn all I can about this phenomenon. I'd very much like to unravel the mystery of why there are different energetic types of humans. How long has this been going on? What is the purpose? Etcetera. Once I can prove it, I can persuade others to accept it."

"Have you studied Arrazi?" Dun asked.

"They're extremely hard to pin down," Dr. M answered. "I can't see auras and so have no way of knowing if I'm encountering an Arrazi or not and they are, for obvious reasons, not fond of revealing themselves."

Giovanni leaned forward, raking his fingers through his curls.

"If they haven't recently killed, their auras look normal."

"Well, I *am* working on addressing the issue of laypeople seeing auras," Dr. M said with a boyish glee. "Would you care to see how?"

Dr. M pushed buttons on a keypad embedded in the smooth wall. "I need you all to stay seated," he said.

I felt a slight buzzing vibration in the chair beneath me. Giovanni's eyes, round with alarm, met mine. The walls around us suddenly burst from glossy black panels to panels of movement and color. So like the photograph of the leaf that I'd first seen in Mrs. Boroff's greenhouse at school, the walls had become life-size displays of the auras of everyone in the room.

The outline of our bodies could be seen with starry dots of color sprinkled like constellations over our physical forms. From there emanated the luminous beauty of our auras, undulating and morphing, as wispy and changeable as clouds.

Mari gasped. I'd never seen her with such a look of wonder on her face. "That—that's what you *see*?"

Dun waved his hands over his head and the projection on the wall mirrored his movements, sending tufts of color swirling out from his hands. Even the auras of the flower arrangements on the table radiated in small bubbles of light on the wall. My teacher, Mrs. Boroff, would have loved that. Rather than the still photographs of Kirlian photography, it looked like Kirlian video. For my mother, Giovanni, Abraham, and me, this was no different from how we saw the world every day.

Tears filled Mari's eyes as she looked from each person in the room to the wall. "Oh my God," she said in a voice soaked with awe. "We are so beautiful." Her gaze met mine.

I nodded.

"You're pure light. You look like an angel, *prima.*" I reached across the table to squeeze her hand, but her eyes were still on the wall, watching our energies collide with blue-silver sparks.

"I will never be able to unsee this and wouldn't want to," Dun said, leaning back in his chair. "How is this possible, Doc?"

As I suspected, Dr. M confirmed that it was technology borrowed from the methods of Kirlian photography. He explained that there were transparent electrodes in the seats, floors, walls, and ceiling, and that the images were projected via computers onto the walls. "As far as I know," he said, "it's the first of its kind. I'm quite pleased with it, as are my investors. Obviously, they see huge marketing potential for such an invention. Why shouldn't everyone be able to see auras?"

"You're kidding, right?" I said, agitation rising. "I sure as hell wouldn't want the Arrazi to have this technology. Who would benefit most from this invention? That's the important question." Dr. M looked away for a moment, which made me suspicious, but his aura remained clear of grime or fear. "Your investors," I said. "Who are they?"

"I'm not at liberty to divulge."

I cocked my head at him. "I thought you said there were no secrets here. Are they the Arrazi?"

"Of course not!" No ball of black, deceitful smoke puffed from his mouth.

"Have you ever heard of the Society? The name *Xepa*?"

"Neither. Are you quite all right, Ms. Sandoval?"

"Fine," I said, though I was unable to calm my suspicion and anxiety, which showed in the display of my aura on the wall, though I doubted anyone but the Scintilla in the room could translate it. Everything I'd learned about reading auras told me Dr. M was being honest, but the holes in his aura perplexed me. Secrets hung in a person's field like pulsing sores. This, this was something else.

FORTY

Cora

After dinner, most of us headed to the rooftop garden to relax and get acquainted. My shoulders were tight with anxiety, which I could only pin on Dr. M's evasiveness when I'd asked him about his investors. Mari had been reluctant to leave the dining room and its walls that enabled her see the world the way the Scintilla did, but finally agreed when Teruko invited her. From the back, she and Teruko looked remarkably similar with their short black bobs. Teruko's hair was tipped with deep pink, though, like a black silk paintbrush dipped in bubble gum.

They were deep in conversation about auras and energy and how Teruko came to be here. She always knew her grandfather could see auras because he'd read hers many times. She had tried to research online what he had told her about his aura being silver and unlike anyone else's, but could find nothing until she came upon information on a seminar that Dr. M was giving in Japan. She went. He had asked the audience if they'd ever heard of anyone with a purely silver aura. She was the only one who raised her hand. He convinced her to bring her grandfather to Ireland.

Dun walked silently beside them. I was suddenly distracted by Mari's spliced aura. The same swirling pink that had been directed so often at Dun was split in half, projecting toward Teruko. A delicate twirl of attraction danced from Mari's belly across the air to the boy *and* to the girl. The girls' arms brushed lightly, causing Mari's aura to flare a deeper shade.

I looked from Mari to Dun, Mari to Teruko, trying to connect the dots, draw new lines between what I believed to be true and what I was seeing.

Mari glanced my way and fixed me with a stare. It was amazing how fast her aura flashed to anger when she caught me observing so intently. Her colors morphed from warmth to warning. Her chin thrust up a fraction of an inch, a show of pride, but she looked away too fast to seal the deal. Was I reading this correctly? Did she actually think she could hide anything from me?

Dun fell out of step with them, trailing behind like a forgotten puppy. His own colors were retracted and forlorn, a dirty bluish-green. When he looked back over his shoulder and saw me watching, he stopped and waited for me to catch up. "How's my girl?"

"If I don't say peachy—"

"I'd totally understand." He slipped his arm around my shoulder. "You've been through more crap in the last two months than some people go through in their entire lives. You're strong, girl."

I looked up at him, my best friend. He must've seen the question in my eyes because he said, "I always knew you were strong. But the still waters kind. Mari is strong like…" He watched Mari as she laughed at something Teruko said. His aura reached for her as his attention did. "Mari is strong like waves."

"Relentless and predictable," I joked.

"They rush at you, then pull away."

We came to a bench between two trees and sat down. Red lanterns cast spots of light on the garden path. "So, why haven't you guys admitted to me that you're crushing hard on each other?" I thought again of Mari's apparent attraction to Teruko.

Dun started to protest with a lot of started and stopped sentences before he leaned back and surrendered. "Yeah. Okay. Fine. We weren't sure whether to lay it on you with everything else that's going on. But I don't get her. One minute she's fire-hot." He waggled his eyebrows at me. I elbowed him. "Then she's totally cold."

"She's always been like that, Dun."

"I know. But it's different when your heart's on the skewer and she controls the heat." He laid his head on my shoulder and I patted his cheek. Could it even end well? She was into him, too. That was clear in the colors.

Giovanni approached, regarding us with creased eyes and uncharacteristic fidgeting of his fingers. "Hey," I said. Giovanni still stared, like he didn't know how to start over with me since our cosmic-oneness spat. We were still charged from it. I could feel the zing of frenetic energy pulse between us.

"I'm going to bed," Dun said, with a final glance through the trees to where Mari and Teruko sat together in rapt conversation. This ordeal couldn't be easy on either of them. They should have stayed in Chile with Mami Tulke. Though, my grandmother's grieving AWOL stunt was the reason they'd jetted to Ireland in the first place. I was upset that our phones didn't work inside the safety of the compound. Dr. M explained that he'd had many of what he thought were confidential conversations on a cell phone only to find out that they weren't. For our safety, he said, we couldn't make any calls.

"G'night," I said, giving a quick peck to Dun's cheek. He shuffled off to his room.

Giovanni sat in Dun's place. "Can I put my head on your shoulder, too?" he asked with a smile in his voice.

"No. I reserve that spot for lovesick friends."

"Still applicable."

I decided to ignore that comment and instead asked if I could spend the night with the Dante book. I'd requested a computer in my room and I intended to continue exploring our possibilities even as Dr. M pursued his. The problems between the Arrazi and Scintilla weren't likely to be solved on just one front. This was a multilayered offensive. Or defense. Whatever.

It was war.

"*Si*. Of course," Giovanni said. "What are your thoughts?"

"I can't sit around here like I'm in some luxury hotel and while away the hours in between being poked, prodded, and interrogated. I *need* to keep looking for answers. I want to know more about Dante Alighieri's life. I feel like if we go ahead and take the mental leap, just go with the theory that he knew about Scintilla, then follow what appear to be his clues, it's as though he's leading us somewhere, maybe to some knowledge he had seven hundred years ago. Maybe to find a clue that will save us."

Giovanni nodded, absently it seemed.

Was he even listening? "Somehow? Maybe?" I sighed. The more I talked, the nuttier I sounded. "I don't know. I'm sure it's crazy. I'm sure countless other Scintilla have been trying to find a cure for centuries."

"No, Cora. Not crazy. We have to pursue every path. That's what I'm doing. That's why I support Dr. M's work. If he can discover a way to, how did he say, *regenerate* our energy? Then maybe his work could help us. We'd be less weak." He spat that word like it was poison. "We're easy targets right now. We have to level the playing field or it's only a matter of time." He stood and held out his hand to help me up. "Come. Let's go get your book."

I thought I'd read and search online on my own, but Giovanni wanted to help. I didn't mind. We slid the rice-paper door open to the night, reading and typing to the soothing sounds of the water fountains and the far-off current of Dublin traffic. This facility felt like another world. It was hard to believe we were still in Dublin, still close to Clancy Mulcarr and the hive of Arrazi. It was hard to believe I was still so close to Finn.

My soul tightened with the harsh memory of seeing him at the party. How strange and agonizing to act like strangers, to dance around the truth of our history. The worst kind of pretending was pretending that you don't want to fall into someone's arms again. How do you unbind your heart? How do you unsee the look in someone's eyes? How do you untaste their lips? How do you unfeel love?

How do you unexperience their moving on?

By moving on, myself.

I glanced at Giovanni stretching his long legs out on a chair perched in front of him. His sandy brows bent in concentration over *Paradiso*. His silver aura rolled like the sea as he read, calm but in perpetual motion. It reminded me of the silvery-blue ocean back home in Santa Cruz. I wondered if I'd ever return to that place. I'd have a new family with me. I knew that.

He caught me looking and smiled. "Listen to some of these

phrases from canto twenty-eight. *From the Pure Spark... From that one Point hang Heaven and nature all... Whence orders three with trinal rapture ring."*

I leaned behind Giovanni and read over his shoulder, my fingers stinging with energy as I placed my hand on his back. Again and again, I read the canto. Words jumped out at me: *pure spark, heaven, three, trinal. Three with trinal rapture ring.* I didn't know what it meant, but the more we read, the more convinced I became that one of the world's most famous poets knew the truth.

"I found some things, too," I said. Giovanni removed his feet from the chair, pulled my hand, and led me around to sit in front of him. "Guess who was one of Dante's biggest fans?"

"Who?"

"Michelangelo. Apparently, he revered Dante. Even wrote sonnets about him." I slipped my hand from Giovanni's to go and grab the laptop. *"All that should be said of him cannot be said for too brightly did his splendor burn for our blind eyes.* He also said of Dante, *Ne'er walked the earth a greater man than he."*

"Maybe he's just being overly exultant in his description of Dante. Figurative."

"Could be. But get this." I turned the laptop around so Giovanni could see. "Get a load of how Michelangelo signed some of his works." Giovanni and I stared at the emblem; three connected circles so much like the triple spiral, my breath had halted when I first saw it. "He called the signature the *tre giri* and—"

Silver beams projected out from Giovanni like lasers. "Means three circles. And you're thinking it's a nod to the *tre giri* in Dante's *Paradiso*?"

I grinned wide, thrilling at the discoveries that were piling up. "Exactly. When asked about the signature, Michelangelo said, *contemplation of the three circles raises the thoughts to heaven*. My mother's journal said that the Scintilla hold the keys to heaven, or something like that." I slipped the key out from under my shirt. "My grandmother gave this to my mother. The key, threes, and the triple spiral, all of them connected by one word: *heaven*. I know in my gut that all these things are linked. I *feel* it." Elation that we might be onto something made my skin tingle.

Suddenly, Giovanni leaned forward and placed both hands on the sides of my face. I stopped talking, stopped speculating, stopped thinking clearly. The voltage of his hands swirled heat on my skin, warming my open lips with sparks.

"Your aura lights up this room when you're excited." He scanned my face before a hopeless look passed over him and he dropped his hands. "It lights *me* up."

"We—well, we can't help that," I said. "We're, like, superconductors."

His eyes darkened in that way they did when he was thinking something he wasn't saying. He studied me and then looked out beyond me, to my aura. I was sure he'd be able to see the ripples of conflicted feelings I experienced when he held my face, but he wasn't looking at my aura anymore. He was looking *into* me.

"Cora—"

Insistent banging on the door startled us both.

FORTY-ONE

Finn

"What'd you do to him?" Saoirse screamed at her brother, slipping her hands under my arms in a futile attempt to lift me from the floor. Even if she were feeling normal, she couldn't lift me. She was a sparrow and my body had become deadweight over legs that could not support me. I was weak and needed to kill, I knew that. But this was different, like being struck with sudden paralysis.

"Get up. Stop acting the maggot," Lorcan said, now towering over me.

"I can't!" I said, ineffectively trying to move my legs and feet. The words had barely left my mouth when Lorcan grabbed a fistful of my shirt and heaved me upward. Even then, my legs could not hold me, and I buckled to the chaise as though I were frozen from the waist down.

All three of us looked at one another as a grandfather clock taunted with its heartbeat.

"Explain this!" I yelled, though feeling less bold since my arse was firmly planted on a chair and I was forced to look up at him. "One minute you threaten that I'll not be able to walk out of here, and now this?"

Lorcan looked muddled—not superior, not satisfied, but confused. "Jaysus, that's the second time today that something like this has happened," he said, uncharacteristically diffident. "I don't understand it." He walked to a cupboard, pulled down a decanter and a glass, and poured himself more than he surely needed. He was already sloshed, as it were, and I was unable to stand on my goddamned feet. This was not a time to drink *more*.

"You two think Lorcan did this?" Saoirse scoffed, then turned to him. "Please. I know you believe you're God's gift, but *hexing* people? That's grandiosity at its finest."

"*Sortilege*?" I wondered aloud.

Lorcan narrowed his eyes and took another swig.

"You—*you* have a sortilege?" Saoirse asked him. "Nobody does. Not anymore. How is that even possible?"

Lorcan threw up his hands, sloshing the amber liquid on the floor and the front of his trousers. "I couldn't tell you what the hell is possible!"

The fear in his eyes made me nervous. I gathered this was a new development, and that scared the crap out of me. We didn't need any more superpowered Arrazi running around. "You've taken from a Scintilla," I accused, breathless. His mother couldn't possibly pretend she believed there were no Scintilla around if her own son had his sortilege.

"If I did, I didn't know it!" The smug smile I had expected when I fell to the floor now spread slowly over Lorcan's face. He looked to the floor and back up with a start, nodding to himself. "Ah," he said, lifting his glass in the air like a toast. "I'd wager it was the party girl. The one with the knife on her creamy back. I *knew* there was something different about her when I attacked her. Aye, I believe I *did* take from a silver one. She was a delicacy."

Every drop of blood drained from my body and pooled in my stomach. *Cora.* He'd attacked her. My God. While Clancy and I were out at that damn cottage being lackeys for the Society, looking for them because there'd been an Arrazi tip, Lorcan had pounced on her. I could hardly let myself envision it. "You—you didn't kill her, did you?" I barely choked out the words while not daring to look away from my fists curling into the sides of my useless legs. I was afraid that I'd betray myself right there.

Please. Please say you didn't kill her.

"Of course I didn't kill her, you eejit. She was with the Society. Had the ring 'n' everything. As soon as she shoved it in my face, I backed off."

Saoirse put her hands on her hips. "Wait, the Society wants all the silver ones dead. They wouldn't have one in their ranks, would they? This makes no sense."

My head spun. I wanted to pin Lorcan to the floor with knives, but I had to put that out of my mind for the moment so I could think clearly. I didn't understand. Where would Cora have gotten a ring to get into the Society? "Tell me about this ring."

"Only those within a certain level have the rings. My mother has one. Your uncle Clancy has one. This girl had one. It's the only reason I didn't kill her, and even then it was damn near impossible to stop myself."

Controlling the shaking that had taken over my body was proving impossible. Thankfully it could be masked as Arrazi need. All I could think of was Cora being drained of her beautiful energy by that thug. How afraid she must have been. How alone. What had happened to her after he attacked her? I should never have walked away from her, especially not there. I had thought I was helping her.

"My God, yes," Saoirse whispered. "She's the reason this has happened to me, isn't she? I'd never felt anyone like her. Incredible. Do you suppose I'll I get my power, too, from being so near her?"

"I don't know," I answered through a clenched jaw, hating the hope in her voice. "She might not have even been a Scintilla," I said, trying in vain to deflect their attention from Cora. But it was ineffectual. Of course, now she was all any of us could think about. It killed me. I wanted them to know nothing of Cora and what she was. But Cora had done this. It was her foolish idea to infiltrate that party.

Even as I inwardly chastised her, I was proud of her guts to fight for answers. She could have run. Should have. Instead, she was sniffing out the right trail, the same trail I was on.

Lord, she was brave.

"All I know," Saoirse said with a rigid set of her thin shoulders, "is that I felt pulled like a riptide to her. Even after we walked away, I wanted nothing more than to turn back. I haven't been right since. And now, now my energy is fading so fast I fear it'll be a matter of hours before I have—I have to kill someone." She gulped loudly, swallowing the hard, bitter truth.

"Do you know her?" Lorcan asked me. "I watched you talking with her. Pissed me off that you'd moved in on her, especially with you bein' there as my sister's date 'n' all. Who is she?"

Both stared at me expectantly. "I—I thought I knew her," I stammered. "She had a damn mask over her face, for *fook's* sake. But when I spoke with her, I realized I was wrong. She—she was a stranger to me."

Lorcan seemed satisfied but Saoirse's shrewd eyes lingered too long on my face. Finally, she plopped down next to me and sighed, cradling her head in her hands. "I'm more tired than I've ever been."

"I know. That's me, as well."

"Go take care of that already. I'm going to bed," Lorcan said with a wave, walking from the room. How could he be so indifferent about his sister's first time?

"I can't move my *fookin'* legs!" I yelled to his back, but he laughed and kept walking. If he could do this to me, he could undo it. Though, clearly, he wasn't going to do so at the moment. Bastard. Using my arms to scoot back farther into the cushions, I fell into them and closed my eyes. Saoirse did the same, sighing heavily next to me. I knew we were both thinking the same thing, and we were both staving off the inevitable.

Soon, it would be do—or die.

Saoirse jiggled my arm to wake me. Her already-pale face had whitened to a ghostlike hue. Morning had come, and no relief with it. Not from the soul-consuming hunger for someone's spirit, not for the affliction Lorcan had seemingly placed on me. I tried, but still couldn't wiggle my toes or move my legs.

Despite my revulsion at doing what was necessary to stay alive, I was becoming frightened for myself. If I couldn't walk, if I couldn't find someone to take from, how in the hell was I supposed to stay alive? Or help Saoirse? Helping her get through her first kill was one of the reasons I came. I was already sick. Now my situation was dire. I was caving in on myself, imploding into a black hole of need.

I felt for the old envelope and pouch from the wooden heart in Ultana's office, glad I'd taken the chance to poke around while I could. They were still tucked in my jeans pocket. I was eager to be alone to open the envelope and find out what it contained.

"I'm worse," Saoirse said in a miserable voice, shuddering. Her pink lips were cracked, as if she were dehydrated. I knew her insides felt just as parched, just as thirsty. We huddled together, shivering in the morning light.

"Get Lorcan," I said. "We need him to undo whatever it is he's done to me. Both of us are running out of time."

"I already tried," she said. "It was all I could do to do make it up the stairs. Once I finally roused his smelly, snoring arse, he said something about you learning a lesson and went back to snoring."

My teeth ground together. "Someday, your brother and I are going to have a moment of serious reckoning."

"Get in line, Finn." Silence, then. Silence that stretched on for a good hour. Then another, before she looked up at me, trembling. "What are we going to do?"

FORTY-TWO

Cora

"Anything you want from the outside world?" Mari asked, breezing into the room in a web of thrilling colors. My cheeks were burning both literally and metaphorically from Giovanni's intimate touch. Mari's knock at the door had interrupted... something, and if pressed, I couldn't say if I was relieved or disappointed. "Teruko has to go for supplies tomorrow and take a report to some mucky-muck investors, and since I'm, you know, *normal*, I get to go, too."

"Is that a good idea?" I asked.

"Who knows how long we'll be stuck here? Any opportunity to get out in the real world is one I'm gonna take. Besides, that mad scientist doesn't want anything to do with me. He's only letting Dun and me stay here because of you."

"Of course, but—"

"No buts. Place your orders now. We're heading out kind of early."

I told her to call Mami Tulke while she was out, and to

see what information she could glean on these mucky-muck investors, then whispered to her about getting me some *girl stuff* and candy. I'd about kill for some Hot Tamales. She nodded. "And you, *señor*?"

"That's Spanish."

"Whatever."

Giovanni shrugged and she left. I was surprised to feel the pang of jealousy that she was going to get to be free tomorrow. Free and normal. Would I ever feel either of those things again?

The next day, Teruko and Mari's absence hit Dun noticeably hard. "I'm normal, too," he pouted.

Truthfully, I thought it was mean that they hadn't asked him to go. Though he did stick out like a sore thumb in the streets of Dublin. I patted his back. "Sorry. But I'm glad you're here. I have a job for you," I said, lowering my voice to a whisper. "I want to find out more about Dr. M's work. He's been really open, but I want to find out what he *isn't* telling us."

"What do you want me to do?"

"I love that you're in, no questions."

"Soul-snatching lunatics are trying to kill my best friend. Helping you snoop around some high-tech lab is the least of my worries."

Giovanni entered the common room, leading Claire by the hand like a big brother. It surprised me, but was sweet. She obviously liked him, as she had a huge grin and was chatting happily. It had to get lonely around here, with no other kids. Teruko's grandfather, Abraham, wasn't around. Then again, neither was my mother. I hoped they'd found good company with each other.

Abraham had a placid silver aura, one I was sure my mom would appreciate being around.

I tried to get a firm grasp on Claire's peculiar aura. It flashed like Giovanni's and mine, but only occasionally, and so quickly, it could be a trick of the light. Her head whipped to look at me. Startled, I tried to smile, but her eyes were so unnerving. "Hi, Claire," I finally said. Kids had never made me nervous before.

"Claire has been telling me how she's lived here as long as she can remember," Giovanni said.

"Really? Do you go out much?" I asked her.

"Never."

"Oh, wow."

"Tell me what America is like," she said. "I have a tutor here and she teaches me lots of things, but"—she inclined her head conspiratorially and lowered her voice—"I think she leaves stuff out."

I laughed. "Do you? What would you like to know?"

"Are loads of people dropping dead all over America like they are in other places?"

I blinked. How could I even answer that? "How is it you've heard of people dying?"

"With my ears."

Dun snickered.

"That's a pretty serious thing to be interested in. Isn't there something fun you'd like to know about America?"

"Fun seems pretty banal in the face of deaths," she said haughtily, stunning me. Her frank manner and intellect reminded me of Giovanni—the part that drove me insane, anyway. This child was certainly unusual, especially for her age.

"Now, Claire," Dr. M interrupted. He entered the room with his frenetic energy that reminded me so much of my dad's second wife, it made me miss her. I wondered how she was doing. "Is that polite breakfast conversation?" he asked. "Run along. Your schoolwork awaits."

Claire affected a pout but flounced off, disappearing through one of the doorways.

"Could we get a tour of this joint?" Dun asked Dr. M. "If I'm going to be stuck here for the duration, I'd like to know the lay of the land a bit." I bit the inside of my cheek. He was quick. No time like the present.

Dr. M looked bothered by the request, but when he saw all of our expectant faces, acquiesced. "Very well. Come along."

It was confounding how anyone found their way in the facility, as most doors were not marked. We followed silently as Dr. M showed us around the lab we'd seen during our initial experiments. We also knew what was on the top floor, and we'd been in the lobby. From my memory of the night we'd arrived, there were at least one or two more floors to the building, as well as the underground parking garage.

Every door, every elevator, every damn file cabinet had a scanner that would recognize only certain people's fingerprints or voice commands. "Start a fight," I whispered to Dun. "Take out the doctor. I need to separate." I jerked my head toward Giovanni.

"Dude!" Dun yelled at Giovanni. "Did you just mad-dog me?"

"Pardon?" Giovanni asked, completely perplexed. "*Dog* you?"

"Don't give me that Grey Poupon answer, you uppity son of a bitch!" Dun pushed Giovanni square in the chest, sending him reeling into Dr. M. I registered the intensity in Giovanni's eyes as he scrambled toward Dun. Dr. M picked himself off the floor and moved to separate them. I backed away slowly, then took off running.

Peering carefully around corners to avoid the ever-present staff, I tried to distance myself as much as possible. A little time alone, that was all I needed. We were putting an awful lot of trust in Dr. M and his motives. As Giovanni had once said to me, no one does something for nothing. Who funded these magic walls and this high-tech research?

Not like an office would have Dr. M's name on the door. That would be wishful thinking. So I started pushing doors, looking through windows. One room looked like an opulent office, probably Dr. M's, but of course I couldn't get in. I turned another corner and came upon the medical exam rooms where I'd been taken each morning for blood tests, my temperature, more questions. The doors were open and, at the moment, no one was around. The exam rooms were more sterile and devoid of personality than any doctor's office I'd ever been in, so I doubted I'd find anything in them. But there was a touch-screen in each room where our information was entered.

No expectations. Vague hope, maybe. That was what I felt when I touched the screen in the first room. It immediately asked for a password. I tried the next exam room and the next. The last one was directly across from the elevators. I had no idea how much time I'd have before I was found. I reached my sweaty hand to the screen, but an idea made me pause. Could I get a memory from the keypad? Surely, the same numbers would be entered over and over. Would that imprint the device in a way I could feel? I closed my eyes and hovered my hand over the display. A five-number code materialized in my mind and dissipated like smoke. I mouthed a silent plea and keyed the numbers in. A home screen popped up.

I touched the tab for "Patients." Easily a dozen people had medical records stored—too many of them with a red DECEASED notation. I gulped hard. Who were these people? *How* had they died?

I scrolled by Claire's name, but then paused, scrolled back to it, and clicked.

Five years old. Born in Dublin. IQ of 152. That explained her mature conversational abilities. I read further down with a slight pang of guilt. This was none of my business, right? Method of gestation: *in vitro fertilization*. Mother was listed as Class III Human, whatever *that* meant. Father listed as Class I. I gasped, disbelieving what I read next.

Paternal father: *Giovanni Teso*.

My mouth went dry. A million questions zinged through my mind. Could this be true? Who was the mother? Did Giovanni know? Was he keeping this from me? Was this why he'd wanted to come here so badly?

The shuffle of footsteps and Dun's overly loud talking reached me. I hit the close file button and jumped on the exam table. No sooner had I done that than Dr. M appeared in the doorway. His eyes flashed to the now-black screen, then back to me. "What are you doing in here?"

"The fighting…it frays my nerves. I take on people's energy. I—I can't handle the stress of that. I had to find someplace quiet. Those two are constantly at each other." Dun's lips pursed together in an impressed smile. A silver storm of agitation flared in Giovanni's aura. "I'm not feeling well," I said. "Maybe the guys can walk me back to my room? That's *if* you're behaving yourselves now," I tacked on for good measure.

Giovanni growled out an exasperated sound. Surely he

wanted to be as far away from Dun as possible. That situation, I could diffuse. But there was a knot in my stomach the size of a boulder. Now that I thought about it, Giovanni had been here before. Claire *did* very much resemble him. The mass of curls in her light hair. The way she looked at you as if she were standing on a dais. Her formidable brainpower. And he had been holding her hand…

I rocked on my heels, beyond impatient to be alone with Giovanni. I could feel the scientist's eyes on our backs as we got in the elevator. Dr. M activated the keypad and pushed the button for the top floor.

"Find anything?" Dun whispered when the doors closed.

Giovanni pushed between us. "What—you're saying that was all a ruse?"

"Shhh," I hissed, glaring at them.

"Why is your aura pulling back from me, Cora? I'm not the one who did anything wrong."

"You can see things like that?" Dun said. "Freaky. I need to sit Mari down in front of that wall again. See what's really going on with her." He put his hand on my shoulder. "I bet no one can lie to people like you, can they?"

"I'm about to find out," I said, glancing at Giovanni as the elevator doors opened.

FORTY-THREE

Finn

"Christ! The two of you have a bloody death wish?" Lorcan yelled.

Bleary-eyed, I blinked up at him. He looked like blazing *shite*, but I was certain I looked worse. His hands were on his hips as he surveyed us, shaking his head like we were two errant children in need of a stern lecture.

"You reckon I should army-crawl myself out of here, dragging my useless legs behind me, Lorcan?" It took enormous effort to speak. I felt like I'd been ripped up out of a coma and told to swim the English Channel.

Lorcan steadied himself like he was about to throw something, pointed one finger at me dramatically, and said, "Your legs work perfectly now!" in a booming, commanding voice.

Nothing. I strained with colossal effort. My legs wouldn't move. It was nearly funny. Except it was *my* goddamned legs we were talking about. Worse was that any fight I'd normally have in me was completely spent. I was wasting away. Saoirse was, too.

She hadn't even woken up. I slid my arm out from under her, rubbing the tingles out of it.

"As much as I hate your cocky arse," Lorcan growled, "it'd be mine on the line if I let you die."

"Not to mention your sister."

He prowled back and forth, taking twice as long as the average person to come up with what was obvious to me. He was either going to have to carry us out of here and help us find someone, or bring them to us. I was near to vomiting. Finally, his slow brain caught up. "Well, I either gotta take you two to kill, or bring you some fresh meat."

"God, Lorcan…" Saoirse mumbled.

"Pick one, little sister, cause you and lover boy here are lookin' like you might die on me any minute."

"Be a hero, for once," she told him.

Lorcan turned on his heel and walked out, slamming the front door.

(M)uch like the night on the boat, my conscious awareness lifted up and away like a helium balloon slipping out of a careless hand and soaring up into the sky. I'd feel the slip, wake with a start or a gasp, then drift again, my body bobbing as if we were on the air.

Next to me, Saoirse was a statue. Her tiny face was marble against the fire of her hair. I closed my eyes and slipped into a dream where her hair was made of crimson maple leaves that crumbled and deteriorated into the soil of the earth.

I woke and shook her, my hands so numb that I wasn't sure I'd actually touched her. Nothing. Gripped with panic that she'd died, I tried to shake her again, harder. When I stilled, I realized I could *feel* the faintest trace of life in her.

Barely.

The door flung open and a load of scuffling could be heard in the entryway before Lorcan appeared with someone over his shoulder. I tried to focus, but my eyes were bleary. He set a figure down on the floor and went back outside. Shortly, he returned with another person, half conscious, and dropped her on the floor. Two young women. I sighed, forcing down the bile that rose up in my throat. No doubt these slight girls were easier for Lorcan to subdue. I blinked and forced my eyes to center on the face of the girl nearest me.

Every cell in my body screamed shock as loud as it screamed hunger.

Jaysus, it was Mari.

"*Where* did you find these girls?" I rasped. *This isn't happening...*

"Little minxes were making out in a van by the side of the road. Was stupidly easy to sneak up on them, actually, they were so *into* what they were doing. Though, this one," he said, with a malicious shove of the toe of his boot against Mari's arm, "was a right pain."

"I—I can't kill her."

"What do you mean you *can't* kill her?" He rolled both girls on their backs. Their feet pointed in separate directions, but their heads were next to each other, two black-haired dolls. They were breathing but totally out of it. He either took from them or knocked them unconscious. Probably both. Of all the people in the world he could stumble upon, it had to be Cora's cousin? I'd rather die. I didn't care. There was no way I was going to kill Mari.

Saoirse stirred next to me. Her eyes fluttered open and widened when she saw the people dumped on the floor like corpses. Even that wasn't enough to keep her conscious. She was in worse shape than me. Lorcan hefted his sister up and plopped her on the floor next to the delicately pretty Asian girl.

"Lorcan, please! You have to find other people. Get them out of here. I know one of them." It had to be said. Nothing else would do. "You can't expect me to kill someone I know."

Saoirse looked up at me with sadness, but she was too weak to speak. Her head lolled back to look at the girl's face. She reached a shaky hand and smoothed the pink-tipped hair from her cheek. The girl opened her doe eyes and looked bewilderedly at Saoirse inclined over her. One improbable tear fell from Saoirse's eye and landed on the girl's cheek, like Cora when she'd leaned over me and saved my life. Except this was giving death.

With a panicked gasp, Mari came to and pushed herself up, but Lorcan shoved her back down with his boot.

"Hey!" I yelled, useless to move or defend her.

As soon as she heard my voice, her head rolled to the side. Her mouth opened in surprise. "You. No freakin' way!" she gasped, grabbing for the hand of the girl next to her who, I just realized by her arched back and limp arms, was already being drained by Saoirse. Saoirse's eyes were closed as she killed. "Teruko!" Mari cried. "No…" She punched Lorcan in the shin and scrambled to push Saoirse away from her friend, but Lorcan grabbed Mari by the hair and pulled her back, hissing to his sister to *finish it.*

As color returned slowly to Saoirse's face, all had drained from Mari's as she watched her companion die. Lorcan hauled Mari to her feet and shoved her onto her knees to face me.

Clapping resounded in the room.

Lorcan, Mari, and I turned toward the source. Ultana Lennon stood in the doorway with a look of pure amusement. "What have we here?" she asked. "A *killing* party?" She tsked. "Don't you know you're not supposed to hold a party while Mummy's away?" Her tone was teasing, but with a knife-edge to it. Though when she looked at her daughter hovering over her first kill, pride was evident in her eyes.

"They were dying, Mother. Both of them lying here like sacks. They waited too long." He pointed at me accusingly. "Look at him now, still refusing to nourish."

Ultana leveled a gaze at me that was every bit a challenge. How on board was I? Could I be trusted? Was I one of the Arrazi's fine young men? Prove it. All of that beamed from her callous stare.

I looked from her to Mari, whose dark eyes—very much the large, almond shape of Cora's—pierced me with incredulity and fear.

"You unbelievable prick," Mari said. Mari wouldn't die without a fight. I didn't know her well, but I knew enough. I was reeling. I needed to ask her where Cora was, if she was safe, get her out of here somehow. But everyone's eyes were on me, waiting. "Not here—I need to do this alone—" I started, but Lorcan cut me off.

"He says he knows her," he said with a shake to Mari's shoulders. "Says he won't kill her."

The hope that passed over Mari's expressive face killed me. I had no idea how I was going to get her out of there.

Ultana strode over, pulling her glove off her one hand with her teeth as she approached. "All the more reason to finish her. We can't simply let her walk out of this house, now can we? If Finn is"—she tossed a withering look at me that was all condescension and spite—"too *obtuse* to see that obvious fact, then I will kill her myself." She grabbed Mari's chin and yanked her face toward hers. "We clean up our messes."

Forty-Four

Cora

"Tell me what was the meaning of that charade back there," Giovanni lit into me as soon as we entered my room. "You wanted to look around, obviously. Why not trust me with that information before you stuck your *mad dog* on me?"

I fought a grin at his improper use of Dun's words. "I do want to talk about trust."

He put his hands on his slender hips and cocked his head sideways. "Yes?"

"Can I trust you? *Really* trust you?"

Giovanni took me in his arms and looked down into my face with concern. "I'd do anything for you. You *must* know this by now, Cora."

I watched his face, unwilling to completely abandon the old ways of reading people. But I also watched his aura. I was getting better at analyzing silver, as my mom had said I would. I needed to read him clearly. I wanted to trust, but after Finn, it was so hard. "Pure honesty. I'm asking for that, okay?"

He fingered a curl near my temple, but his eyes never wavered or betrayed any nervousness. I, on the other hand, wished he'd stop touching me so tenderly. Intimately. He was making me flutter with his electric touch and starlit attention.

"What do you know about Claire?"

His gaze went from starry and open to perplexed. "I know what you do. That she's adorable, but with a mystifying aura. She is clearly very bright and—"

"She's yours."

Giovanni's hands dropped to his sides like lead weights were attached to his wrists. He stepped back, clearly stunned. "Ex-explain."

"You didn't know?"

"Cora! Jesus! Explain!" He paced back and forth. "I can't comprehend what you are telling me," he said in a freaked way, so desperate that I suddenly believed he had no idea about Claire. I stepped to him and wrapped him in a hug. I wasn't prepared for his desperately clutching hug in return. His arms encircled me; his hands splayed out over my back as he pressed me to him. His chin rested atop my head; his heart hammered in his chest. "Please tell me what you're talking about," he whispered. "I don't believe what you are saying."

"I read it in her medical file," I said, infusing my words with calmness, though my insides were quaking. "It said you're the father."

Holding on to me like a life preserver, he stumbled back and sat on the edge of the bed, his hands sliding a streak of sparks over my hips.

"Look at her, G. It's obvious."

Giovanni's eyes were a palette of bewilderment, anger, hope-fulness... "I want to go see her. I want to see Claire now."

"You don't want to confront Dr. M? He created a child from your…um…genetic material." I didn't even want to think about how *that* was obtained. "Without your permission or knowledge."

"Yes, yes…but Cora, don't you understand?" He grabbed my shoulders, his voice desperate and urgent. "If what you're saying is true, she's part of me. Family. My blood."

I understood. Giovanni had lost everyone he loved in one swoop. "But—but we need to talk to him right now. If he's capable of doing something so underhanded and morally wrong, who knows what else he's capable of?" I pulled his hand and he followed, bewildered but willing.

No sooner did we step to the door and open it than we faced my mom and Abraham standing on the other side. Abraham looked demolished and his emotional state was obviously affecting my mom. "We're leaving to talk to Dr. M about something," I said. "What's wrong?"

"Abraham is worried," my mother said. "It's getting late and Teruko and Mari have not returned."

"Maybe they're just enjoying themselves, enjoying being out," Giovanni said, but Mom shook her head violently and began pacing in circles. I didn't like to see the shadows of her locked-up self. "No, no, no. He's a seer. A clairvoyant. He saw a vision of something terrible happening to Teruko," she said.

Dread hit me like a cold wind. "And Mari?" I couldn't bear to lose anyone else. "What did you see, Abraham?"

Stooped and frail, his firm grip surprised me when his shaky hand grasped my shoulder. His answer came out in one cracked rasp. "Death."

FORTY-FIVE

Finn

"Kill me, you foul Arrazi hag. But if you do, I won't be able to tell you where the Scintilla are hiding."

Ultana's grip instantly released from Mari's chin. But then, quick as a whip, she slapped her. Hard. Mari's head snapped back, equally fast, and even though tears glossed her brown eyes, she stared hard at Ultana, daring her to do it again. I had to hand it to Mari. She was tough and fast on her feet, but I badly wanted to believe she wouldn't tell them. She was a scrapper and she was buying time.

"How do you know of the Scintilla or the Arrazi?" Ultana asked in a measured tone, though her breathing pitched with anger. I liked to see her taken so off guard.

Mari's trembling chin lifted. "You'd love to think the world is ignorant about people like you. But you'd be shocked," Mari said, rubbing her cheek. "Soon, the world will know all about you and the Scintilla. I bet they lock every last one of you up when that happens."

Something deadly but fearful passed in Ultana's eyes. "Locked up," she said, her face an inch from Mari's, "is something I will *never* be." Mari's chest heaved forward. She screamed.

"No!" I yelled. "She comes from a Scintilla family!"

I shouldn't have said it, but it was the only thing that would stop Ultana from killing her right then and there. Mari gasped and bent forward with her hand over her heart, struggling for breath.

"Get up, boy!" Ultana barked at me. I was having trouble focusing. Adrenaline had gassed me up only so much.

"He can't get up," Saoirse said to her mother. I'd nearly forgotten she was there. She stood, completely restored, with a dead girl lying at her feet.

Mari bit her trembling lip when she looked down at the open but lifeless eyes of the girl. "Teruko…" she whimpered.

"Lorcan put some kind of spell on Finn. He can't move his legs. That's why Lorcan had to find someone and bring them to us."

Ultana's head jerked to look at her son.

"Finn was talking to a girl at the party," he stammered. "A silver one, but how was I supposed to know? I'd never felt it before. I wanted her spirit, Mum," he said like a boy who'd wanted candy. "I attacked her but stopped when I saw her Xepa ring."

Ultana looked at me after a lengthy pause, where I'm sure she was wondering how in the hell a Scintilla got a ring to pass herself off as a member of the Society. "You have secrets, Mr. Doyle."

My energy flagging, I swallowed hard and tried to take in a full breath. "Don't we all?"

She chuckled. "Indeed. Kill soon or you'll die with yours. Lorcan dear, where did you find these young women?"

"In a van, by the side of the road."

Mari struggled to stand. Her eyes were on me when she said,

"I want to talk to Finn alone. I will only talk to him." Mention of the van clearly scared her.

Ultana ignored her. "Return to the van, son," she said. "Surely it's registered to someone with an address. We can start there."

"Want me to bring another warm body?" he asked.

"No need. Finn will make his choice. We will either have two dead bodies on our hands"—she looked at me—"or three."

Lastly, she addressed Mari. "We may not need you for information after all. And clearly, though he needs you in order to live, Finn's pesky conscience won't allow him to do with you what is necessary. You've bought yourself hours, at most." She patted her own cheek. "I'm feeling a bit peaky myself, and I have no compunction about using you."

Mari's nostrils flared as she glared at Ultana with no effort to disguise her contempt. "This world would be so much better without people like you. How do you live with yourself?"

"I've had *many* years to adjust, and I find it quite easy to live with myself. You learn over time to keep what you must and to discard what is not useful. So you see, I have discarded my chafing conscience. It's a trifling thing meant to keep us marching in line. I am Arrazi. I do not live by other people's rules."

Forty-Six

Cora

"Death?"

I fought for each demanding breath. I couldn't face death. Not again. I used to associate black with death. Dark oblivion. White was the color of death now. But Abraham didn't say anything about the Arrazi in his vision.

"How? Can you see how it happens? When?"

Abraham lifted my free hand and traced a spiral in my palm. "I only hear a song of death," he said in his Japanese accent, his finger circling over and over. "It is louder now."

Adrenaline flooded my body and sent my silver aura spiking around me. The four of us stood in the hall, our Scintilla auras flaring. Seriously, what had I done in another life to deserve this fresh, hot hell?

Giovanni grabbed my hand and held it. "We'll go look for them."

"Thank you," I said, giving his hand a squeeze. After the inconceivable news he'd received, it was incredibly sweet for him to suspend that, for now, and see if we could find Mari and Teruko before her grandfather's vision of death could come true.

If it hadn't already.

We all ran down the hall toward the elevators. A white-clothed attendant asked if we needed assistance.

"Yes," I said. "We need to see Dr. M right away. It's an emergency."

"I'm afraid Dr. M is not currently present in the facility," the man said, his curious gaze falling on each of us in turn. The tuft of black that flew into his aura from his mouth sent me into a rage.

"Not pres—where is he? I know you're lying. Call him! It's an emergency! We need to know if there's a way to reach Teruko. She and my cousin may be in danger and every second that we stand here wasting time is time that could be spent helping them!"

"Hey," said Dun, poking his head out from his room with pillow creases in his cheek. "What's with the rowdiness?"

A ripple of concern passed over the attendant's placid face and then faded. "I'm sorry. The doctor cannot be disturbed."

Giovanni clutched the man by his shirt, lifting him to his toes. "*Disturb him.*"

Dun ran over as I pushed the elevator button. "If you can't contact him, then tell him we had to go. We need a car so we can go look for the girls. Who is in charge of the cars around here?" I jabbed my finger on the button again. Unresponsive.

Dun touched my shoulder. "Cora? Look for what girls? Is it Mari?" he asked with a stricken look. I nodded.

The man held up his hand to me, blocking me from the elevator control panel. "You cannot leave the facility, miss. It is prohibited."

A few awful beats of silence followed before at least three of us shouted for an explanation.

I kicked the elevator doors and very nearly kicked the man. "'Prohibited' is not a word I'll accept right now! I'll be damned if you're going to tell me I'm not free to walk out of this facility!" I turned to Giovanni. "I'd never have agreed to come here if someone was going to make me a prisoner again!" The same despairing panic that had overtaken me in Clancy's keep arose in me.

Giovanni's response was to give the guy another hearty shake by his shirt like a cloth doll. "You punch in the elevator code and help us get out of here or be responsible for the lives that are lost."

I reached for the buttons with the intention of doing what I'd done with the computer earlier, but before I reached it, I felt stinging hot voltage nick me in the side of my neck. Screams rang around me like broken glass bells. My muscles folded in half. The hallway rotated in distorted angles as I fell to the floor. Clouds of silver drifted down like stars.

My body jerked as if I'd been falling. My eyes sprang open. A flat, firm bed was underneath me, harsh fluorescent lights above. In my groggy state, I tried to move but couldn't. Every limb was pinned to the table. Even my head was strapped down. I struggled to loose myself, but it did nothing but exhaust me. Despair was a tempest raging from my chest outward, a mix of disbelief and hopelessness. A hot tear trickled down my temple. I hadn't realized I was crying. But of course I was. How could I not?

My cousin was missing, possibly dead, and I was trapped like some kind of rabid animal in this enigma of a research facility. "Hey!" I screamed. "Hey!" An excruciating amount of silence passed before I heard someone moving and the telltale grunts of the same struggle I'd just endured.

Angry words in Italian wrapped around me like shiny pearls. Giovanni.

"I'm here with you," I gasped. The sound of struggling stopped.

"I'm going to kill someone," he said, the bloody promise of vengeance dripping from the knife of his words. Giovanni was obsessed with retaliation in a way that I wasn't, but at times like this, I could see his point. "Is anyone else in here?" he asked.

"Cora?" my mom's soft voice called out. I really *could* kill, thinking of my mother, frightened and trapped. She didn't deserve another day in captivity. Not. One. More. We thought we were safe.

"I love you, Mom." My words, a staccato attempt to calm her and—and what if I never had another chance to say them? What if we never had the opportunity to be a mother and daughter? What if these last couple of weeks, these fleeting moments, were all we'd ever have? There was a stream of things running through my head, but the only thought that rose to the top over and over again was, "I love you."

Dun was the last to come to. He yelled out a warrior's cry after battling the straps with no success. His anguish stoked my own. I wanted to scream with him. The longer we lay here, the worse our chances of saving Mari and Teruko. "Abraham?" I asked, wanting to ask him exactly what he'd seen in his mind's eye. I'd find a way out of here, but that was one step. How could I find the girls in a city as big as Dublin? *Please let him be wrong.* "Abraham?" I called again.

"He's dead," Dr. M said from somewhere in the room. The strike of a hammer.

Mom began to cry.

Dr. M approached and stood over me, looking down with an expression so sympathetic that I vowed to slap it off him when my hands were free. "His heart failed with the shock from the electrodes. I'm sorry to have to resort to such medieval practices, but you must know it is not acceptable to attack my staff."

My back teeth ground together so hard that pain shot through my jaw. "The longer you rob us of our freedom, the longer it will take to find Mari and Teruko. Abraham said that—"

"I'm well aware of the situation, Ms. Sandoval. We used a tracking device, and the van has already been recovered. Regretfully, the girls were not found."

"So you have no idea what happened to them?"

"I do have some idea. I'm going to release your restraints now. There's footage from the van I'd like to show you. I trust you won't be exhibiting any more aggressive behavior."

"*Don't* trust me," I growled.

That seemed to amuse him. "Fair play. You can trust me, however. You can trust that you will severely regret it if you fight." He shook his head sadly. "All of this is so unnecessary. We're on the same team."

With the metallic click of a latch, one of my arms came free. A quiet, efficient worker helped to undo the rest of my straps. As soon as the last restraint fell away, I bolted upright, swung my legs sideways, and kicked Dr. M in the stomach. He flew backward into a metal cabinet. I leaped off the table. Immediately, a gun was pointed in my face.

I shoved the barrel away. "Untie everyone, now!" I rubbed my chafed wrist and looked at the man with the gun. "You're *really* going to kill one of the most rare and valuable possessions on the planet?"

"Come with me," Dr. M said with his hand on his stomach where I'd nailed him. He showed no indication of doing as I'd demanded. I instantly felt five years old. He had colossal audacity to turn his back on me, but I realized his helper was right behind me with the gun pointed at my back, and I didn't know what his orders were. And there was Dun, the only non-Scintilla among us.

"Untie my family!"

Dr. M flinched but did not respond. "Bring Giovanni with us, as well," he told another man who nodded, soon joining us with a very pissed-off Giovanni. If they could read eye-speak, they'd see that we had nothing on our minds but kicking some ass and getting the hell out of there. Real guns, though? This was new.

I'd grown so accustomed to being afraid of the silent kill of an Arrazi. I hadn't thought of real weapons being used to threaten us. If Giovanni used his sortilege with real guns, too much could go wrong. I hoped he had the same thought. Before anything went down, I needed to see what Dr. M could show us of Mari and Teruko's disappearance.

Dr. M pushed some buttons and video footage popped up. A camera was obviously mounted in the dash of the van, and we watched as Teruko and Mari faced each other, knee to knee, locked in conversation. I'd rarely seen Mari so enamored and vibrant. Then Mari did something totally unexpected. She reached out and caressed Teruko's pale cheek. It was incredibly tender for the girl I'd always known to be tough as steel. Teruko leaned into Mari's hand, graceful as a cat leaning appreciatively into affection. They smiled shyly. My throat swelled with tears.

Mari leaned forward, held Teruko's face like a rare treasure, and kissed her waiting lips.

There was such scorching beauty in that kiss. I remembered that mix of feelings with Finn, like he was the only fire I wanted to warm by, the sweet and the sensual heat of craving. My stomach fluttered with the memory of our first kiss in the forest.

I was right about her attraction. *Oh, Mari...why didn't you tell me?* Maybe, I hoped, maybe they went off for a walk together. Maybe they were okay. Maybe they'd come back and have a love story. Then I thought of Dun. In order for Mari to have a love story with Teruko, she couldn't have one with him.

While they kissed, the camera showed someone approaching from behind the van. Both girls startled and turned toward the passenger's side door. I bit back a yell. To a normal person, it looked like the guy was simply talking to them through the window. But as Mari reached to slug him, as their bodies drooped and then slid sideways without him ever touching them, I knew they'd been weakened by someone taking their energy. Though the footage was grainy and the man's face was only from the side, when he opened the door and yanked Teruko out, I gasped with recognition.

"You know that man?" Dr. M asked.

I shuddered with the memory of his bulky mass on top of me, smelling like a mixture of old pickles and whiskey, and ruthlessly stealing from my soul. "Yes. I've been attacked by him."

"That confirms my suspicion," Dr. M said. "An Arrazi."

My bones felt like they were made of ice. "Yes. He is."

"This is the one who attacked you the night of the party?" Giovanni asked, the glint of steel in his voice.

I chewed my lip as the footage showed him jerking Mari out of the car by her arm, throwing her over his shoulder like a small child, and disappearing behind the van. The thought of Mari being hurt by him was sickening. I bent forward, feeling faint, and felt Giovanni bathe me with soothing energy, which I accepted without argument. Watching that video was torture. Surely that Arrazi would kill her. He had a coppery sadistic streak that I could feel in his energy. She had no Xepa ring on her finger. No ace up her sleeve. He would have no reason to stop.

The song of death was loud in my ears.

FORTY-SEVEN

Finn

Ultana raked her eyes over Mari, pondering, I supposed, what to do next. I prayed it wouldn't be to kill her. I also prayed Mari would keep her antagonistic gob shut. "Daughter," Ultana said with false sweetness. "Come here, please."

Saoirse walked to her mother with timid steps. "Yes?"

"How are you feeling, dear? Now that you've conquered your hunger?"

My fingers dug into my palms.

"B—better, Mum. Stronger." Saoirse's eyes were trained on the floor.

"Wonderful," Ultana said, trailing a finger under Mari's chin. Mari's nostrils flared, but she didn't flinch. "I'm willing to bet there is the sweet spice of Scintilla in this one's aura. Would you like to know how *that* feels in your blood?"

"Stop this," I said. "She has information we need. You don't have to play this cat-and-mouse game with someone…someone like *her*. It's low." I raised my chin. "Beneath us."

"I'm not a mouse!" Mari roared. No, she wasn't. I gave her a warning look and her eyebrows pressed together.

"I can get the information from her. Let me alone with her." My heart hammered. I was on dangerous ground. I needed to try to help Mari, but I also needed Ultana to trust me. This was the edge, and I was teetering over it.

"Saoirse, take our guest to the spare room on the second floor." She looked down at my legs. Saoirse reached for Mari, who jerked her arm away.

"Don't touch me! I'll kick your scrawny little ass!"

Saoirse looked at me, pained, then to her mother, and in that moment, her body went rigid, her eyes hardened. I wasn't the only one being tested by Ultana. Saoirse leaned in toward Mari and spoke low, "I am capable of killing you in less time than it takes for you to threaten me."

Ultana sneered.

The fight in Mari's face fell and her voice softened as she looked down at her friend, dead on the floor, then looked up to meet Saoirse's gaze. "You cried as you killed her. I don't think you want to kill. That, right now, is just one of the differences between you and me."

Saoirse led Mari from the room with one hand on the small of her back. Ultana and I were alone but for the dead girl on the floor. We considered each other.

"Finn, I like you," she said. "I want nothing more than for the Arrazi people to gain strength and status in this world. You want that as well, right?"

"I'm going to be honest with you, Ultana," I said, swallowing the pit in my throat. "I wish our strength and status didn't depend upon annihilating another race." She was too shrewd to serve an outright lie to, and I was already on thin ice. With Ultana Lennon, I had to mix my truths with deceit. Someone like her would swallow them better that way. I wanted nothing more than to ask her direct questions, pull the truth from her, and take off to save Mari, but I was afraid she'd feel my obvious sortilege as it affected her. Even if she now knew that I had contact with a Scintilla family, I didn't want her to know I was one of the rare Arrazi who'd taken from one. I had to bide my time. Not to mention the fact that with my legs, I wasn't taking off anywhere.

"I want to thank you for helping Saoirse. I recognize how hard the first few times can be…for some. You'd do well to banish your conscience as well. You must trust me when I tell you that *our* survival absolutely depends on *their* annihilation. Mine. Yours. Our families. I have big plans for you, and if you stop fighting what is natural, things will be much easier. You could go far, live a *very* successful life. Accept what is."

"Thank you. I'll do my best," I said, tight-jawed but attempting to sound contrite. She and I had very different measures for what made a successful life. I still didn't plan on living out one that included years of killing. I'd stick around long enough to know in my heart I'd done everything I could to help Cora and find answers. If I died after doing that, my life would have been a success.

Lorcan burst through the door moments later. "The van is gone, Mum."

Ultana sighed. My hopes rose that this would give Mari an edge and keep Cora's location a secret. For now.

"We need to dispose of her," Ultana said, motioning to Teruko like she was a piece of rubbish.

"What do you do with…the bodies…after?" I asked, genuinely curious.

Lorcan bent and scooped the girl off the floor. "Arrazi bloke nearby, he's a director at a funeral home. Cremates them for our family."

"Got it all worked out, haven't you?"

"Bet your arse. There's a whole world of logistics you obviously know nothing about."

Ultana plucked scissors from the top of a table and bent over the girl in Lorcan's arms. She was such an odd woman. Volatility ran under the surface, and I feared what she'd do next. At the same time, I had to look. Everything Ultana Lennon did was a possible clue. She held the scissors close to Teruko's head and snipped a lock of her hair where the black bled into bright pink. She laid the scissors down, and then picked up the hair between two fingers, like one would the stem of a rare flower, and held it up to the light. After that, she slipped her hand into Teruko's pocket and fished out a euro.

She didn't offer an explanation. It had the creepy effect of a serial killer taking mementos. Except this wasn't *her* kill. She walked out of the room with both items. Very soon, I heard the opening of the glass cabinet and the clinking of the coin being tossed into the collection plate.

Forty-Eight

Cora

"I fear the worst," Dr. M said as we stared at the monitor that replayed their fate over and over. "I have no idea how to find them."

I tried to appeal to him even though I seethed. "You have to let us out of here. We came to you with the genuine wish to work together to find answers. We've trusted you. You cannot keep us prisoner."

"I can, actually. For your own good. The fact that there are different energetic classes of humans is one of the best-kept secrets in human history. Have you thought about why that is? It is for your safety that I must confine you. You watched that monitor. Look what happened today. They're getting more brazen every day."

Giovanni's arm brushed my shoulder. "But neither Teruko nor Mari is Scintilla. Their abduction could have nothing to do with this."

"By an Arrazi?" I reminded him with my arms crossed. "It's connected. Maybe they know we're here."

"Right," Dr. M said, with a worried look. "If you're out there, what's to stop them from taking you?" He pointed at both of us. "*You* are the prize here. You are the coveted ones."

"You mean hunted."

"Semantics. You are wanted for what you *are*. I'm trying to replicate your energy so that we can offer it to them peacefully."

"Offer?" I asked. "You mean sell it to them, for profit."

"How do you intend to create our energy?" Giovanni asked. "By producing genetic offspring?" I knew it was only a matter of time before he swung the bat of truth at Dr. M. "I know what you did. I know that Claire is mine."

"Donating sperm does not constitute ownership, Mr. Teso. You signed the papers when you were here five years ago."

I threw up my hands. "Talk about semantics. It's his DNA! And he wasn't even an adult when he signed papers. What you did was wrong. How could you make a *child* without someone's consent?"

Dr. M stared at Giovanni for a moment. I couldn't help but feel there was another silent conversation I didn't understand. "I can't genetically create a Scintilla. I've tried every method, to no avail. It comes to this—artificial means of creating a being with the energy of a purebred Scintilla has proven impossible. Claire was my grand experiment. And"—he sighed dramatically—"my grand failure. I don't know why this is so. Perfectly normal humans can artificially proliferate, but not the Scintilla. I can only conclude that realizing the aim of regenerating Scintilla energy will only be achieved by *natural* means. I believe that is the missing component. It's the only theory I've been unable to test in a controlled environment. I must test out this hypothesis with the two of you. Everything else is years in the making and we're running out of time."

His last statement pinned me in place. My head buzzed,

whirling around and around, spitting out question after question. *Did he just say what I think he said?*

Giovanni stood in stunned silence. I already knew he desired a world with more Scintilla so we could somehow decimate the Arrazi and win our freedom once and for all. But if I understood correctly what Dr. M was getting at, it was the most ridiculous plan I'd ever heard. "The two of us cannot populate this earth with more Scintilla, you insane piece of—"

Dr. M pointed his finger. "Be careful what you say now, dear Cora. You have *no* power here."

"You don't get to tell me I have no power over my own body!" My pulse rocketed so high, I felt like it was about to burst out of my chest.

"This is all about power," Giovanni said, still too calm, too level. I watched him carefully, aware that his life had definitely prepared him to be more cunning than I. "You want something from *us*. We have more power than you realize."

"This is about the world ripping apart at the seams," the doctor said. "This is about survival, not only for one species but of humankind on Earth."

"This is about money *and* power," I said. "The only two things men like you care about. You want us to believe that you suddenly subscribe to the 'world is going to hell in a handbasket and we're the saviors' theory? I don't even buy that theory, and it was my own father who first suggested it. Clancy Mulcarr told me that we were worth a fortune on the black market. This is about either money or power, or both. No rational person would suggest what you're suggesting if there weren't something in it for them. I've heard enough of this," I said, turning away. "I *have* to go find my cousin."

Dr. M ignored my statement. "You get to save at least one

Scintilla from being sold on the black market. Don't accuse me of wanting to profit from you. I could have sold all of you already if that were my aim."

My blood turned to ice. "Who will we save?" But before he opened his mouth to speak, I knew. I stood and stepped close to him, thrusting my hand at his chest. "You're threatening to sell my mother?"

Two more men entered the room, armed, waving their guns in my face. That made four. Hands clasped my shoulders from behind. Giovanni pushed me behind him to shield me.

"I may not see auras, but I can see plain as day that you're enamored with her," Dr. M said to Giovanni. "We don't have the luxury of time. This is the only theory I've not yet been able to test because I've never had a pure Scintilla female to test before now. It's vital to my research and to the survival of Scintilla all over the world." He smoothed his hair back. "I have no doubt that you'll be *motivated,* both of you, to let nature take its course for the greater good."

I pulled from Giovanni's arms and lunged for Dr. M, not caring about the men and their guns. Would they shoot me if I was so valuable? "My mother has been through hell! How can you do this to her?" I screamed. "And you're just going to wash your hands of Mari and Teruko? I swear you will pay for this. I swear it. You are an evil, opportunistic son of a bitch."

It was Giovanni who pulled me back and held me against him.

Dr. M pinched the bridge of his nose like I was an exasperating child. "Cora, in war, a great many atrocities can be justified. I am called upon to do things that might seem wrong to some. What you're being asked to do, by comparison, is rather basic." He pointed to a door. "Through that door is another world where the only thing that you need concern yourself with is how willing you are to not only help save your mother, but your whole race. Use your time wisely. You won't have much of it."

The men motioned with the tips of their guns for us to go through the door. I looked to Giovanni and he blinked hard. At least in the short term, it would get guns out of our faces. With five men and four guns, he couldn't risk using his sortilege to disarm them. The time for combat would have to wait. Now was a time for strategizing.

I had to get us out of this place, all of us. I shoved past Giovanni and kicked the door open. "He's the worst kind of crazy, Giovanni. He's crazy with a cause. Oh my God." I gasped. "That's what the holes mean. He's not lying. He's imbalanced. He thinks he's going to change the world. Coming here was a mistake."

We were sealed in what looked like an apartment. There was a living room with plush couches, a television, warm lamps. More frickin' fish.

"The last time I was here, I was fifteen. I thought he wanted to find more Scintilla, to help keep us safe. I knew he wanted to re-create our energy, but I thought he meant scientifically. I was young and desperate, and when asked to donate sperm, I assumed he wanted to run tests on it. I had no idea he'd go this far, Cora. None."

"We can't give in," I said. "Even if we did do what he's demanding, what do you think would happen after that, huh? You think he just wants to be *Uncle M* to a posse of our Scintilla babies? No way." I wore a path back and forth on the carpet. "No way is this happening." My hands clenched. My body shook violently. My every breath was snatched out of my mouth before I could fight for another.

"Cora—"

"No!"

Giovanni stared at the ground. "I was going to suggest we try to sleep. We need to think. We need a plan to get out of this appalling forced intimacy. I will not stand before you and say I don't want you. But not like this. *Never* like this." His sad blue eyes glossed over. "My dreams were always of you facing me with love in your eyes, tilting your flower of a face up to me to be kissed, offering your lips because…because you wanted me, too. I'd never want you coerced. God, Cora…it takes something potentially beautiful and twists it into something so ugly."

I wasn't surprised at what he said. I knew. I'd fought similar yearnings, because while they may have been right in some corner of my broken heart, they were wrong to the whole of it. Would I ever let the light shine in again, even if it was a lesser light than the one it knew with Finn?

"Say something."

"What you feel," I said, unable to admit my confused feelings, "is as much of a farce as what Finn felt for me. We are what we are. We cannot help *attracting* each other. It's an illusion from our energy, a mirage."

"By that description, you will never believe in love."

"No," I said, the press of hurt spreading like a weighted blanket over my body. "I don't believe in love anymore."

"It's not love you don't believe in, Cora. It's your own lovability."

What did it matter what I believed? We weren't locked up in this pretend house to talk about love. The reality was too horrible. My cousin was missing, and we were prisoners again— and we were being asked to create a life to save a life.

FORTY-NINE

Finn

Lorcan wordlessly carried the body out of the house and drove away. It was an ugly business, all of it.

My desperate thoughts immediately turned to Mari, upstairs. How could I get her out? Cora had already lost her father. I couldn't let another of her family be taken. Mari didn't deserve this. No one did.

"I can't make your legs work, but I can keep you company until they do," Saoirse said, startling me from my thoughts. She stood in the doorway with something in her hand. Color had returned to her face. Though she was still pale, peachy warmth spread like a crushed flower on her cheeks.

I was a wilted weed in comparison.

"What's happening with her?" I asked, pointing upward and struggling for the energy to talk. "You know how I feel about this. I can't kill someone I know."

Saoirse pursed her lips. "It's a sticky situation, all right." She sat down, facing me. "My mother has made it clear that the girl—"

"Mari."

"…that she can't walk out of here after what she's seen and knows. If word got out, the world would accuse us of murder."

"We *are* murderers."

"Still," she pressed on, "I think the only thing keeping her alive is the information she dangled. She's either very smart or very rash. Since I do know my mother wants to find three Scintilla, she'll let her live until she's sure she can't help her get them."

"How do you know your mom wants three?" I asked, intent on getting the truth from her. "Why three specifically? What's the significance?"

"Wow. That's a lot of questions. I'm not sure I can answer them all, but I—I feel like I can tell you anything," Saoirse said, though her eyes showed resistance. It was interesting, watching her fight. I realized I'd better pay attention to the level of fight in a person to truly know if they strained to hide a truth. There were more ways to deceive than an outright lie.

"I overheard my mum telling your uncle that three Scintilla together were vital. I only caught the tail end of the conversation, but she told him that it could liberate us."

"*Liberate?*" Knowing my selfish uncle, he took whatever Ultana had told him and decided he'd pretend to be her humble servant, then go off and benefit from finding and keeping three for himself. Still, knowing *why* three was their goal would be good knowledge to have. I planned to ask my mother if she knew anything about the significance of three as soon as possible.

If they were smart, Cora and the others would split up. Their collective energies were already enough to cause Arrazi to take notice. That was how Clancy had found their little cottage rental. Arrazi might not be able to see auras, but they could sniff them on the wind like mongrel dogs.

"I don't know what my mother meant by 'liberate.' She confounds me half the time, and the other half, she's so secretive I never know what's truly going on. She's free with her knowledge of our history—a locked door when it comes to her dealings with the Society. I think she's trying to protect Lorcan and me."

Her hand fell to my arm and she squeezed softly, her eyes sincere. "I think I've said enough, except"—she paused and touched her fingers over her lips—"I want to thank you, Finn, for being here for me for one of the worst moments of my life. I'll never forget how you tried to help me through it. I know it's hard for you, too."

She set a deck of cards on my dead leg and smiled, her body language switching from serious to playful. "The least I can do is keep you company until you aren't our reluctant guest anymore."

"Saoirse, seriously, I can't dodder with cards at a time like this."

She slid the cards from their box into her palm. "I'm just going to give you a reading. I believe the cards can help."

"Tarot cards?" I guessed, having a quick look at the deck. "I've never had a tarot card reading before."

She set the deck down between us. Her head bent over the cards in concentration, and a stray bolt of red hair dangled down against her cheek. "Okay, Finn, hold one thought or one question in your mind."

No worries, there.

Saoirse shuffled, and with quick practiced flicks of her wrist she placed three cards on the chaise. "Past, present, future," she said, tapping each, one by one. "For past," she said, flipping the card over, "the High Priestess reversed. This is a card about secrets and knowledge withheld. It indicates there's something in your past that you haven't fully dealt with, perhaps denying something you know deep down is true. It could also mean you're worrying excessively about someone else's problems." Her eyes blinked toward the upstairs floor before she turned the second card over.

"This is your present, the Nine of Swords. Nightmares? Memories haunting you? Basically, Finn, you're spending lots of time stressing and obsessing about this corner you feel you're trapped in."

The cards for past and present were pretty accurate.

"For future," she said, flipping the card over. "The Two of Cups." Her voice ended on an up-note of surprise. I had no idea what that card meant, or why it caused a slip of a smile to lift one side of her mouth.

On the card, a man and a woman stared deeply into each other's eyes. They each held a golden chalice from which they poured the contents from their own cups down into a single cup between them. Two snakes rose and twisted together above the man and woman.

"What's that snake symbol? I've seen it somewhere."

"You've seen it because physicians use it. Likely, it's on your parents' doctoral certificates. It symbolizes healing and balance. In tarot, the two snakes rising up represent duality. The fact that they're intertwined represents their union or reconciliation of opposites."

"Duality?"

"The dark and light within us. Pouring their separate cups into the single cup depicts that union. They are offering of what they each uniquely have and combining them into something greater."

"And the red lion's head?" I asked. "What's that about?"

"It's called the caduceus. It's a symbol of strength and cour-age. Also, of attraction, or passion. Fire energy. It speaks of the beauty and power when two come together and become one," she said with a blush unfurling on her chest. She'd been looking down at the cards the whole time as she spoke, but tilted her head and gave me a shy, sideways peek. "The Two of Cups is a lover's card."

I shot a surprised glance at her and swallowed hard. "Is that right?"

"Yes," she said, her voice descending to a demure hush. "It suggests that it may be the time for you to join with another and work in partnership. It—it would be a very favorable time for that." She locked stares with me. "According to the cards."

Saoirse's body tilted closer. "I shouldn't…" She bit her lip as her exploratory sea-glass gaze roamed my face. The bend in her brows showed uncertainty before an inner truth displaced the question in her eyes and she leaned fully forward, brushing her lips softly, tentatively, against mine.

The intimate contact with another was comforting even as it stunned me. Her mouth was warm, inviting. There was a sweet hesitancy in her kiss, and the dude in me wanted to draw that out, see what fire was underneath the restraint. I felt a rush of surprise and flattery, but I didn't want Saoirse. I didn't want shy and restrained. I wanted intensity. I wanted to be pushed up against a tree. I wanted Cora.

It was always going to be Cora.

It wasn't that I never wanted to be kissed again. It felt damn good. But the impression was much like having ale when all you want in this world is a glass of whiskey. Good, damn enjoyable even, but not what I *really* wanted. I gently pressed my hand to her collarbone and ended the kiss.

Hurt flashed in her eyes.

"I'm sorry, I—"

"Don't be. I don't know what possessed me." She stood and the tarot cards spilled to the floor. "That's bad luck," she said, looking down.

She'd taken the Two of Cups personally, I realized. But when I saw that card and listened to her explanations of it, all I could think of was Cora and me. We could not be more opposite. "Duality" could not be expressed more perfectly than how we were made so different. When Saoirse had said "reconciliation of opposites," stubborn, irrepressible hope welled up in me.

"I had every intention of never acting on that impulse." A mortified look passed over her. "I can't believe I kissed you. I feel like a right fool."

"No, don't," I said. "Go on. I feel wretched. You're lovely. Very lovely, Saoirse. But it's like I said before, I'm ruined."

Her brow shot up. "Ruined? I figured you were being dramatic."

"I don't know if I'll ever love anyone else. I mean, I know you weren't talking love and it was just a kiss and all, but—"

"She must have been something incredibly special, Finn."

"Aye. She was that."

"What happened?"

The doorbell rang, a welcome interruption, and Saoirse went to answer it. Clancy's deep, booming voice pounded like a heavy stone tossed across the marble floors. Hell. He was the last person I wanted to see right now, and I didn't want him anywhere near Mari. He followed Saoirse into the room.

"What's this, lad?" Clancy said, seeing me on the chaise. His vest strained against his belly and he kept his hands in his pockets as he looked me over with a concern I hadn't seen in his eyes for some time. "You need to kill."

"Aye," I admitted. "And Lorcan seems to have put some kind

of hex on me." Why lie? Clancy should know that Lorcan had a sortilege, and I wanted to see if my uncle would know any way to help me since Ultana hadn't been interested to try. I think she liked seeing me helpless, a fly paralyzed and dangling in her web.

"What happened? *Exactly* what did he say?"

"He said if I repeated something I said to him that I'd not be able to walk for a day."

"So, it wasn't an outright curse? It was, if you do *this* then *that'll* happen?"

"I don't see the difference. The outcome is still the same. I can't *fookin'* walk."

"There's a great bit o' difference. Something being dependent upon something else is a wily curse in that it leaves it up to you whether or not it befalls you. The power is all yours. It's known as a *geis*. It can be a curse or a blessing but is entirely dependent upon your obedience to it." He scratched his beard. "I've not heard of someone having that ability in eons. You're saying that lump of an empty head can do this?" Clancy looked to Saoirse and tipped his head apologetically.

Saoirse shrugged. "I happen to agree, so no offense taken."

"Too bad he can't be muzzled. I had no idea he had a sortilege. Do *you*, child?" Clancy asked her.

"No."

"How did he get it?"

I knew my uncle's mind would leap straight to the right conclusion. Maybe it'd do him good to know Ultana and Lorcan Lennon were much more dangerous than he thought.

"He took from a Scintilla. Can the *geis* be undone?" I asked.

"Not that I know of. You'll have to wait it out. You're lucky he didn't say 'forever' rather than a day."

"Why are you here?" I asked with a profound edge to my voice.

"Mind yourself. Ultana has a message for me from the head of the Society."

"Who *is* the head?" I asked, quickly slipping the noose of truth around his neck.

Clancy immediately sensed what I'd done and gave me a reproachful look. He seemed to fight it as Saoirse had but finally said, "Don't be impertinent, boy. I don't know who the head of the Society is. I don't even know if *she* knows. Trails are less worn the higher up the path you go."

Ultana came in, gave me a curt nod, and whisked Clancy away. I heard her office door open and close down the hall. I fervently wished for two things: that she'd not notice anything amiss in her office, and that she'd be as cagey as I suspected she was and say nothing to my uncle about Mari being upstairs. Mari's life depended on many things, most of which I had little control over at the moment.

All too soon, their meeting concluded. My uncle popped his head through the door and winked. I had no idea what that meant, but it set me on edge. I was not Clancy's coconspirator. Gone was the warm relationship we once had. It was another of my losses.

There was a time when I preferred his company over my parents', especially in the last few months when their insistence that I give up my music in favor of medicine increased and when their restrictions grew more severe. Uncle Clancy seemed to counter that with full support of my music, as he was a musician, too. He'd shown trust in me with the business of running the pub, and he encouraged my longing for more freedom. He was the reason I got to go to America. Now I knew why.

My heart throbbed sorely with the betrayal. I once loved and respected my uncle.

Love has the most potent ability to crack you.

"I passed a job your way," Clancy said in a low voice, waggling his bushy white eyebrows like this was the most grand news ever. "After you're up and moving, of course. You're right useless as you are now. I'll inform your mother." He laughed on his way out the door.

"Useless," I muttered. Unless I could find proof otherwise, all Arrazi were useless.

Fifty

Finn

"Your uncle places a great deal of faith in you, Finn." Ultana leaned against the doorframe with her arms crossed. "I offered him a very important job and he's asked that *you* be entrusted with it. I'm not certain what to make of his request. I'm not naturally inclined toward trust until it's conclusively earned."

"I'm not going to fall all over myself to convince you to trust me, Ultana," I said, irritated. I was struggling to stay alert. She had to play with me when I could barely keep my head upright? Saoirse made a sound from the other side of the room but quickly scurried out when her mother glared. I knew a baited hook when one was dangled in front of me, and I didn't want any part of a job of Clancy's.

I'd seen him at work.

"Sometimes trust is a leap of faith," I said.

"Faith." Her black lace-up boots tapped on the floor as she approached and lifted my chin, forcing me to face her. But for the wrinkles that stretched from it, the V on her face was as clear as a branding. There was no way it was a birthmark. "I have faith in very little," she said. "Faith is a barren plate for those who hunger for certainty. In this world, nothing is certain."

"Don't touch me like I'm a child," I said, jerking my chin from her grasp. My fists clenched against the urge to shove her away, but I didn't honestly think I had the strength. My own death was imminent and I didn't care by whose hand it came, so long as it came after I accomplished the only thing I lived to do. Beyond that, the only death I feared was any death I caused.

Ultana laughed, slapping her one hand on her thigh. "Oh, but I do have faith in your ability to keep me amused." Her tone turned serious again. "The Society has many holdings and companies all over the world. Despite your obvious suspicion of their motives, you might be interested to know that one of their Japanese subsidiaries funds important research that is vital to our future survival." She bent low and looked me in the eye. "You're very keen to find a way to live without killing, are you not?"

"Wouldn't you rather live without killing?"

Her eyes turned skyward, thoughtful. The thin, veined skin around her eyes folded as she squinted, considering my question. I couldn't believe how long she took in thinking it over; nor again, how her profile so mirrored that of the Michelangelo drawing in her office. Her gaze returned to me. "Killing can be *inconvenient*, at times. This is why it's vital that research continue on synthetic ways to manufacture the energy we need. If successful, then distasteful events such as what transpired today in my home won't have to happen again."

There was a quickening in my gut as I pondered the possibilities. Hope rose in me like frothy cream. "I'd love to know more about this research." I had no idea people were working on this while I was out killing trees.

"Your uncle said you'd say that. One of the Society's holdings is a facility here in Dublin that has been working tirelessly on energy research. I've been expecting a report to arrive via courier about an exciting new development at the facility, but no one has arrived. While the researcher seems to be enormously devoted to the work and is doing his due diligence, it's high time for a visit to see the developments in person."

That didn't actually sound so bad. "I want to go," I assured her, excited because of the potential *and* because I'd felt the first tingling of sensation in my toes.

"Of course you want to," she said, looking down at the wiggling movement of the blanket at my feet. Nothing escaped her notice. "As soon as you *fall all over yourself* proving that I can trust you, you will be permitted to go."

A tidal wave of sensation suddenly washed from my feet all the way up my legs. As fast as it had been taken from me, my mobility had returned. Lorcan's *geis* did say "a day" and it must have run its course. Because I was so weakened in spirit, I fought to stand, but once I did I towered over Ultana, which was a much more comfortable vantage from which to face her. "Trust me. I'm ready. Finding a way to be free of this hell is the only thing I'm interested in."

She smirked. "Excellent. Come with me."

With every stair we took, my anticipation sank lower. I knew where she was taking me. And I knew without a doubt, like a brainless mackerel, I'd taken her bait. When someone has what you want most, they wield the hook.

Ultana opened the door and strode in. I was more on guard, fully expecting someone with Mari's temperament to be at the ready to bash our heads in. I was actually disappointed she wasn't—even more so when I saw why.

Mari was restrained by ropes to a wooden chair. Her head

bobbed oddly when we walked in. Her aura felt weak to me, like a pulse thrumming faintly through layers of clothing. It was enough to spike my raring need, however. She looked disoriented. There'd obviously been a row of some kind with Ultana. Swelling encircled her left eye from which she peered sidelong at us.

"Finn and I were just discussing trust and faith," Ultana said. "He feels trust is a leap of faith. I feel it's a gift bestowed after demonstrable acts. Where do you stand on this?" she asked Mari. My stomach knotted with dread and palpable hunger. It took every bit of strength to tamp it down.

Mari licked her swollen lip and fought to pull her chin up. Her eyes blinked heavily. Ultana had obviously depleted her aura already, but she found the strength to laser a stare that had enough hateful spite in it to burn a hole in iron. "I have *faith* in the fact that I'd beat your ass if you weren't a monster. I *trust* you know this and that's why you've tied me up. To make it a fair fight 'n' all."

Jaysus, could she not control her mouth for even one minute? I shook my head and gave Mari a warning look from behind Ultana. Ultana turned to me. I thought she was about to say something as her upper lip curled into a sneer, but without taking her eyes from me, she backhanded Mari as hard as I'd ever seen a woman hit someone.

I leaped forward but halted when Ultana held up her stump of a hand, and from Mari's scream I could tell she was being taken from. "Move again, and I will kill her." Mari gasped as Ultana released her hold on Mari's spirit. "I will ask the questions," Ultana said, slightly panting. "And for every dissatisfactory nonanswer she gives, *you* will take from her."

"No."

The malicious look I received chilled me. I'd been stupid not to fear Ultana Lennon. "Are you putting this common human's life before your own? You do this, and I will give you the first opportunity to get what you so desperately want. You could save so many people."

"You said they were working on it, not that it had been achieved. I'm willing to die to save her, yes."

"Your death will not save her!" she bellowed, spit flying from her lips. "You do this, Finn, or I will kill her right here, right now."

It was all I could do to look at Mari. But she deserved for me to look her in the eyes. "Please, Mari. Tell her what you *can*," I said, hoping she understood that I didn't want Cora's whereabouts compromised. I wanted this all to stop. If this research facility had a possible solution, then maybe no one else would have to die. I could barely get the next words out, but I needed Mari to know. "There is no part of me that wants this. I do *not* want to do this."

Mari blinked a slow blink of understanding.

Ultana stood next to me. "You know of us because you have family who are Scintilla?"

"I didn't say that. He did."

"No point in denying it. I can taste it. How many of your family are Scintilla?"

When Mari didn't answer me, Ultana nudged my arm. I had zero practice with any kind of finesse. All I could think of was what my father had told me. *There are ways to make it easier on them.* Imagining the *anahata* for the heart chakra, I directed my energy on Mari's heart center, trying to pull gently from her spirit. Her head jerked up when I started. A look of pain and loathing flashed in her eyes. I stopped and Ultana leered at me, muttering under her breath about weakness. Mari's energy pumped through my blood, giving me a momentary hit of vigor. I hated that I felt like a tiger wanting to lunge at the prey in front of me.

"How many?" Ultana asked her again.

"If you're going to kill me anyway, what's my motivation to tell you?" Mari asked. Ultana's response was to nudge me, harder this time. I held my breath and pulled from Mari's aura again. Traces of intoxicating Scintilla energy ran through her soul.

Mari cried out, tears dropping onto her lap. "Three, that I know of."

Just what Ultana wanted to hear.

"Are they in Ireland?"

"Screw you."

Ultana shoved me aside, and Mari's body jerked forward so hard, the chair screeched on the floor. Ultana released her hold, and Mari's head arched back in a yell. Not a cry, not a whimper— a primal scream. She was angry and shook a traitorous tear from her cheek when she looked at me. "They are scattered." Mari gasped. "To the winds," she said, "because—because they know the Arrazi want three of them."

I held in my relieved sigh, but still Ultana looked at me with suspicion. If what Mari said was true, it was possibly the smartest thing the trio could have done. Though I worried for Cora to be alone, and for her wee mother as well.

"How do they know the Arrazi seek three?" Ultana asked.

Mari hesitated too long, and Ultana practically knocked my rib out with her elbow. I took from Mari again, if only to spare her the agony of Ultana's viciousness, drawing Mari's sweet aura slowly as I could from her body. My self-control was faltering. I needed completion so badly. I desired that flame that burned within her. I shook with want but kept Cora's sweet face in my mind. I could control this. There had to be a way out.

"You know about baby rattlesnakes, Finn?" Mari gasped when I stopped. She was completely slumped over, her black hair pointing like sharp charcoal pencils toward the floor. Her body swayed in the chair, but the ropes held her mostly upright. "The baby ones…are the most…dangerous," she said in halted speech. "They can't control their venom. Careful the baby ones."

I didn't understand. Was Mari using what little chances she had to take jabs at me for my lack of finesse because I was a young, inexperienced Arrazi? Was she saying that I was hurting her more than Ultana? That didn't seem possible. It felt like code.

"Where are they?" Ultana asked.

Mari struggled mightily to look up. Dread pooled in my gut. She wasn't going to play along. I both admired her and was infuriated by her.

"Stop this," I begged Ultana. "Maybe she doesn't know. Or, if she does, she can obviously keep their whereabouts a secret, so she can keep us a secret. Let her go! I'll do anything you want. Let her go." I wasn't aware that tears flowed down my cheeks until I saw the perplexed look on Ultana's face as she touched one, almost as though she'd never seen tears before. "I'm begging you, Ultana…"

"Do it, you pussy!" Mari screamed at me through her own tears. "I'm not going to tell her what she wants to know."

"My thoughts exactly." Ultana cackled. "Enough of this. Kill her now or I will kill her myself. I very much want to."

"Come here," Mari said weakly. Her eyes implored. I slid onto my knees in front of her, shaking with dread and desperation and hunger. "I know you're trying, but I'm not leaving here alive," she whispered. "We both know that. *Please*, Finn… Better to be you," she said softly, a sob escaping. "I'd rather be a part of someone who loves her."

"I can't."

Behind me, Ultana gave an impatient call of my name—a

warning that her tolerance was through and time had run out.

"Please…"

I placed my hands on Mari's face and lifted it up. "I'm so sorry," I said, looking into her eyes. "Forgive me."

I shook as I hugged Mari and held her close to me, stroking her hair while siphoning her aura into mine. A knife was at both our throats. Next to Cora, Mari was the bravest person I'd ever known. Slowly, gently, I pulled from her until I felt a snap of release, and a seismic blast of strong and vivacious energy amplified in my own. The full weight of her head fell to my shoulder.

Nauseating desolation cut me as though my being was filleted by a giant blade. Deeper guilt than I've ever known dragged its nails across the raw pink of my soul. I kissed Mari's temple. Full of strength and fury, I leaped to my feet, spun around, and pinned Ultana Lennon to the wall by her neck. "I will never forgive you for this," I spat. "I'll kill you before I ever do your dirty work again."

A raspy laugh erupted from her. What on earth could she find so comical when a man had his fist clutching her throat, more than ready to pinch the life from her? It satisfied me to see her skin turning white around my fingertips, my nails digging into the loose flesh.

"Save your worthless gift of forgiveness for yourself, lad," she choked. "And don't threaten me. I've been on this earth too long. You think a threat from *you* is going to intimidate me?" she said in a fit of maniacal giggles.

"It should." My hand rose to clutch her face.

Her gaze shifted over my shoulder before something struck hard and low at the base of my skull. Immediately, I swayed on my feet and fell to the floor. The last thing I saw was Ultana looking down on me with disdain. "Your ignorance is your biggest weakness."

Fifty-One

Cora

"Those men with guns…you know how they burst in on us when I shoved Dr. M? They were watching somehow. They've *got* to be watching us, don't you think?" Giovanni and I lay side by side in the only bed in the room. Another day had come and gone and we'd figured no way out of the makeshift apartment. There were no outer windows. Food was delivered through a metal door that my head wouldn't fit through. No one would answer our repeated yells for help.

I'd slept maybe three hours per night over the past two nights. Stress, worry, and exhaustion smudged black circles under my eyes. I'd never bitten my nails before, but now they were chewed down to the raw pink parts.

Giovanni pulled my fingers away from my mouth. "If he plans on watching *everything*, he's a sick voyeuristic fu—"

"Shhh," I whispered into his ear. "The only way we're going to get out of here is if we pretend. We have to make him believe we've accepted what has to happen." A loud, awkward gulp followed. "If he does, he'll take me out for more testing, I'm sure."

"I don't see how we're going to get out of here otherwise. Every hour is another stone stacking the odds against Mari, your mother, and Dun. Claire must be taken from this place, too. I won't let my child live under his thumb any longer."

"I know. It's been two days. The longer we take to do something, the less time they have. I don't think Dr. M will buy it if we just tell him the deed is done. We have to operate on the assumption that nothing is private. Our only chance for escape is to first get out of this room."

"If I get even one toe out of this room, they'd better prepare for a fight to the death."

"Yes," I said, feeling bloodlust heat me. "If you can pull one gun into each hand and toss me one like a movie stunt, we'd at least be armed." My stomach rolled at the thought of those big black guns. I'd never fired a gun in my life. "I have to find my mother and Dun, you must get Claire, and hopefully we'll get everyone out of here in one piece. I'm sick about Mari. Between her and my mother, I can barely stand the worry."

"I've been watching you. I see that," he said. "It's killing me to see you this way."

I smacked the pillow, rolled away from him, and went to take a shower. As hot water cascaded down my back, I was surer than ever that my plan could work. It would be the most phenomenal acting job of our lives, but if we convinced Dr. M we were on board, then he'd likely give us more freedom—false freedom that I planned to exploit to earn the real kind.

You'll never be truly free, my inner voice chided.

I toweled off and dressed, steeling myself to go out and act on my idea. Immediately. Nothing was more important to me than getting my family somewhere truly safe.

If there *was* such a place in this world…

Giovanni looked me over as I approached, hair wet, legs bare, with nothing but a large shirt to cover me. It took everything in me not to cut and run back to the bathroom. I took a deep, calming breath, reminded myself why we had to act this out, and stood before him with my palms sweating.

"Kiss me."

He took so long to reply, it was excruciating. "Please," I murmured, and then spoke louder, just in case. "I want you to kiss me."

Auras betrayed everything and his was no different. Auras spoke the truth, even when people thought they were keeping their emotions in check. His extended for me even as his arms stayed at his side. He bit his lip, another tell.

"Try to look at me with loving eyes, because I don't think I can stand to see disdain when I kiss you for the first time," he said. His voice was so tender and vulnerable, it made me realize he was as nervous as I was.

"I do see you with loving eyes, G." His brows drew up into a question; his eyes showed a sincere desire to believe me. "And this won't be the first time you've kissed me," I reminded him, recalling his passionate kiss when I'd saved his life, remembering being flipped over and his body covering mine, his hands holding mine above my head. I flushed, the memory adding more flapping to the chorus of wings already in my belly.

He narrowed his crystal-blue eyes lit with mischief. "If I do it right, it will feel like the first time. Every time."

Nerves planted my feet in one spot. I didn't know how to begin the charade but, as if in a dream, I somehow floated toward Giovanni, movement tickling the pads of my feet. Looking down, I realized the rug was ribboning in front of me because he pulled it with his sortilege, drawing me slowly to him.

He stepped forward over the mini-mountains of rug, his silver aura ticking off the beats of his heart. My own aura jumped in step with his, danced to his as it tended to do when we were close. This was all a ruse, pretend, but my body wasn't playing fair. It was in a state of willing anticipation as he reached out, remembering the way he coaxed want out of me without even touching me. My body desired to be touched. If I let myself imagine hard enough and deny why we were in this room, then I could see Giovanni with fresh eyes. I could see him the way I might have if Finn had never existed.

Openness and heat rolled off him. His energy was a force that collided with mine even before we touched. I backed away from it like a child trying to tiptoe away from the surge of a wave. My back hit the wall.

The look in his eyes sent a shock wave of exhilaration through me, and before my brain could process it, deconstruct it, or overanalyze it, his hands were pressing the wall on either side of my head, his long frame leaning forward without touching me, but almost, so close. His mouth hovered so close to my mouth. My breathing intensified, my heart pounded, and he hadn't touched me. He was teasing me. Again.

I reached up and clasped the back of his neck, yearning for the ferocity he'd once shown to reemerge. He was such a take-charge guy. Where was that now when I was nervous down to my hair follicles? But he didn't advance. He drew it out, practically *causing* me to want him. He stood tall and raised his face out of my reach, looking down at me with unmasked intensity.

"You're trembling, Cora."

"I—I know. You're making me nervous." Even my voice was quaking.

"I'm making you excited." I tried to deny it, but he put his finger over my lips as he'd done the day we first met. "Your aura shows me the truth."

I turned my head away, feeling as exposed as if I were standing naked. It occurred to me that I soon might be. *We are playacting. Faking. This is all pretend.* Giovanni bent and peered into my face. "Kiss *me*," he pleaded, softly. "Please, don't make me feel like I'm yet another person bending your will."

We looked deeply into each other's eyes. We both understood this was a dangerous game we were playing, dangerous on two levels. In a game of pretend, what was real and what was false could twist and cling together like strangling vines until you weren't sure which was which. There was an undeniable situation happening beneath the surface of our lie. As his face shone down on me with sincerity and tenderness and heart-wrenching disclosure, my heart opened to let him in.

I placed both palms on his chest, feeling the current shoot through my hands and up my arms. The pulse in his neck fired faster. It was there that I kissed him first. The soft, velvet spot of skin fluttered under my lips. He exhaled a soft moan into my hair.

Nerves fell away as I lost some of my internal battles. I tasted his skin, marveled at the increase in energy that flowed stronger between us when I dared to lower my walls. It was powerful, primal at its molten core. From there, it spread outward, enveloping us both in what looked silver to my eyes but *felt* like pink and yellow blushing into the red of desire at its tips, like a rose.

Stone-still but gazing down at me with unveiled want, he kept his arms on the wall. This allowed me to tiptoe out of my resistance to the situation. We *had* to pull this off. Dr. M had to believe we really had sex. Yet I was shocked to feel that the more I touched Giovanni, the more I wanted to. My hands wrapped over his rounded shoulders, over his arms, and ran down the coiled length of them, feeling strength in the hills and ridges of his muscles. He was so controlled. His tapered fingers clawed into the wall, but he didn't move them. Not yet.

Both of us breathed faster. Time buffered, cocooning us, shining a spotlight on where we stood chest to chest—two people whose complicated lives had become knotted by a strange destiny.

I stood on tiptoe and kissed his lips, softly at first, shoving acidic guilt down as I did. When our lips met, his control faltered. His hands slipped from the wall. He clutched me to him, burying one hand in my hair and the other at the small of my back. Opening our mouths to each other was like unlocking a vault of secret wants and unspoken yearnings, and we explored all of them with each kiss.

With a flick of his hand, the comforter on the bed flew to the footboard. He scooped me up and carried me, his kisses never stopping. He planted them on my cheek, my neck, my temple, and my waiting mouth. So gently, he laid me down and stood over me, his broad chest rising with fast breaths as he yanked his shirt over his head and dropped it on the floor. I studied his lean but muscular body—the height and commanding presence of a Viking, the languid prowl of his Italian ancestry. Objectively, I had to admit that Giovanni was striking. Sexy.

He crawled over me, his eyes traveling up my body as he did, their depths darkening with want. The blanket rose up and hovered over us like a magical cloud. I was grateful, knowing he shielded me. I closed my eyes as I pulled my own shirt over my head, throwing it off the side of the mattress.

I didn't expect him to stop and stare at my body in astonishment. I started to cross my arms. "No...*sei molto bella...*" he whispered in Italian. "You're *so* beautiful. So beautiful."

He lifted my hand and kissed the ivy marking on my finger, then turned my hand over and placed his lips on my palm where the moon etched my skin, its spiraled design blending into the life line and heart line and the pulse at my wrist. His lips brushed over each triangle on my forearms. His curls tickled my cheek and neck as he bent his head and kissed my shoulder where the key had marked me.

There was something incredibly intimate about him kissing my scars.

Slowly, he lowered himself over me. Like flint striking on steel, when our skin touched, sparks flew off in every direction. My nerves hummed, my toes tingled, my insides curved like metalwork under fire. The sensations glowed in our auras, wrapping sparks and heat around our tangled arms and legs. Our kisses grew more urgent.

"I—okay—wow," I whispered. "This—is very—convincing. Anyone would *have* to believe that we—"

Giovanni stopped and held my face between his hands. The look in his eyes was all seriousness. "It's not them I'm trying to convince, Cora."

He pressed against me, showing me in the most primal way that there could be *no* doubt his want was genuine. Mine was, too. My head swam with thoughts, my body with sensations, my being with new light. It was amazing how much light could sneak in through a tiny crack. Part of me wanted to cry.

It was another good-bye.

His head pulled back, barely, and he spoke in a hush against my lips. "I'm the one person who doesn't *need* your energy. I don't want to take from you. I want to give to you. That's how I know I love you. I will never hurt you. I—I love you."

Our enormous lie to fool Dr. M was wrapped in truth as Giovanni stamped his words on my body and my heart with sparks and kisses.

FIFTY-TWO

Finn

I had vague memories of being collected by my uncle and brought to my bed at home. My skull pounded with a lump the size of an orange, and my stomach was racked with nausea that would come whenever I stood. I'd shut up in my room in a haze of pain and guilt. I wouldn't talk or shower or eat. Mari's death played over and over in my mind. I rolled in the mud of it, coating myself with the filth of my evil.

I don't know what I proved. I only knew that killing Mari was the worst sin I'd ever committed, and that I'd never live a day without pain over what I'd done. I deserved that pain. Pain was my currency, my payment for existing.

Every life has value. But killing someone you know and respect exacts a price that an anonymous life wouldn't charge. Ugly, but true. Ugly truths are blatant. You can't turn your head away, can't dilute them. Ugly truths impose, demand to be seen. Ugly truths eat you from the inside out.

No matter how I replayed the moments over and over in

my head, even when some part of me conceded that Mari would have died by Ultana's hand, and that I'd tried to be mercifully kind compared to how Ultana would have done it, it didn't take away the scarlet letter I'd branded on my own soul. I'd killed a member of Cora's family—one of her two best friends.

Worse was to think of things I could have done when it was too late. If Ultana had started to kill Mari, could I have jumped in front of her? Would Ultana have been knocked forcefully backward the way I'd been when I'd tried to take from Clancy's aura? There were scores of possibilities that were beyond my ability to try. It was forever too late.

I was damned.

I already knew I'd never be worthy of Cora. But now I was unworthy of forgiveness. Not Cora's, not God's. If my last act was to attempt to find out if an artificial means of energy for the Arrazi had been discovered, then I'd satisfy myself with that. I'd become one singular need: knowledge.

The first thing I did when I was alert and feeling well was to open the envelope I'd taken along with the pouch from the wooden heart in Ultana's office. The yellowed parchment fluttered in my hand as I carefully unfolded it. It looked to be a legal document with circular stamps all over it. Everything was written in Italian, but using a translator online I pieced out the most important part: *The dust in here was removed from the carpet where laid the box and the bones of Dante Alighieri.*

I peered into the pouch again and had to concede it looked like ashes. God in heaven... Could this be? It took no time at all to find the news story. In 1865, someone had scooped up material from Dante's tomb in Ravenna, Italy, divided it among six pouches, and had the remains authenticated with six certified letters. One was found in the ceiling of the Italian Senate in 1987, and the other in the National Library in Florence in 1999. Four were still missing.

I could now account for two of them.

Why on earth would Ultana Lennon have two sacks of dust from Dante Alighieri's bones? She obviously collected things, strange things, but this was macabre. Coincidence wasn't something I believed in, especially when two Arrazi women, Ultana and my mother, had obvious interest in the Italian poet. Was he important to the Arrazi somehow?

I called my mother at the hospital to ask.

She sighed into the phone. "There have been many notable people throughout history who were givers or takers of light," she told me above the hectic noise in the background. "I don't know if Dante was Scintilla or Arrazi. I only know some people believe he had discovered why we were created this way and may have known how to stop the cycle we all hate."

My breath hitched.

"But he was killed before he could divulge anything. Time has windswept the rumors, but the old families haven't forgotten."

"Someone didn't want his knowledge to get out."

"Son, that has been true throughout our history," she answered. "We've all been complicit in the secret."

"If Dante knew how to stop this cycle, then whoever silenced him would be an enemy to both the Arrazi *and* the Scintilla."

"A common enemy?" my mother said with a note of astonishment. "I'd never quite considered that."

I had to admit, it was hard to imagine a scenario where the Scintilla would ever see the Arrazi as something other than their worst enemy.

After we hung up, I also explored the meaning of the Two of Cups. That tarot card became a haunt, popping into my mind spontaneously, usually when I longed for sleep. When I typed in "reconciliation of opposites" I saw many posts: some about alchemy, others on enlightenment, and interestingly…the number three, triads, and triangles.

Three was the apparent metaphysical superglue of numbers, joining all things opposite.

Triangles, in particular, interested me. I recalled the rock my father showed me the day I returned home from my boat. Two overlapping triangles represented the heart chakra, the place I should focus my efforts when murdering. Obvious that it should be easier to kill through the heart. Who needed a rock to confirm that? Wasn't that what poetry confirmed?

Still, it seemed odd that this geometric symbol carried so much meaning throughout time and history—not only to a variety of beliefs throughout the world, but to my kind, the ones who kill more kindly if we kill through the heart.

"Reconciliation of opposites" also produced posts about ancient Egypt and the ankh. The ankh, seen in so many early hieroglyphs, was a symbol meaning "the key of life"—key to the eternal spring, the waters of life, or the elixir of life. The many descriptions of this ancient key braided philosophies of life force, death, and immortality.

Interesting. Pouring from the Two of Cups was the water of life.

Seemed that the history of humanity was full of recycled philosophies.

I riddled over it for hours upon hours until my eyes crossed with fatigue.

Then the call came.

I didn't think it would. I'd threatened Ultana's life. I'd figured all hopes of seeing the research facility she'd dangled in front of me were forever lost. Not even Saoirse had called since I'd left their house. I'd become a flea on the black sheep of humanity. Why hadn't Ultana cut me off?

Lorcan had called me from within ten minutes of my house so I took the fastest shower I could and ran outside. My feet faltered when I saw that he was picking me up in a nondescript black van.

"Still having trouble walking, Doyle?" he sneered.

"So it was you who clubbed me. Should'a known."

Lorcan cast a quick quizzical look my way. "I *wish* I could claim that one," he said emphatically. "Hey, maybe my wee sister clobbered you," he said, erupting into a fit of mocking laughter.

As I climbed in the van, a memory hit me of the day I took Cora to see her childhood home and we'd been followed by a black van, very similar. I said nothing, but felt the creep of suspicion on my neck.

Lorcan drove to the address we were given. It was in a dodgy old part of Dublin, known for its Magdalene asylums back in the day. The institutions were supposedly meant to "rehabilitate" women from lives of prostitution and thievery but were run more like prisons, locking women away against their will for enforced labor. There still wasn't much by way of improvement of the area, but when we rolled up to the research facility, it was obvious that it was well funded *and* well secured.

The men who came out to greet us were too curt, too quiet. It was my policy never to trust people who said too little, or too much.

This Dr. M, he was the latter. Maybe that was why his lackeys were so quiet—they couldn't get a damn word in edgewise. Another reason not to trust him: he was too fidgety and nervous and kept looking at Lorcan with pinched eyes. "Have we met somewhere before?" he finally asked Lorcan.

"Not at all."

Dr. M's brows bunched in consternation. Clearly, this surprise visit didn't sit well with him.

Unbeknownst to them, we were armed with a master key to every door and every lock in the building. We were shown into a waiting room with a fish-tank floor, and through a series of offices. "There must be more to this facility than pretty floors and offices, Dr. M?" I said, impatient. "What progress have you made in creating a form of energy that can be used to stop the... senseless killings?"

I had no idea if he knew what we were. I played it cautious, but I wanted answers. Lorcan didn't seem to know what to ask or why we were there at all. He was Ultana's eyes, I guessed.

"Please see here," Dr. M said, ushering us into a lab with walls of machinery, computers, and copper wiring. I half expected Frankenstein's monster to pop out of a cabinet and block-walk right over us. "The biometrics lab takes specimens and measures their electrical output and—"

"Specimens?" I interrupted.

"Of the three energetic breeds of human," he answered.

"You've run tests on—on *all* kinds? The givers *and* the takers?"

"I've never met an Arrazi—that I know," he said. "But we've tested a third kind of people who claim to take energy from others."

"I see. But where do you find the special ones?" I asked, aware that I sounded overexcited, too intense.

Dr. M gave a secretive smile. "We have scouts, so to speak."

Scouts. I was sure my temperature dropped ten degrees. People who were paid to bring Scintilla in... "Right. I've heard about those."

Dr. M looked at me with curiosity but didn't press. "Let me show you some of our most exciting innovations."

We entered a shiny black room with nothing in it but a big rectangular table. It looked like something Hugh Hefner would have in his mansion. In the 1980s. During a very lacquer-rich period. I laughed. "This is what you're paid for?"

"Bring her in," Dr. M said to one of the ever-present Japanese aides.

Within minutes, a woman was pressed into the room. She was small and blindfolded, and obviously very scared. It took but a moment to recognize her. Without conscious awareness, I must have stepped forward. I realized I'd reached for her, instinctively. I wanted to wrap my arms around her, protect her. She scuttled backward, away from my Arrazi energy, which surely she identified and felt. Her back hit the slick black wall of the room and she shook her head.

"I—" I switched to Irish, hoping desperately that what I said wouldn't be understood by Lorcan. Not only did my parents speak it, but I'd been sent to Dingle to refine my Irish. I'd hoped he was one of the many who didn't speak our native tongue. "*Tuigim do eagla. Ní bheidh mé Gortaítear tú. Bhuail mé tú aon uair amháin, nuair a, nuair a bhí tú aontaithe le do fear agus do… do rúnda álainn. An bhfuil sí anseo?*"

I understand your fear. I won't hurt you. I met you once, when, when you were united with your man and your…your lovely secret. Is she here?

Every word was carved from my frozen mouth, afraid to reveal more than they might already know about this poor woman. She'd suffered so much already. But I had to ask.

Already, her hands were outstretched in front of her as if to ward off the energy she couldn't see but could feel. Only now, she was reaching *for* me. I stepped forward. Her hand splayed out and stroked the air around me. Like a blind person, knowing a face only by touch, she was molding my aura, feeling my unique blend of energy. Though I couldn't see her eyes, I could see the moment that recognition dawned on her face. Her fingers clamped down on my wrist.

"Do you mind telling us what the hell you're doing?" Lorcan said.

A corner of my mind warned that I still had to play the part, but I was beyond answering. Cora's mother was pouring something of herself into me. Injecting me with visions: of Cora, of all of them, being attacked with some kind of electric shock instrument. Waking in a room, firmly bound to hard tables. Cora and Giovanni being led away by gunpoint. Not seen since.

Her fingers left my skin and the vision stopped. Adrenaline surged through me. They were here! Of course. The Society was funding research to generate Scintilla energy, and the doctor himself had just told me he tested on humans of their kind. How did my *eejit* arse not make the connection? Did Ultana know there were three in this facility?

My gaze raked over the doctor.

"Excuse me," Dr. M said, trying to assert authority. "I am fond of saying that we do not keep secrets here. I'm afraid I do not speak your tongue and would like for you to cease from using it with my patients." I acted apologetic, but my body was a hive of buzzing activity. He cleared his throat.

"I wanted to put her at ease. She is obviously very scared," I said.

"Yes, yes. Very well. A demonstration of the room."

When his hand reached for a panel on the wall, my body

tensed in preparation to leap for Cora's mother if needed. But when the doctor pushed the switch the only change was the sudden appearance of the mesmerizing cascade of colors projected onto the walls around us.

Even Lorcan was dumbfounded. His mouth hung open as he peered at the walls, at the auras we could sense like bloodhounds but never see before now.

My own aura was still white but might as well have run bloodred with Mari's murder. Lorcan had some white in his aura, which wafted out from his body like an exaggerated cloud. He had a lot of orange and some of it not so clear, like it was mixed with other, darker colors. I swear it lightened and changed as he stared at the walls.

The focus of Lorcan's gaze and of mine was Cora's mother, the only Scintilla in the room. Silver sparks flew from her like a mosaic of mirrors reflecting luminous light from her core and out through her astral body. If this was what emanated from Cora, no wonder I'd been captivated. It was a lake of such shimmering beauty, I yearned to connect with it, to dive in and be *part* of it. Sparkling crystals of light, love, and everything beautiful a human could hold.

It was the most astonishing and lovely miracle I'd ever seen.

Lorcan stared, openmouthed. Was he as affected as I was?

Christ, they couldn't want all of the Scintilla dead!

I had to find Cora.

"You'll excuse me," I said, ignoring the doctor's protestations. "I've been told that no one in this facility will hinder my ability to look around freely." I hoped Lorcan would be too stupid or too unmotivated to follow. I got very up-close in the doctor's face. "I believe you *do* keep secrets here," I said, hitting his heart chakra with a tentacle of energy as a warning. His eyes rounded. "This woman is *not* to be harmed."

"My goodness, who would want to harm her?" Dr. M chirped. "I simply covered her eyes to protect your anonymity as I've always been instructed. I want nothing but her safety."

I gave a quick nod. "Indeed," I said, looking over my shoulder at Lorcan. "Then remove her from this room"—I lowered my voice to a whisper—"and away from *him*, immediately."

A small control center.

From the looks of it, that was what I'd entered after wandering through halls that all looked so much alike, I feared I was simply running in circles. I'd used a master key that Lorcan gave to me to bypass the locks on many rooms. This particular room intrigued me because it was right off a larger room with multiple gurneys lined in a row. All of them had white harness straps dangling like spider legs under each table. It was the room in the vision from Cora's mother.

Panels of computer monitors lined the wall, dark but illuminated with red record/play buttons. A large blackout screen hung above the monitors. Out of curiosity, I pulled the cord and it snapped and recoiled upward, revealing a large glass window much like one in a police interrogation on a TV show. Beyond the glass, I saw bursts of movement. I moved closer to the glass to determine the source. When I did, my head flinched in surprise. Not what I expected at all.

Two people rolled around passionately under the covers in a bed. I flushed. This Dr. M was a raunchy bastard. Did those people know they could be seen? Feeling like an utter perv, I turned my back on the lovers and made to leave, but the door flew open as I reached for it.

"What are you doing in *here*?" Dr. M asked with barely masked anger, his balding head beaded with sweat.

Lorcan brushed past me and walked toward the window. He let out a lascivious whistle. "Mmm-mmm, Doc. What have we— Hold on… Well, bite me wicked arse and call it candy. *That girl?*" The howl that came from Lorcan sent cold drips of uneasiness down my spine. "Hot damn! I know how she feels underneath me and her aura *is* delicious. Bitch has got a bite, though," he said, his fingers running over his cheek, which had sported a half circle of red since the party. "Who's the bloke that has her in a compromising position this time?"

I spun around.

Dark curly hair flew within the white covers as they rolled over, oblivious to their audience. Her back was to us, bare but for one distinguishing mark—the knife. I felt like one had been driven hard into my chest.

Without thinking, my hand slammed on a switch next to the window. The light changed in the room we were in. *He* noticed and sat up. Giovanni peered around Cora's back. Lorcan pushed another button and we could hear Giovanni's flagrant curses in Italian.

Cora slowly turned. Time snagged, stopped. Light caught the spiral of dark hair that hung over one eye as she looked over her bare shoulder.

Our eyes met.

I didn't know what Dr. M was saying, or what crude comments Lorcan was spouting after he waved to her and said, "Hi, doll." I only knew that the girl I loved, the one person in this world I wanted to save even beyond myself, was gathering a blanket around her body and walking slowly, wordlessly toward me.

Her hair was wild from *his* touch. Her lips were plump and wet with *his* kisses and slightly open in bewilderment. Her eyes, her beautiful green eyes, confused, blinking as she realized what was happening. She opened her mouth to speak, looked from me to Lorcan to Dr. M, and pursed them. A closed book.

I wished I'd never made it off my boat. God could strike me dead on the spot and it would be a favor, though God owed me no favors and wouldn't spare me this pain.

Giovanni was suddenly next to her. His arm wrapped possessively around her shoulders. "You could help us. You know you could, you Arrazi bastard. At least save *her*!"

How on earth could I save her? This facility was controlled by the Society, and they had them, three of them, whether Ultana knew it or not. After this, she'd surely know. Lorcan would tell her immediately.

Lorcan waved his finger at Giovanni. "We're not going to save her life. And I'll tell you what, *you* will never save her life, either," he said. "Or you will die."

"Lorcan!" I yelled. That simple word "or" was an evil spell coming from his mouth. My God, he'd cursed Giovanni and by doing so, Cora. I may have hated Giovanni, now more than ever, but he was the only one who seemed to care about her as much as I did. And she, him. That was bloody obvious.

Torture was standing there, hoping that she'd say anything to explain what I'd just seen, anything to comfort the gash in my chest.

Instead, she focused on Lorcan and her face turned from astonished to vicious. "What did you do with my cousin, Mari? And Teruko? Where are they? Did you kill Mari?" Tears streamed down her face. "I know you killed her," she said to him, dissolving to sobs. "I know you did…"

"And you." She slammed her palm on the window, hitting me

with such a savage glare that I recoiled. "This is the second time I've been prisoner while you're on the *free* side of the wall!"

I had no idea what to do, but I couldn't help them at that moment. It was obvious that I knew them personally. Seeing Cora so stripped, her pain raw and unmasked, resentful as a caged animal, was like having teeth ruthlessly clamp down and rip my heart to shreds.

Lorcan crossed his arms over his chest. "So you *do* know her? Why don't you tell her what happened to her cousin?"

Cora's eyes slanted to me, agony and questions in their green depths. I leaned my head on the window, flogging myself with whips of guilt. "I do know this girl," I said to Lorcan. To deny her now, when she was about to find out what I'd done, would have been shameful and cowardly. "I've loved her," I answered. "Every day."

My voice sounded like the brush of dead leaves to my own ears. My heart beat too thick and heavy to be dead. I opened my mouth to tell her about Mari.

"Liar!" she cried, both fists beating the glass. "Look at what you're doing, who you're here with!" It shouldn't have surprised me that Cora possessed such ferocity. She'd always coursed deeper than she'd shown.

"Cora, I—"

"Your love was a lie!"

She called my love a lie? It was the only real thing in my heart. Inside, something snapped. "You want to hear something true?" I yelled back at her, not caring that I'd lost control, that I deserved every drop of her hate. I slammed my own fist on the glass against hers. She didn't flinch, didn't back off from me. Just stared at our hands pressed with glass between them. God, she was so close…

"That bastard that you're in there having *sex* with…" It sickened me to even say the words. Inexplicably, her eyes flitted to Dr. M and then back at me, pained. "You want to know his darkest secret? The blackest hole in *his* heart? My mother told me all about it after she met him in Clancy's cell. He's *paid* to find and bring in his own kind! Ask him how much money he got for your precious little Scintilla head!"

She opened her mouth, but then closed it again. And I saw she'd bitten her lip so hard, a welt of red blood sliced across it.

No more words. I had to get out of there. I'd done enough damage.

FIFTY-THREE

Cora

Finn turned his back.

Of all the moments in the world, he'd looked in on *that* one. My chest felt like someone had hacked out my heart with a long, corroded nail. He'd been so angry, treated me like I'd had a choice and had made the wrong one. Choices my ass.

Not only did Dr. M leave me no choice, but Finn being Arrazi left me none, either. Was I supposed to pine away for the rest of my life for someone who I could never, ever be with? Finn would never know that he was always in my mind, my heart. I was pushing him away, pushing him uphill like a boulder, one that I would always be chained to. No matter what I did, or how I tried to leave it behind me, it would always roll back at me. My love for Finn would always flatten me.

Still, even if he was angry, how could his pride be more important than my freedom?

How could he have shown up with that Arrazi piece of crap who taunted me about Mari? I still didn't know what happened to her. But Finn did. How could he hear Giovanni ask for help and just…just leave?

Giovanni would never know how much of myself I'd given to him. It might not have been my full heart, but it was as much as I had left. Now it was smashed in my outstretched hands. I felt the air charge around me as Giovanni's hand reached for my back.

"Don't touch me."

I stood with my eyes closed, seeing only two palms pressed together against the glass. Finn and I would always be divided by something impenetrable.

"What he said—"

"Is it true?" I turned and shoved Giovanni in the chest with one hand and clutched my blanket to me with the other. He stumbled backward, his face insolent as a child's. He opened his mouth to speak, but I saw it in his eyes. "I know it's true. You told me—nobody does something for nothing, remember?"

Bitterness roped around me and squeezed so tight, I felt the welts of it inside and out. I swiped the tears away with the back of my hand. "My family, my *real* family, is here because you brought us here. We are prisoners again, because of *you*. And you're *profiting* from it? How much?"

"You're not letting me explain—"

"Nothing you can explain will erase the fact that you used me for your own benefit. This is the secret Finn's mother saw in your eyes when they found us at Clancy's. I stupidly assumed it was your telekinesis. I assumed and you never corrected me." Revulsion and humiliation rocked me so hard that I shook. "You were using me. Oh my God, in the *worst* way! Were you getting paid to try to screw me? How much for a Scintilla baby, huh? Ugh, this is sick."

I flung myself away from his reaching arms and reaching aura. Degraded down to my soul, I wrapped the blanket around me tighter, went to gather my clothes that lay crumpled on the floor, and ran into the bathroom. Once the door was shut and locked, I collapsed against the wall and sank to the cold floor, shivering—in complete shock.

Blades of truth jutted into my chest.

Mari. Her name was a twist of the blade. I didn't know if they'd killed her, though my heart told me she was dead. If it wasn't that Arrazi, then I probably had Clancy Mulcarr to blame. My mouthy, freaky, feisty, sparkly cousin was gone. How could this be happening?

Another blade, that Finn could see me behind the glass, knowing I was in danger, and still walk away. And what was *his* part in all of this? How did Finn end up on the other side of that window, in Dr. M's facility with that Arrazi son of a bitch who took Mari?

The blade of truth Finn had thrown about Giovanni had hit its mark, deeply. I bled inside from the betrayal. No wonder Giovanni had been so pushy about Dr. M, always bringing it up. Money was a *great* motivator. I always thought it was odd that he'd had so much cash available. I also blamed myself for agreeing to come when my gut wasn't sure. Every decision I'd made in the last two months had led to nothing but death and disaster.

I couldn't trust anyone.

Least of all myself.

It was awful not being able to scream my truth in Finn's face. I was gagged by my very situation, muzzled for my mom's survival. Stupid to worry about what Finn thought. Yes, I *was* feeling something, many things, with Giovanni, but always Finn was in the back of my mind. I couldn't escape him. It was Finn I'd compare everyone else to. Every other love was counterfeit—tin in the face of the gold. I slammed my palm on the cold tile. Damn it. Was Finn always going to feel like a home I could never return to?

I had to stand in front of him, head up, silent but crumbling inside. I knew if I opened my mouth, Finn had the power to pull the truth from me in front of Dr. M., the one person I *needed* to buy the farce that Giovanni and I were actually having sex. I could only stare and let them all believe the lie. Luckily, Finn didn't ask me outright. Hell, he even helped corroborate it when he yelled at me. He'd sold it hook, line, and sinker because he believed it himself.

Giovanni knocked softly on the bathroom door. "Cora? Let's talk, please. You must hear what I have to say."

"How many chances have you had to tell me the truth?" I asked, not moving from the floor. "What I *must* do is get my family out of here."

He sighed against the door. "You no longer include me when you say family."

"You don't know what family means."

"I don't. How could I? But the situation is not what you're thinking."

"Shut up! Stop talking. Honesty doesn't mean as much when you're giving it to buy forgiveness. You're still just looking out for yourself. You were always looking out for yourself."

FIFTY-FOUR

Finn

My torn and bleeding knuckles throbbed as I dialed the phone. Lorcan would have to deal with the fact that his van took a few punches. The bastard had cursed *her* by cursing Giovanni and callously volleyed her cousin's fate back at me. I wanted to confess to Cora. She deserved to know. But then, then everything got out of hand. It would be a matter of minutes before Lorcan alerted his mother about the Scintilla at the facility. I had to find a way to get them out of there before it was too late.

Saoirse answered on the fifth ring. "Lorcan is probably going to call your mother. Can you please run interference if you can? I'm asking you as my friend to do this. The girl…the one who ruined me…" *God, I was ruined.* I couldn't tell Saoirse she was Scintilla. She didn't need to know that. She needed only to know that I was asking for help. She owed me. "She's being held inside this facility. You have to buy me time to help her, Saoirse. I'm begging you. I helped you when you most needed it. Now, I need you."

"Okay, Finn. Okay. I'll do what I can."

I scribbled a note and left it on the driver's seat of the van.

> Urgent. Your mother sent a car for me. Instructs that you make no phone calls until you get my call. Get the van away from the facility for your own safety and drive it to "Hell." Wait there.

I had to smile at telling Lorcan Lennon to go to Hell.

My father had been out of town for two days of a month-long stint with the Defence Forces. He couldn't help me. I called my mother and was told she was in surgery. I had noticed how many people worked for Dr. M in that facility. I was outnumbered at least twenty to one and had no idea what ways they might have of stopping me if I tried to free the Scintilla by myself. My next move was a complete gamble, but I was desperate. I ran a block away, hid behind a metal grate, and called my uncle to come right away, giving him the address of the building where I hid.

While I waited, I watched Lorcan wander out from the facility with Dr. M. They glanced around for me, shook hands, and Dr. M returned inside. Lorcan paused when he got in the van. He pulled away shortly, and I ducked down as he passed, hoping to God he and Clancy wouldn't see each other on the road.

Minutes later, my uncle arrived.

"I know where the Scintilla are. All three of them." Clancy didn't react, but his neck turned red the way it always did when he was riled. "Ultana is quite possibly about to know where they are as well because Lorcan was with me. It comes down to this— she wants three Scintilla. You're trying to find them before she does. Whatever power she thinks that will give her, I figure you intend to claim it for yourself."

His head jerked up, surprised. "Your sortilege is frightening,

Finnegan. You have the potential for there to be *nothing* you can't know just by asking."

"Don't patronize me. Right now, all I want to know is whether you'll help me rescue them and keep them out of Ultana's hands. I'm not stupid enough to think you want them to play cricket. But it's a fact that Ultana sides with the Society, who wants the Scintilla dead. Between that devil and the devil I know, I choose you. I have to get them out of there, and I can't do it alone. You don't want the Society to know you already had possession of the three once," I said, drilling him with his own secret. "I will tell Ultana how you've been going rogue unless you help me now without hurting any of them."

"Aye, Finn," my uncle said, looking straight into my eyes. "I'll help you."

"We both know you're only about helping yourself, so cut the crap. You will not hurt them or I'll kill you. I swear it. Hurt them at all and you won't live to see tomorrow."

Fifty-Five

Cora

"Cora," Giovanni knocked on the door to the bathroom sometime later. "Dr. M said he wants to see us." His voice was urgent. This might be the time to make our move. I wasn't sure how long I'd sat on the cold floor, but my body was tense and stiff as I stood and opened the door.

"With luck, he'll want to meet outside of this place." At the first chance, I intended to break free of this compound or die trying.

I would rather die than be anyone's prisoner, ever again.

Giovanni reached for my hand, but I slid out of range and shot him a warning look.

"He conned me, too," he said. Hurt and defensiveness filled his voice and showed in his retracted aura.

"Con artist got conned?"

He turned away.

"There's no excuse for not telling me. I thought we were lost *together*." My voice cracked on "together" and it pissed me off.

I'd known Giovanni was wily from the minute I'd met him, and yet I trusted him. Time and time again, I proved to be too naive to trust my own judgment. I wished my father knew how his protective bubble had rendered me ill equipped for this harsh world.

I yanked on my pants, slid my feet into the flat slippers they provided, braided my tangle of hair, and waited like a coiled snake on the foot of the bed, prepared to strike when the summons came. Giovanni was ready, too. He hung off the small love seat's edge, ready to jump.

I stared at the window, wondering if we were being watched. It had been an ugly scene with Finn and his Arrazi friend. Even after Finn stormed out, the guy stared at Giovanni and me. I thought a lot about that stare. It was hard to read. Gullible me would have thought there was wondrous awe in his gaze, but gullible me had gotten into enough trouble. He was nothing but a killer.

Before they came for me, I had to find a way to give Giovanni a secret message. I scooted off the bed and walked up behind him. His whole body tensed when he felt me approach. His back was rigid and straight as he leaned forward on his knees. I leaned over the back of the couch and pulled his shoulders toward me. He slumped against the seat, letting me wrap my arms around his neck. On the side away from the mirror, I whispered in his ear.

"I'm going after mine. You go after yours. We'll get out of here, whatever it takes."

His right hand reached up and around and stroked the back of my head. He turned sideways slightly. I started to pull away, but he held my head close. "And after?"

I swallowed hard as I tried to say the harsh truth. "I can't depend on someone I don't trust."

"I would die to save you, you know that?" he said with quiet ferocity against the edge of my mouth.

A buzzer rang, and the metal door slid open. Dr. M stood in the doorway. Two men, both armed, flanked him. The spark of Giovanni's energy fueled my own. As I glanced quickly at Giovanni's aura, I could see we both struggled to hold our intensity in check. His face was impassive, almost bored-looking, but his aura flared so wildly, it hooked around me and combined with mine. If this were the dining room, they'd see that we were an enormous ball of silver fire, ready to fight.

The young men strode forward. "Turn around," one ordered Giovanni. Giovanni did as he was told, and the man pulled his arms behind his back and slipped a zip tie around his wrists, pulling it taut. Gone was one method of defense and attack.

Dr. M kept one hand on a Taser at his waist as the men led us out. We walked in a line down the long hallway toward the elevators. A million possibilities whirled through my mind. Could Dr. M somehow be electrocuted in that high-voltage dining room of his? Would we go into the biometrics lab where I could wrap some of that copper wiring around his neck? *My* sortilege was useless. I couldn't kill him with a memory.

We stopped at the elevators and suddenly a horrid memory intersected with dire need. An emergency ax gleamed through the glass of its red case next to the elevator doors. My eyes sought Giovanni. The silver corona around him splayed and jabbed. Before I could do anything, the elevator arrived and we were ushered inside.

"Where are you taking us?"

"We're moving you, my dear, to another location. I had no idea that our financiers had Arrazi working for them. Frankly, it's a very dangerous situation, indeed." He turned to me, intense and sweating. "I know you think I'm the enemy but I'm not. I was misled—"

"Let us not talk of being misled," Giovanni snarled.

Dr. M ignored him. "I'd have never known what those two men were if you hadn't said it. They could have killed us all in an instant. They could have taken you." Sweat beaded on his bald head as he spoke in an ever-higher pitch. "I'm so close to the answers. Soon we will know if one theory of mine holds water." He glanced at my stomach. "Soon."

"I will not leave here without my mother and Dun."

"Where is Claire?" Giovanni asked.

"Everyone is to meet downstairs. We will take you where no one will ever find you, don't worry."

That was *exactly* my worry.

The elevator door opened at the parking garage level. Dr. M stepped out into the garage. Giovanni turned his back to the doctor, drawing the Taser at Dr. M's waist through the air, into his bound hands behind his back. He fumbled and squeezed the trigger, hitting one guard who jerked and fell to the ground. The other guard lifted a gun and I rammed my shoulder into his stomach. The gun fired, blasting a hole in the ceiling of the elevator. My ears rang. Giovanni shocked the second man, and I leaped from the elevator and pressed the button, closing it on the two men.

I kicked the red firebox and yanked the ax out through the broken glass as Dr. M snatched the stun gun from Giovanni's hands and fired. Giovanni fell in a contorted heap at our feet.

Dr. M raised the Taser at me.

I didn't see myself, or the doctor. For one blinding moment, I saw my mother hacking off the hand of her attacker. The residue of that memory accumulated with my own fury and desperation.

Pure blind rage pushed my arms up. I stepped to the side as he fired and swung the ax as hard as I could. Pain shot up my arms as blade connected with bone. Screams filled the air. Dr. M's hand and the Taser fell to the floor at our feet as he shrieked and bled. I scooped up the weapon and fired it at him.

"Cora!" Dun came running up the ramp toward me but was blocked by a barred gate, which was accessed by a fingerprint security panel. "I can't open it," he yelled, clutching the bars separating us.

I fought down the nausea that threatened to overcome me as I picked up the doctor's dismembered hand and pressed a clammy finger on the pad.

The gate rose into the ceiling. Dun ducked under it, ran forward, and hugged me. "Holy crap, that was the sickest thing I've ever seen!"

"Where's my mother?"

"We were all walking toward the vans when we saw the fighting start. Goddamn, girl," he said. "That was some serious ninja shit you just pulled off. When I saw what you were doing, I went kapow all over the dude that was guarding us and ran over here. I don't know how much time we have, I only punched him unconscious."

Dr. M moved and I pulled the trigger again and again. His body rippled and twitched with each hit. It wasn't until Dun pulled me against his body and wrapped his arms around me that I realized I was wailing.

Giovanni began to come to, and both Dun and I helped him to his feet.

"Claire," I gasped to Dun. "Is the little girl with you?"

"No. I think she's still inside. They were supposed to be bringing her down."

Giovanni's head bobbed but his words came out clearly. "Leave me here. I have to find her. You get yours. I get mine, remember?"

I regretted ever saying that. It was anger talking. I couldn't leave him. Then I'd be no better than Finn. "No. We'll find her," I said, gritting my teeth. Sunshine streamed in through the garage entrance. We were so close…

I looked back toward the facility, toward who knew how many guards or guns or Arrazi might be lurking. Out of the corner of my eye I saw a figure, small and tentative as a doe in the woods, stepping cautiously toward the sunlight. My mother. She was moving instinctively toward freedom. "I have to get her." I ducked out from under Giovanni's arm. He sagged against Dun, whom I handed the bloodied ax to. "Get his hands untied if you can," I said, and ran.

She'd reached the street and was running thoughtlessly down the sidewalk when I caught up with her. "Mom!" I said spinning her around. "Stop. They're still back there. Dun and Giovanni and…and the little girl. We can't leave them."

Blinking against the harsh sun, my mom opened her mouth to speak but the sound of screeching tires cut her off. A car pulled up. Bodies piled out. My mother's eyes turned from bewildered to horrified as two men jumped out. As a sharp puncture sunk into my arm, I saw what had caused her face to morph to terror.

Clancy Mulcarr.

The sky reached out and smacked me down.

Clancy

Had

Found

Fifty-Six

Finn

It was incredibly hard to pull myself up out of the mental quicksand that my uncle had thrown me into. The needle was wielded by a man I'd recognized: Ultana Lennon's driver, the one with the scarred mouth. He wasn't Arrazi—no competition or threat. Was Clancy in league with her all along? Why would the same guy who worked for Ultana also be a henchman for my uncle if they weren't working together? How the hell could he lie to me?

Maybe he didn't lie. Clancy had promised not to hurt Cora. An angry puff of laughter escaped me. He never said anything about not hurting me.

Scheming bastard. I should have dug his heart out with that shovel when I'd had the chance.

I pulled myself to sitting. I'd been unconscious for some time—that much I could see by the slant of the sun between the ramshackle buildings. The Society's research facility was a few doors down. I knew in my gut I was much too late, but I had to go in. I had to see for myself that Cora wasn't there. Maybe I was wrong about him and Ultana. Maybe Clancy would have no way to get past the security. I felt for the master key. Still there in my pocket, thankfully, or I'd have no way to get in the building myself.

I stumbled to the front entrance and nearly fell backward when the doors opened and three people tumbled out. Cora's mate, Dun, wielding a goddamn bloody ax, Giovanni Teso, and a wee lass who couldn't be more than five in years. Giovanni had her cradled in his arms. Damn if she didn't look like his own fair child. Dun bled from a deep gash in his hand, and he met me with a surprised but challenging glare.

I held up my hands in surrender, as if that meant anything. I could take from them all without a touch and they bloody well knew it. "I'm not going to hurt you," I said. Though I wanted to hurt Giovanni. Visions of his hands on Cora's fine skin flashed in my mind. Yeah, I wanted to hurt him.

"Not much of an exciting fight then." Dun panted.

"Where's Cora?" Giovanni bellowed so loudly the little girl tucked her head to his neck in fright.

My gut caved in. "Please tell me she's with you. Because if she's not—"

"Of course she's not with us. She ran outta this place after her mother over two hours ago," Dun said. "We haven't seen her since." Giovanni continued to stare at me with unmasked suspicion.

I raked my fingers over my head and mumbled profanities a small child ought not to have heard.

"Dude?" Dun asked.

"Clancy's got her. I know he does. He's got them both. He stabbed me with a needle of something and left me unconscious on the street. We've got to go to my place, see if he's taken them there." I looked at Giovanni. "Like before."

"Why should we believe anything you say?"

"I'm not Cora's enemy," I said pointedly. "I'm an Arrazi, yes. I can't *fookin'* help that. But I am a man and I have free will about who I help and who I hurt. Please. We have to get you off this street, and we have to find her before it's too late."

There was far too much staring going on and not enough movement so I walked away. Hell with 'em. We didn't have all damn day to deliberate. I had to get back to the manor. I heard the discussions going on behind me as I got out my phone and called for a cab. When one pulled up within minutes, the group ran my way.

"Ho there," said the driver when he saw the bloodied ax and the warrior who carried it. "What kind of trouble you be bringin' with you? I want no part of it."

"No trouble," I said. "We don't bring trouble. We bring money, and lots of it. Get us there and it's yours."

Dun rested the ax between his feet, but his hand stayed firmly gripped on the handle. "I figure if you're willing to walk away from one Scintilla, one crazy-pissed Indian, and a child of questionable heritage, you're more concerned about finding Cora than killing us."

"Bet your arse."

We were uncomfortably quiet on the way. Even the child was quiet, though I noticed her staring at me more than once. She had a peculiar energy about her and even more peculiar eyes. I was drawn to her but also strangely intimidated. Odd.

"Not this gate again," Giovanni protested as we pulled up. I actually felt for the guy. He'd escaped, only to come full circle where he'd started.

I paid the cabbie a fortune and we piled out of the car. If the situation hadn't been so urgent, I'd have laughed at my mother's expression as she opened the door and gawked at the four of us. "There is no rational explanation to account for what I'm seeing," she said.

"Mother, Clancy has Cora. I'm sure of it. Please, hide them in the lighthouse and keep them safe until I return."

"I'm going with you," Giovanni said, setting the girl at my mother's feet. The tender look my mom bestowed on the child made me sure she'd be okay. Giovanni noticed, too, but his voice shook when he said, "Please…Claire's all I have," and it made me wonder what had happened that he didn't count Cora on his list.

"Where we goin'?" Dun asked. With that ax dangling from his hand, he truly looked like every bad old American Western I'd ever seen.

"Your hand needs stitches quite badly," my mother said to Dun.

Giovanni stepped to Dun. "Protect her," he said, placing his hand on Dun's shoulder. "She's my daughter."

Whoa. So I was on the right track. "Let's go," I said. "We'll take the car."

We drove into the back end of my property as far as the car could travel. When we hit the woods where Clancy's secret prison was located, we got out and ran through the trees.

As soon as we reached the path that led to his underground lair, I motioned for Giovanni to be quiet and follow me. Voices bounced through the trees and we ducked. I peered around the trunk and saw a van with the engine running. Exhaust curled into the evening air. A man slammed shut the back doors to the van and climbed into the driver's seat. "She could be in there," I said. "We have to follow. C'mon."

It was maybe impossible to track the van in the time we'd have to spend running back to my car, but there was only one road that exited onto the highway from Clancy's edge of our sizable property and we could intercept the van if we were fast enough.

My energy flagged as we ran full-out to reach my family's side of the property for the car. When the hell would I be able to go longer without taking? The constant urge was wearing on me. Giovanni and I ran across the gravel, threw ourselves into the car, and sped onto the highway. Our strained spirits filled the car with a thick sludge of tension.

We approached the T in the road where the van should pass, if we hadn't already missed it. I'd block the van with our car. I'd stand in the road myself, if I had to.

"You could kill me now," Giovanni said, his fingers tapping on his leg.

"Yes."

"I know you want to," he said. "For taking her from you."

My teeth scraped together. "Don't give yourself that much credit, man. You don't deserve her, either."

His mouth opened to respond, but then the van came into view before we reached the intersection and sped past. "Damn it!" I pulled out behind it. It was definitely in a hurry to get where it was going, making it hard to follow without being obvious about it.

"Do you think she's in that car?" Giovanni asked in a voice that was as tight as a new guitar string.

"I do think it's possible, yes. The question is, how are we going to rescue her and her mother?"

"Can you attack them, as an Arrazi?"

"I can't attack another Arrazi, no. And they have syringes with some kind of sedative."

"Yes, they used one on Gráinne when we were attacked at her old house the night we escaped from yours."

"*Shite.*"

The van pulled onto a familiar road, one both Giovanni and I recognized as the entrance to Newgrange. I turned off my headlights and stayed back a ways. Instead of pulling into the historic site, the van continued past it and rambled down a narrow private lane. We pulled over and watched it roll to a crawl, turn, and drive in reverse up to a hill.

Quietly, we got out of the car and crept closer. Because the back of the van was opened toward the hill, we could not see much when the man opened the doors and pulled someone out. I heard the squeak of a gate as they went through.

"Now," Giovanni said, rising from his crouch.

I pulled him down by his arm. "*I* have to be the one to do it," I said.

Even in the gloom of darkness, I could see the disgusted look he gave me. "Why, so you can be her knight in shining armor again? I don't think so." He rose to standing and I grabbed his arm. The violent gust of Scintilla energy he threw at me sent me into spasms of hunger. I released his arm.

"What Lorcan said to you back there at that lab was a curse. It's his sortilege. Trust me, if you save her life, you will die, just as he promised."

"I would die to save her," he said through clenched teeth. His eyes flashed hotly. I believed him.

"Well, as much as I might have wished for your demise, my friend, let's save that as a last resort, shall we? I'll go in first. If I don't come out with her, you do as you wish."

Before I could start off toward the van and the hill beyond it, we heard the sound of someone running, and we ducked behind the car. A hooded figure in black darted past us and through the gate.

Giovanni sprinted forward. I leaped up and tackled him.

Fifty-Seven

Cora

Consciousness came slowly, like emerging from under deep black water. No dreams. No thoughts. Just heavy pressure. Oblivion. They'd obviously injected us with the same thing my mother got hit with before. We were in the back of a van, rumbling and swaying on a curved road. I tried to sit up but my hands were tied in front of me and my body felt weighted and uncoordinated. The van skidded to an abrupt stop and the back doors opened, framing two dark silhouettes.

One grabbed my feet and yanked. I slid toward the door, my back scraping on the metal floorboard. My mother was pulled out after me. I teetered, trying to gain my balance and bring my mind fully up to the surface.

In the darkness, we were pushed through grass wet with dew that made my feet cold and soaked my pants below the knees. I shivered under the half-lidded moon. It looked bored.

Clumps of brush and trees dotted the hilly grass. The trill of water flowed nearby. Having been blindfolded in the van and barely conscious, I had no idea where we were now or how long we had been traveling. We could be on the other side of Ireland for all I knew. My eyes kept straying to my mother's back as she was led in front of me. I had the urge to step in the impressions her tiny feet left in the damp grass. Her head dipped low, gazing at the ground as if she couldn't care less where we were headed. If my own shadowy despair was any indication, I could only imagine hers at being back in the clutches of Clancy Mulcarr.

Still, hope was a feral bird inside me. There had to be a way out of this.

"Ah now," Clancy said, chucking me under the chin. "Don't look so low. You won't be my prisoner forever. This time, little spark, I *am* going to kill you."

Okay, so no.

We stopped at an ancient scrolled gate set between two brambly, overgrown hedges. It screeched in the gloom when one of the men pushed it open and shoved us through. In the predawn light, it looked like a gate guarding nothing but a pile of dirt. I squinted into the darkness and realized it *was* a pile of dirt…dirt with a door. This was similar to pictures I'd seen of Newgrange before it was excavated. Another burial mound? Possibly one of the many dots I'd seen when standing upon Newgrange? I recalled the tour guide saying that there were many others all over the Boyne Valley that had yet to have been excavated.

Why this place? On the postcard of the triple spiral tucked inside my mother's journal she'd written, "Origin story?" Sickeningly poetic that this should be the place of the conclusion.

Clancy pulled out a ring of keys and fumbled in the darkness for the right one to unlock the apple-sized padlock hanging from the arched wooden door in the side of the mound.

"Welcome home," sang the man behind me—a non-Arrazi.

"Where's the other van, do you reckon?" he asked Clancy.

Clancy glanced back. "Shut it. They'll be along soon."

A match was struck and three torches lit, casting an orange glow inside the mounded room. It was the kind of damp and cold that soaks through your skin and coats your bones with condensation. Would I ever know warmth again? I reached for my mother's bound hands. With sadness in her eyes that was darker than the night, she clung to my hands and pressed her forehead to mine.

As soon as our heads touched, an urgent blast of memories funneled into me.

Looking down on a bare and fresh baby on her chest, pink-skinned, black-haired, and content to nestle against her mother's warmth. The baby glowed with pure innocence, the fire of life, and a raging silver aura that was more massive than hers. The most intense love emanated through the memory, and I knew that baby was me.

Flashes of milestones: My first crooked smile. My first sweet utterance of "mum-ma," wobbly steps on plump, roly thighs into her outstretched arms. Smooshy openmouthed toddler kisses. The sweet, woodsy smell of my curly hair.

Mom was using her sortilege to tell me there wasn't a moment of my first five years that she'd forgotten.

My head spun with images. I swayed slightly, fighting to stay on my feet despite the heady infusion of feeling and memory pouring from her to me. Tears coursed down my cheeks, but I held in my sobs for fear they'd hear and break us apart.

She was only doing this because her bird of hope had been shot down. I wanted to flinch from the burning of my skin and her hopelessness. But we held on, forehead to forehead, even after the visions faded like burned papers rising up into the sky.

Mom and I stared at each other in the torchlight, tears streaming down our flickering faces. Lambent silver danced around our bodies and connected. Yes, we were one. We always had been. When death approached, maybe especially so, nothing mattered more than the love in life and our connection with those we love.

The men yanked us apart and told us each to sit on separate slabs of stone. There were three of them, roughly five feet long, positioned together in a triangle. Intricate veins of carved spirals laced over each stone. The triple spiral was evident on at least two from where I stood. Could these be the three missing curbstones from Newgrange? They looked like they'd puzzle in seamlessly with the other enormous stones encircling the famous tomb.

Rough hands pushed me backward on the stone until I was lying down, sealing a chill through my shirt. The same was being done to my mother. Clancy stood over us, hands folded in front of him, looking immensely smug.

"Creator, sustainer, destroyer," Clancy said, walking in a slow circle around my mother and I, flat on the stone slabs. I watched his black shadow rise and lengthen on the slope of the curved ceiling like a black flame. "Some say that is what the triple spiral signifies. Some would say God is the creator, the Scintilla are the sustainers, and the Arrazi are the destroyers."

"So," I spoke, my voice shaking from the word "destroyer." "You're doing what you think you were created to do? Destroy the sustainers? Who would fulfill the Scintilla's role then, huh? Who will live my purpose after you kill me? Your thinking is totally slanted."

He reached down and squeezed my cheeks with a rough hand. "Even among supernatural humans, some are destined to do more than we were created for. I am one of those. I know the *true* meaning of the triple spiral."

I hated to admit it, but I actually wanted to hear what he had to say. The significance of the triple spiral had taunted me, and even if it was the last thing I'd hear, at least I'd die with one less question in my heart.

"Never could get your three, huh?" I goaded. "So end my suspense and tell me why you want three of us." At least he might have my mother and me, but not the satisfaction of three Scintilla he'd always wanted. Despite my anger, I prayed Dun, Giovanni, and Claire had made it out of Dr. M's and were hiding somewhere safe.

Outside, the sound of muffled footsteps approached. Clancy nodded to his bulldog helper and the door opened. I craned my neck, cold stone biting my cheek.

Clancy prowled the dank tomb as he spoke. "The closest the ordinary, ignorant humans have ever come to the truth about the power of the triple spiral is"—he stood over me and looked down with such smug satisfaction that my blood turned to ice—"maiden, mother, crone."

As the last word left his lips, a tiny old woman was shoved into the earthen cavern. She was small, but her eyes gleamed in the dark with puma-like ferocity as she peered into the murky room. She looked like an old-world villager from a hillside tribe— flowing skirt, apron, multiple rings on her hands, and colored scarves. There was something familiar about the determined set of her jaw, though…

"Mami Tulke!" I yelled, sitting upright, but Clancy stuck his boot in my chest and knocked me backward. My head hit stone with a jarring thud that rang my ears.

Mami Tulke threw her body over me, whispering in Spanish. *"Oh niña, lo siento mucho. Traté de venir por ti."* She was sorry. She tried to come for me. The man pulled her away and dragged her to the third stone—the one reserved for the crone.

"How did you get my grandmother?" I yelled. "Why?" Every time I thought things couldn't get worse…

"You led me right to her, my dear," Clancy answered. "I read it in the journal that was with your belongings. Gráinne's writings were quite intriguing, especially the part about meeting another Scintilla when she went to Chile."

"Giovanni?" I asked, hoping to draw out information. Did they have him? Had he escaped Dr. M's at all? "You no longer need him?"

"He will be sold like chattel on the black market, luv." Clancy clapped his hands together. "Grand. That settles the how. Now, for the why of it." He pointed a fat finger at me. "You represent birth, Cora. Dear Gráinne, you represent life." He stopped at the sandaled feet of my grandmother, who was still spitting and struggling. "You represent death." His voice rose to an exultant tenor. "All three phases of life itself, in their most powerful energetic form, are offered up before me at the most sacred site of our kind. An Arrazi's holy grail."

This was what he'd wanted all along? "Why? Tell me why." In one swoop, he'd eliminate three generations of my family. How could this be his grail, or anything close to *holy*?

"Some say that once an Arrazi takes the entire spirit of a Scintilla into his own, he will obtain their sortilege and never have to kill again. Those are nice notions, to be sure, but not nearly enough. I take the life of you three, the symbolic and energetic essence of life's cycles, and I become *free* of the cycle—free of life's cycle. I live *forever*."

"Greed!" spat my grandmother. "Who believes in such prophesies?"

"The whole world believes in prophesies," he said. "What do

you think the book of Revelations is, old woman?"

"You *actually* think that you'll live *forever*?" My heart churned erratically with every word he said. "What if you're wrong? Then you only succeed in killing three valuable Scintilla," I said, appealing to his greed.

"It's been done before. One woman has already proven it, and now I will. Every queen needs a king. You three will die, and this time, my lovesick nephew isn't going to help you."

I turned my head away, a tear seeping from my eye into the stone. "He's had chances to help me and didn't."

"May it be a comforting thought to you before you die to know that he *did* try, and he failed."

I had no idea what that meant. Clancy had attacked me right after Mari and Dun had run into Finn at the waterfront. Finn's brutish Arrazi friend had attacked me outside the party, *and* Finn left me to wither away in Dr. M's facility. If helping me was Finn's aim, he did fail. Impressively.

A surprised squeak of a scream rose from either my mother or my grandmother, but before I could register what had caused it, I felt the searing rip of the energy around my heart. Clancy stood in the middle of the triangle of stones, pulling our platinum energies out of each of us simultaneously. A vortex of silver rose from our chests, spinning, blooming like a mercury-dipped rose in the air above us.

I tried to scream, but my voice caught in the painful cyclone and swirled away on the wind of his thievery. Clancy's head tipped back in rapture. His arms slowly lifted up as the energy of the three of us rose higher and higher. His aura was morphing from a grimy reddish-brown, like dried blood, to blinding white. My vision blinked in and out as I drained. I felt like a vast desert, cracking under the harsh cloak of a frozen, dry winter. I tried to fixate on my mother's and grandmother's energies. If I could divert my own to them, could I save them? Buy them time?

But our auras became indistinguishable in the storm. To my eyes, our light mixed and spread out above us, a galaxy of shimmering stars.

When the wind scattered me to the stars...

Fifty-Eight

Cora

Clancy's aura expanded into a cloud of white as he pulled life from the three of us.

My grandmother turned and our eyes met. She blinked heavily and gave a slight nod, like resignation or permission. Her gaze was suddenly torn from mine to something behind me, and I felt a blast of cold air. For one heart-wrenching instant, I thought it was my final moment, my soul leaving my body forever. But the rustle of black fabric swooshed over my chest momentarily as someone leaped over me. Clancy Mulcarr flew backward. The yank on my energy slackened, then released.

"Ultana?" he gasped, clearly afraid, and in awe. "How—?"

"You're a disobedient little peasant," a woman's serrated voice said to Clancy. "I counted on that. As if I'd let *you* have the three." A medieval blade jutted from her hand, and she had it pointed right at him.

"You've been spying on me?" he asked, incredulous. He hadn't moved from the floor, but sat like a scolded puppy. "So, it's not true then? The legend of the immortal woman?"

"True, to be sure," she answered. "I am the White Goddess."

Gasping for breath and barely able to see clearly, I peered at the back of the person who'd saved us. This lady was *immortal*? Was it a sortilege? Was it even possible? She'd sacrificed a maiden, mother, and crone before? The woman turned and surveyed us with cold eyes.

The wild bird in my chest fluttered and…fell.

It was the Arrazi woman from the masked ball. The necklace of locks dangled from her neck. She pointed a stump of a hand at my mother like a condemnation.

"I did tell you our day of reckoning would come, Gráinne Sandoval," she roared in a delirious voice, pulsing with disturbed excitement. "Thirteen years since you severed my hand, and thirteen years I've watched that little hovel of yours, waiting for you to return. I have pictures of this girl—your long-lost daughter—there with Finn Doyle. My men almost caught them, too." Her sneer turned into a cruel smile. "They aren't the first Arrazi and Scintilla to find themselves drawn to each other. Opposites *do* attract. However, if I have my way, they *will* be the last."

The cavern was quiet but for the spit of the fire in the torches until Ultana spoke again. "It's been a long time, but it will have been worth the wait when I absorb every drop of your light into mine."

"Please stop this!" I yelled through a hoarse throat. "She took your hand. You don't need to take her life!"

"The White Goddess has no need for an eye for an eye. That's the recompense of the equal, and none of you are *my* equal." She spun in a circle within the triangle, her dagger slicing the air above us. "Together, you are the maiden, mother, and crone. Separate, you are nothing but coins in my pockets."

"Why the maiden, mother, and crone, White Goddess?" I asked, trying to cool her fire with flattery. A walnut of fear blocked my throat. "Clancy thought he'd live forever if he killed us. If you're already immortal, then why do *you* need us?"

Clancy appeared as interested in her answer as I was.

She laughed. "I don't *need* you, tiny spark. I need you dead!" Her voice lowered. "Every last one of you. When the last light goes out, when the last Scintilla dies, the truth dies with you. That is my tedious job, and I want it finished."

"What is the truth that will die with us?" my mother choked out. Her voice sounded so far away, like she was half dead already. I tried to send her energy, but it felt like scraping gray dust from the bottom of a well.

Ultana laughed. "It's genocide, dear. We've been eradicating you for millennia. You're nearly wiped from Earth and good riddance, too."

Mami Tulke smiled wryly as she stared up at the earthen ceiling. What? What could make an old woman smile in the midst of a bizarre human sacrifice? I had so many questions for her, and despaired that I'd never get the chance to ask.

Ultana's voice rose higher. "The Scintilla will be smeared from the pages of history, and *I* will be celebrated for doing so."

My ability to brown-nose had run its course. "Celebrated by whom? The Arrazi have wanted to use us, collect us, even profit from us. If you'll be celebrated, that means there's someone else whose opinion you grovel for. You'll be celebrated for doing someone else's dirty work. Whose? The Society's? It's not why do *you* want us dead, but why are you being their attack dog? Why do *they* want us dead? What is Xepa, and why are they using Arrazi like you and Clancy to get to us?"

"I *am* the Society, girl. Xepa is my answer to every patriarchal secret society that has ever existed, and I've eclipsed them all. Within Xepa's hierarchy, there is none above me."

An Arrazi controlled Xepa?

"You still haven't said why you want all Scintilla dead. Why? How can that be in your best interest if we are a source of power for you? My grandmother is right, it's greed. It has to be. You want our sortilege. You don't want anyone else to have it, including your fellow Arrazi. Right?"

She leaned down, peering into my face with discerning, callous eyes. Her face was so close to mine that I thought I saw the letter *V* branded into the side of her cheek. "Ah," she whispered, evading my question. "You're curious about my scar?" Her fingers lit on it momentarily, betraying a bit of insecurity. She pointed at my forehead where my mother had branded me with love. "You're scarred, too."

"You have *no* idea."

My body was a minefield of memories. I didn't know what mark I bore from those precious moments with my mother. I might never know.

"I was branded as a thief hundreds of years ago, back when they used such barbaric punishments," Ultana said, her hand floating to her marred face and down to her necklace. "I excel at picking locks for which I have no key." Then, her scrutiny traveled to my throat and she ruthlessly ripped the silver key from my neck. "*She wore a key like Janus which opened up the gates to the invisible world.* I see I'm not the only thief in this room."

I didn't dare look at my grandmother. I still had no idea where she'd gotten the key or what it unlocked. *Gates to the invisible world?* My mother had been so scared about the key being found that she'd had it buried in the forest. The Scintilla desperately needed to know what that key opened, and now it was in the enemy's possession.

"The Arrazi are the lowest of thieves," I said.

Ultana glanced at my bound hands, unfurled my fingers, and slowly tugged the Xepa ring from me. "This is also mine."

The second she touched me, I latched onto her energy with every bit of strength remaining. I didn't know if I could purposely summon her memories into me, but I had to try. My present mind faded into the background as pieces of her history surged forward. She had a *vault* of sortileges to choose from. They spun past my view. Making sense of her many years and many powers was like sifting through shards of mirrors. Ultana was *very* old— unnaturally, impossibly old. I couldn't know for sure if she was immortal. Maybe her abnormally long life was a stolen power from a long-ago Scintilla, one of many silver souls she'd ruthlessly killed.

She snatched her hand away with a wary look burning in her eyes. "You are a thief," she accused. "You steal memories."

"You're not immortal. You're lying. I saw it in your history. Anyone can kill you. Clancy here could kill you for lying to him, for pretending to be more powerful than you are," I bluffed, desperately hoping he might seize the opportunity. Let them feed on each other.

The anger that exploded from her made it obvious that *she* was wholly convinced of her sortilege to live forever and that she resented my nerve. "You doubt my immortality? You know of others who have lived as long as I?" she said, reaching for me but catching herself before our skin made contact.

She was afraid of what I might see.

I pressed on. "With no proof, I think it's easy to say and impossible to believe. Prove how powerful you are once and for all. Who could ever challenge you? Your faithful peasant here will regale the Arrazi with the tale. You have that sword. Use it to silence doubt."

"I could use it to silence you."

I fought to keep my voice steady, like I'd run out of give-a-damn. "Great. Let us see the awe-inspiring power you possess before you silence us all."

She raised the blade. I dared to hope, but she pointed the spiked tip at my chest.

"I don't believe in you," I whispered shakily, shrinking with fear now that the sword was piercing the skin over my heart.

Those eyes that had seen so much death showed no trace of fear at all as she whipped the blade away from my chest and drove it into her own stomach. She looked almost pleased, overcome with emotion, as if she'd wanted for so long to thrust a blade into her body.

"You're not going to live forever." My heart surged so hard it was almost unbearable to breathe. Seeing the blade protrude from her stomach curdled my own. "You *can* die, you mortal bitch. And when you do, I hope you rot in hell."

Drops of fear rained into her eyes until they were full with it, but her smile was still confident, triumphant. "Hell," she gasped. "Dante's great icy hell... The *Inferno.*" My eyes must've lit upon hearing his name because she added, "Oh yes, he said the same thing to me when I killed him for trying to cleverly spread the truth with that book of his. Why is it you Scintilla always threaten me with hell? The life of an Arrazi *is* hell!"

With no warning, and as Clancy did before her, she outstretched her arms and immediately tore through the three of us with her Arrazi energy. The hilt of her sword protruded from her gut and the tip stuck like a fang from her back. My chest heaved forward, her pull infinitely more violent than Clancy Mulcarr's, or Griffin's before him. This woman was a ruthless monster and a much more efficient killer. And, despite the gash through her middle, she was devastatingly alive.

Too soon, her aura detonated in white.

I quickly looked from my grandmother to my mom, realizing in horror that there was no beautiful torrent of silver coming from my mother's chest and rising above her to join with ours. Her silver stream of light was...just...*gone,* her body still as the stone she laid upon.

I searched the air above us, watching the clouds of silver like a sailor does before a storm.

Reaching was like fighting gravity. I couldn't lift my bound hands from my stomach, but I wanted nothing more than to touch my mother one last time before my own light left me. I could only lift them enough to cross them over my own chest— as I once had in the hospital in my futile attempt to protect my spirit. I watched, helplessly, as my silver aura surged from my body toward Ultana against my will.

The word "no" barely had time to pass my lips before all breath was sucked out with it.

Swirling and vibrating with the tempest of violent silver waves, another "no" resounded. Finn's energy swept into the room.

Finn leaped in front of Ultana, whose eyes had been closed as she drank from our souls. We'd soon be empty cups. Did he realize she was taking from us? Once her energy hit Finn, she'd take from him, too. I tried to yell a warning.

Inexplicably, instead of falling to his knees when her rope of spirit latched onto him, the woman was thrown backward, hitting the wall with a terrible cracking of bones. Her head lolled forward. The impact pushed the blade forward. It slipped from her stomach with a sickening wet sound.

My aura hung suspended above me, then funneled back down, into my gasping body.

Clancy leaped up, but Finn grabbed the bloody weapon with one hand and savagely pushed his uncle backward. He fell down next to where Ultana leaned, barely conscious. Not dead. If she were dead, her white light would be dead as well, but it burned brilliant white, fueled by the light of my mother's life.

I turned my head into the cold stone, sobbing.

Finn sliced my binds apart with the sword and gingerly slipped the rope from my wrists. I stared at his forehead, which was wrinkled in concentration. He avoided my eyes. Then he untied my grandmother, who rolled off the rock, crawled over, and knelt next to my mother, murmuring prayers in Spanish.

I fell to her side. Mom's bound hands reminded me of the handfasting she and my dad had performed at their wedding, symbolically tying them together forever. Now they were joined in death. I bent my lips to kiss her hands. Tears streamed onto the soft pads of her fingers. Too soon, someone lifted her up and away from me.

I gasped at the silver aura. Giovanni? He clutched my mother possessively to his chest.

"Where are the other men?" I asked.

"We drugged them with their own syringes," Giovanni said and carried my mother out into the new morning that had been her last. I choked with sobs, leaning my head against the stone, and then pushed myself shakily to my feet.

"Never in your life did you make such an abysmally wrong choice, lad," Clancy groaned to Finn, who stood between the two Arrazi on the floor and us. Finn was one of them but guarding... *us*. He towered over Clancy with clenched fists and the sword dripping blood into a small dot in the dirt. "You're betting on the losing side!" Clancy roared, his deep voice thunder in the small tomb. A shock of his white hair fell over his forehead as he yelled. "Have you given no thought to how this will impact you, our family? You've killed us all!"

Finn's voice was calm and measured, very much like his mother's. "I'm thinking more about how this will impact the world."

Ultana's head bobbed up with effort. "Clancy, you duplicitous bastard. You've been on the losing side as well—your own. Finn *wants* to die. After this betrayal, he will *surely* get his wish."

"Not before you do!" I screamed, grabbing the sword from Finn and rushing forward to finish the job. I'd drive it through her so many times my mother's soul would escape and fly to heaven.

Finn grabbed me from behind. "No, Cora!"

"Some—someone needs to pay," I moaned. "My mother... my father...Mari."

"I know, luv. I know. But Ultana has information. More than anyone here, I reckon," he said against my ear. "If she dies, then what she knows dies with her."

I shot a look at Clancy. Everything in me wanted to drive the blade through both of their ruthless hearts. I shook against Finn, fighting to be free. "I want this to be over."

Scarier than feeling murderous toward the two Arrazi who were responsible for the inhuman deaths of my family was the *absence* of compassion. Hate like I'd never known wound through every inch of me.

"Kill us, puppet," Clancy challenged. "But it won't be over."

I kicked my foot toward Clancy. "You killed Mari, I know you did. I want you to die. When you do, who will come after us then? She said it herself, she *is* the Society, the enemy. Who will even care if you're dead? If she's dead, then no one will give any more orders to destroy us."

"You *can't* kill me, stupid girl," Ultana coughed.

Finn coaxed the knife from my hand and moved in front of me. He looked directly in Ultana's eyes. "You made it very clear that protection, money, and power were to be secured by all Arrazi who do the Society's bidding, including your own family. If you rule Xepa, then who rules you? Who threatens your family? Or were those all lies?"

All eyes were on her, waiting for that answer. Even Clancy watched eagerly for her response. We'd thought the Society was the ultimate enemy, but was it? Ultana squirmed and kicked in agony as she clutched her bloody stomach much like my father once had. She was fighting Finn's sortilege, fighting not to answer.

But something else I noticed—her light, it was fading, folding into her physical body slowly, inch by inch. She was either very scared, or...*very* wrong about herself.

God, let her be wrong.

Let her answer his questions in time.

"I believe I know who she protects with her silence," Mami Tulke rasped from behind me. She shuffled forward, kicking up centuries of dust with her sandals. "She will not tell you."

"She has to tell him," I said. "Finn's sortilege is to pull the truth."

"I see," Mami Tulke said, looking at Clancy. "You forced me to use my sortilege, my ability to shield, so you could skirt this boy's sortilege to obtain the truth. You used me to deceive him. But," she said, pointing a gnarled finger at Ultana, "this woman will not speak the truth against her will. Our powers do not work on her. I tried to shield as she was attacking us and could not."

"Christ, Clancy. That's how you did it, how you lied to me?" Finn said. "I was a fool to think my power would guarantee honesty. Worse," Finn said, dipping his chin, "I was a fool to want to believe you."

"Yet the boy doesn't have to speak the truth himself," Ultana said with a smirk. "Why does this girl you've risked everything to save think that Clancy killed her cousin? Since honesty is so revered here, does she not deserve to know the truth?"

"What? What truth?" I asked Finn.

Finn angled his head to look at me, but his eyes stopped short in a way that made me cringe. What did he know?

"That key in your hand," Mami Tulke interrupted, motioning to Ultana. "It does not belong to you."

"You know this how, old woman?" Ultana asked, tiredly.

"I know this because I'm the thief who took it." Her wrinkled mouth split into a proud smile when Ultana's eyes grew wide. She nodded. "You know from where I stole it. That's the truth you don't want to speak."

"Where did you get the key?" I asked my grandmother, my body quivering. I felt so cold that the room undulated, dreamlike, and my body felt strangely disconnected from my head. My mom would tell me to ground myself. Stay present. Be strong.

Mom.

Mami Tulke's hand gave a dismissive wave at my question. "The church."

"What church?" Finn asked. "Where?"

"*The* church," Mami Tulke spat, exasperated. "I took it from *the rock*, the keeper of the keys of heaven. It comes from the Vatican."

"*Cristo*," Giovanni whispered. He'd come back in from outside and was listening at the doorway. His arms were heartbreakingly empty. Astonishment rounded his eyes, and his mouth hung open. "*The Vatican?* She *stole* the hand of Saint Peter from the Vatican! It's been an unsolved mystery for years." He laughed nervously, incredulous.

"You're telling me that I've been wearing a key around my neck that was hidden inside a hand, a hand that *you* stole from one of the most famous statues in the world?"

Ultana chuckled and a bit of blood sputtered from her mouth. The way she appraised my grandmother could've been described as admiration. What? Honor among thieves? Her puffed breaths came faster as she clutched her wound. Her astral body was thin as smoke around her upper body and head and diminishing into the air. She gasped and leveled me with old, knowing eyes. "*A mighty flame follows a tiny spark.* Run, little Scintilla. Run. Because as long as there is a God on their altar, you will always be hunted."

FIFTY-NINE

Finn

Ultana Lennon had no more words after that.

Cora stood, unmoving, and stared down at the old Arrazi. Was Cora aware of how violently she was shaking? I yearned to wrap my arms around her. She needed to cry. She needed to kick and scream and release the pain that rippled from her body so strongly that it hit me in gusts. How was she even standing? I stared at her profile in the flickering light. Cora was the strongest person I'd ever known.

"Mortal after all," Cora said, startling me from my gazing. She bent and slid the key from Ultana's open hand. "Her light's gone out."

"Who ran her through? You?" Giovanni asked me, stepping forward and requesting the sword with his outstretched hand. "I'll finish this." He motioned toward my uncle.

I denied him the weapon. "In actual fact, the blade was in her stomach already when I ran in." She'd blown back when her energy hit me. That was when I'd seen the sword in her stomach.

The only person in the room who hadn't been tied up was my uncle. "You stabbed her?" I asked Clancy.

Clancy rested one arm on his knee and ran a hand over his bearded face, tinting it with brown dust. He shook his head. "Cora taunted Ultana like a schoolchild. I can't believe Ultana fell for it. Truly, I can't believe she died. How did you know she wasn't immortal, girl?" Clancy asked Cora.

Cora's voice was flat, dead as the air in the room. "I didn't. But she was alive for hundreds of years. I saw it in her memories."

"Well," I said, "seems that too many years were spent fertilizing her egotistical pride rather than pruning it."

I could barely see that Giovanni had a syringe hidden in his hand when he lunged forward with no words and with no warning. He grabbed Clancy by the hair, yanked his head over, and shoved the needle into the side of his neck. Clancy's eyes were wide with shock before he was overcome by the drug.

The prey attacked the predator.

"No!" Cora yelled, too late. "Dammit, G. He couldn't follow us as long as he was conscious. That's how he followed us to the shack before. He was put under and was able to use his sortilege. Jesus. He'll track us until he comes to."

Giovanni threw down the spent syringe. "Then let's finish it."

Cora's grandmother shuffled over and took Cora's hand and led her outside. They went out into the cool air and stood mournful watch over her mother's body while Giovanni and I dragged the two thugs into the burial tomb. We went back outside, and I walked over to the door and clicked the lock in place.

"We should kill them, you know we should," Giovanni said to Cora. "If we don't, we'll face them another day, and next time we may not walk away."

"Not all of us *are* walking away," Cora choked out, looking down at her mother's sweet face. That woman had known too much sorrow in her short life. I watched Giovanni stare mournfully at Cora's mum, too. It was the first time I felt bad for him. This tribe of Scintilla had suffered enough losses.

"I want them dead, but I don't want to be a murderer like them," Cora said.

Giovanni's hands clenched into fists. "It's not the same as what they do. I will do it," he said. "With no guilt."

Cora spun toward him. "You think I'm weak for not wanting to kill them? I *do* want to. And that's what disturbs me. I want nothing more than for them to stay in that tomb and never come out." She held up her hands. "And what of all your talk of connectedness? Of oneness, huh? If vengeance is a volley hit back and forth, how does it ever end unless someone refuses to strike back?"

"The fear you'll have in facing them again might be the steep price you pay for peace within yourself," I said, though I looked at my feet when I did.

"How do you find peace with yourself, Finn?" Her voice was hard, but I could tell she wanted to know if I'd genuinely come to terms with being an Arrazi.

Finally, I looked up, feeling a sharp sting when I met her eyes for the first time since we stared at each other through the glass window. "I haven't. I never will."

SIXTY

Cora

Finn stood with us, but apart.

I sighed. He'd voiced my feelings exactly when he said fear was my price for inner peace. Of course he understood, though I doubted fear was *his* currency. From what he said, to the look in his eyes and his aura, guilt was his currency. He'd had to kill to stay alive. While I abhorred it, I couldn't deny being happy he was alive. He'd helped us, helped me. Again.

That meant something.

Giovanni's eyes rolled over Finn, but not in the derisive way I'd expected. I didn't know what had happened between them that they showed up together, but there was something hopeful about an Arrazi and a Scintilla standing side by side in a field of wet grass and sorrow.

"So, we're just going to leave them locked up in there? I suppose they could die anyway," Giovanni said with an optimistic shrug. "Who'd find them way out here?"

"That will be up to chance, won't it?" I hardened myself to

thoughts of their fate. Hopefully, they'd be trapped long enough for us to get far away—a head start. At least Ultana wasn't one we'd ever have to worry about again.

Finn bent and scooped my mother into his arms. How long could we stay in each other's presence? His aura was colored but weak—water with fine swirls of paint in it.

Like the labyrinth of lines curving over and over again on the triple spiral, our good-byes were always guaranteed to circle back around.

In the car, my mother was laid out across my lap as well as Giovanni's. I found myself roping small braids into the hair around her face. Every so often, a silver strand of hair would peek from among the black and my heart would pulse and swell with a mixture of both love and unthinkable grief. I'd never forget the unique light of my mother. She gave me my own. Seemed like a reckless thing for a Scintilla to do.

"Why did they have me at all?" I found myself asking no one in particular. "If they knew what I could become?" Everyone who could answer that question was gone. Finn's eyes jerked to me. "Of course. Arrazi children wonder the same thing."

He gave one affirming nod. "Perhaps more so."

"Where are we going?" Mami Tulke asked.

"To lay Gráinne to rest," Finn answered quietly, pulling onto a road that I knew led to his house.

"Why would I bury my mother at your house?" But then, where on earth *would* I bury her? I heard her strained voice in my head saying, *Take me home.* I couldn't bury her at the home she shared with my father. It wasn't safe. Ultana had said it herself—she'd been watching that place for years.

Finn's eyes caught mine in the rearview mirror. "We won't be here long. You'll understand soon."

"Claire is there with Finn's mother," Giovanni said. "And Dun. We need to get them and go someplace safe."

"Safety doesn't exist for us," I said, aware that my voice sounded rigid and skeptical, and I hadn't agreed to go anywhere with him.

"Oh, you mean like how you encouraged everyone to go to Dr. M's for safety when you were profiting from it?" Finn fired at him.

"On my life I didn't know what Dr. M was going to do to us. I needed money. He paid me to find others like me. For *research*. He'd never hurt me in the past. I had no reason to assume he was bad." Giovanni's eyes pleaded for me to believe him. I noticed his hands were placed over my mother's folded hands on her stomach.

"Okay."

Finn slammed his hand on the steering wheel. "What? You're going to take his word?"

"Yes. You're here. He'd *have* to tell the truth, wouldn't he?"

"I'm not so sure anymore," Finn said.

"That man," Mami Tulke began in her jagged accent, turning to Finn. "He said Cora was in another room and he would kill her if I didn't protect him from other people's powers."

"I wondered how he lied," Finn said, with a sympathetic look to Mami Tulke. "I was arrogant and too stupid to realize he might have found a way around my sortilege. I'm sorry he used you like that to get to your granddaughter."

She patted his arm with her wrinkled hand. "You are a good human."

"No. I'm Arrazi."

Her chin rose as she appraised him. "Still good."

"He comes from good people," I told her. "He and his parents helped us escape before when—when Dad died."

Mami Tulke twisted in her seat and looked at me, first deep in my eyes and then down to my mom's head in my lap with her black hair cascading over my knees. My grandmother's chin trembled. "I believe Arrazi are either taught to hate, or they hate themselves for what they are forced to do," she said. Her gaze turned again to Finn. "Stay with the light inside of you. Light is there."

Finn's jaw clenched. "If it was, I wouldn't have to steal it."

He drove through the gate and edged the car to the far side of the driveway near the grassy cliff where I once sat on a sunny afternoon, reading my mother's journal. He got out and helped Giovanni scoot out of the car with my mother's slender body clasped against him. I wanted, more than anything, to carry her in my own arms, or to touch her, kiss her, pull her back from where she was. I wanted more than anything for her not to be dead. To have a chance at a happy ending.

My heart twisted and wrung out the useless wish. Every time someone I loved was taken from me, my heart would shrink more until there was nothing left. Is that how I would be taught to hate? Is that how I'd stray from the light in me?

Giovanni carried my mother's body as we followed Finn across the lawn toward the rounded head of a boulder jutting from freshly turned ground. I ran ahead of everyone. Words had been carved into the stone.

> "OH, MY FRIEND, ALL THAT YOU SEE OF ME IS JUST A SHELL
> AND THE REST BELONGS TO LOVE."
> —*RUMI*

I sank to my knees, placing my hands on the marker. Tears spilled down my cheeks, and my bottom lip trembled so hard it was difficult to speak. "You buried my father," I gasped, with one hand over my stunned heart. Cutting remorse had consumed me every minute since I'd had to leave my father's body behind in that tack shed. I'd never expected or even thought…

I looked up at Finn standing next to me. The fact that he had done this for my father overwhelmed me with gratitude. Without rational thought, I threw myself into him, crushing us into a tight embrace. "Thank you," I said, shaking with tears. He clutched my back and held me as tightly as I was holding him. His body shook against mine.

It was impossible to separate the feelings competing inside of me. The pain, grief, anger, fear, love—all of it coexisted. I inhaled Finn's familiar scent. Listened to the beat of his heart like it was the last falling notes of a song I'd never hear again. It was my own thievery, knowing it would likely be the last time I'd smell him, feel him against me, and let his warm colors envelop me.

My truth reared up against my will. No one made me feel this way. He was still the hearth my heart warmed itself by. He was still my other half. I'd tried to let him go. It was inexplicable, but my Scintilla soul still longed for his Arrazi soul. He was home, and it didn't matter how many times I turned my back on it. He was still home.

"I might have been wrong about you," I said into his neck. "Love is what we do every day. It's in our actions. I was stupid and cruel to assume you were incapable of it. You'd never have done any of this if you didn't love me."

Finn let out a choking cry and squeezed a bit harder. "I—I'm sorry," he said, pushing me away and stumbling backward. My chest seized up. "I can't…" Sorrow creased his eyes as he slowly backed away from me.

He didn't want my talk of love anymore.

His aura was thin as mist, the colors muted. He was weakening, but not totally in need yet. I was such a lovesick fool that *he* was the one strong enough to remind me how unsafe I was in his presence.

"I'm so sorry. So sorry." Tears cascaded from his soft eyes, over his high cheekbones. "I did everything I could think of to save her. Ultana was never going to let her leave."

My breath caught. "What are you talking about, Finn?"

"When it came down to either me or Ultana, Mari *asked* me to be the one to do it." Finn sobbed into the heels of his hands. "I've hated myself every second, especially for not thinking to jump in front of Ultana when she was taking from Mari, like I did today. That's how I got the idea, but it came too late for Mari. Oh God, forgive me. You've lost more than anyone should have to. I'm so sorry, luv."

That "luv" was both a balm and a bullet, but I was struggling to fathom what he was saying. "What—what are you telling me? You're saying that Mari *asked* you to kill her? And *you*—" Stumbling over that word, I fought to finish. "And you did?"

"No," Mami Tulke gasped, pressing her palms together and lifting them to her lips like a prayer. She stumbled backward.

I backed away from both of the boys who had betrayed me so deeply that I'd never be the same girl who gave away pieces of herself.

A blast of blackened, scorched energy flew past me. Dun leaped onto Finn, pinning him to the ground. His aura blazed with rage, swirling around him like a hurricane. He raised his fists and pummeled Finn. Blow after blow landed on Finn's body and face. Blood spurted from his nose. Darkened his split lips. Finn did nothing. And he could have. We all knew it. He closed his eyes and took the beating like it was rain falling upon him.

Dun's punches slowed, like he'd spun himself out, and a part of me was relieved. But when he fell forward and off Finn, I realized his aura had been attacked. Not fatally. Just enough to stop him.

"Damn you, Finn!" I screamed, rushing to block Dun. This seemed a further betrayal after what he'd done. I would beat him unconscious myself. I raised my fist, but my own aura was attacked and I tumbled to the ground.

"Not...me..." Finn groaned, breathless, bloody.

"Enough!" a severe voice yelled from behind me. Ina Doyle smoothed her hand over her black hair, while shooting daggers at Dun and me. She cocked an eyebrow. "I won't have it. I am a mother, above all."

Finn rolled to his side, clutching his ribs. He struggled to draw breath. "I'll never stop—"

"Shut up!" I sobbed. But he didn't.

"I'll never stop being guilty, hating myself, feeling sorry. God, I'm so sorry. I'll never stop wanting to be dead rather than be what I am. And until I am dead, Cora, I'll never stop loving you."

For a few minutes, our cries floated on the morning air.

"What will you do now?" Finn asked in a thick voice.

I was too dazed to answer. All emotion, all feelings were sucked into a black hole somewhere inside of me—a place so deep and inaccessible that it felt like they would never rise up again. Utterly numb, I could only operate on the most base level, that of survival.

"She will come to Chile with me," Mami Tulke said with finality.

"Shhh," I said, standing and reaching for her hand. I needed someone's hand or I was afraid I'd implode right there, next to my mother's dead body over my dead father's grave. "Clancy's soul is on a string," I said, parroting my mother's words. "He might hear us."

Multiple looks drifted up and around as if we'd actually see the astral specter of Clancy Mulcarr floating nearby, eavesdropping, watching.

"Mami Tulke, you're the only family I have left. I know I'll end up with you someday, if I'm lucky. I want you to take Giovanni and the—his—little girl with you. Keep them safe until I can join you."

"Until?" Giovanni asked. "Where do you think you're going?"

I ignored him and kept my eyes fixed on my grandmother. "Tell me why you took this key from the Vatican," I pleaded, presenting the silver relic on my outstretched hand. "Please."

"Every generation of Scintilla speaks of us as the *keys to heaven*," Mami Tulke said, her face bunching like old, mangled paper. "Who thinks they have exclusive ownership to the keys to heaven?" she asked. And when no one answered she spoke more forcefully. "The church!

"It was a wild impulse to go, yes. Keys to heaven. But as I stared at Saint Peter with his pointing finger and his keys, I noticed that the hand was removable. I became obsessed with the idea that Saint Peter had something to hide." Her eyes shone with pride as her chin tilted up. "I was right, *mija.*"

"He may have been hiding a key, Grandma, but we don't know to what. We don't know why. If I'm ever going to stop this, I have to find out."

Ultana had said many things in the tomb, but she did confirm that Giovanni and I had been on the right track. Dante Alighieri knew the truth and had been trying to share it with the world. What the totality of that truth was, we still didn't know. The thing

Ultana said about being hunted as long as there was a God on the altar could've been a lie just like her immortality was. Either way, I was going to Italy. "*Paradiso…*" I murmured to myself.

"You—you said *Paradiso*?" Finn asked, squinting one eye that was already swelling. "I have a—a thing to show you," he said, being equally as careful not to say too much. "I found something about Dante at Ultana's that you might want to see."

"Okay," I said, discomfort mixing with curiosity.

Giovanni approached me. "Why on earth, Cora?" He'd already surmised where I was headed, of course.

"Dante, the key, Ultana's warning…I believe the truth is there."

"The danger is there. I will go with you," Giovanni said. "It's truth I need to know, as well. You cannot go alone." When I shot him a warning look, he lifted his proud chin and said, "Tell me no, and I'll still trail you. I'll be your shadow because it's the right thing to do."

"Giovanni, you can't save her life," Finn said with effort. He then looked at me. "Let me go with you. Giovanni has had a *geis* put on him by Lorcan Lennon. He's the bloke who attacked you, the one who was with me at the facility where you were being kept. And he's Ultana's son. Cora, you must believe what I say. If Giovanni saves your life," Finn explained, looking from Giovanni to me, "he will die."

I gasped. Unbelievable.

"These boys are right, you shouldn't go alone," Mami Tulke said.

"I have to go." I motioned to my mother's body. "I can't let this stand. And I'm going alone. For the survival of our kind, it's best if we split up. None of you are coming."

"I don't understand exactly what you hope to achieve," Finn

argued, struggling so hard to stand that his mother rushed to aid him. "Especially alone. To avenge your parents' deaths? You'll earn your own. Ultana could have been lying. Everything she said could have been lies."

"What if I could end this? I inferred from Ultana that Xepa was under the thumb of someone at the Vatican, and if that's true, the church put my parents in the grave. How can I stand by and let them put the truth in the grave and bury all of us as if we never existed? Whoever *is* behind all of this is close, so close to eradicating us all, and they're using the Arrazi to do it. I have to find out why."

"I'll go," Dun said. He was still sitting on the ground. His eyes were rimmed in red from crying. "I'll go anywhere to help keep you safe. I'm not losing my other best friend," he choked out a vow.

"Cora, please." The plea came from both Finn and Giovanni simultaneously. They cast sideways glances at each other as the morning sun crested over the tops of the trees and shone down on us.

"Finn, you once said to me, 'How can mankind evolve if we aren't searchers of truth?' I *have* to keep searching." Finn looked away, stewing in his own words. I glanced at Giovanni. "I have to do this, have to keep moving forward. It's the only way to fight for the truth and stay in the light."

I stared down at the key in my hand and intentionally eased out the memories it held: triangles, pyramids, the Star of David, Borromean rings, which reminded me of Michelangelo's monogram, trefoils, the trinity, and three-headed gods... Along with all of the images, the triple spiral was there. The triple spiral...

"I need to go back to Newgrange," I said. A new idea sent fresh, urgent excitement coursing through me. "I need to go there right now."

SIXTY-ONE

Cora

Everyone erupted into argument as I ran toward the car. I had to touch the ancient stone. The spirals would tell me what truths they stored—wouldn't they?

Shouts and pleas bounced off me as I reached for the door handle. Finn's hand was suddenly over mine. I shot him a warning look that said I'd blacken his other eye if he tried to stop me, but he opened the car door for me with a yielding nod.

I pleaded with Dun to stay with my grandmother and watch over her until we returned. No matter how helpful Finn's family had been, I couldn't leave her alone with Arrazi.

Finn, Giovanni, and I jumped into Finn's car. "You mind explaining," Finn asked, pulling a tiny bit of skin from his split lip, "why you aim to go *back* toward the scene of your near-death? This is bloody insanity."

"Your charming Irish banter still needs work," I said. "I have to touch the stone to access the memories."

"Your sortilege?" he asked.

"Yes. There must be memories in the stones, and if there are," I said, glancing at what I could see of Finn's triple spiral tattoo, "they mean something to all of us. From the moment I dug up this key, I've been wearing clues around my neck. It wasn't until today that I saw how they might fit together."

Arrazi worked for Xepa to find and kill the Scintilla, we'd confirmed that. But our focus on Ultana's secret society only served to deviate us from the larger truth—she worked for someone else. Xepa wasn't the top of the pyramid. From that moment until my last breath, I'd scrabble and climb and fight to find out who or what was at the top.

Giovanni squeezed my shoulder. "We must be quick about this, Cora. We have no way of knowing how long the sedative will last. Surely Clancy and those men will find a way to get out of the tomb, even with the lock on the door."

"I won't need much time."

"I don't like this," Finn said.

I felt the tumbling rocks of nerves in my stomach, but I wouldn't be stopped. Fear was a wall to plow through on the way to where I wanted to go. Once the idea about the triple spiral struck me, I couldn't let it go. If I never set foot on Irish soil again, I'd always wonder about the truth of the ancient symbol. If my power could unlock that truth, I had to try.

I steeled myself for what lay ahead. Regular people were dying in greater numbers, and genocide was the fate for anyone who just happened to be born a Scintilla—like the crime was just in existing. A shift was taking place on Earth, and with the natural disasters, it seemed like it was self-destructing along with everyone aboard. Would our cries ripple into the universe? Amid the raging beauty of the world and some of the people in it, it often felt treacherous, fragile, chaotic, and dark. Lies were the black soil being heaped over all of us. I wanted to believe in the raging beauty again. It made my heart ache before the fire of resolve pumped through it. I guess I was fighting as much for me as for everyone else.

If it was my last act, I vowed to be the light that illuminated the truth.

Acknowledgments

With all of my heart, I thank Sydney and Cooper and my friends who've been so understanding about the passion, time, and commitment I give to my work. Without your support and love, this wouldn't be as meaningful. Hazel, I owe you a million cups of cocoa.

I am eternally grateful (and still pinching myself) for the continued opportunity to see a dream realized. Thank you, Michael Bourret. Thank you to the Entangled team who work so hard to magically transform my words into real-live books! To my editor Karen Grove, I'm raising my glass to our continued partnership. Thank you for believing so strongly in my stories.

Thanks to Stacy Abrams, Kate Fall, and Nicole Steinhaus for their additional editorial guidance and shrewd eyes on both *Scintillate* and *Deviate*. To Pamela Sinclair and Kelly York for the beautiful cover designs. Heather Riccio, you're a publicity wiz and a great advocate. Thank you for the amazing behind-the-scenes support.

To actress Caitlin Rose Mahoney, for being the living embodiment of the sweetness and fire that is Cora Sandoval. To Sam Deas for being a perfect, swoon-worthy Finn. And to Brett

Staal for bringing Giovanni to life. So much gratitude to the entire cast and crew of the *Scintillate* trailer. What an amazing thing you all made together. Blew my mind!

Thanks to Jason Roer (www.cohortsandconspirators.com) for your creative vision and the know-how to make the best book trailer ever! I also thank you for your cheerleading and countless hours of putting up with my revolving door of doubts, elations, worries, and ideas. You've been one of life's surprising gifts.

I'm indebted to my dear friends who critique and beta read for me. I sincerely appreciate the gift of your time and expertise.

Thank you to my YASI sisterhood (www.yaseriesinsiders.com) and to Sophie Riggsby and Katie Bartow (Page Turners Blog and Mundie Moms) for your part in making this the best debut year an author could have!

The Sandoval family was such an important part of my young-adult life that I had to name a character in your honor. Thank you.

Wee one = Thea

Readers! The biggest tackle-hug thanks for your kind words and enthusiasm, and for making my dream come true—that my story would land in the hands of people who would "get it" and enjoy it. This past year of school visits, reviews, messages, bookstore readings, and signings has been a gift and a constant reminder of why this is one of the best jobs in the universe. Thank you!

Keep reading for a sneek peak of
ILLUMINATE
Book 3 — The Light Key Trilogy
by Tracy Clark

*But already my desire and my will were being turned like a wheel,
all at one speed, by the Love which moves the sun and the other
stars.*
—Dante / *Paradiso* / *canto XXXIII*

ONE

Cora

*T*he keys to heaven.

That phrase scratched a deep groove in my brain. I fingered the silver key pressing against my chest as Finn drove Giovanni and me to *Brú na Bóinne* — Newgrange, in Yankee speak. The key was much weightier since I found out it had been stolen by my grandmother from a statue of St. Peter at the Vatican. What was the connection between the key in my hand and the fact that it came from the hand of a saint at one of the most hallowed religious sites in the world? My key couldn't be a *literal* key to heaven, could it? Mom's journal said that the Scintilla were *the keys to heaven.* How could either of those things be true?

Death was the only door to that domain.

My parents had both walked through it. Mari, too.

But I learned that souls don't bleed warm and sticky. The bleed of a soul is stinging ice.

I bet it doesn't feel that way when you die naturally. I bet a natural death is like warm steam rising from a bath, languid and ambitious as it stretches its wings and sails upward.

Both my father and my mother died the cold way. Surely I'd be killed likewise. I intimately knew the icy bleed because I'd already been attacked numerous times by the Arrazi, and every time it felt like the frozen blade of an ice axe stabbing into my chest and splitting me open for my silver aura to spill out.

Pain battered my temples and tension gripped my muscles until they felt bloodless and limp. Soul so angry. Body so damned tired. I'd have to climb the steep stairs out of my weariness to find the truth and use it to stop the slaughter of Scintilla, and innocent humans as well. My circle was shrinking. I had so few people left.

The two boys in the car with me had my love, but my love for them was a receding wave that had swept my heart out to sea.

One was a liar. One was a killer.

The car rolled to a stop in front of the Visitor's Center where Finn ran in for admission tickets. We were uncomfortably close to the tomb where just hours ago, we'd left Clancy Mulcarr unconscious on the floor next to Ultana Lennon's dead body, but I had to shove that fact in a corner of my mind in order to do what I had come here to do.

Tickets in hand, we entered the ancient ruins and ran up the path that led to the megalithic tomb. Each of us climbed the ladder leading over the large curbstone in front of the tomb's entrance. Finn and Giovanni stayed close to me. Together, we stepped inside the dark, cool monument and stared at the giant stone bearing the marking that seemed to connect the Arrazi and the Scintilla through history.

I reached out with shaking fingers to touch the triple spiral. Would the stone itself tell me the truth?

The energy that swirled from the triple spiral was palpable and robust, tingling my fingertips before I even made contact with the stone. I placed my palm flat on the engraving and closed my eyes, waiting to feel my mind spin into a vortex of memory. But I didn't spin. Visions didn't form a tempest in my mind. I remained stubbornly rooted in the present, where all my questions stacked like bricks on top of me. There was energy in the rock, yes, but it was a scratched record. Like reaching my arm into a swirling hum of white noise. Indistinct residue. So many hands had touched this stone over the years that I could pull nothing clear from the static but a faint image of breathtaking spirals of light.

The grooves of cold stone pressed against my head as I leaned forward in frustration. This damn monument had lured me since I was a child, and now it taunted me by holding tight to its secrets.

Ultana Lennon had convinced Clancy that the spirals represented the *maiden, mother, and crone,* and that if he killed me, my mother, and grandmother, he'd become immortal. She'd tricked him. It was a false trinity used by Ultana's twisted mind to ensnare and kill the remaining few Scintilla. She used Clancy to find us, and in the end, she murdered a most precious Scintilla—my mother.

I stared hard at the trinity of interlaced spirals. My mind stretched for connections, fought to understand a mystery that had been around since before the time of Christ. Thousands of years before. After a few moments of staring and thinking, an astonished breath puffed out. "A false trinity…"

"What?" Finn asked.

A glimpse of his triple spiral tattoo could be seen just at his neck where his pulse fired rapid and steady. When I first saw Finn's tattoo in the hospital, I'd recalled that the true meaning of the triple spiral was unknown and that people of various beliefs had hijacked the symbol to suit their own philosophies.

"No one knows what this design really means," I ventured. "But some mistakenly think it symbolizes the holy trinity. The trinity isn't an original idea, though. It's an evolution of ideas from many belief systems, some older than Christianity," I whispered, recalling my mother's writings in her journal and the research we'd done. "If Ultana had been telling the truth that someone won't stop hunting us as long as there's a God on their altar, then all the memories I pulled from the key make more sense. Why would the spiral be in those religious images if it weren't connected? Why would my grandmother steal the key from the church in the first place?"

I grew more excited as I slowly pieced things together. "The religious symbols, the persecution and death of those who dared to believe differently... Those were deeds of the most dominant religion in the world over many centuries."

"Not just one religion," Giovanni said. "Many have killed and still kill for their own special brand of God. I can't see that God would want a thug kingdom populated by murderers, but then I'm just being logical," he added with a cynical tone.

Finn wiped his forearm across his lip, still bloody from when Dun beat him after he confessed to killing Mari, though he described it as a mercy killing. I swallowed hard. That reality was a coarse lump of salt in my throat, in my heart.

"According to Ultana," Finn said, "a religious organization— possibly at the Vatican, as that's where your key is from—has targeted the Scintilla and hired the Arrazi to eradicate them. Why?"

"That's the question," I said. "What truth can be so scary to them that they'll break their own commandments to conceal it?"

Giovanni leaned against the stone with his arms crossed. "I still don't understand how the spirals play into this..."

"It's a trinity. Threes... The church has taken many pre-existing ancient symbols and made them their own."

Finn's hand rested over the spirals on his chest. "I'm Catholic," Finn said. "Born and raised. But I know from history that many of the church's symbols were adapted from earlier pagan symbols. It's a brilliant conversion tactic, really. Take something people already believe in and alter it just enough to make it their own. It's how beliefs are stolen." His brown eyes pierced mine. "It's how followers are created."

"Okay," I said. "Confirmation that I'm headed to the right place."

"*If* Ultana was telling the truth," Finn said, eyebrows arched skeptically. "It might have been a deviation from the truth. You could be going to Italy for nothing."

I ignored his comment. They'd already tried to convince me I shouldn't go. I'd lost my father, my mother, and my best friend. I no longer cared about "shoulds". "Finn, keep tabs on the Arrazi here so we know what they're up to. Giovanni, you have to go with my grandmother to Chile. Keep her and Claire safe. See that Dun makes it home to California. As for me…I'll find out if we're finally on the right trail and, if so, why they want to bury the *keys to heaven*."

We emerged from the chill of the tomb into the morning sunlight, blinking to adjust our eyes. I squinted at the dark outline of a group of people standing directly in front of us, blocking our path out of the ruins. A familiar energy sent a blast of terror through my body, and I clasped both Finn and Giovanni's arms.

As my eyes found focus, the Arrazi came into view. Before I could utter a word or move, their knifelike energy reached out and plunged icy hands into me and just as quickly pulled back. A chilling greeting.

The gravel crunched under my feet as I skidded to a stop and stared in shock at the Arrazi who blocked our escape from New-grange. I cringed, bracing myself for the strike of the axe.

Giovanni and Finn both thrust a protective arm in front of me. Pure fear swelled through my palms as I clasped each boy's arm. Dread rippled off them and buffeted my sides. I forced myself to breathe.

Beneath a thick layer of fear, bubbled molten hate. I stepped forward, shaking with a curious blend of rage and exhaustion that made me feel almost invincible, like I'd lost concern over my own death. I was sick of running, sick of living in fear, sick of losing the people I loved.

"The last I saw of you, you were drooling on yourself in a tomb," I said to Clancy. I almost taunted him about Ultana, the head of Xepa, and how her dead body sprawled next to him when we left them. But her son stood at his side, staring at me with eyes slashed to thin, speculative slits. Had Clancy told him of his mother's death?

"I told you this was a bad risk," Finn grumbled next to me.

"I'm at risk just waking up every day."

"Did you really think I'd not know where you went?" Clancy asked, stepping toward me with a smile, as if we were old friends. "Haven't we been down this road before, pet?"

"Pet?" Giovanni yanked his arm from my grasp and shoved his way in front of me. "Cora will never be something you stake claim to, ever again."

"Stop," I whispered to Giovanni, reaching up to clasp his shoulder. "You save my life, you die. Is that such a hard rule to remember?"

His head turned enough that I could trace the noble slope of his nose and see the determined attitude of one blue eye as he snarled, "Yes."

His Scintilla energy sizzled under my palm so ferociously that I fought the temptation to pull away. Instead, I tried to calm him the way he'd done for me so many times, but I was too dark, too angry to produce any positive feelings.

I had nothing to give.

Giovanni's shoulder tensed as I squeezed harder and whispered, "You can't afford to think like that. There's someone else depending on you now." There was a slow blink and an almost imperceptible nod. He understood. Giovanni had to worry more about taking care of his newfound daughter, Claire, than protecting me.

A series of crunching thuds resounded around us, like sledge-hammers hitting gravel. A chorus of shrieks filled the air as bystanders pointed at a group of tourists who lay in a heap, their limbs piled chaotically over the top of one another.

"Stop!" I screamed at Clancy. They were innocents who had

nothing to do with our drama and wouldn't believe it even if they were told. But Clancy's bushy white brows were bent in consternation at the pile of dead bodies, and I realized I hadn't seen the Arrazi hook their auras into the bodies to take and kill. Yet, there they lay—dead. *What…?*

I'd thought the Arrazi were responsible for the drop-dead people. Could my father have been right? Was there a phenomenon randomly striking down clusters of people? And was I the antidote, as he'd suggested? My gut still said no. But it seemed like it could have something to do with us, with this ugliness of a war between two unique types of human. I just didn't know how.

The park wasn't crowded. It had just opened, but all the tourists were packed around the dead bodies, some snapping pictures and video with their phones. I couldn't be caught on film again at the site of another incident. I wanted to turn my head away, shield myself, but I didn't dare take my eyes off the Arrazi.

Their eyes hadn't left us for one second.

Clancy smiled widely. Before I could even guess what he found so amusing, he lifted a finger and, all at once, the Arrazi lashed their ensnaring auras at the living, pulsing crowd and siphoned their colors from their bodies. Giant tubes of color flowed from the tourists into the bodies of each Arrazi.

People died as they ran for their lives, their life force sucked from them, even as they hugged one another for comfort. Bodies fell like crushed flowers. And we could do nothing to prevent it.

Thunder cracked as the Arrazi's auras exploded in a white as blinding as the lightning that shot overhead. The cloud of pure white energy surrounded them and reached for us like a misty, noxious vapor.